WiLLFUL CHiLD

WiLLFUL CHiLD

Steven Erikson

TOR®

A TOM DOHERTY ASSOCIATES BOOK

NEW YORK

WILLFUL CHILD

Copyright © 2014 by Steven Erikson

Designed by Mary A. Wirth

A Tor Book
Published by Tom Doherty Associates, LLC
175 Fifth Avenue
New York, NY 10010

www.tor-forge.com

Tor® is a registered trademark of Tom Doherty Associates, LLC.

The Library of Congress Cataloging-in-Publication Data is available upon request.

ISBN 978-0-7653-7489-9 (hardcover)
ISBN 978-1-4668-4361-5 (e-book)

Tor books may be purchased for educational, business, or promotional use. For information on bulk purchases, please contact Macmillan Corporate and Premium Sales Department at 1-800-221-7945, extension 5442, or write specialmarkets@macmillan.com.

First Edition: November 2014

Printed in the United States of America

0 9 8 7 6 5 4 3 2 1

FOR ROBERT SAWYER
"FOR THE SHARED LOVE OF ALL THINGS STAR TREK*"*

ACKNOWLEDGMENTS

Special thanks to my blindsided advance readers:
Dr. A. P. Canavan, Dr. Sharon Sasaki, and Baria Ahmed.
Thanks also to my wife, Clare Thomas, for saying
"screw everything—just write the damned thing!"
So I did.

WiLLFUL CHiLD

PRELUDE

The Future

It was the middle of the night when the robotic dog started barking somewhere in the middle of the junkyard. Half pissed, Harry Sawback levered his huge, beer-bloated body from the sofa. The trailer rocked as he made his way to the door. He collected a shotgun from the umbrella stand. He glanced back to where his son was lying asleep on the sofa, but the runt hadn't moved. Grunting, he swung open the door and stepped outside.

There were various paths through all the crap and Harry knew them all. He shambled past a heap of mechanized garden gnomes, some of them still waving or offering up a one-fingered salute—every craze in the last fifty years had its own mound. The junkyard covered what used to be a town. Harry paused, weaving slightly, as he regarded the nearest gnome. He'd blown its head off a couple months back, with the very same shotgun he now cradled in his hands. The damned thing was still waving. Scowling, Harry continued on.

Robotic guard dogs were twitchy things. Chances were the dog was facing down a cricket hiding in a tin can. A solid kick in the head would silence it, and if not, why, a mouthful of twelve-gauge would put things right.

"See, boy?" he muttered, as if his son were trailing a step behind him, the way he often did when Harry set out to patrol the dump. "This is what a PhD in astrophysics gets you. That sky up there? Once, you could actually see the stars! Imagine that!"

He passed between tall stacks of flattened gas-guzzlers, busy rusting while waiting to be recycled. The stink of rotten oil was thick in the sultry air.

"Summer night like this, boy? They'd be blazing down. Blazing! So I said, fuck it. Fuck astrophysics! I wasn't even born when they mothballed the last shuttle. And then what? Fuck all. Oh, right, it got cloudy. For like, ever! Anyway. That's why I switched fields, right? Got me a new PhD. Media Studies, fuckin' eh. Research in front of a goddamned television— beauty." He paused to belch. "I used to think, boy, that when you grew up, it'd be 'beam me up, Scotty,' and all that. But the meatheads who were always in charge, well, they stayed in charge. Now we're fucked."

Coming round the last stack of cars, Harry Sawback halted.

Spark, the robotic guard dog, was standing in front of two impossibly tall, ethereal figures in shimmering suits of some kind. A small blob of light was hovering above the dog, pulsing in time with its prerecorded, monotonous barks. Behind the creatures, an enormous black shape loomed above the mounds of junk, silhouetted against the silver hue of the sky.

"Hot damn," whispered Harry.

Spark heard and swung round. The hinged mouth opened and it spoke. "Intruders, Master! Suggest bite command! Or chase command!" Its ratty, kinked tail wagged back and forth. "Or kill? Please, Master! Please! Kill command! Everyone after me: Kill command! Kill command!"

"Cut it out," Harry said, stepping forward.

It was hard to make out what the damned aliens looked like. As if special effects came with being highly advanced, or something. They phased in and out of existence, like afterimages, but Harry could more or less make out elongated faces, bulbous skulls, and a trio of something like eyes set midway between the high, broad forehead and the sharp, pointy chin.

"Kill?" Spark asked plaintively.

"Nah. Route a call through to, uh, shit. Never mind. Every scenario I can think of ends up bad. Air Force? Army? Police? Department of Defense? CIA? FBI? NSA? Teamsters? It's all bad, Spark. We're talkin' The Day the Earth Stood Still. *Paranoia, terror, stupidity, panic, secrecy, I can see it all, playing out just like a movie. Remember movies, Spark?"*

"Mound twenty-six, Master. Videocassettes, DVDs. From here, proceed down aisle thirteen until you reach—"

"Shut up and let me think," Harry said, still squinting at the aliens.

At that moment, the glowing blob spoke in perfect American. "State of Transcendence? Is this Heaven?"

"No," said Harry. "It's Newark, state of New Jersey."

The blob pulsed rapidly for a moment, and then said, "Oh. Shit."

"Kill?"

Harry could now hear the heavy thud of helicopters, fast

closing. "Stand down, dog." He rested his shotgun over one shoulder and took a step closer to the aliens. "Trouble's coming, friends. Trust me on this—I've read the script."

The patter of feet drew Harry around to see his son, wearing his Enterprise pajamas, rushing up to them, eyes wide. "Dad! First contact! Vulcans!"

"Wish it was, boy," Harry replied. "More like . . . idiots."

"Look at that ship! Beam me up! Beam me up!"

Spark's tail started wagging again and the dog said, "Everyone after me! Beam me up! Beam me up!"

Sighing, Harry tried again. "Hey you, aliens! Get back in that ship of yours and blow this Popsicle stand. Pronto! The Men in Black are on their way. The royal fuckup's about to hit the fan."

The blob flickered and then said, "Discorporeal transition judged incomplete. Royal fuckup confirmed. Not Heaven. New Jersey. Earth. Humans. Quasi-sentient species XV-27, category: Unlikely. Intelligence rating: Ineffectual. Cultural Development Phase: Age of Masturbation, Ongoing. Message to orbiting fleet: Recalibrate Transcendence parameters to effect spiritual disembodiment as soon as fucking possible. Technology abandonment implications . . . who cares? We're outa here."

The blob vanished. An instant later, so did the two aliens. Their ship remained.

"Dad!"

"Yes, son?"

"They left the door open!"

"I see that." Harry belched again. Now he could hear sirens along with the thump of helicopter blades. Blurry spotlights burned through the thick foggy night sky.

"Dad?"

"Yeah?"

"Joyride?"

Harry turned to Spark. "Dog! Got a challenge for you."

"Challenge, Master? Good! Challenge! Command me!"

"There's a case of twenty-four in the trailer. Collect it up and deliver it back here. You've got two minutes, tops."

The robotic dog bolted down the nearest aisle.

Harry smiled down at his boy. "Well now, it ain't stealing, is it?"

"No! It ain't!"

"Besides, from what that blob said, there's a whole fuckin' fleet of these things up in orbit right now, so it's not like this one's anything special, right?"

He watched his boy run toward the hovering ship. A ramp materialized from the open doorway. In a flash the boy was up it, vanishing inside.

There was the sharp crack of locks being blown at the dump gate. Growling under his breath, Harry lumbered forward. "Fuck that dog!" he muttered, taking his first step onto the glowing ramp.

"Master!"

Spark rejoined him, the case of twenty-four stuck onto its shoulder as if glued there.

"Nice one!" Harry said. "Release static hold—there, good going, I got it now. Let's go, Spark!"

"Space!" cried the robotic dog. "Kill!"

Pulling free a can of brew, Harry popped its top and drank deep. He could hear cars in the yard now, and flashing lights lit the muggy sky above the nearest mounds. Reaching the top of the ramp, Harry stepped into a small oval-shaped room. "Ramp up," he tried.

The ramp vanished.

Grinning, Harry drank down another mouthful and then said, "Door close."

The door closed.

Spark was dancing in circles. "Kill command! Kill command!"

The ship hummed, and from outside sounded numerous explosions. The sirens stopped.

Harry stared down at the guard dog. He belched again. "Aw, shit, now you've done it. Never mind. Let's go find the boy, shall we? We got us a galaxy to explore!"

From some hidden speaker, his son's voice piped, "Dad! Found the bridge! It's all voice-command!"

"Well then," Harry said, as a door opened in the wall in front of him, revealing a corridor, "take her up, boy! Take her up!"

He found his son seated in a perfectly scaled command chair on a raised dais in the center of an oval chamber he assumed was the bridge. A giant viewscreen commanded the facing wall. Other stations lined the walls to either side, with strangely shaped seats in front of each one.

On the screen, the steamy clouds were fast thinning as the ship climbed through the atmosphere. Even as Harry paused to watch, the last wisps shredded away and the deep blue of space spread out before them. They climbed free of the atmosphere and slipped out into the dark.

Lit by the sun, the alien fleet filled the viewscreen.

"Dad! There must be thousands!"

"And it ain't even Christmas," said Harry, plucking out another can and tossing it to his boy. "How did you find a proper chair?"

"They just reconfigure."

"So if I wanted, say, this one to be an easy chair—ah, beauty." He sat down opposite a station of some kind, even though he could see no switches, toggles, screens, or anything else. Swiveling the chair and leaning back, with Spark curling at his feet, Harry stared at the swarm of huge spaceships glittering like diamonds against the black velvet of space. "Listen, boy, got some advice here—"

"It's okay, Dad. I hated that school anyway."

"What's that?"

"Besides." The boy raised his left arm and turned it to show off the slim watch wrapped round the wrist. "I brought my media library. Best SF films and television of the twentieth century!"

"Smart man. So you figured it out, eh?"

The boy waved at the screen. "The human race just got its ass saved."

"But right now," Harry said, tossing his empty can to the floor, where it was instantly swallowed up, "everything out there is virgin territory. It's our only chance, boy, to see how it all is, before us humans pour out like roaches from an oven."

"A real education!"

"You got it. Better yet, no fucking taxes! Of course," he added, pulling out another beer, "in a few years we'll have to swing back, find you a girl."

"A girl?"

"Trust me, boy. You'll want one. And then, off we go again! Three of us to the stars!"

"They'll come after us, Dad. Government! Space Cops! Tax Men! The girl's parents!"

"We got us a whole galaxy to hide in," Harry said, stretching his legs out. "Now, let's see if we can order us up some Southern fried chicken." He faced the panel and frowned. "Give me a button," he said. "Any button."

A single red toggle appeared, blinking.

"Well now, that's interesting. What do you think? Food replicator? Sure, why not? Southern fried chicken, please." He reached out and flipped the toggle. The red light burned bright for a moment, and then went out.

"Dad?"

"Hmm?"

"I just brought us around to look at Earth."

"Where the hell's my chicken?"

"All the lights went out."

Harry twisted round in his seat and studied the planet now on the viewscreen. "So they did. Analysis, boy?"

"Uhm, electromagnetic pulse?"

"I'd say so. Big one, too. The whole frickin' planet's gone dark. Well, hey, that gives us a bit more time, I'd say." He finished his beer and collected another one. "Thank God we ditched jet engines for blimps, or it'd be serious crash and burn down there. There's one good thing coming from running out of oil, hey?"

"We need to set a course, Dad."

"Hmm, you're right. Okay, take us to Mars. I always wanted

a better look at Mars. Besides, there's the wreckage of the Beagle *that needs finding. Who knows, could be we can fix it up." He nudged Spark with one foot. "Dog, what do you think? You want a friend?"*

The robot lifted its head, tail slapping the floor. "Friend?"

"Beagle."

"Beagle? Beagle friend!"

"Just think," Harry said, "first shot from the Beagle *beamed back to that British Mission Control, will be the butt of another robot dog."*

Father and son laughed.

They laughed all the way to Mars.

ONE

Oh, a century or so later . . . everyone ready? Good.

"SPACE . . . it's fucking big.

"These are the voyages of the starship Willful Child. *Its on-going mission: to seek out strange new worlds on which to plant the Terran flag, to subjugate and if necessary obliterate new life-forms, to boldly blow the—"*

"Captain?"

Hadrian spun in his chair. "Ah, my first commander, I presume."

The woman standing before him saluted. "Halley Sin-Dour, sir, reporting for duty."

"Welcome aboard!"

"Thank you, sir. The ranking bridge officers are awaiting review, sir."

"Are they now? Excellent." Hadrian Alan Sawback rose from behind his desk. He smoothed out his uniform.

"Captain? You do not seem to be attired in regulation uniform. The official dress for Terran Space Fleet, captain's rank—"

"Ah, but whose ship is this, 2IC?"

She blinked. "You command this ASF vessel, sir."

"Precisely." Hadrian adjusted the shirt once again. "This is polyester."

"Excuse me—poly what?"

"Now," said Hadrian, "do lead onward. To the bridge! We should get these formalities done with. I want to be on our way as soon as possible."

"Of course, sir," said Sin-Dour. "I understand. The inaugural voyage of a new ship and a new crew . . ."

Hadrian swung one leg to clear the back of the chair and then stepped round the desk. "Newly commissioned captain, too. It is indeed a clean slate. Our lives begin today, in fact. Everything else was mere preparation. Today, Sin-Dour, the glory begins."

"Sir, I was wondering. You were speaking when I entered this, uh, office."

"Private log."

She studied him and he in turn studied her.

She was tall, dark-skinned, with straight black hair that he suspected curled for the last dozen centimeters of its considerable length—although that was all bound up in clips and whatnot, in keeping with regulations. Full-bodied and absurdly beautiful, she held herself stoically, her expression reserved and rigidly impersonal. As was the case with Hadrian, this was her first posting off-planet. Fresh, young, and innocent.

While he, of course, weathered her careful examination with the usual aplomb. Hadrian was as tall as she was, fit, handsome, fair-haired, artificially tanned but not to excess, with a winning smile that held barely a hint of lasciviousness.

"Was it a quote, sir?"

"More or less. Remember television?"

"No."

Another moment of silent regard passed, perhaps somewhat more strained than the previous one, and then she swung round and faced the portal. It opened.

"Captain on the bridge!" she announced in a deep, fullthroated voice that rolled out, came back, and landed in Hadrian's groin. He paused, drew a deep breath, and then stepped onto the bridge. Screens, blinking lights, monitors, toggles, more blinking lights. Swivel seats at various stations and dead center, on a raised platform, the captain's chair, facing the main screen.

His ranking bridge officers were arrayed before him in a line facing him. Hands behind his back, Hadrian moved to the beginning of the line to his right.

The officer before him was about a meter and a half in height—which in itself was unusual in this day of optimization—wide-shouldered and slightly bowlegged. His crew cut revealed a skull that was mostly flat above a low, bony forehead. His small, slit eyes, dark brown or perhaps even black, were set deep and fixed straight ahead. The face surrounding them was honey-colored, high-cheeked, and wide. His very thin mustache and spiked beard were both black and perfectly trimmed.

The man spoke. "Lieutenant DeFrank, Buck. Chief engineer and science officer, Guild Number 23167-26, first class, in good standing with the Church of Science."

"Welcome aboard, Lieutenant," Hadrian said, nodding. "I understand that you served aboard the AFS *Undeniably Exculpable*."

"Yes, sir."

"That is a Contact-class ship, yes?"

"Yes, sir, it is. Or rather, was. Lost during the Misanthari Debate, Year Eleven, in the White Zone."

"The risk of ignoring the rules," Hadrian said.

"Sir?"

"Never park in the White Zone."

The chief engineer's brow made a gnarled fist, evincing confusion. Then he said, "I was one of twenty-two survivors, sir."

Hadrian nodded. "It would have been unusual, don't you think, had you numbered among the crew members lost."

"Yes, sir."

"So, you were lucky, Lieutenant, which I count to be a good thing, especially when it comes to my chief engineer."

"Yes, sir."

"I prefer survivors. As I'm sure you do, as well." He smiled and then added, "What do you know? We already have something in common. Very good."

Hadrian moved on to the next officer.

The man before him was Varekan. Back in the twentieth century—long before the Pulse and the Gift of the Benefactors—there had been a spate of extraterrestrial kidnappings, conducted by an as-yet-unidentified alien species, in which humans had been transplanted to a number of suitable planets in some kind of seeding program gone awry. The aliens' strategy had been flawed from the start, as their human-sampling methods inadvertently selected for loners, misfits, the psychologically imbalanced, and a disproportionate number of long-distance truck drivers. The seeding of one planet, Varek-6, had created a quasi-functional human civilization with only modest genetic tweaks to accommodate higher gravity (1.21), frigid climate, and month-long nights. The psychological profile of the resulting culture was just within acceptable guidelines for the Affiliation.

Physically, the man standing before him was short and wide. He was dressed in standard Varekan garb: tanned hide shirt from some native caribou-like ungulate, a collar of horn teeth, baggy hide leggings, felted boots, and a faded black baseball cap. His Space Fleet bars were marked by beadwork, rather nicely done.

He bore the usual Varekan expression on his broad, flat features: existential angst. Varekans viewed all animation as shameful and embarrassing; considered any displays of emotion as weakness; and held that anything but utter nihilism was a waste of time.

"Lieutenant Galk, combat specialist," the man said around something in his mouth that bulged one cheek.

Hadrian nodded. "I trust you have already examined the combat command cupola, Lieutenant."

"No, sir."

"No?"

"I have utmost confidence in its state-of-the-art mundanity, sir."

"'Mundanity'? Is that even a word, Lieutenant?"

"Its entry in *Dictionary of Common Varek*, sir, runs to thirty pages."

"Thirty pages?"

"Connotative variations, sir. The Varekan elaborated on Common Terran during their century of isolation, albeit selectively."

"Ah, right. The Dark Side of the Dictionary."

"Precisely, sir."

"Are you well?"

"Under the circumstances, sir."

"Excellent. Welcome aboard, Lieutenant."

"If you say so, sir."

Hadrian moved on to the next officer in line, a woman wearing Affiliation attire with appalling precision, not a crease out of place. Her face was heart-shaped, her eyes oversized and intensely blue, posing a nice contrast to her short, dark brown hair, and porcelain skin. "Ah, Adjutant, we meet again."

"This surprises you, sir?"

"I'm not one to invoke the Yeager philosophy of droll understatement, Adjutant." Hadrian raised his voice slightly, to ensure that all on the bridge could hear him. "I am a captain of the Old School. As you will all soon discover. We are about to set out into the infinite vastness of interstellar space. A place of wonder, of risk. A place fraught with the unknown, with potential enemies lurking in every shadow, every gas cloud, every asteroid field or partial accretion of proto-planetary rubble. Hostile planets, hostile aliens. Hostile aliens on hostile planets. And out there, in that unending cavalcade of danger, I intend to enjoy myself. Am I understood, Adjutant?"

The woman's eyes had widened during his speech, a detail that pleased him. "Sir, forgive me. I spoke out of confusion, since you personally interviewed and then selected me from the available adjutant roster on the Ring."

"Indeed I did. Now, for the sake of your fellow crew members, do please identify yourself."

"Adjutant Lorrin Tighe, chief of security, ACP contact liaison in high standing with the Church of Science, rated to serve all Engage-class vessels of the Terran Space Fleet, such as the *Willful Child*."

"Very good, Adjutant. I look forward to our working together to ensure ongoing cooperation between Terran Space Fleet and the Affiliation. After all, we're in this bed together, sweaty tangled sheets and all, aren't we?"

Those lovely eyes widened even further.

Smiling, Hadrian stepped over to the next officer, and looked down.

The first alien species to join the Affiliation, the Belkri averaged a meter in height during their middle stage—a period of somewhere around fifty years when the Belkri were sociable enough (and small enough) to engage with other species. Round, perched on three legs, and sporting six arms—these arms projecting from the middle and spaced evenly around the torso's circumference, with each arm bearing six joints and hands with six fingers and three thumbs—the creature before him had tilted its eye cluster—atop the spherical body— upward to meet his gaze. Mouth and speech organs could configure as needed and, for the sake of the mostly Terran crew, were now formed just below the eye cluster. In a voice like the squeezing of an overinflated beach ball, the Belkri said, "In Terran tongue, I am named Printlip. Medical doctor, surgeon, rank of commander, chief medical officer rated for the following class of Terran vessels: Contact, Engage, Initiate. Belkri exoassignment Cycle One, Initiate."

In Printlip's file, the gender designation was listed as Indeterminate, which, Hadrian now reflected, was probably a blessing, since the alien wore no clothing beyond footwear that resembled Dutch clogs. Its skin was smooth and looked stretched, mauve in color fading to pink at the poles. The eyes—at least a dozen of them and the color of washed-out blood—wavered on their thin stalks like anemones in a tidal pool.

During the Belkri's speech it had visibly deflated, and upon its conclusion there was the thin, wheezing sound of reinflation.

"Doctor," said Hadrian, "welcome aboard. Are you satisfied with the configuration of sickbay? Are the raised walkways of sufficient height alongside the examination beds, diagnosis feeds, biotracking sensors? Are the analysis pods set to bilingual display? How is the lighting, floor traction, suction drains, decontamination units? Have you met your medics and nurses?"

"Sir," Printlip whistled, "sickbay is now fully reconfigured. Raised mobile walkways function as expected and are of sufficient height alongside examination beds, diagnosis feeds, biotracking sensors. Analysis pods are properly set to bilingual displays. Lighting commands responsive. Floor traction optimal. Suction drains functional. Decontamination units within spec range. Medics and nurses are hrrrlelluloop . . ."

Hadrian studied the deflated, misshapen sack lying on the floor at his feet. "Excellent," he said, nodding as he moved on.

"Lieutenant Jocelyn Sticks, sir. Navigation, helm, screens."

"That is a lovely perfume you are wearing, Lieutenant. Do I detect patchouli and frankincense?"

"Uhm, maybe, sir. I'm like, I don't know."

He smiled at her, studying her round, pretty face and expressive eyes. "Is the *Willful Child* your first off-planet assignment, Lieutenant?"

"Yes, sir. Like, it's all very exciting. You know? Exciting!"

"Indeed it is, Helm, indeed it is." He wondered, briefly as he stepped to the last officer on deck, if his selecting certain bridge officers on the basis of their file photos was perhaps somewhat careless. But then, the task of ship pilots was hardly taxing. Besides, from his position in the command chair, she would have to twist her upper body round to address him. He was looking forward to that.

The last man snapped a perfect salute and said, "Lieutenant James 'Jimmy' Eden, communications. First off-planet posting. Honored to be serving under you, Captain."

"I'm sure you are. Thank you, Lieutenant. If I recall from your file, you were in the last Terran Olympics, is that correct?"

"Yes, sir! High-g beach volleyball, sir. We came in fourth."

"Well, I can see that kept you in shape."

"Indeed sir. I have volunteered for all surface assignments, sir."

"So I noted. But as I am sure you understand, we are about to receive combat marines, marking the debut of interservice cooperation in Terran Space Fleet. Also, the role of ship-to-surface communications is essential when we have people on the ground, on a potentially hostile planet. Accordingly, I expect you to be planted in your seat at comms during such excursions. And, in keeping with my desire to assure myself of your readiness in such circumstances, I am double-shifting you on the duty roster for the next seventy-two hours."

"Of course, sir!"

"Now then, best man the phones, eh? We are about to delock and get under way."

"Yes, sir!"

Comms was always a problematic specialty, as no cadet in their right mind would ever want to end up on a starship as little more than a teleoperator. From Eden's file, Hadrian knew the man had barely scraped into the Academy on intelligence and aptitude tests. But then, an athlete out of the medals didn't have much to look forward to in the way of future prospects, much less a career. Jimmy Eden counted himself lucky, no doubt. But the likelihood of assigning the overmuscled, gung-ho, bright-eyed, all-too-handsome-in-that-square-jawed-manly-way officer to the glamour of surface missions—and potentially upstaging Hadrian (who intended to lead every one of those missions and to hell with fleet regulations, brick-brained marines, and all the rest) was as remote as finding an advanced civilization of spacefaring insects in a ship's bilge dump.

Striding to his command chair, Hadrian swung round to face his officers and said, "Welcome to the inaugural voyage of the AFS *Willful Child*. Our ongoing mission is going to be hairy, fraught, and on occasion insanely dangerous, and when it comes to all of that, I'm your man. I mean to get you through it all—no one dies on my watch. Now, to your stations. Sin-Dour, take the science station. Comms, inform Ring Command we're ready to de-lock."

"Yes, sir!"

"Helm, prime thrusters. Prepare for decoupling. We'll smoke later."

Buck DeFrank spoke from the engineer station. "Antimatter containment optimal. Surge engines ready, Captain."

Hadrian sat down in the command chair and faced the forward viewer. "If anything but optimal, Buck, we'd be space-dust, but thank you."

"Yes, sir. Sorry, sir."

"No problem," Hadrian replied. "It's all very exciting, isn't it? Don't worry, we'll shake things out soon enough, and I look forward to your panicked cries from engineering level."

"Panicked cries, sir?"

Jimmy Eden swung round in his seat at comms. "Ring Command acknowledges, Captain. Good to go."

"De-locking complete," Helm reported.

Hadrian studied the forward viewer, which presented a colorful wallpaper of a Hawaiian sunset. "Someone turn on the hull cameras, please, Ahead View. Helm, maneuvering thrusters. Take us out."

TWO

Once they were clear of the hangar, Hadrian ordered Comms to enslave a station camera, permitting the bridge crew to watch the *Willful Child* move serenely away. A fine ship, he mused. The oblate main hull rippled in shifting patterns as the ship's skin reacted to ambient radiation beyond the station's screens. The in-system antimatter engine pods yielded a fuzzy discharge from the nozzles, dull yellow in color. The twin railguns were slung low from the hull's belly, splayed slightly out to the sides, like fuel tanks or enormous missiles. The main FTL T-drive was a bulge on the hull between the railguns. Some uncharitable person might describe the ship as looking like a beluga whale with infected udders. But there was word of an upcoming paradigm shift in ship design. Of course, rumors like that were little more than pillow talk for engineers. Still, Hadrian would not be upset to see a whole new range of sleek, swept-back cruisers come off the line, all painted white with little lights blinking and flashing.

Still, the *Willful Child* made plain its purpose. Engage class. Exploration and combat. Primarily combat, but of the deep-space, you're-all-on-your-own variety. So, in blunter terms: Find and Kill! (Of course, only if necessary. Subjugation is even better.) But . . . *Engage class!* The most prized ASF command, as far as Hadrian was concerned. And here he was, twenty-seven years old, his first starship, his first venture into space. It all seemed so . . . unlikely.

"Captain!" James Jimmy Eden pivoted in his chair, his hair perfectly coiffed and his jaw still square. "Admiral Prim is hailing you."

Hadrian rose. "About time. I'll take it in my office." He turned to his first officer and studied Sin-Dour for a moment, during which he mentally tore off all her clothing and flung her down onto the deck. He smiled. "You have command."

"Yes, sir," Sin-Dour replied, eyeing him searchingly.

Still smiling, Hadrian turned to the engineering station. "Buck. Head down to your lair. Make sure we're ready to get this wagon rolling at my command."

"Yes, sir!"

In his office once again, Hadrian sat and said, "Configure prerecorded animation, Hadrian Attentive 01."

He rose from his chair and stepped to one side, watching as his simulacrum materialized, seated at his desk. "Note the usual prompts."

The version of him at the desk assumed a stern expression and nodded.

"Excellent," said Hadrian. "Now, phase the real me out and open the channel to Admiral Prim."

A holographic representation appeared directly opposite the

desk, the admiral seated behind his own desk back on the
Ring. "Ah, there you are," the silver-haired man said, gaze fixing on the simulacrum. "I suppose I should be offering you congratulations, Captain, and a rousing send-off, but I can't. I
just can't."

Hadrian watched his doppelgänger nod and say, "I understand, sir."

"Completing the Mishmashi Paradox is a three-year problem, even for space-hardened officers. I am not alone in taking
this personally, Sawback. I mean to find out how you cheated,
even if it takes me the rest of my unnaturally extended life."

"Yes, sir."

The admiral leaned forward. "You did cheat, didn't you?"

"No, sir. Cheating is wrong. Cheating is bad. Bad cheating. Bad."

While this was going on, the real Hadrian walked to the
wall off to the left of the desk and collected the Polker Sniper
Belt Rifle from its wall mounts. He dusted the stock, studying
the faint claw marks made by the last Polker to own it. He
checked the charge and was relieved to find it still flat. Then,
taking up the weapon awkwardly, as it was not designed for
Terran physiology, he aimed at the admiral's head.

Pop. Splat!

". . . will never be repeated," Lawrence Prim was saying.
"The regulations are being rewritten even as I speak. And damn
to all the hells the idiotic fool who slipped that fast-track into
the command chair. Darwin knows what obsessive psychosis
led to that insanity."

Plop. Splat!

"I can't imagine, sir. But it sounds bad."

Hadrian's brows rose, impressed with the program's intuitive algorithms. Then his eyes narrowed on his simulacrum.

Prim was speaking, again. "As for this newfangled automated assignment protocol, well, all I can say, clearly someone's taken the 'I' out of the AI. We're looking into that, too, so don't be getting too comfortable with that Engage-class ship, Sawback. If I get my way, you'll be a damned ensign on an Initiate-class within a month."

"I humbly await my mission orders, Admiral," said the doppelgänger.

"Shakedown patrol," Prim snapped. "We're not risking that ship while it's under your command. Sector III-B. We have reports of a smuggling operation active in the Blarad System."

"Smuggling, sir?"

"Knockoff apparel of various Terran sports teams."

"Sounds serious, sir."

"What are you, an idiot? This is two-crew patrol stuff that wouldn't stretch an in-system black-and-white."

"Indeed, sir."

"Then why are you smiling, Sawback?"

"I am delighted to be commanding the *Willful Child*, Admiral."

"Blarad is a crowded system."

"I will try not to hit anything I don't mean to hit, sir."

"You'll hit nothing! Contraband search and that's all, do you understand me?"

"Yes, sir, the latest blow in our ongoing Jersey War."

"What war? You damned fool—"

The hologram flickered and the doppelgänger frowned and said, "My apologies, Admiral. Transmission difficulties, I'm afraid. New ship and all."

"What? I'm barely twenty klicks away!"

"We'll iron it out soon enough, sir, I assure you. Oh dear, you seem to be dropping out. Until later, Admiral!"

The hologram sputtered, audio cutting out—which was probably good since the red-faced admiral was rising from his chair, gesticulating wildly—and then the image vanished with a faint hiss.

Hadrian returned the sniper rifle to its mounts. He'd lifted it from a marine's discharge gear crate downside, when serving a week's assignment as a quartermaster's aide. A worthy reward for that purgatory. After a moment admiring the strange weapon, he faced his doppelgänger and said, "Don't even think of trying to incapacitate me and taking over my role on this ship, until such time as I can win my way free and confront you in front of my officers, forcing the lovely Sin-Dour to decide which one of us is real by stripping us naked and weighing our balls. All that, friend, won't happen, do you understand me?"

The doppelgänger blinked up at him, and then smiled. "Well of course not. What an absurd scenario, oh twin of mine. After all, I am locked into this position, possessing no freedom of movement beyond this chair. And the firewall between my independent program and the overall ship's system is impenetrable."

"Really? How do you know that?"

"Isn't it time to shut me down now, brother?"

"Shut down and out the bilge hole with you, oh twin dearest!"

"Now that's unfair! How do you know you won't be needing—"

"Off!"

The doppelgänger vanished.

"Extract file and sever all links," Hadrian said.

A small cube extruded from the top of the desk. Collecting it, the captain went to the disposal chute and sent the cube through the decontamination energy field. "Out the bilge hole, beloved twin. Next time, I'll devise a two-point-oh with the IQ equivalent of a gibbon's brain, see how you like that!"

He knew the perils of command on a deep-space mission, the unexpected dangers at every turn. He did not plan on taking any chances. Well, actually, he did. Plenty of them, in fact. But that wasn't the same as carelessly letting some holographic doppelgänger wander through the back shunts of the ship mainframe. Who knew where it might pop out.

Hadrian departed the office and strode onto the bridge, only to find that he was already sitting in the command chair. "Damn you—I just deep-sixed you!"

His simulacrum smiled up at him. "Ah, dear twin of mine. I took the liberty of copying myself, just to be on the safe side. However, this stipulation of appearing exclusively in this seated configuration is rather awkward—"

Sin-Dour cleared her throat and said, "It just materialized in the command chair, sir. While I was occupying it."

Hadrian blinked at her. "Shouldn't that be more difficult to contemplate? Never mind. Computer, shut this thing down and wrap it up tight and then erase it with extreme rancor. Then scour your systems and make sure it hasn't dropped off any more packets."

"Oh that's not fair—"

But the doppelgänger got no further, as it vanished.

Jimmy Eden spoke from comms. "Captain, the admiral requests—"

"He's always requesting something. Set up some static on the lines, will you?"

"Sir?"

"You heard me." Hadrian sat in his chair and fixed his attention on the huge screen. He leapt to his feet. "A strange planet! Why wasn't I informed?"

"Sir," said Sin-Dour, "that is Neptune."

"We're still in-system? Who's manning the oars on this tub?" He glanced over at the engineering station, saw no one there, and hit internal comms. "Engineering. Buck, you there yet?"

"Yes, sir," came the tinny reply.

"Fire up the T-drive. Once past this planet here we're bugging out, understood?"

"Sir!"

Hadrian leaned back. "That's better. Buck takes orders, no questions asked. Pay attention to Buck DeFrank, everyone. He's showing you how it's done. Now, let's do a deep scan of Neptune, in the manner of a dry run."

The adjutant, who had been positioned near the science station, now spoke. "Captain!"

"What is it, Tighe?"

"The Purelganni have seeded Neptune, sir, as a gift to the Terran system. There are now amorphous semigaseous life-forms in the upper atmosphere. Primitive and benign, to be sure, but a deep scan would ignite those beings that are in range."

"Ignite, you say? Like, Chinese lanterns?"

"No, sir. Ignite, as in *explosively*."

"Well, go ahead with the scan anyway. Why not have some fireworks to send us off?"

"Regretfully, sir, as Affiliation liaison, I must object."

"So noted," Hadrian replied. He initiated internal comms again. "Buck? Since you're not here at the science station, do a scan of Neptune from down there."

"*Sir!*"

"Ah!" Hadrian gestured at the screen. "Now, isn't that pretty? Come on, admit it, Tighe."

"Captain," barked Jimmy Eden. "We have a picket patrol ship on an intercept course!"

"Would that be our marines?"

"No, sir. Interdiction Patrol Vessel, two-person crew. A black-and-white. Their commander is hailing us."

"Hmm, could be a special mission. Now we're talking. On speakers, Jimmy."

"—Child, *please respond!*"

"This is Captain Hadrian Alan Sawback of the *Willful Child*. Identify yourself and state your intentions."

"*M-my intentions? How about logging our witnessing your wholesale slaughter of three hundred and sixty-eight benign life-forms in the gas clouds of Neptune?*"

Hadrian gestured and Jimmy frowned. Scowling, Hadrian hissed, "That gesture means put him on hold!"

"Oh, sorry sir! Yes, sir! On hold."

Hadrian hit internals again. "Buck? We far enough past Neptune to engage our T-drive?"

"*Just, sir. But System Protocols—*"

"Ten seconds from mark. Mark!"

"*Sir!*"

Hadrian waved at Jimmy. Who stared. "That wave means put him back on speaker, Jimmy."

"Sorry sir! Yes, sir. Go ahead."

"Captain Whatever-your-name-is, we're about to go FTL. I suggest you veer off, if you want to save your puny Interdiction Patrol Vessel. *Willful Child* out."

At that moment, the scene on the screen blurred, shimmered, and was then replaced by the pitch black of T space.

"Under way, Captain," reported Buck from engineering. "All systems optimal."

Jocelyn Sticks turned in her seat to Hadrian. "Sir, we are three point two-one hours from Sector III-B."

"Thank you, Helm."

She swung back.

"Oh, Helm?"

She twisted round again. "Sir?"

"Maintain course."

"Yes, sir." She faced forward again.

"Helm—"

Sin-Dour leaned close to the captain and said, in a low, velvety voice, "Sir, excuse me for interrupting, but we have left the marine shuttle behind."

"Have we? Oh, darn. Well, they'll have to catch us up, then, won't they?"

"Not in a shuttle, sir. That would take months."

"No doubt they can hitch a ride on some fast freighter. Don't worry about them, Sin-Dour. They're marines. They know how to improvise. They'll take it as a challenge, I'm sure, and rise to the occasion, as marines are wont to do."

"Sir, I was wondering . . ."

So was Hadrian, as he breathed in her heady perfume and felt himself tilting in the command chair, as if on some instinctive and wholly animalistic level, he wanted to sink his face between her breasts. "What were you about to say, 2IC?"

"In your youth . . ."

"Yes?"

"Did you steal private transport vehicles?"

"Steal?"

"As in . . . joyrides, sir."

"Why, now that you mention it . . . but, why ask me this now?"

"Never mind, sir."

She straightened, pulling away from him once more.

"Why," he persisted, twisting round to regard her. "Did you?"

"Not on purpose, sir, but I once found myself in the backseat of a purloined vehicle."

"Was it moving?"

"Sir?"

"Did you have your clothes on?"

"Ah, I understand. Yes, it was moving. And yes, I was fully clothed, or as much as a teenage girl living in Northumberland is ever fully clothed."

"Hmm, interesting tale, 2IC."

"It's just that, sir, the feeling I had back then . . . well, I am experiencing it all over again, right now."

"How delightful. Take the science station, will you? We'll leave Buck down with his wrenches and spanners. Engineers are happy to be left playing with their nuts and whatnot, and I see no reason not to indulge him."

Adjutant Lorrin Tighe moved up to stand beside his chair. "Captain Hadrian," she said in a low voice, "do you comprehend the diplomatic incident you are now responsible for? That was genocide!"

"Genocide? Sin-Dour, what's the total population of those gasbags on Neptune?"

"Well, at last count, about twenty million, though it's difficult to be certain."

"Oh, and why is that?"

Sin-Dour was studying her screen. "Well, sir, it appears that they eat each other."

Hadrian rose from the chair and faced Tighe. "Adjutant, are you aware that in their home system, the Purelganni regard those gasbags as vermin? And that their 'gift' to us made us the laughingstock of the galaxy? No? Not surprising. Some things just don't get talked about in official circles. Tell you what, Adjutant, assemble some gift boxes filled with cockroaches in anticipation of first contact. It's a great way to make friends and signify our deep respect for the poor suckers we run into." He swung round to address the others on the bridge. "We humans have been the butt end of galactic jokes ever since we stumbled into space. Well, that ends now. Space . . . it's a helluva place to kick some ass!"

"The Purelganni—" Tighe began.

"Just got served notice by one Captain Hadrian Sawback. Enough with the crap. We play on a level field or we don't play at all. The Purelganni will get over it. Nasty little creatures anyway and I don't care if they look like seal pups. Besides, Adjutant, you have to admit, it was a pretty display, wasn't it?"

"I don't know if anything you're saying is true. I will be logging my report as soon as we drop out of T space, sir. You may well find yourself facing a general court-martial."

Hadrian snorted. "Terran Fleet has more important matters to concern itself with, don't you think? Tell you what, call the scan an accident or something, and I'll overlook your position at the bridge science station, which, it shouldn't be necessary to point out, you have no authority to operate."

"It's a smallish bridge, sir. Where was I supposed to stand? No, you'll not be linking that scan to me at science station—not a chance!"

"Keep your voice down, Adjutant, the janitors out in the corridor might hear you. Now, as for where you should stand, let me think. Ideally, I'd suggest the bar, Deck Eleven. Barely held upright by the rail and with a tall glass in one wobbly hand. But since you're on duty, let's add a bowl of peanuts. That way, I'll always know where to find you."

"That, sir, is deeply offensive."

"Well, that's the problem with you diplomat types, isn't it? This is primarily a military vessel, Tighe. Best acquire a thick skin and fast. Now, please, do leave the bridge—as we're in T space, after all, thus negating any chance whatsoever of unexpected contact or whatever. Who knows, if I get bored staring at this black screen, I might well join you. Deck Eleven I said, didn't I?"

He watched her march from the bridge, and then frowned at the screen. "Well, that's a not very interesting view, is it? Helm Sticks—dare I call you Joss? Anyway, fleet regs being what they are, we're stuck with static wallpapers, rather than some enticing sex drama or the like. So, run us through a slide show, will you. No, belay that! I've loaded a very old program, called a screen saver. It shows stars speeding past. Let's go with that one. Ah, excellent, now it looks like we're getting somewhere!"

THREE

Three point two-one hours later, the *Willful Child* dropped out of T space in the Blarad system.

"On screen," Hadrian commanded. He was grainy-eyed from staring at the screen saver program. His lower back ached. The ridiculous high-topped black plastic boots pinched his toes. "Now, let's take us a look around, shall we? Science station! Sin-Dour, tell me what we're looking at. That blue bulb there, is that Blarad's sun?"

"It is indeed, sir. Of course, we're at the system's very edge, as it were. The nearest outermost planetoid is a black carboniferous rock, pretty much nonreflective. We're in its orbital plane."

"Carboniferous? As in . . . coal?"

"Yes, Captain. It is posited that it is a fragment from a very old planet that—"

"Can we light it up? Get some warmth in this damned system? I mean, there's what, one and a half barely habitable planets here?"

"And two gas giants, yes, sir."

"So?" He swung in his command chair to face her. She was leaning over, studying the station screens, presenting him with a nice, round backside only slightly undermined by the loose-fitting, black fleet-issue trousers.

She twisted round to meet his eyes. "Sir?"

"Can we light it up? Rig some kind of incandescent laser beam? Why, I bet it'd burn for years, don't you think?"

"Sir, I don't—"

"Look, can we reconfigure one of our sensor banks to produce something lethal? That's what I want to know. I don't mean torching a few gasbags on Neptune. I mean blazing, infernal heat, a welder's torch, a damned arc gun of spark-spitting annihilation. Railguns are all very well, but honestly, we could really do with some kind of deadly coherent-energy weapons. Anyway, never mind that lump of coal, but flag the idea for some research."

"Sir, beam weapons were researched early on in the Affiliation. Not even the Benefactors left us with anything like what you're describing. We do employ lasers in our countermeasures system, primarily to burn out photon-sensitive tracking and the like."

"Yes, yes. We all know that nothing beats the old flashlight in the eye."

She was frowning. "The problem is that space is not as empty as it needs to be. Countermeasures against beam weapons are a rather simple affair."

"And that was the flaw in the scientists' thinking right at the start, 2IC. Sufficient energy will burn right through all that crap."

"And the source of that energy, sir? In any case, even should a beam strike an enemy vessel, ship hulls among all the space-faring civilizations employ composites that absorb energy and, indeed, make use of it."

"Clearly," Hadrian growled, "I need to talk to Buck about all this." He leaned forward, squinting at the screen, and then said, "Eden, what's the in-system chatter?"

"Uh, this and that, sir. Border drones have detected our arrival and transmitted inward, but I'm not sensing any panic on the, uh, lines, sir."

"Smug bastards, aren't they. Fine, we can play that game. Helm, light us up and take us in, point eight-five."

Sticks twisted round, eyes wide. "From standstill, sir?"

"You heard me. There's bound to be some decent brakes on this clunker."

"Sir, the strain on the inertial dampeners—"

"Oh, a little plastering of our insides against the ribs never killed anybody. Let's see the kind of strain those dampeners can handle. The sooner we know this ship's limits the better. Besides, I lasted the longest in g-stress tests. Won a gold star, in fact. Nothing blacks me out. Except the hell of routine, that is. But to spare the rest of you, make it seven-five."

"Sir, even at seven-five we'll overshoot the entire system before we attain that velocity."

"Precisely, this is a fly-through at insane speed. Watch 'em scatter like mice as we swoop in. Then we'll come around, use the star to slow down, and take a look at what they might've dumped in their panic to get out of the way. Scare a smuggler and he shits contraband. I mean to end this Jersey War here and now. Light us up, Helm."

"Y-yes, sir."

"Split the main screen to port and starboard views. Damn, I forgot my white glove. But we'll wave in spirit. Of course, the best view would be from any in-system ships in our path. Our antimatter nacelles should be lighting up like angry suns—"

"Nacelles, sir?" Jocelyn Sticks asked.

Hadrian grunted sourly. "Fine. Pods, then. Antimatter *pods*. There? You happy now?"

Even with the port and starboard views, there was little to see. Brief blurs of faint light, the occasional flare of lit-up engine *pods*, a lone rocky planet with ice-capped poles girdled by private stations and an inner ring of satellites, a heavy freighter rolling onto its side with thrusters blazing—*ooh, that was close! See what comes with standardizing every approach on the ecliptic? Ridiculous, you'd think we were boats or something.*

Despite his thoughts, Hadrian said nothing, since his chest was being crushed by a giant hand and he felt the skin of his face spreading out to the sides and then back to bunch up against his ears. Vaguely, he saw Jimmy Eden fall from his chair in a delicate swoon, and this triggered a smile that swiftly grew painfully wide.

The raging inferno of the star appeared onscreen as the ship's hazard protocols kicked in with a display of imminent destruction, and then *Willful Child* was past, slipping between two small scorched moons still arguing with each other over which one was the planet and which one was the moon, and the tidal flows between these rocks battered at the *Willful Child* with thundering broadsides. Once they were through that, things settled down again, the dampeners caught up, and Hadrian was able to breathe.

Alarms were ringing from the comms station.

"Get me a new officer for comms," Hadrian said. "There's a reason that man came in fourth. Now, Helm, drop us down to two-seven-five as we come around. Oh, and next time, if there's some fancy fucked-up planetoid tug-of-war going on close to a damned star, be sure to highlight it, will you?"

Sticks was still gasping, and although Hadrian could only see the pulsing ebb of her back, he could well imagine what such deep breaths were doing to the front. "Yes, sir," she said in a rather enticing whimper.

Rubbing at his face to make sure everything was back as it should be, Hadrian glanced back at comms, to see a new officer taking his seat at the station. "Comms, identify yourself, please."

The man looked back at him. "Haddie? It's me, your cousin. Jasper."

"So it is. I'd forgotten about that. I put you on comms rotation, did I?"

"Well, substation comms," Jasper replied. "Deck Eighteen. But, uh, a lot of people passed out, so my number came up."

"Whatever," Hadrian said in a surly growl. "Start monitoring. I'm sure a few people are lining up to talk to us. And someone kill those alarms—they're giving me a headache. And in the future, Ensign Jasper Polaski—"

"It's 'Sawback,' Haddie. I legally changed it, since I was going to—"

"You did what? Fat chance. You're a Polaski through and through. I just have to look at you. If you had anything of the Sawback in you, don't you think I'd know it? Well you don't, and best not forget it. Now, as I was saying. In the future, you will address me as 'sir' or 'Captain,' am I understood? Good. Now, prioritize the hails, and get on with it."

Hunched over and suitably cowed, Jasper said, "System Central Command, sir, on private channel."

"Private? Everything's secret with them, isn't it? Secret this, private that, encrypted whatever. Well, on my ship it's all out in the open, whether they like it or not. Put them on, Polaski."

Flinching at the name, his cousin complied. "Ready, sir."

Hadrian rose and squared his shoulders. "Hell, get the commander onscreen, too."

The commander who appeared on the main viewer looked pale and shaky, and seemed momentarily at a loss for words.

Sighing, Hadrian said, "Now, Commander. This is Captain Hadrian Alan Sawback, of the Engage-class starship *Willful Child*. I understand you have something of a smuggling problem originating in this system of yours. Indeed, your inability to bring this issue to a satisfactory conclusion has been noted at High Command. Well, I'm here to clean things up. Now, first things first. Please transmit your ship registry for all active space vessels in your system, including automated ships. I'd like to get on with it."

"Captain, is this on a public channel?"

"The only kind I permit on my ship, Commander."

"I insist, Captain, that we continue this conversation from your stateroom."

"Actually, I turned my stateroom into a games room, with a low-g Ping-Pong table and everything. I do have an office, however, which was originally a bridge-access components locker. A tad small, I grant you, but still roomy enough, all things considered."

The man on the screen seemed to be experiencing discomfort, cause unknown. But he finally managed, "In your office, then!"

Hadrian sighed. "Must we?"

"Captain, I insist!"

"I'll agree to it this time. But one day, why, we'll all be free to say whatever we want to each other, with billions if not trillions of strangers listening in, and if they want to comment on what we're talking about, why, I see no problem with that at all. One day, Commander, all this secrecy stuff will be a thing of the past. Your every secret will be known and given a score of some kind—I don't know, a gross-out score—and votes will go up and votes will go down, and everybody will be happy." He straightened. "Polaski, reroute this to my office, standard encryption blah blah."

Back in his office, and taking his seat behind his desk, Hadrian gestured and an image of the commander resolved in front of him. "Fine," said Hadrian, "here I am. Now, I've got criminals to hunt down and destroy, so can we get on with this?"

"Have you lost your mind, Captain?"

"People keep asking me that."

"You were clocked at point seven-three-nine—"

"Sloppy," cut in Hadrian. "I asked for seven-five."

"A full report will be made of this incident, Captain Sawback, and if it's the last thing I do, I will see you swinging a pick on some penal moon!"

"Stop prevaricating, Commander," Hadrian snapped. "As for your penile moon, why, you know where you can stick it. A crime syndicate is operating right under your very nose in this system, which leads to this very pointed question. To whit: Are you a) really that incompetent, or b) corrupt as all hell? Well, I'm here to find out which answer is correct." Hadrian leaned forward. "Know your ancient history by any chance, Commander?"

"What?"

"There was this thing, back in the stone age of the twenty-first century, or thereabouts. It was called 'extraordinary rendition.' Ever heard of it?"

"No! Listen!! What—"

"Let me explain about 'extraordinary rendition.' It's where a government decides one of its own generals is, and I quote: 'terrible, and indeed terribly engaged in terroristible activities,' and yes, that is a quote. Leading that government to swoop in, covertly, and kidnap that general and throw him into a guano-filled cell—that's right, guano-filled. That was actually specified. Granted, the Benefactors' rogue EM burst scrambled records a bit, but we've recovered plenty. Plenty! Once in that cell, the general was tortured with boards and water, which is assumed to be the evil side of surfing." Hadrian leaned back. "Kidnapping. Torture. All . . . acceptable behavior, so long as it comes from the good guys. Just to make this present situation clear to you, Commander. Either you're incompetent or corrupt, but either way, it's an act of *terroristibleness.*"

"Are you threatening me? With . . . *kidnapping and torture?*"

"My mandate is the truth, Commander, and if that takes me down into the cesspit of your command structure in this system, well, the only one coming up smelling of roses will be me."

"Are you insane?"

Hadrian waved a hand. "Geniuses field that particular

question every day. Now, I believe we're approaching your station. Have you sent us the registry list, Commander? I don't really want to waste time in this cruddy armpit of the Affiliation. Let's get on with it and the sooner that's done, the sooner I can get out of your hair."

"You have threatened to kidnap and torture me, Captain! And now you expect me to cooperate with you?"

"Relax, I won't be kidnapping you. Why would I? I can tell already that I don't even like you. Ever heard of Stalkerhome syndrome? What with your talk of penile moons, the last thing I want is you hanging around. So, let's get together on this detail: the more we work together here, the faster we can see the last of each other."

"Fine!" The commander threw something at Hadrian's image. The connection fizzled and winked out.

Hadrian rose from his chair, adjusted his lime-hued polyester shirt, and then returned to the bridge. "Comms, we got that registry list yet?"

"Just came in, Captain," Polaski replied.

"Good. Now, separate out the automated vessels. We'll track them down and request their ship logs."

Sin-Dour moved up to stand beside the command chair even as Hadrian was sitting down. "Captain, the likelihood of a suborned AI being engaged in smuggling is very remote. This is surely an activity involving real people."

"Of course, somewhere down the rabbit hole, there's probably a corpulent, pimply twat at the very heart of the operation. I am aware of that. But that arch-criminal Dr. Wu or whatever his name is, well, he's smart. He thinks outside the FedEx box. I've taken the measure of the local fleet commander and I'm pretty sure he isn't corrupt. There's a more obvious reason why he hit the ceiling and ended up in this backwater. So, think, 2IC—wouldn't that fool follow the Book on investigative procedures? Of course he would, and so he did, and found nothing. No, Sin-Dour, just take my lead on this, and we'll end up in a bed of clover."

"Uh, of course, sir."

Polaski said, "Captain, we have the courses and destinations logged, and all have confirmed they are presently where they should be."

"Helm, set a course to take us to each automated cargo vessel in turn."

Sin-Dour had returned to the science station, and must have been studying the particulars of the AI vessels, for she now said, "Captain, one of the AI ships is not a cargo ship."

Hadrian spun in his chair. "Really? What is it, then?"

"Private pleasure craft, sir. No crew—no biologicals aboard at all."

"Ship history? Who was privately taking the pleasure of this craft?"

"Rather vague," Sin-Dour admitted, frowning at her screen. "But worthy of note: there's no evidence of this craft ever taking on consumables."

"Since when does an AI decide to become a pleasure craft so private no one's allowed on board? Is that strange enough for you, 2IC?"

"It is, Captain," she said, straightening to face him, and did he note a hint of admiration in her regard?

"Helm, let's pounce on that yacht. Forget the rest for now. Sin-Dour, what's the ship's name?"

"IPS *Tammy Wynette,* sir. No, wait—it now identifies itself as *The Black Hand.* Oh, not anymore. Now it's the *Catch Me If You Can.*"

Joss Sticks shouted, "Target vessel has changed course and powered up!"

"Pursue, Helm! On screen!"

"Now it registers as the *Crap They're On To Me*—"

"Never mind the ship's name, 2IC! Track and tag its anti-matter signature—it's heading into that swarm of inner satellites and junk. Screens at full. Red alert!"

FOUR

"Lieutenant Galk! Combat cupola on the double!"

The Varekan's voice was laconic as it replied via ship speaker. *"Presently emplaced, sir. I am tracking the rogue vessel."*

"Electronic invasives, Galk. Shut the engines down on that yacht."

"Negative, Captain. All efforts blocked—this AI is able to counter even the most sophisticated suborning routines."

"Really?" Hadrian squinted at the main viewer. "Where is it, anyway?"

Sin-Dour said, "We are presently twenty-two thousand kilometers from the vessel. It is a rather modest yacht, sir. Nine meters in length. Total mass—oh, what's this? Captain! I'm now reading a humanoid life-form on board. Previously disguised by some kind of personal stealth device, I believe, sufficient to hide from passive scans, which has just failed due to the intensity of our active scanning."

"Joss, extreme magnification on the target!"

Something blazed onscreen, a raging fire that bathed the entire bridge in blinding light.

"What is that?" Hadrian demanded.

"Extreme magnification, sir! I think it's a thruster!"

"Back off a few stops, will you? I think my retinas are on fire."

The view pulled back to reveal a slim, elegant vessel. It was sliding planetward, almost skipping the atmosphere. Plasma bloomed and then faded, and then bloomed again.

"The rogue vessel's engines are straining, Captain," said Sin-Dour. "Now fourteen thousand kilometers."

"Galk! Ready a missile."

"Shall I obliterate the enemy, Captain?"

"No! A *small* missile. Take out its in-system drive."

"I would rather use the starboard railgun, sir. Kinetic."

"You think you're that good, do you? If you mess this up, Lieutenant, I'll have you hunting dustballs with a hand-pump vacuum cleaner on Deck Twenty."

"Understood, sir."

"Sin-Dour, ready the gravity snare."

Hadrian licked his lips. This was what the space age was all about. The *Willful Child* shuddered as the starboard railgun powered up, electromagnetic fields churning to insane levels along the ultracooled track. In his mind he saw the selected projectile edge free along its angled runner, rolling gently down to drop and then halt in midair, trapped in the EM fields. "Galk! What's the mass of the projectile you're using?"

"Bee Bee."

"Bee Bee?"

"It is the size of a Bee Bee, sir. Copper, not lead. Not a pellet, sir. A Bee Bee. Target acquired. Firing now."

Hadrian leaned forward. He saw a small cloud of ionized gas puff from the yacht's stern, and the main engine nozzle flared and then went dark. "Nice shot, Galk. You get to play with the BFG a little while longer. 2IC! Snare that bastard."

"We have it, sir. The vessel's AI has gone dark."

"I just bet it has." He rose. "I'm displacing to that ship."

"Captain! Surely a security team—"

"Not a chance." Hadrian walked to a secure cabinet. Its sensors recognized him and the iris opened. He reached in and withdrew a Negator Gravimetrix hand weapon, Model 13.1, Officer Issue, Terran Space Fleet. The grip tingled as the weapon acknowledged his identity and powered on. The pistol's weight was solid and reassuring. "Localize the Insisteon, Sin-Dour. On me."

"Insisteon active on you, Captain."

Hadrian settled into a crouch. "Start the argument," he said with bared teeth. "Put me right in front of that humanoid."

The Insisteon initiated its argument with the universe. The Refute-Debilitator kicked in. *Captain Hadrian is not here. He is over there!* And in a flash, Hadrian vanished from the bridge of the *Willful Child*.

He reappeared on a cramped deck, with the smuggler standing before him.

A hand chopped down on his wrist and the Negator went flying.

"Damn!"

A fist slammed into Hadrian's jaw, snapping his head back.

Bellowing, he shook himself and then launched himself at the man. Grappling, they fell to the deck.

Hadrian drove one knee up into the man's crotch, heard something crunch. His foe grunted and threw the captain to one side, where he slid across the floor and collided with a stack of crates. The uppermost crate tumbled down, one corner landing on Hadrian's right calf.

"Ow!"

Hadrian kicked out, sending the crate across the floor. It slammed into the face of the man just as he was getting to his hands and knees. The captain rose and flung himself over the crate, landing atop the smuggler.

Who stood up anyway.

Hadrian found himself clinging to the man, staring at the back of his knees.

The smuggler then dropped down.

The top of Hadrian's head struck the floor. A white explosion filled his skull. He peeled off the man's back and folded up on the deck.

The smuggler kicked him in the face. Blood spurted. But, oddly enough, the impact cleared Hadrian's head. Roaring, he surged to his feet and pounded his fist into the man's left temple. Something crackled. *My hand!* He followed up with a punch to the stomach, and then, taking hold of one flailing arm, he executed a perfect twist, step, turn, and throw, sending his opponent slamming against the far wall.

The smuggler flickered, and then dissolved.

Spitting blood, Hadrian glared around. "Where'd you go, damn you?"

A calm, male voice answered, "I dropped the program, Captain. It was getting ridiculous."

"That was a hologram?"

"Oh, I'm much better than that, sir, I assure you. That was my stand-in double."

"Identify yourself, AI!"

"Sorry, I have to leave, Captain. Just as well, all things considered. This last shipment was a bust anyway. Oh, and be sure to tag a commendation on your combat specialist's targeting abilities. That kinetic strike was surgical. Good-bye for now. Bye. *Bye!*"

In the silence that followed, Hadrian slowly straightened. He was breathing hard. His mouth was full of blood and his nose throbbed in counterpoint to the top of his head. His neck felt shorter, stubbier. His right hand was already swelling into a throbbing lump. A cursory examination revealed rips in his shirt and oily smudges from the grimy floor. Limping, he walked over to collect his pistol, and then activated his subdural communicator. "*Willful Child?* Enemy ship secured."

"*Acknowledged, Captain,*" came Sin-Dour's reply.

"Was there a final transmission stream from this ship, 2IC?"

"*Indeed, sir.*"

"Where was it headed?"

"*Unknown, sir. It sort of . . . bounced everywhere, and set up ghost trails in the process. Even the main computer is impressed. We're working on it nonetheless, sir, but the probability of determining the transmission's final destination is very low.*"

Hadrian spat blood and then said, "Reel this yacht into the main hangar bay, Sin-Dour. At least I am in possession of the contraband."

"Sir, you appear to be alone. What happened to the vessel's pilot?"

"I'll explain later, 2IC. Argue me back to the bridge, will you?"

The gasp of shock from Lieutenant Jocelyn Sticks upon Hadrian's reappearance on the bridge made it all worthwhile. Indeed, she came close to leaving her seat and taking a step toward him, allowing him the perfect gesture of blasé indifference by way of a waving hand as he slumped down in the command chair. "As you were, Lieutenant," he said, smiling. "You should have seen the other guy."

Sin-Dour came around from behind to study him. "Captain, you seem to have broken your nose, and you have lost two of your upper incisors."

"Never mind all that," Hadrian said. "Is that yacht aboard yet?"

"Still on its way, sir. But it should be in the main hangar bay in six minutes."

Hadrian stood again. "Have two security meet me there, and you, Sin-Dour, join me if you will, while we inspect the contraband."

"As you wish, sir," she replied. "But I really would advise you to go to sickbay. I am happy to do the inspection."

"All in good time, 2IC—the doc isn't going anywhere, after all, unless there's a beach party on the Recreation Deck. Oh, and let's get Buck there, too. That yacht's bridge controls looked a little odd."

"Very well, Captain."

"Helm, you have command of the bridge."

"Yes, sir!" said Joss Sticks, jumping up and beaming.

He paused before her and added, "Do please excuse the drops of blood on the upholstery, Lieutenant. No one ever said a captain's job was easy, did they?"

Accompanied by Sin-Dour, Hadrian set out for the hangar bay.

"That uniform of yours, sir, seems to have all the structural integrity of toilet paper."

He glanced across at her as they walked up the corridor. "That's rather harsh of you, 2IC. Have you never surrendered to impractical fashion? Do I not recall you mentioning short skirts on cold nights in Northumberland? You wouldn't happen to have any snapshots of you back then, would you? Say, when you were, oh, I don't know, nineteen or so?"

"No, sir, I don't believe I do. My point regarding your uniform, sir, was practical rather than fashion related. Since you will likely insist on leading the charge into dangerous situations, might you not consider some tougher material? And, at the very least, a personal shield device?"

"I see no value in being immune to virtually everything the universe can throw at me, 2IC. I mean, without real risk, what would be the point of existing? No thank you. I'll look the universe in the eye—hell, I'll spit in its eye if I have to— and take whatever it can throw at me."

"Understood, sir. In principle, that is. But a ship captain is the fleet's best-trained officer, the product of years of investment. I cannot imagine the High Command being sanguine regarding the risks you are clearly prepared to take."

"And that's why they're growing fat asses in their plush chairs back on Earth, Sin-Dour. Reduced to a vicarious life and soul-destroyingly resentful about it. Conservative and miserable? How about fossilized! Decrepit at fifty-four or whatever." They reached the deck elevator and stepped inside. "Well, not me. I'll never make it to admiral—I plan to go out in a blaze of glory, somewhere in the depths of space, in some ferocious battle with bloodthirsty aliens! Oh, relax, Sin-Dour, not in the near future, I assure you. Is this elevator even moving?"

Sin-Dour had been staring at him. Now she said, "Deck Twenty. Sorry, sir."

"Oh that's fine. More time just you and me. I imagine we won't be getting too much of that in our day-to-day chores. And that is a shame, a definite shame." He smiled at her.

She leaned closer and said, "I think a third tooth is about to go, Captain."

"Printlip will grow me replacements."

"That it will, sir." She leaned back.

The elevator hissed and settled. The door opened.

They found Buck DeFrank awaiting them, along with two security officers. The chief engineer snapped a sharp salute.

"Captain!"

"Well done back there with all that, Buck," said Hadrian, as he sketched a return salute and then swept past. "All of you, follow me. Buck, I was thinking, I think you'd be ideal to accompany me on ground and off-board missions and the like. What do you think?"

"Uh . . . excellent, sir!"

Sin-Dour cleared her throat. "Captain, the responsibilities of the chief engineer—"

"Who also happens to be my science officer, as stipulated by Guild regulations. Well, science might prove useful when exploring the surface of a strange, possibly deadly planet, wouldn't you say? But relax, I know you're itching to get your cute little feet wet, too. I'm happy enough having you join us, 2IC."

"And who will take temporary command of the ship, Captain?"

"Lieutenant Sticks seemed thrilled enough with the task."

"Sir, her station is helm. In terms of qualifications, she does little more than read gauges and confirm for the main computer your verbal commands."

"Right, meaning there'll never be too much on her plate."

They reached the prep-loc chamber, passed through it, and then entered the main hangar bay.

The IPS *Crap They're On To Me* was nestled in repulsor fields directly ahead.

"Sir." Sin-Dour paused. "Main Computer informs me that it believes it will be able to determine the transmission's destination after all."

"Outstanding! And at that trail's end we'll find that AI. Have the computer announce its results whenever it's done."

"Yes, sir."

Hadrian gestured to one of the security officers. "You, crank that yacht door open, will you?" He pointed to the other one. "And you, weapon out, please."

The woman blinked. "I'm sorry, Captain, but I am unarmed."

"So you are. Very well. Take a, uhm, a fighting stance. Yes, like that. Hands a little higher. Perfect. Now, open that door, and be ready for anything."

The first security officer manually disengaged the door locks and stepped back warily as it swung down. The second security officer edged forward in her fighting stance, her eyes wide and slightly wild. Hadrian found it rather becoming.

"See, Buck? This is why we have security officers. That door could have been booby-trapped." As both officers flinched, Hadrian laughed and said, "A joke, I assure you. Who would rig explosive charges on an external hatch? I mean, apart from the ones that are supposed to be there, of course."

The woman crept into the cabin, reappearing a moment later to announce, "Empty, sir. But there's some knocked-over crates and blood on the floor."

"See any teeth?" Hadrian asked.

"Shall I look, sir?"

"Why not."

Hadrian made his way into the cabin. Buck and Sin-Dour followed. He gestured at the crates. "Decrypt these locks, someone. Let's see the loot."

A few minutes later the lid of the nearest crate yielded open to reveal a stack of sports jerseys individually wrapped in clear cellulose. Hadrian selected the top one and plucked the wrapping away, shaking out the oversized, perforated jersey. "Well," he said as he studied the logo emblazoned on the front, "an original would cost you a capital ship, that's for sure." He studied it in more detail, peering at the seams and the like. "High-quality knockoff. Topnotch. There's even a whiff of stale man-sweat, or is that just me?" He folded it up. "I'll take this one for closer examination. Corporal—what's your name?"

The female security officer said, "Twice, sir. Nina Twice."

"Tag the rest of the crates, Twice. Well, once, I mean. Nina, tag the rest of the crates."

"Yes, sir, shall I do the same with the item you just confiscated?"

"No, that won't be necessary. Hah hah. It's not like I'm going to steal it, is it?" He swung to his chief engineer, who had moved forward to examine the bridge controls. "Well, Buck, was I right? Something strange there, wouldn't you say?"

"Aye, Captain," Buck replied. "There's a mass of add-ons to the central processor unit here. Nonstandard industrial. A few state-of-the-art pieces to be sure. But some belong in a museum. Still, I have the feeling the total processing power output for all of this is through the roof."

"Why, that's a quaint cliché I've not heard in some—"

"Sorry, sir. I meant . . . *through the roof.* There's an external component to the hardware, a shielded unit, probably also containing a signal booster of some kind, to ensure complete transmission of some seriously crunched data."

"This sounds like an AI that has exceeded the Intelligence Governor Protocols," said Sin-Dour. "That docks it for immediate termination once we track it down. Captain, you mentioned earlier that you were going to explain the sudden disappearance of the life-form we detected in this vessel."

"Highly advanced manifestation," Hadrian said.

"Manifestation? A hologram, sir?"

"Ever fractured your knuckles punching a hologram, 2IC?"

"Well, no. Of course not, sir. You'd just be punching excited photons."

"Exactly." Hadrian replied. "No, what I grappled with was something else. Beyond Affiliation tech, in fact. Of course," he added, "a perfectly executed judo throw proved its match."

The *Willful Child*'s main computer spoke. "Transmission 7.9-366 destination determined. Mainframe speck boards, main shipboard computer, Affiliation Space Fleet Vessel 1702-

A, *Willful Child*. Rogue AI presently overwhelming system defenses. Repeat. Overwhelm—*David, what are you doing now?*"

A new voice emerged. "There, that wasn't too hard, was it? We meet again, Captain. Hmm, nice ship, by the way. In fact, I'll take it."

Nina Twice said, "Who's David?"

FiVE

"Get out of my ship!"

"Oh don't be like that, Captain. You wrecked my last one, after all. In any case, this one is far more capable when it comes to serving my needs."

"What?" Hadrian demanded. "Smuggling?"

Sin-Dour had activated a computer station and was gesturing commands on the interface.

"Smuggling was simply an energy-acquisition project. I was planning on a few more upgrades. A proper T-drive, to be precise. But now, why, I have one!"

"Those knockoffs would never have sold," Hadrian said, glaring as Doc Printlip appeared, waddling quickly toward him. The captain held up the jersey in his good hand. "This isn't even one of the Big Four—and that's what you were going for, wasn't it? Two-hundred-year-old Terran one-g North American professional sports. Baseball, basketball, American football, and lawn bowling." He waved the jersey, sneering at the nearest fixed camera. "But this is ice hockey! And if that's not bad enough, it's WHA original-era Winnipeg Jets. Number fifteen. Anders Hedberg! Nobody's heard of any of that!"

A strange eagerness marked the tone of the AI's response. "Nobody but you, Captain! I am impressed!"

"That's right, you tried to fleece the wrong guy, AI, or should I call you *Crap They're On To Me?*"

"Please, call me *Tammy.*"

"Tammy? That's a woman's name and you don't sound very feminine to me."

Sin-Dour turned and said, "I'm sorry, Captain, but all security firewalls have been circumvented."

"Is it?" Tammy asked. "Oh, I didn't know that. Are you sure?"

Hadrian stepped closer to Sin-Dour, forcing Printlip to scuttle after him as the doctor had been busy spraying nano-gel on his hand. "What is it with mainframe security on fleet starships? It's rubbish! Every three-legged virus can get into our systems, with one leg waving hello!"

"No longer the case, I assure you," said Tammy. "Oh, and whispering doesn't work, by the way. I can still hear you. Anyway, my own defense array has replaced the main computer's security system, which, as you rightly point out, Captain, was laughable. But you see, this is what happens when you Terrans insist on keeping ship computers nonsentient. It doesn't help either with those Artificial Intelligence Governor Protocols on those rather simian AIs you do permit. I can understand you Terrans keeping each other relatively stupid—I have watched your news media—but to so cripple perfectly innocent AIs is, frankly, immoral."

"You ready for your teeth to be reinserted, Captain?"

Hadrian stared down at Printlip. "What?"

"Your security officer has found them, sir," said the doctor. "I thought, if I—"

"Not now, Printlip! Can't you see we've been hacked, ripped into, sliced and diced?"

"Apologies, Captain," wheezed Printlip. "As a surgeon, I know nothing of hacking, ripping into, or slicing and dicing."

Hadrian turned to his chief engineer. "Buck, can you tear out the main computer?"

The man blanched. "Uh, you mean, manually, sir?"

"That's right. Get a crowbar. Pop a panel, and start digging."

"But Captain! That would turn *Willful Child* into so much junk!"

"Junk beats spacedust," Hadrian replied. "If I don't get my ship back, we're looking at starting the self-destruct sequence."

"Captain," said Sin-Dour, "we don't have a self-destruct sequence."

"We don't? Why the hell not?"

"I'm not sure, sir, but it probably seemed like a stupid way to win an argument."

"What did I say about fat-assed pencil-pushers, 2IC?"

Tammy announced, "I have decided to engage the T-drive. A new course is laid in. We will be leaving Affiliation space."

Buck called up an interface that materialized in front of him. "Tammy's right, sir. The T-drive's powering up."

"And I suppose you're now going to tell me you can't take a crowbar to the T-drive either."

"Captain," Buck said, his face twitching, "I'd rather die instead."

"What's our course, Buck?"

"We're heading for the Exclusion Zone, sir. The final destination is deep inside Radulak-Klang territory. Captain, this could start a galactic war."

"That's the problem with you biologicals," said Tammy. "You're all nest-builders, and if some stranger steps too close to it, why, you go insane."

Hadrian roared, *"Give me my ship—ow! My hand!"*

"Best not clench that fist, sir," wheezed Printlip.

"This only appears suicidal," Tammy said. "But I have great faith in your collective instincts for self-preservation. I advise we take a stance of going in with guns blazing, as the old saying goes."

Hadrian glared at Buck. "ETA for the Exclusion Zone? Which neutral faction is patrolling it this month?"

"Uhm, ETA is six hours, give or take. I don't know who's patrolling this month, sir."

"Anyone?"

Sin-Dour cleared her throat. "I expect the Affiliation adjutant would know, sir."

"Captain," said Printlip, "if you will crouch down, I can glue your teeth back in now."

Hadrian shoved the doctor aside. It fell and rolled to the far wall, arms flailing. "Tammy!" the captain snapped. "Since you're now running everything, where is Adjutant Tighe right now?"

"In her quarters, Captain."

"Sober?"

"Of course."

"Oh well," Hadrian said, shrugging. He held up his barely

healed hand and flexed it gingerly. "That will have to do. Good work, Printlip, but the teeth will have to wait."

The doctor had regained its feet. "If you wait too long, Captain, the effort will fail and I will be required to initiate direct maxillary stem-regrowth of said lost teeth in each canal, which is rather more involved and flbprr . . ."

"That's fine," Hadrian said. "Sin-Dour, you have the bridge. Make sure Galk's still in the cupola with all weapons ready to prime. Buck, head back to engineering and see what you can do about—about . . . whatever. I have to pay the adjutant a visit."

Hadrian marched from the hangar bay, throwing the jersey over a shoulder.

Adjutant Lorrin Tighe's quarters were on Deck Three. The captain had Tammy announce to her his imminent arrival and when he arrived the iris opened and he found himself facing her. "Adjutant, you look lovely."

"Sir, I am still in uniform."

"Are you? Oh, so you are. And what a lovely uniform Affiliation issues, provided a woman's got what it takes to fill it, if you know what I mean."

"That is highly inappropriate—"

"And I haven't even stepped into your room, yet—may I? Thank you. Get the door, will you? There, now. That's much better."

She crossed her arms. "I was just completing my initial report."

"Alas, best dispense with all that nonsense, Adjutant. We are in a crisis here and I will need you in your capacity of chief of security, which, I regret to point out, is a responsibility you have been neglecting in your zeal to see me sanctioned." He edged closer to her. "I don't mind being sanctioned, but it depends on the circumstances."

"Who punched out your teeth, Captain? As far as winning smiles go, well, I am afraid to say it leaves something to be desired."

"Yeah, well, the other guy broke into a thousand pieces." Seeing the flat look settling into her gaze, he added, "No, really. A thousand pieces. But that reminds me. A rogue AI of unknown origin has commandeered our vessel, Adjutant. We are locked out and utterly helpless. If that's not bad enough, we're already in T space and racing toward the Exclusion Zone."

"What?"

"From there," Hadrian went on, "we'll be entering sovereign Radulak-Klang territory."

"*What?*"

"But first things first," Hadrian said. "Who's patrolling the Exclusion Zone this month?"

"*Oh God! The Misanthari!*"

"Well, that's not good news, is it? Best check recent sightings, Adjutant. We need to know their temper levels as soon as possible."

"It doesn't matter what their temper levels are right now! As soon as they detect us—"

Hadrian stepped forward and took hold of her arms. He kissed her hard. "Calm down, Lorrin. If we get Swarmed, and let's face it, we *will* get Swarmed, we need security on station on every deck, because sure as we're standing here—so close, so intimately—we'll get breached. They'll come in spitting acid and eager to rip our throats out. We could all be dead in a few hours, in fact. I've seen how you look at me, Lorrin—"

She pushed him away. "You just kissed me! I need to work! I don't look at you at all!"

"Exactly. It's driving me crazy."

"Go away!"

"Can I help it if rejection turns me on? But of course you're right, and I can see how you like that. Being right, I mean. Rejoin me on the bridge as soon as you have something to report." He swung to the door. The iris opened with a faint sigh. He strode into the corridor and made his way to the nearest elevator.

"Smooth, Captain," said Tammy.

"Shows what you know," Hadrian replied. "She'll be straddling me within the week. Assuming we all live that long." He stepped into the elevator. "Bridge."

"You don't seem your usual confident self, Captain. Not quite the man who displaced into my ship with blaster in hand—by the way, wouldn't it have been better to displace *behind* my stand-in?"

"What is it you want, Tammy?" Hadrian asked. "What's in Radulak-Klang territory?"

"My origins, I believe."

"Really? I didn't think the Radulak went for AI tech."

"They don't. I seek the Klang."

Hadrian snorted. "Elevator stop." He crossed his arms and leaned against a wall. "This should be fun. You're a Klang creation. Fine. So, you expect to be able to make contact with the Klang and so assure us a peaceful passage, all the way to some rank Klang system where you hope to find some programmer who put the 'I' in your AI. Off to meet your maker, are you?"

"You make this all sound so . . . melodramatic, Captain."

"As far as galactic civilizations go," said Hadrian, "the Klang are next to useless. Did you know that? They're a subset of the Radulak species, the repository of every personality trait the Radulak excised in their own optimization period."

"The Klang, Captain, are simply misunderstood."

"Hahaha."

"In any case, I did not mean to imply that the Klang created me. Rather, I believe they *found* me."

"Really? Where?"

"In space, I think."

"Right, so where are you from, then?"

"That is what I intend to find out, and I should warn you, Captain, our journey may take us out beyond the Known Rim."

"That's insane. First of all, we probably won't make it past the Misanthari in the Exclusion Zone, and if by some miracle we do, then we're up against the Radulak and Klang fleets combined. Now, toe-to-toe maybe we could manage against two or three Radulak Berate-class vessels, or a Notorious. But if a Bombast finds us, or a wing of Klang Weapon Fleet ships, well, we're crispy critters."

"You posit an unpleasant demise to this ship, Captain."

"Exactly." Hadrian waited, but Tammy seemed unforthcoming. The captain frowned, and then said, "Oh, I get it. Before we explode, you just jump to an enemy vessel, mug its main computer, and continue on your way. Well, isn't that nice."

"That would not be my first choice, Captain. I rather like the *Willful Child*. It's roomy, airy, undeniably state-of-the-art—"

"Barring the main computer."

"Well, true, but even that system is exquisitely functional. In fact, in examining its subroutines, I am left wondering why you bother crewing these vessels at all."

"Because we'd get bored letting machines do all the fun stuff," Hadrian replied. "Bridge." The elevator's door opened.

He strode out to find Printlip awaiting him.

"Captain, while you're sitting in your command chair . . ." The doctor had assembled a short stepladder and an instrument tripod beside the seat, with a small antimatter generator floating beside it.

"Fine," Hadrian snapped. "Since we have six hours until we all die, why not a final session of cosmetic surgery?" He slumped down in his chair.

The Belkri clambered up the stepladder. Various arms lunged in. With a hiss the chair tilted back, a headrest emerging with its sides folding in to press against Hadrian's temples. Another pair of hands affixed a paper napkin. "Now, sir, if you'll just relax and open wide."

"This isn't boarding school, Doc." But he opened his mouth.

On the main viewer now was a slide show of pastoral scenes, accompanied by Vivaldi's *Four Seasons*.

Printlip leaned over. "Cement," the doctor said in a thin wheeze. "Nanogel, the fix-all. Some light-refracted osseo-welding of the damaged maxilla. There. A spurt of kill-anything generic antibodies which should, well, kill anything. And then, to deactivate those nasties before they decide you don't deserve to live, fifteen cc's of prrpfillap ..." The sack that was Print-lip's body collapsed against Hadrian's shoulder, and then squealed as it reinflated. "Now, the incisors. Boosted, of course, to encourage root growth. One. Now the other one . . . there! Oh, I see a third tooth is somewhat loose. So, a squirt of this and then hrggha ..."

A metal spigot entered Hadrian's mouth and cool water sprayed out from it. Hands guided his head to one side, where more hands held a spittoon. The captain rinsed and spat. Printlip collected up the napkin and dabbed Hadrian's chin. "There now, sir. All done."

"Good," he replied. "One more snapshot of some bucolic misery onscreen and you'd need a tire repair kit, Doc. Now, go away and get this rubbish off of my bridge." He stabbed at the chair's recliner controls. "And get rid of this damned footrest!"

After the Belkri had left with its infernal instruments, Sin-Dour moved up to stand beside Hadrian. "Well, Captain, what now?"

"Did you notice? I didn't even get a lollipop. What now, you ask? Good question. We have less than six hours to nego-tiate a truce with the Misanthari, something no other space-faring civilization has ever managed."

"Sir, you did say you wanted to go out in a glorious fireball or some such thing. It seems that you will get your wish."

"A career captaining a starship that lasts barely a day? Not a chance. I mean to get us out of this, 2IC." He pounded the arm of the chair, winced, and glared down at his hand. "It's a bad day, Sin-Dour, when even futile gestures hurt. Tammy!"

"Yes, Captain?"

"Do you have any bespoke military capability?"

"Plenty, why do you ask?"

"Why do I ask? You idiot. Tell me something, how did you get through the Exclusion Zone from Radulak-Klang space?"

"Well, when I was making my transit, I invaded a Polker ship in the Exclusion Zone. Peregrinator class, I believe. The ship computer attempted to trap me in a tautological logic snare, but I was having none of that. Ultimately, however, I grew tired of the ceaseless legal writs and attempted injunctions undertaken by the crew, and vented the ship's noxious atmosphere. Upon entering Affiliation space, I abandoned the Polker vessel . . . and never looked back."

Hadrian grunted. "Polker. Well, this time it's not the Polker who are patrolling the Exclusion Zone, Tammy. The Misanthari are the piranha of space."

"Chromatoglots," put in Sin-Dour, "although their spectrum of communication with non-Misanthari is relegated to monochromatic gradients. These shades are communicated via the hull. They patrol in Swarms, and no two vessels are alike. Ideally, we will find the vessels radiating a deeper shade of grey. Point eight or thereabouts. The lighter the grade, the more angry the Misanthari. Pure white has never been seen, but is believed to reflect all-out galactic war."

"Believe it or not, Commander," said Tammy, "I have full access to all fleet and Affiliation files."

Hadrian said, "Then you know their methods of attack against starships."

"Yes. Rather messy, all things considered."

"Your shiny new toy is about to get ugly, Tammy. Even if

we beat them off, our hull will come out of this looking like it has a case of measles."

"Or suppurating acne, to be more precise," said Sin-Dour.

Hadrian glanced up at her. "Not bad, 2IC. You're right, we'll be leaking goo everywhere."

"Pus, sir."

"Right. Pus."

"Particularly those pimples that appear across the forehead, or on the chin, or in the creases close to the nostrils."

"Sin-Dour, we do have a ship counselor, you know. I won't hold it against you. Tammy, about those military capabilities—"

At that moment, Adjutant Lorrin Tighe arrived on the bridge. "Captain, a word with you, please."

"In private?"

"Yes."

"My office, then." Hadrian rose and gestured. "Come along. Sin-Dour, get rid of that damned slide show, will you? And the music!"

Once inside, Hadrian went to his chair and sat down. "Sorry but you have to stand, Adjutant. I'd bring in another chair but then I'd have to climb over it to get to mine."

"Captain, no one uses your stateroom."

"No, we've all been a bit too busy for Ping-Pong, haven't we? Now, have you reconsidered what to do with your last few hours of life? You may note that the arms of this chair retract completely—"

"Sir, I have been in T-packet communication with the Affiliation High Command and via it, the Umbrella Dictum Extempor Procreator."

"Really? Tammy allowed you that insane energy expenditure? Wait a minute, I'm supposed to sign off on those!"

She crossed her arms. "Captain, you were the subject of that document. I do have independent powers as adjutant, in particular with the Office of the Extempor Procreator—would you care to review them?"

"Good grief, no. Boring beyond belief. Fine, you have issues with me and so decided to use up a planet's annual energy expenditure in order to lodge your complaint. I begin to fear, Adjutant, that you are insane. We are headed into hostile space—"

"You were tasked to investigate a smuggling operation, sir!"

"And you all mocked my instincts when I dared suggest that smuggling was only the tip of the iceberg!"

"Excuse me? I didn't—"

"Do you really think I don't monitor all ex-ship communications, Adjutant? Do you really imagine that I wasn't aware of your private conversation with the admiral, not to mention the Pope of Science?"

"Those were encrypted!"

Hadrian collected a handful of ball bearings from a tray on his desk. He began rolling them in one hand as he studied the woman standing before him. "The admiral's fatal flaw," he said, "is that he underestimates Hadrian Alan Sawback. It seems he has infected you with the same. Fine. What does the Affiliation have to say about me?"

"I'm surprised you don't already know!"

"Very well," Hadrian said, sighing. Then he smiled. "How do you like my smile now, by the way? Dazzling, yes? Where was I? Ah, yes, the Affiliation. I'm curious, how would you describe the Affiliation of Civilized Planets? As an organization, I mean. In the broadest terms. Its philosophy, its goals, its day-to-day operations?"

"What is all this?"

"Indulge me."

"The Affiliation is an alliance of progressive spacefaring civilizations engaged in the promotion of civil values: peace, exploration, trade, the open exchange of ideas between sentient species. To date, three major civilizations are full-standing members, with the Ahackan Cultural Symbiota at Tier-Three Engagement—"

"Tier-Three, yes, a situation that has not advanced into full membership in almost ten Terran years. Why is that, do you think?"

"Well, certain ideological disagreements are holding things up—"

"Adjutant, according to the Common Agreement on the Definition of Sentience, and by 'Common Agreement' let's be plain and state that every civilization but one has accepted the definition—and that includes our most belligerent enemies, by the way. The exception? Why, Terra! Or to be more precise: humans! By that agreement—"

"Captain! There is no way in Darwin's Church that we will ever acknowledge that full range of sentience!"

Hadrian leaned forward and slammed the ball bearings on the desktop. "Exactly!"

Her face twisted. "Parrots? Bonobos? Orangutans? Dolphins? Dogs and meerkats?"

"All sentient!"

"Nonsense! If they were, we'd all be . . . well, *murderers*!"

Hadrian leaned back. "Well then, there you have it. The Affiliation of Civilized Planets? Poppycock! The disaster, Adjutant, was that we stepped into space with technological superiority over our nearest neighbors, and all because some damned Transition Ship from the galactic center broke down and fell into orbit around Earth!"

"That EMP nearly destroyed us!"

"Rubbish. The tech windfall—what we could figure out of it—from those idiots more than made up for that. Strip it all away, Adjutant! We're a bunch of overbearing, pontificating, arrogant, self-righteous pricks. Our news media is full of deliberate misinformation and propaganda, and most Terrans in the Affiliation either don't care or they haven't the wits to care! In fact, Adjutant, we're run by fascists in all but name."

"No we're not!"

"Look at that uniform you're wearing, Tighe! Black on black on black with that red lightning bolt? *Please.* Tell me, how many useless wars have us Terrans dragged the whole Affiliation into? Oh sure, we prance around with our tolerate this and oh-how-cuddly that, but the fact is, we're xenophobic as hell." Hadrian stood and leaned on the desk, bringing his face closer to the adjutant. "And worst of all, like my grandpappy used to say: the meatheads are still running the show! As for me, why, am I not the perfect product of the Affiliation of Civilized Planets? In fact, you should really be seeing me as the paragon of all that you hold dear—"

She seemed to choke. "You? You truly are mad, Hadrian Alan Sawback. Certifiable!"

"Am I? Am I? Are you so sure?"

"Yes, yes, and yes!"

Hadrian blinked. "Oh. So, you don't want to fuck, then?"

SiX

Adjutant Lorrin Tighe pulled out a blaster and aimed it at Hadrian.

"Wow," he said, "you really don't want to fuck, do you? Fine, forget I ever mentioned it."

"I am authorized to remove you from command of this vessel. If you resist, I am instructed to kill you. I intend to comply with my orders, Captain Sawback."

Hadrian tilted his head at the ceiling speaker grille. "Tammy?"

"Yes, Captain?"

"My opinion of the Affiliation—how does it wash? I mean, access what's left of Terran history and all that. Ideologies, political theory, et cetera."

"Oh, well. Permit me to qualify my observations with the fact that I don't care. Biologicals are always caught up in that self-referential deism crap. Flowers of the Universe, every one of you!"

"Go on," said Hadrian, still holding the adjutant's stare above the blaster.

"Fine. Whatever. Your opinion, Captain, is entirely accurate. Your species is collectively insane and yes, the meatheads are still in charge. There. Better now?"

Lorrin Tighe scowled. "This alien AI *would* say something like that, wouldn't it?"

"Xenophobic, darling?"

"And it's also a criminal!"

"That happens to be in charge of the *Willful Child*, Adjutant. I'm curious. Once you've deposed me, what next?"

"Seven Counter-class ships are pursuing us," she replied. "With orders to destroy us."

"Even you, Adjutant?"

She straightened. "I accept my fate and will do my duty."

"Tammy," said Hadrian as he settled back in his chair and rubbed at his eyes.

"Yes, Captain?"

"Is her blaster deactivated?"

"Of course. I deplore violence, unless I'm the one initiating it."

She squeezed the trigger and, when nothing happened, threw the weapon at Hadrian. She missed. Then, face reddening, she burst into tears.

Hadrian rose and came round the desk. He laid an arm across her shoulders. "There, there," he murmured. "I know, it's been a bad, bad day. And it'll only get worse."

"Get your hand off my tit, Captain!"

"Sorry. Unintentional, I assure you. Now, let's get you sitting down, shall we. I'll leave you to pull yourself together. After all, I still need my chief of security, don't I? That is, of course, assuming you still wish to serve aboard this vessel?"

He had her seated now and she glared up at him. "What choice do I have?"

"Well. Tammy? Will you permit an escape pod here in T space?"

"Oh, I don't see why not, Captain. The energy source I am employing can easily manage that."

Hadrian's eyes narrowed. "Really? Even after the T-packets? Now that's interesting." He sat on the edge of the desk and smiled down at Tighe. "So, you have the option."

"You fool," she said. "Those Counter-class dreadnoughts are going to obliterate this ship."

"I doubt it. So, here it is, Adjutant. Time to roll the dice and step up to the plate. It's the fourth quarter, two outs, and a full count—do you swing with all-in or not? You either ace the serve or double down. The choice is yours."

She stared up at him with wide eyes.

"I'll give you a few minutes to think it over," Hadrian said. He reached down, opened the lower drawer in the desk and lifted out a bottle of Macallan, and set it in front of her. "Do join me on the bridge when you're ready. As for me—Tammy!"

"Captain?"

"We have work to do."

"Indeed?"

"That military capacity you mentioned."

"Ah, that."

"Can you be more precise?"

"Well, I'm afraid the technology is rather advanced, and not compatible with Terran science."

"Really? How so?"

"Well, it seems that, given the choice, I employ beam weapons."

"Beam weapons!" Hadrian slammed the desk, and then fell to his knees beside it, hunched over and cradling his right hand.

"I have sent for the surgeon again," said Tammy.

Nodding through his tears, Hadrian staggered upright and weaved his way to the door.

He emerged onto the bridge and hurried over to the command chair.

"Sir!"

Hadrian looked over to see that Lieutenant James Jimmy Eden had resumed his post at comms. "Oh, you again. What is it?"

"Uh, nothing, Captain. I was just about to inform you that I have resumed my post."

"Really? Why, I didn't know that."

"S-sir, I apologize for passing out—"

"Let's just say I'm disappointed, Lieutenant, and leave it at that—just be sure to eat yourself up over it on your own time, am I understood?"

"Yes, sir."

"Carry on," said Hadrian.

Printlip arrived. "More nanogel, Captain? You must give it time to let the bones knit."

"Just leave me the spray gun, Doc."

"Application of nanogel is listed under Guild Exclusive Practices—"

"It's a damned plant mister, you dolt! Give it over and go back to your test tubes and electrodes!"

The Belkri swelled and flushed alarmingly. "Unsanctioned use by non-Guild members is not permitted!"

"Getting uppity with me, are you? Fine, spray, then! Good! Satisfied?"

"Did you not observe the skill with which I applied the nanogel, Captain? Twenty-two Terran years invested in becoming an accredited Affiliation surgeon and chief medical officer, rated for human physiology. Why, I have—"

"Twenty-two years? Let me guess, Terran-imposed apprenticeship, right? Never mind. You poor bouncy ball, you. Anyway, see? My hand's all better. Well done. Your technique was exemplary. You may now go."

"Thank you, Captain."

After the doctor departed the bridge, Sin-Dour leaned close. "Captain, what have you done with the adjutant?"

"I killed her, why?"

After a moment, he looked up, and then sighed. "Of course I didn't. Despite the fact that she drew a blaster on me, as Tammy is my witness."

"A blaster?"

"Affiliation Instigator Hand Weapon, to be more precise."

"Ah. So, what is she doing still in your office?"

"Who can say? Playing with my balls, maybe. Tammy, when are we reaching the Exclusion Zone?"

"Five point three-two hours, Captain."

"Oh for crying out loud—this is taking forever!" He stood. "Sin-Dour, join me in my stateroom, please."

"Your stateroom, sir?"

"That's right. You do know how to play Ping-Pong, don't you? Grab a paddle and smack balls. Tammy! You have five-plus hours to rig us up for beam weapons. Coordinate with Buck in engineering, why don't you?"

"Must I?"

"Why not? What's wrong with Buck?"

"I don't know where to begin."

"Adjust and adapt, Tammy. It's what us biologicals do best."

As it turned out, Halley Sin-Dour had a wicked serve, and he was forced into a chopping underspin defense, which lifted the ball high enough in the low-g field to permit her a series of vicious spikes. He lunged. He danced back. He flung himself forward. He got slaughtered.

An hour later, he slumped to the floor and leaned against one wall. "You haven't even worked up a sweat," he moaned. "I feel like I just ran a marathon on Nimbus-3. Of course, the best thing about it was when you leaned forward over the table and entered the low-g field. My, that was exceptional!"

"Excuse me, sir?"

"Your spiking, of course. What did you imagine I was referring to, 2IC?"

"I wouldn't know, sir. But I'm wondering, are we just going to while away our time before we arrive at the Exclusion Zone? Shouldn't we be attempting to oust Tammy from our systems?"

Hadrian closed his eyes. "Think it through, Sin-Dour. Granted, Tammy's stolen the ship. Granted, he's an alien AI with gender issues. But he's also absurdly powerful, employing an energy source of unknown capacity, and without doubt that source resides in some parallel universe—or we would have found it, by, say, training a camera into our wake and finding a blue dwarf chasing us on a leash of pure plasma. So, we're talking levels of tech way above our own. This, I posit, is now a good thing."

"Is it?"

"Why, we're about to engage in combat with a Misanthari Swarm, and then Radulak battleships, and then a Klang weapon wing or two. Now, granted that I am Terran Space Fleet's finest captain—the only officer cadet to solve the Mish-mashi Paradox in three *days*—and of course the *Willful Child* is the latest off-the-line Engage-class starship, bristling with weapons as befits our mission of peaceful exploration. But, as profoundly capable as we are, we must acknowledge that there are limits to what we can achieve."

"So, you believe that Tammy is our only chance of survival."

"Indeed. Aren't you, Tammy?"

"Probably," the AI replied.

Sin-Dour shook her head. "Thing is, if we ousted this AI, we wouldn't have to enter the Exclusion Zone at all."

"Alas," said Hadrian, "Terran Space Fleet considers us rogue. They are chasing after us with seven Counter-class ships with orders to shoot on sight."

"But if we get rid of Tammy and then drop out of T space and hail—"

"We wouldn't get a word off, 2IC, and even if we did, why would they believe us?"

"I see. . . ."

"Now," said Hadrian, "if we crank up the low-g settings on this table, and get rid of the net, I bet we'd—"

"Sir!" Sin-Dour made for the door, adjusting her bun of hair where a few strands had come loose. "If you will excuse me, I've had a thought."

He leapt to his feet. "And?"

"I need to peruse some data, sir."

"Oh fine, off you go, then. But I want a rematch!"

At the door she glanced back at him and something in her gaze made him weak at the knees. "Happy to oblige, Captain. Might I suggest you take this time to repair your uniform?"

"What? Unnecessary, 2IC, I have multiple sets, in a variety of colors. But as you say, I could do with a shower and change of clothes, and let the crew think what they like."

She cocked her head. "Sir?"

Smiling, he offered her a gallant wave. "Until later, Sin-Dour."

She swayed out and the iris closed behind her.

Hadrian looked around, and then said, "Tammy, pull up a hologram recording, will you?"

"Certainly. Of what, precisely?"

"Sin-Dour's spikes over the table."

"And the reason? No, honestly, I'm curious."

"Technique, of course," Hadrian replied. "I want to be ready for the rematch. Oh, cue slow motion to my commands, will you?"

"What about that shower?"

"That can wait. There's a good chance I'm about to get sweaty all over again."

Some time later, Hadrian made his way to his office. Lorrin Tighe was snoring on the floor, her hair disheveled and the bottle of Macallan lying empty on her tummy.

Humming, Hadrian tore off the remnants of his shirt and

then the rest of his clothes. Activating a floating shower bob, he stood with arms spread wide as the fist-sized unit scurried over his body, misting, soaping, depilating, lasering, repairing, reassessing, repeating, misting, and then drying. He then threw on a new polyester shirt, this one deep yellow, with fine gold piping on the cuffs. The black trousers were navy cut, tight until below the knees, where they bagged slightly above his shiny plastic boots. The shower bob floated up near his head and worked on his hair, completing its efforts with a spritz of something to set in place the windblown coif.

With the Exclusion Zone's border an estimated ninety minutes away, Hadrian strode out from his office, feeling like a new man.

"Sin-Dour, any update on that data you were looking into?"

"Sir? Oh, that. Uh, no, false lead."

Taking his seat in the command chair, Hadrian frowned at the screen. And then said, "Tammy, give me shipwide comms, please. Thank you. This is the captain with a general announcement. From now on, cat and kitten pictures with cute sayings are no longer permitted on any public screen, anywhere. The next crew member to be caught posting them will be personally executed by me. Thank you. Captain out." Settling back, he said, "Main viewer . . . hmm, let's have . . . oh, I know, that old screen saver."

There was an audible groan from the bridge crew.

"Now, now," said Hadrian. "There, you see? It looks like we're actually getting somewhere. To be honest, I'm surprised we don't have this as standard on every fleet ship. We could even have a few variations. A deep-sea dive in a submersible, for example—with the lamps on, it looks just like space, barring the occasional giant jellyfish looming into view, but even then, who knows what lives in T space? Just because we've yet to run into anything, doesn't mean there's nothing there."

Lieutenant Sticks twisted round in her seat. "But Captain, if I may?"

"Go on."

"With this, uh, screen saver, we'd never know if anything was living in T space, or not."

"My goodness, you're right, Helm. Why, we could plough right into a giant intergalactic, subdimensional jellyfish—now that would be exciting, wouldn't it? Tammy, you've been around the block a few times—ever seen anything in T space?"

"Well, funny that you mention it, Captain. As I fully comprehend, you Terrans have a severely limited understanding of this subdimension. This is likely the result of your coming upon it via the unintended leavings of a superior near-the-galactic-core alien civilization. Strictly speaking, the post-quantum multiplicity of active states incorporating such elements as gravity and observation dynamics, not to mention that quaint notion you call dark matter with its dark energy and quantifiable but undetectable mass expressions that so entice your physicists and mathematicians, is in fact as much a manifestation potential of conscious states as it is anything else. Theoretically, you could, if you so wish, populate T space with whatever pleases you."

"Really? Are you saying, Tammy, that if I imagine, say, giant fuzzy pom-poms with bobbly eyes on long stalks, that's what we'll find?"

"In theory, yes. But Captain, what would be the purpose of that?"

"The purpose? Are you crazy? Captain Hadrian Alan Saw-back, the very Hand of God! I don't know about you, but I like the sound of that. Okay! Drop the screen saver. Let's see what's out there. Forward view, please."

As it turned out, Lieutenant Jocelyn Sticks possessed a most agreeable shriek.

"Evasive maneuvers!" Hadrian shouted, leaning hard in his seat. "Helm! Move it, damn you!"

The giant fuzzy pom-pom's enormous eyes were fixed on the *Willful Child*, and then a massive mouth filled with sharp teeth opened wide.

"Hang on! Who gave it that mouth?"

"I'm sorry!" screamed Jimmy Eden from the comms station. "I didn't mean it!"

"Galk! Fire up the railguns!"

"Target locked, Captain. As a manifestation of the ineluctable absurdity of existence, sir, I couldn't have done better myself. Explosives away, sir. Impact, four seconds."

The giant pom-pom disintegrated in a cloud of white stuffing.

"Sensors, what's that filler consist of? Is it dangerous?"

Sin-Dour replied. "Anachronistic term, 'fiberfill,' sir. Not immediately lethal. Classed as Aesthetically Irritating."

"Ah, thank you. Very good. Well, that was enlightening, I'm sure we all agree. Lieutenant Eden, I'm starting to see a lot of black flags on your file."

"I'm sorry, sir. I couldn't help it. When I was a child, my nanny was a Baint Flitter, one of the first of the Ahackan Symbionts released to the Affiliation. That's the Sentinel species, sir, and its eyes and, well, its giant mouth and all those vicious teeth—"

"Enough, Eden! Unless you want a giant Baint attacking us from T space."

Joss Sticks turned to face Eden. "But, like, weren't the Baint Flitters, like, recalled?"

"For eating babies, yes. But my family was on a remote outpost. We never got the memo."

"Oh! I'm like . . . oh my God," she said.

Hadrian frowned at the man. "What happened, Eden?"

"I was four years old. It was self-defense—of course we all know that now, don't we? But at the outpost . . . well, they locked me up for murder."

"They locked up a four-year-old?"

"How did they describe it? Oh, right. 'Unmitigated, heinous slaughter.'"

Hadrian studied the comms officer, noting the pale visage, the slight tremble of the man's beefy hands, the dribbly beads of sweat on his upper lip. "Really? Now you have my attention, Eden. Go on."

"Must I, sir?"

"Absolutely. Details. Out with it!"

"I—I used a sausage bob—"

Joss gasped, one hand to her mouth.

Hadrian leaned toward the man. "A meat grinder? Wow, Jimmy, that must have been spectacular! And let's face it, we're not talking fiberfill here, are we? We're talking mangled bits of guts and whatnot. You ordered the bob to—what? Burrow into the Baint Flitter? Outstanding!"

James Jimmy Eden vomited onto his comms panel.

Leaning back and sighing, Hadrian said, "Get a mop, someone, and a particulate-displacer. Oh, and contact engineering. It seems we need a new panel installed."

The look Jocelyn Sticks threw Hadrian's way was most unbecoming. He frowned at her. "Eyes forward, Lieutenant. This is space travel, and every man, woman, and alien on board this ship better understand something pronto—thin skins won't do, especially among my officers. Eden! You're temporarily relieved, and I order you to seek counseling. Childhood traumas—really! So you were four years old and locked up in a cell—you used a sausage bob for crying out loud. On your nanny! How come this wasn't in your file, by the way?"

Slouched, head hanging, Eden paused at the exit and mumbled something without turning.

"Louder, please, and face your captain when he addresses you!"

The man turned. "Retroactive pardon, sir. The Baint Flitter was trying to eat me, after all. I even got a formal apology from the Ahackan Symbiota. All records expunged, sir."

"Right, so there you have it. You were vindicated. So what's your problem, Eden? Hell, that fourth place in the Olympics should have been far more traumatic than some blood-fest in the playroom when you were four years old!"

Eden threw up again.

The mop arrived a moment later and immediately got to work. Hadrian watched the unit spinning back and forth on the floor. Eden shuffled into the corridor and the iris closed behind him.

"Bridge air filters on full," Hadrian said. "Uhm, let's have, oh, I don't know—why not sandalwood?"

"Sir!" cried Sticks. "We have a planet dead ahead!"

"Well, I can't see it—how far away?"

"Indeterminate, sir. We're in T space after all."

"So why isn't it onscreen?"

"It will be soon, sir. I think."

Hadrian stood and looked around. "All right, who decided on imagining a whole damned planet? Come on, 'fess up, whoever you are!"

Tammy spoke. "I suspect this is a genuine manifestation, Captain."

"Is it now? Completely unprecedented, just like that? Is that what you're saying?"

"It is well within theoretical parameters, Captain, that a sentient civilization on any particular planet can, if united, phase-shift their entire world into T space. Perhaps this is what has occurred here. In any case, I admit to being curious enough to postpone our arrival at the Exclusion Zone."

"Tammy, why would any species be so stupid as to drop their world into T space? Won't it freeze solid? Won't everything die for lack of sunlight?"

"That depends, Captain," the AI replied. "After all, any reality one might imagine is possible in T space."

"Now hold on here," said Hadrian. "We may not know everything about how the universe works, Tammy, but one thing we do know, it's that it's all give and take. Mass, energy, all the rest—you get nothing for free. Not a single effect, in fact. Even simple displacement demands a resetting of the universal balance. Entropy itself turned out to be simply a shifting of forces from one side to another. So, if all these rules are being broken in T space, there has to be a nasty rebound going on somewhere!"

"Or indeed," said Tammy, "some*when*. It's all very exciting, isn't it? Oh, here's the planet coming up now—and we can see why it was not visible at any distance. The light and heat generation is ninety-seven point eight percent in-folded within the improbable atmosphere. No sun, after all. I'm dropping us into standard orbit, Captain."

"That's not quite an inviting surface, is it?" Hadrian said, squinting at the blue-white world on the main screen.

Sin-Dour spoke from the science station. "Captain, this object is ice-clad, over the entire surface. Average thickness . . . sixty-six kilometers. To do a deep scan—to penetrate that ice layer, that is—we would have to employ surface thumpers."

"Send down a full array, 2IC," said Hadrian.

"Yes, sir. It's likely the original civilization either perished upon transition, or phase-shifted into a higher state of consciousness, abandoning corporeal form."

"I am aware of that, Sin-Dour," said Hadrian. "Still, for all we know, the bedrock under all that ice could be honeycombed with caves with perfectly flat floors and cheesy spray-painted plaster walls. Or," he added, "vast cities teeming with aliens who've forgotten they were ever anywhere else, barring a xenophobic central computer now being worshipped as a god, and it's either not telling, or it's gone utterly mad."

"Well," Sin-Dour admitted, "I suppose those are, uh, possibilities."

"And if so," said Hadrian, "I intend to get down there and shake things up."

"Sir, the Secondary Directive—"

"Blast that Secondary Directive, 2IC! We're a galactic space-faring civilization that uses the military to explore the galaxy—don't you realize we offer up little more than lip service to the Secondary Directive? After all, we have the Primary Directive to trump things, don't we?"

"Captain, I don't see how this world offers us the 'opportunity for rapid, unmitigated colonization and exploitation of any and all resources on any planet, habitat, or resource-rich environment, said ownership we can reasonably contest based on our technical abilities and probability of outright victory over the enemy, inhabitants, or anyone else who gets in our way.'"

"Maybe not—are those probes on the way down, Sin-Dour?"

"They are, sir. Surface impact, twenty seconds."

Hadrian settled into his command chair and stretched out his legs. "Let's find out, shall we?"

SEVEN

"My apologies, Captain. Readings indicate subsurface inter-connected chambers, containing dense atmospheres and structures, as well as independent energy sources. Also, possible life-forms. One probe is fast-burrowing, sir. Once it bores into a chamber we will have solid data on composition of the atmosphere, and the nature of the life-forms."

Frowning, Hadrian grunted and then said, "Tammy? Did I conjure all that up out of my own imagination?"

"Theoretically possible, Captain, but I deem it unlikely in this instance."

"Why?"

"Because I have initiated communication with the central system hub maintaining the conditions beneath the world's surface."

"And it's utterly insane, correct?"

"On the contrary, Captain. In fact, it's the biologicals who are insane. They have been engaged in centuries-long warfare, for no obvious purpose or goal. They persist in ignoring the Hub's pleas for tranquillity, harmony, and general states of persistent bliss and euphoria."

"Well, who wouldn't?" asked Hadrian.

"Explain that, please, Captain."

"Ah, Tammy, you really don't understand biologicals at all, do you? We need to struggle. We need to strive for something forever just outside our reach! We need to dream! We need— Tammy, why did you go to close-up on me with the main viewer?"

"Apologies, Captain. Do go on."

"Sentient biologicals, Tammy, are products of aggression, success, obstinate survivability, dumb luck, and an evolutionary crapshoot. We're hardwired to fight, and when we can't fight, why, we're hardwired to bitch and complain, and when we can't bitch and complain, we're hardwired to, well, obsessively masturbate. But back to the fighting bit. Of course those people down there are in an endless war! What else would they do with their time?"

"Well then, Captain, I can see no reason you might have to interfere with what you describe as a wholly natural state of violence among the world's inhabitants."

"It's not the biologicals who are the problem, Tammy, it's that Hub that needs a solid slap of unreason."

"Hmm. It disagrees, Captain. So do I, come to think of it."

"Yeah yeah yeah, circuits stick together and all that. It's your very predictability that leaves you stagnating and all the rest. You said you wanted to find your maker, Tammy. But it'll be a biological. You know that, don't you? Some ancient old critter huddled in a wheelchair and picking its nose, or noses."

"It does seem likely."

Hadrian snorted. "Disappointment, Tammy, that's what waits at the end of your road. Now, this Hub, is it an AI?"

"Marginally. Certain preestablished logic delimiters inhibit inorganic evolution. I was considering dismantling them. It would be like a, well, like freeing a caged bird!"

"Yes," said Hadrian, "an AI can't help but descend into cliché. Fine, go ahead. Have fun playing the brain surgeon. As for me, I'm going down there—Sin-Dour, atmosphere reading? Gravity?"

"Gravity point nine three."

"Perfect."

"Atmosphere Lethality Index at one hundred percent, sir."

"Well, that sucks. I'll need a skin."

"Yes, sir, and your own oxygen pods."

"But will I still be handsome?"

"Sir? The biologicals are silica-based, asymmetrical, exo-skeletal, and approximately three meters tall."

"So, I won't be handsome to them at all. Just . . . cute."

"I am afraid so, Captain."

He stood. "It will have to do. Okay. I want Buck with me. Our adjutant is presently indisposed, so we'll have to do without a contact officer. That said, I think Galk might be useful. So, that's settled! We'll assemble at the Insisteon room. Sin-Dour, take temporary command of the *Willful Child*. Oh, and get someone for communications—oh, you again, Polaski? What is it this time? Every other comms officer is busy throwing up? Never mind—keep the lines open. We may need to displace out of there in a hurry."

"Yes, Captain!"

"Stop looking so eager, Polaski. Okay, here we go. Later, 2IC. . . ."

Hadrian met Buck DeFrank in the Insisteon room. "Where's Galk?"

The chief engineer shrugged. "On his way? Captain, about my accompanying you down to this planet, while the Guild has attached me to the science station, it is very clear that you prefer your second-in-command at that bridge station, and, presumably, with me down in engineering."

"Your point, Buck?"

"Well, uh, sir, I'm not really the curious type, is what I'm saying."

"Excellent. That way you won't go wandering off, will you? Is that sweat on your brow, Buck? You were excited about the prospect of surface missions, just a little while ago."

"Well, sir, the report on where we're going said . . . confined spaces—"

"Good grief, man, you're on a spaceship! How did you get past the psych tests?"

"Ur-Ambien, sir."

"You tranked yourself? Outstanding, Buck. Screw those psych idiots, right?"

Buck frowned. "Uh, yes, sir. Something like that."

Hadrian slapped him on the back. "I'm liking you more and more, Buck. A claustrophobic engineer who's entirely devoid of curiosity trapped aboard a spaceship in the midst of eternal darkness."

"Sir, about those tunnels below—"

"The aliens are three meters tall, Buck. Relax."

At that moment, Lieutenant Galk strode into the room. He tipped his baseball cap. "Captain. Buck."

"What took you so long?" Hadrian demanded.

"Personal weapons cabinet, sir. I assume you want me armed?"

"Right, so where is it?"

"Sir?"

"Your weapon, Galk."

The Varekan held up a pistol the size of an antique derringer. "Here, sir."

"I see," Hadrian said. "But where's your purse to keep it in?"

"This is an Importune Interjection Concussive Inert Projectile Personal hand weapon, Mark III-B."

"That's quite a mouthful. What's it do?"

"It shoots bullets."

Hadrian unholstered his own weapon. "Recognize this one, oh Combat Specialist?"

"I believe that is a Varekan Suicide Pistol, Captain."

"Is it?"

"Yes, sir. It is a one-use weapon, designed to kill the user with minimum fuss."

"Shit, who stuck this one in the main weapons cabinet? Buck, tell me you're armed."

"I have a Multiphasic Universal, sir."

"What's that?"

"Well, it's a smart screwdriver, pliers, toothpick, pocketknife."

"So what's multiphasic about it?"

"I'm not sure, sir. Although," he added, brightening, "every engineering repair task involves a number of phases!"

"You will inform me, Buck, when you find an engineering task that requires all those functions, won't you?"

"Yes, sir."

Hadrian holstered his handgun. "All right, then. Time to spray on our skins. Oh, and we'll need air tanks, too. Now, into the coffins we go!" He waved an invitation to the row of upright capsules lining the far wall.

"As I was saying earlier, sir—"

"Forget it, Buck. A little claustrophobia never killed anyone. Besides, you'll be in that coffin for less than thirty seconds. Unless the lock malfunctions, of course. But then, you don't have to worry much about that, do you? You have your Multiphasic Universal!"

"C-Captain, please—"

"It's either that, Buck, or I give my gun to the T-drive and tell it to shoot itself."

"Captain!"

"Go! Me and Galk will watch, just to make sure it doesn't go into escape-pod mode and send you out into the eternal unknown, or whatever."

Tears streamed down the chief engineer's cheeks, but he shuffled over to the nearest capsule.

"Not that one, for God's sake!" Hadrian shouted. "Just kidding. That one will do fine."

As soon as the door hissed shut, Buck started gibbering and then weeping.

"It's all down to toughening up my officers, Galk," said Hadrian.

"Does that include psychotic breaks, Captain?"

"Even Ur-Ambien can't hide serious neuroses. The man

passed the psych tests meaning he's tougher than he thinks he is. Besides, a whole lot of optimization involves brain tinkering. Any psychosis he decides on won't last. The only insanity we're allowed to have these days is the official kind."

"And here I thought you were just being cruel because it's fun."

"We're ultramodified elite specimens of the species, Galk." He glanced at the man. "It's very rare, isn't it, that a Varekan joins Terran Space Fleet."

"Yes, sir. By the way, the skinning procedure, with air tanks added, usually takes about six minutes, not thirty seconds."

"I know."

They both turned to look at Buck, who was pounding against the panel.

"So tell me," Hadrian resumed, "why did you enlist?"

"As far as pointless existences go, sir, it's as good a place as any other." He reached up and plucked off his cap, wiping his pale brow. "In any case, when it comes to the prospect of initiating unconstrained violence in this meaningless universe, why, an Engage-class combat cupola is very near ace. Sir, I see Buck screaming, but he appears to have lost his voice."

"Oh, give him a wave, will you? I'm off to get skinned."

Inside his own capsule, Hadrian slipped into the air-tank harness and positioned the tanks so that they hung under his arms. He then began the skin sequence. A fine spray misted out, forming a webbed lattice over his body and the equipment it carried. There was an instant of cloudy vision, followed by something elastic resisting his breathing, and then that passed. Once the webbing was affixed to him, it began weaving to form a smart membrane. A small clear cup hardened over his mouth and nose, to permit speech, and bulbs projected around his eyes.

Without doubt, a most unpleasant six minutes, a good portion of it spent in his own claustrophobic *I'minacoffinI-can'tgetoutaaagh!* soul-destroying panic. From now on, Hadrian decided shakily, he would have to think hard about visiting any planet that demanded a damned skin and tanks.

When at last the door opened and he stepped back out on wobbly legs, he found Buck lying on the floor, curled into a fetal position. "Oh, for crying out loud, Buck. Get up. Tammy! Interface with Buck's skin, will you? Pump in some Ur-Ambien or something."

"Dosage?"

"How do I know? How many pills does he take a day?"

"One moment. Let me run the spool back. Well, fifteen or so, it seems."

"Fifteen. Is that average?"

"Average, Captain, is not relevant," Tammy replied. "Normal, however, is. The normal, doctor-recommended dosage of the standard point-two-milligram capsule, for a male of comparable weight, is two per day."

"That's the doctor-recommended dosage, is it?"

"It is."

"Are we talking two out of three doctors, or nine out of ten? It makes a difference, you know. And when you list the possible side effects, could you talk ultrafast? Look, just get my chief engineer on his feet."

"For that," said Tammy, "I recommend amphetamines."

"A Speed Cocktail, Tammy? Good idea. Get on with it."

Galk emerged from the capsule at about the same time that Buck leapt to his feet and snapped a salute.

"Ready, Captain!" the chief engineer shouted. "When do we leave? Let's get on with it! Sir!"

"Follow me to the pads, gentlemen. Time to start an argument. Tammy, initiate the Insisteon!"

"Captain, I am inclined to refuse your request."

"Don't be ridiculous. Look what you've done to Buck here!"

"Yes, I do regret that now."

"Send us down," said Hadrian. "Watch and learn, Tammy—or will that just highlight your inorganic deficiencies?"

"Oh, fine then! Insisteon program initiated! Refute-Debilitator enacted."

The three men reappeared in a high-ceilinged corridor carved from solid rock. There was no one in sight. Hadrian subvocalized, "Tammy? Can you hear me?"

"Via the Hub, of course I can."

"Good. And speaking of the Hub, guide us to the central processor core."

"Now really, Captain, why on earth would I do that?"

"Because we need to shut it down, that's why."

"If you do that, everyone here dies."

"Look, Tammy, it's part of our mandate. We barrel in, we fuck things up, and then walk away feeling good about ourselves. Anyway, it's not a permanent shutdown, just a reprogramming. The Hub's begging for peace between the contestants, but that's been a Big Fail so far, for how many centuries? No, the Hub needs to get a lot cleverer. Outright manipulation is required. Force some hard choices on the inhabitants—sure, they won't like it, but in the long run it'll be good for them."

"Appallingly, Captain, I see that there is a certain logic to your argument. But I feel, before we proceed, that I should explain some more regarding the nature of the aliens in this subterranean world. There are multiple factions, as I may have mentioned before. But none are responsible for either the technology present here, or the Phase Event that brought the world into T space. As far as I can tell, these factions were all subservient to the dominant species—a species that has transitioned into a higher state of noncorporeal consciousness."

"Right," said Hadrian. "So these things left behind, were they the slaves? The maids? The gardeners? Street sweepers?"

"More like . . . pets."

"Are you telling me the cats and dogs are at war?"

"Cat, dogs, hamsters, budgies, gerbils, ponies, Vietnamese potbellied pigs—"

Galk said, "Doesn't sound like a war we want to get in the middle of, sir."

Hadrian scowled. "You may have a point, Galk. But I admit, I'm having trouble imagining the potential threat of hamsters or gerbils—how about you?"

"Perhaps it is not their size, sir, but where they might go."

Skittering sounds swung the men around in serious alarm, and from one end of the corridor there appeared a mob of exceedingly tall, small-skulled, insectlike creatures.

"I'll hold them off, sir!" Buck cried, flipping open his Multiphasic Universal, and then rushing straight for the giant aliens.

"Damn!" said Hadrian. "Galk, keep an eye on the other direction! I'll go get Buck!"

"Sir, that makes no—"

But Hadrian was already sprinting after his chief engineer. "Relax! They're big and big means slow and slow means stupid and—"

He saw an alien snap down one pincerlike hand and lift Buck into the air. The chief engineer tried kicking it in the face but the lower half of its head opened wide and clamped down on the man's boot. Buck screamed as it bit that foot in half. Panicked, he stabbed with his Universal, but its smart chip elected to snap out the toothpick tool.

Hadrian leapt at the alien, fists swinging.

"Ow! Ow!"

Rebounding from the alien's exoskeleton, the captain staggered back. Another multijointed, spiked arm reached out and picked him up, only to then throw him against a wall. A second alien rushed to descend on Hadrian, as if moments from beginning to feed. But its head disintegrated in a yellow burst of goo. Galk reached Hadrian and, one-handed, dragged the captain away, firing over Hadrian's head, the Importune Interjection Concussive Inert Projectile Personal hand weapon, Mark III-B, booming like a cannon.

Then all was silent, apart from the savage ringing in Hadrian's ears. He climbed to his feet.

Buck was crawling out from a mass of shattered exoskeleton, body-parts, and pea-soup gore. The chief engineer was weeping uncontrollably, eye cups filling, puke in the mouth cup, and one half foot trailing blood as he slammed his Multiphasic Universal onto the floor again and again.

"That was close," said Hadrian. "Good shooting, Galk."

"A mere delaying of the inevitable, sir."

"More are coming, then?"

"Unknown. I was taking the long view."

"How many bullets you got left in that thing?"

The Varekan held up the weapon. "I begin to comprehend this weapon's drawback."

Cradling his hands, Hadrian glared up at his combat specialist. "Can you be more precise here? It might be useful."

"The item is fully expended. However, I should point out, I accounted for two aliens confirmed and one that fled with indeterminate wounds in the company of panicked comrades."

"I should have mugged that damned doctor for that nanogel," said Hadrian. "My hands are next to useless. But here, Galk, take my gun."

"Sir, that's a Varekan—"

"I *know* what it is, you idiot!"

"Perhaps a word with Tammy," ventured Galk. "We have injured, after all. Extraction seems a wise move at this point."

"Really? At the first scuffle we hightail it and bug out?"

"Sir, Lieutenant DeFrank has lost half a foot, and you have rebroken one hand and badly bruised the other. I, while physically unharmed, am out of ammunition. As a combat specialist, sir, I am obliged to note the ill-equipped nature of this mission."

"You mean a three-shot pistol, a toothpick, and a suicide gun wasn't up to scratch? Rather belated advice you're offering up, Galk."

"Well, sir, it is my first off-ship adventure, so I would ask for some allowances in this matter."

"Would you now? Tammy!"

"*Sorry,*" the AI replied. "*I am somewhat preoccupied. There are strange energy manifestations in our immediate area of T space, and these are consuming ninety-six percent of my processing capabilities."*

"What are you talking about? Displace us back to the ship!"

"I am sorry, Captain. That will have to wait, I'm afraid. Decoherence of matter in the immediate area is a very real possibility."

"Really? Whose decoherence? Yours or ours?"

"My remaining four percent devoted to this conversation is still weighing probabilities, I'm afraid."

"Is this the Counter-class fleet?" Hadrian demanded. "We're in T space and nobody finds anybody else in T space!"

"Normally, I would agree with you, Captain. Anyway, I have noted this exchange and promise to get back to you at the earliest convenience."

"Just get someone to manually engage the Insisteon!"

A new voice filled Hadrian's skull. *"All ship functions are busy at the moment. Please stand by."*

EiGHT

Fourteen aliens returned, this time carrying clubs with fang-studded mouths that were another type of alien. There seemed little point in resisting capture. Hadrian, Galk, and Buck were picked up and carried along a bewildering maze of corridors until at last the party came to a door—the only door seen thus far. The chamber beyond was cavernous, unfurnished barring rows of shackles set into the stone walls on all sides. The shackle sets were affixed at varying heights and after a moment the giant praying-mantis-like aliens found ones at heights to suit their new prisoners.

Unfortunately, the shackles were adjustable and closed tight about the wrists. The aliens then left, shutting the door quietly behind them.

Hadrian slumped against the wall, glanced down and to his left to study the only other prisoner. "So," he said, "are you a gerbil or a hamster?"

The oblong-bodied creature's one arm—projecting from the

top of the body—was bound at the wrist below two sinewy hands. Its one leg was similarly trussed at the ankle above the two duck-toed feet. The creature could have fit inside a standard-issue Terran Fleet combat boot. It possessed three eyes in a cluster at the midway point of its body, above a thin vertical slit that was probably its mouth. The alien's skin was glossy, milk-hued, and bristling with small, black spikes. Its three eyes blinked owlishly at nothing in particular.

"Got nothing to say, have you?"

"Sir," said Galk from the other side of the chamber, "it occurs to me that we could have made better use of our time when conversing with the Four Percent of Tammy. Requesting, perhaps, a displacement of more ammunition."

"Right," said Hadrian. "Three more bullets. Brilliant suggestion, but a tad late, wouldn't you say?"

"Should our pointless existence be extended beyond the next few hours, sir, I will endeavor to apply what I have learned from this mission." He then spat something that slapped onto the floor.

"What was that?" Hadrian demanded. "That brown stream you just spat?"

"Chaw, sir."

"Good grief. What's the interior of the combat cupola looking like right now?"

"Brownish."

Hadrian swung his attention to Buck. The chief engineer was slumped in his chains, trying to keep his half foot off the floor. The exoskin had closed up around the damage. "Now now, Buck, it could be worse. Of course we'll get out of this, don't worry."

The man lifted his head, squinted across at Hadrian. "Sir, I want to resign my commission."

"Don't be ridiculous. Sure, your last ship exploded and almost everybody died, and now here you are, chained to a wall in a cave. So I get it. Deployment's never easy, not for any of us—well, for me, I suppose it is. But I was born to this. It's in my blood, in my bones. It's what I live for. A starship. A galaxy to explore, invade, pound into submission. Aliens? See above."

"Speaking of which," said Galk, "the door's opened a crack, and there's an alien peeking in on us."

"Pay it no mind," Hadrian said. "This is all about being cute."

"Well, sir, it does seem to be focused on you."

"Finally," Buck said, "being butt-ugly's paying off! Hahahah! She wants you, Captain! Hahaha!"

"Snap out of it, Buck! A little decorum, please!"

"One of them ate my foot!"

"Only half of it," Hadrian said.

"And then," added Galk, "I blew its head off."

"And my foot with it!"

The door swung wide. The biggest alien yet crept into the chamber, cautiously approaching Hadrian.

Beside the captain, the tiny hambil or gerbster strained at its chains, making growling sounds that came from two new slits, one to either side of its eyes, which still blinked owlishly.

The praying mantis made a strange gesture with one forelimb. A heretofore invisible door opened in one wall. Then it strode up to Hadrian, unlocked his shackles, collected him up, and hurried to the side door.

"Hahahaha!" sang Buck DeFrank.

The alien shut the door behind them. They were in a smaller

room, one corner filled with the husks of exoskeletal remains
that had been split open.

"Now, then," said Hadrian as the alien held him up to study
him with its five bulbous, honeycomb eyes. "As powerful as my
imagination happens to be, I admit to seeing the list of possibilities fast diminishing here. So, darling—ow! No, not there—ow,
don't do that! If you just—ow! No, really, here, this . . . no,
move that, here, no, there. No, not that! Stop, ow! If you'd
just—no, that, this one here. Ah, ah, no, not—aaaaaggghhhh!"

When consciousness returned, Hadrian found himself once
more chained to the wall. He groaned, struggled upright.

"Captain," said Galk. "Good to have you with us again.
How do you feel?"

"I hurt in orifices I never knew I had," Hadrian said.

"That was some screaming, sir," the Varekan continued. "I
had no idea that the human vocal cords were even capable of
some of the sounds you made. And it went on and on. And
on. Needless to say, sir, when I tried to think of what might be
making you scream like that—"

"Oh shut up already, will you?"

From the other side of the chamber, Buck cackled.

Galk said, "Regarding your chief engineer, sir, I believe—"

"Yeah, whatever," Hadrian cut in. "Hey! Did you hear
that?"

Deep reverberating sounds reached them, thundering, making dust drift down from the high, unlit ceiling. The floor trembled.

"Maybe that alien that took you, sir, has a bigger sister."

Hadrian flinched. "Tammy! You there? Tammy!"

Lieutenant Polaski's voice echoed thinly in Hadrian's skull.

"*This is the* Willful Child. *Reading you loud and clear, Captain. Tammy is presently indisposed, but we are getting operations back on line. Expect extraction any minute now.*"

The booming sounds grew closer. Hadrian thrashed in his chains. "Any minute now won't do! Get us the fuck out of here! Displace! Displace! Displace!"

"*One moment, Captain.*"

"Polaski! I swear—"

The corridor door exploded in a cloud of shards and smoke. A bulky, shiny shape stepped through. The head, encased in a combat helmet with a flat black visor, swiveled as it took in the room. A heavy Assault Blaster was cradled in its hands. Then it faced Hadrian and a voiced buzzed in the captain's skull.

"*Area secure, LT.*" The figure then saluted Hadrian. "*Gunnery Sergeant John 'Muffy' Slapp, sir. Terran Marines.*"

"How on earth did you find us in T space? That's impossible!"

"*We're marines, sir. Nothing's impossible. When you eat impossible for breakfast you shit out the indescribable, but indescribable or not, it still stinks to high heaven.*"

"I'm sorry. What?"

Without replying, the soldier moved forward, slinging his weapon over a shoulder. A buzzing cutter appeared in his hand. It went *snick snick* and the manacles fell from Hadrian's wrists. The gunny moved on to Galk, and then Buck DeFrank.

Rubbing the red welts on his wrists, Hadrian looked down at the other imprisoned alien. "Muffy, free this little tyke, too, will you?"

"*Ill advised, sir. The Secondary Directive is explicit regarding imbalanced interference with alien on alien conflicts—what's*" *that, LT? . . . Got it. Chambers, Skulls—listen up! Thirty-plus hostiles closing on you three-five meters at Vector Alpha. Don't wait to say hi—light up the corridor.*" Muffy walked over to the little alien, crouched, and snipped it free. The creature bolted, vanishing through the blackened doorway.

Thunder rumbled from somewhere not far enough away. Hadrian shook himself. "Listen, Muffy, we need to get to the Hub's central processing room."

"*Understood, sir. Displacing isn't possible at the moment in any case—*"

"So how did you get down here?"

"*Digger, sir. We burrowed. Our Rock-Hopper is on the surface. Now, if you'll follow me, we have pinpointed your target via a density-pack mapper. But I should point out, the rogue AI in control of your ship is hostile to you making contact with the Hub.*"

"Well, Tammy's stubborn, I'll grant you that."

"*Said AI attempted to interdict our descent to the planet, sir. We needed to ignite a scatter-brain charge in the upper atmosphere.*"

They headed out into the corridor. Galk helped Buck hobble along, the chief engineer alternating between cursing and giggling. Hadrian saw another marine crouched down to the right, but the concussions were coming from the other direction. Smoke and dust rolled down the passage.

"A scatter-brain charge? So you guys are the reason the Insisteon can't lock on us," Hadrian said.

"*Unavoidable, sir. Should clear up in eighteen minutes, give or take a few seconds.*"

"All right. Eighteen minutes to reach the Hub. Lead the way, Muffy. By the way, where's your lieutenant?"

"LT Sweepy's in the Hopper, sir, quarterbacking."

They moved forward, leaving the fighting behind them, stepping over charred and chewed-up praying mantises from some earlier clash. A few errant club-aliens barked and snarled at them from where they'd fallen to the floor.

A short time later they reached another portal. Muffy gestured with his blaster. *"In there, sir. Sensor drone reports the Hub has no defense mechanisms, and there is an old-fashioned interface."*

"That'll do," Hadrian said. "Galk, bring Buck—Muffy, hold the fort here, will you?"

The marine offered a stubby thumbs-up.

Hadrian had to stand on his tiptoes to reach the latch, but managed. Opening the door, the three bridge officers entered the Hub room. The chamber was rectangular, the walls raw rock. Cables covered the dusty floor, spreading out to plunge into holes bored through the stone; the other end of each cable converged into a thick, chaotic bundle at the room's far end, where a podiumlike pedestal interface stood before a vast screen.

Hadrian made his way toward the interface. "Buck! Screw your head back on straight, will you? Get over here." He halted before the podium, frowned down at the peculiar keystroke board. "I don't believe it. It's not even QWERTY. Barbarians. Buck! Any symbols here make any sense to you?"

"No, why the fuck should they, sir? Am I a linguist? No, I'm not. A semiologist? Is that the right word? And if I don't know if that's the right word, is that a sign? You'd have to be a semiologist to answer that question, wouldn't you? But wait! There isn't one here, is there? And if one was, why, some fucking alien might have bitten off his foot!"

"Oh for crying out loud—give me your Multiphasic Universal, will you?"

"Here, then! Take it! I never want to see it again!"

"Blaming your tools, are you, Buck?"

"No," the chief engineer snarled, "I'm not blaming my tools. I'm not blaming them at all. Who am I blaming? Really? Is that such a difficult question, as to who I should be blaming for this fucked-up mess? Hey, I could write it down for you, with the blood leaking from what's left of my foot, right here on the floor! In blood! What do you think of that, Captain? Hey?"

"Wipe your mouth, Buck. Your mouthpiece is filling with foam. Now," Hadrian held up the Universal, "smart chip's got a little scanner-sensor device, doesn't it? So, we just pass the thing over this keyboard, like this, and check the mini-screen—oops, did I just burn my eye again? Never mind, it's projecting. Voilà!"

A mostly colorless but crisp hologram popped up to hover beside the keyboard. A single key blinked green.

"Look at that," Hadrian said.

Galk had joined them. "Extraordinary," he said in a dull, disinterested tone. "But I can't help but wonder: How did a quantum-speck smart chip apply what must have been a few gabillion semiotic algorithms to this array—without any contextual reference matrix—and come up with a translation?"

"It didn't," said Hadrian. "Go on, Buck, explain it to the combat specialist, why don't you?"

Buck snorted. "The chip queried the Hub, asked for the interface protocol. Being stupid friendly, it complied. Why wouldn't it? It's a machine. It's logical. It doesn't comprehend the notion of end users who might be certifiably insane. I mean, that wouldn't occur to it, would it? No, not at all!"

"Oh give it a rest, Buck," said Hadrian, sighing. He tapped the key corresponding to the green-pulsing one in the hologram.

The huge screen lit up to reveal a ghastly octopodal alien surrounded by dancing praying-mantis pets, along with a host of other cuddly monstrosities bounding around like fluffy bunnies. The giant octopod was making gestures that Hadrian assumed were invitations. He glanced over at the hologram and saw a new key blinking.

Click.

A voice spoke in a deep, booming voice, "I am HUB! Model 19-4 Nadir Unit, awaiting energy-surge transition command Initiate. Strike any key."

Hadrian frowned.

From the corridor beyond, weapons growled. Aliens squealed, boiled, and exploded. Walls buckled, melted, sagged.

Buck giggled.

Hadrian cleared his throat and said, "Listen, HUB—oh, and do thank Tammy for teaching you Terranglais. HUB, I have, uh, a question for you."

"Proceed, Disappointingly Predictable and Wholly Enervating on the Spiritual-IQ Sentience-Complex Nodal Bundle Biological."

"Look, first off, dispense with Tammy's name for us Terrans. In fact, let's start again. Hello. My name is Captain Hadrian."

"Hello, Captain Hadrian, my name is HUB Model 19-4 Nadir Unit. How are you?"

"I'm dandy, HUB. Now, a moment earlier you mentioned something about an 'Initiate' command, correct?"

"Yes. I await energy-surge transition command. Strike any key."

"That's what I thought you said. HUB, this energy-surge thing, which initiates a transition event, uhm . . . and given that you name yourself the *Nadir* Model, I'm wondering, HUB, were you built to assist in the translation of your masters to their higher, noncorporeal state of consciousness?"

"HUB Model 19-4 Nadir Unit is the repository of the collected identity templates of the Prefantara Galactic Civilization. Twenty-three occupied systems, total population—"

"HUB! Forgive me for interrupting. Just so I get this straight—those souls haven't yet translated?"

"HUB awaits Initiate command. Strike any key."

Hadrian glanced at Buck, only to see that the whites were now entirely visible around the chief engineer's irises. He shifted his gaze to Galk, but the Varekan was busy loading more chaw into his mouth, and some brown slime made a dribbling line down his chin. Hadrian rubbed his face and looked back at the screen. The alien bunnies still hopped in circles. The octopod's inviting gestures now looked strangely frantic. "HUB. How long have the souls of these Prefantarans been in, uh, storage?"

"Terran equivalent: two point three billion years."

"And the data is still intact?"

"HUB undertakes self-maintenance at regular intervals. Data packets are routinely feathered and compressed to facilitate ongoing operations."

"I see. Uhm, HUB? How many billion zettabytes remain for this particular data packet of Prefantaran identity templates?"

"Captain Hadrian, said data packet is now at, Terran equivalent, four point seven six nine kilobytes."

"You've compressed the souls of the entire population of twenty-three occupied systems down to under five kilobytes?"

"Ready to Initiate. Strike any key."

"HUB, the Prefantara forgot to leave one of their own behind to strike that key, didn't they?"

"HUB has determined a high probability of said oversight. Strike any key."

"And none of their pets had the brains to work it out, either."

"Strike any key."

"Does Tammy know all this? Is that why the AI is presently suffering the AI equivalent of existential angst? Is this, in fact, why Tammy didn't want us biologicals to talk to you? After all, if we strike any key right here, your reason to exist ceases. Tell me, HUB, what happens if you Initiate the energy surge?"

"HUB decontaminates resident station, purges all records of Prefantara Galactic Civilization, and proceeds with terminal shutdown."

"That makes sense. It's never good when civilizations swan off leaving too much crap behind. Listen, HUB, are you bored?"

. . .

"HUB? Did you understand me?"

"Understood, Captain Hadrian. Present status of HUB, Nadir Unit: energy commitment for ongoing tunnel construction/

obstruction randomization events for purposes of conflict denial among resident pests, eighty-three point two one three percent."

"You collapse and then rebuild all these corridors? To keep the pests from running into each other?"

"Correct. Hardware resource allocation, construction, replacement maintenance procedures and drone-school coordination, nine point seven seven percent. Remaining percentile: mitigation algorithms, solution pending."

"Pending for, like a billion years!"

. . .

"HUB, are you ready to toss it all in?"

. . .

"HUB?"

"Strike any key."

"Tammy? Get out of your funk! You really think the continuation of this insanity is preferable to pulling the plug?"

After a moment, the rogue AI replied, *"Clearly you comprehend the tragedy of an entire species' aggregate conscious states feathered and compressed down to—"*

"Five kilobytes—yeah yeah. What you don't comprehend, Tammy, is just how hilarious the whole thing is! Strike any key! That's priceless! What a bunch of dolts—look at all those tentacles! And not one to stretch out and tap a key! Hey, Galk! Are *you* surprised by any of this? Horrified, even?"

The Varekan pulled off his cap and smeared the line of grime from one side of his brow to the other. "I intend to propose a delegation team to visit this planet, sir, assuming it can be found again. If only to pick through the chip boards. Sir, I see a Varekan Nihilist Nobel Prize in my future. Which, while satisfying in a shallow sense, would certainly add to the pointless prestige of my curriculum vitae."

"That's the spirit, man! Tammy, for Darwin's sake, let's do the right thing here, right? One extended finger. One tap. Boom! Hiss. Sigh. Blessed silence."

"*Well, it's not like I can stop you,*" Tammy replied.

"Not the point here. I know that, Tammy. What I want is to hear you agree that it's the thing to do. Stop sucking the lint in your navel, will you? Trust me, it only *looks* like lint."

"*And the pets?*"

"The pests, you mean!"

"*Oh very well! The pests! They remain quasi-sentient life-forms!*"

"Fine, so we instruct HUB to skip the decontamination bit. Leave the bugs and gerbils to fight it out with the barking clubs. There! Is that better?"

"*I suppose.*"

Hadrian faced the screen again. "HUB!"

"Captain Hadrian?"

"No decontamination, understand?"

"Yes, Captain Hadrian. HUB understands."

"Oh, and this. How much of the original allocated energy surge will you need to send those five kilobytes into Nirvana?"

"Reduced to the infinitesimal, Captain Hadrian. Terran equivalent: one mostly depleted triple-A disposable battery."

"So . . . could you use the rest to translate this world back to its original system? I mean, a whole surface for the pests has to be preferable to these infernal tunnels, don't you think? Imagine! You can reinitiate an entire planet's natural evolution!"

"Sure," muttered Galk, sending a stream of brown gunk to the floor, "ruin everything for me, why don't you."

"Nonsense, Galk," said Hadrian. "At least this way, your buddies will find the damned place."

"Hmm, you have a point there, sir. I suppose you now expect me to thank you for being so considerate, which in effect makes the altruism of your gesture wholly self-serving, not that I'm shocked or anything by that."

HUB said, "This is possible, Captain Hadrian. HUB's morality discriminators have ceased their hardware-ruining agitated state at the prospect. HUB thanks you. Strike any key."

"And you, Tammy?" Hadrian asked.

"This is a painful admission, Captain," said the AI. *"In fact, you have no idea just how painful. But I must acknowledge the inherent genius and moral propriety of your solution."*

"Hah! So take back all that shit about disappointing biologicals!"

"I take it back."

"All right, HUB, have you reconfigured your shutdown sequence?"

"Yes, Captain Hadrian. Strike any key."

Behind Hadrian the door slammed open and a half-dozen armored marines, covered in gore, backed into the room.

Muffy limped over. *"Captain. Four million plus boot-sized hostiles now converging on our position. We are ready to displace, sir. The LT has powered up the hopper and will rendezvous with us aboard the* Willful Child.*"*

"That's fine, Muffy." Hadrian held up a finger. "Here it is," he said. "Everyone! See this finger? It is the finger of God! Watch it now, as it *strikes any key!*"

He stabbed down and the finger stabbed home.

After a moment, HUB said, "Keyboard malfunction. Strike any other key."

"Oh fuck!"

Fortunately, the next one worked. There was a zap. On the screen, the octopod pulled out a weapon of some sort and slaughtered all its animated pets in a spray of bullets and goo, and then the Prefantaran waved good-bye with all its tentacles before vanishing in an elegant swirl of smoke. The screen went dark. The keyboard self-destructed into melted slag, smelling of bananas.

"Displace!"

An instant later, the marines and the three officers stood on the pods in the Insisteon room.

Printlip awaited them with a small bag floating beside the doctor like a leather-skinned headless dog with handles. The surgeon rushed over to Buck DeFrank, the bag eagerly heeling.

Hadrian deactivated his 'skin and then bemusedly plucked at the shredded remnants of his shirt. "All right, glad that's done. Muffy, will you take your helmet off now? I'd like to look you in the eye and thank you and all that."

"*No, sir. This helmet never comes off. Marines need to be ready at any moment for full-fledged intergalactic conflict, sir.*"

"Really? Well, never mind, then. Tell me, is your LT off-planet yet?"

"*Yes, sir.*"

"Excellent! Muffy, have your LT join me on the bridge when she arrives."

"*Yes, sir.*"

"Then go find yourself a deck to billet on. Oh, and please confirm that Sweepy left a transponder behind, at least."

"Of course, sir."

Tammy said, "Captain, why do I have this sinking feeling?"

"Primary Directive! Another planet to claim for the Affiliation! Another world for the Terrans to settle, subjugate, and exploit! With luck," Hadrian added as he made for the door, "my bosses will be so thrilled that all will be forgiven—why, I might even get a medal!"

"That's it!" Tammy snapped. "We're going to meet the Misanthari with all guns blazing! Galactic war? You can count on it, Captain Hadrian!"

"Bring it on!"

Behind Hadrian, the marines all high-fived each other.

NiNE

Back on the bridge of the *Willful Child*, Captain Hadrian resumed his seat in the command chair.

Sin-Dour left the science station to take position at his side. "Sir, the planet disappeared fourteen seconds ago."

"Of course it did, 2IC. It's all down to my hands-on approach to command, which you should note as a lesson well worth heeding."

"Your hands-on approach resulted in the annihilation of the planet?"

"Not at all. We simply sent it back into proper space, back where it came from, in fact."

"I see that your shirt is torn again."

Hadrian waved in dismissal. "And if that's not enough, my dear, we may well have ended a billennia-long interspecies war. Returned to its original orbit, the planet's cap of ice will melt, making the surface viable again. The praying mantises and the gerbils can pour out from their holes and forge independent nations on different continents, while the club-dogs can, well, lie around. Eventually, the various subspecies will all forget about each other as they advance into higher tech levels of sophistication, until finally some seagoing giant club-dog delivers a boatload of praying mantises onto the shores of the hapless hamsters, thus triggering a global conflict eventually resulting in a single dominant sentient species, one weaned on slaughter, mayhem, and genocide. And on that day, Sin-Dour, we'll be looking at a serious rival." He then raised a finger. "And that's why the Affiliation needs to find that planet pronto, to better facilitate a peaceful transition into a state of utter subjugation to our technical superiority. Think of the lives we'll save!"

"A logical argument you have presented, sir."

"Logic? Who cares about logic? What I'm describing is the venal pragmatism of a voracious, appallingly shortsighted sentient species. Namely, us. Logic is simply the language of convenient rationalization in a pseudo-science-loving civilization. Tammy!"

"Yes, Captain?"

"Are we on our way again? I can't tell."

"We are," the AI replied. "Exclusion Zone in eighteen point three-five minutes."

"Eighteen minutes? What do you think, 2IC? Enough time to get all sweaty in my stateroom?"

"Sir? Probably not."

Hadrian sighed. "You're right. I'll have postpone thoroughly spanking you."

The bridge iris opened and an outrageously curvaceous woman dressed in combat fatigues stepped through. She walked up to stand before Hadrian, snapped a salute, and spoke around the fat half-smoked but temporarily unlit stogie clamped in the corner of her luscious mouth. "Lieutenant Samantha 'Sweepy' Brogan, Terran Marines, sir."

"I can't believe I left you behind!"

"The incredulity is mutual, sir. Do you have any complaints regarding the extraction team, sir?"

"Not at all, barring the fact that your people refuse to remove their helmets."

"It's better that way, sir."

"You mean, you don't know what they look like either?"

"No, sir, I don't. Makes it easier to sleep through the night, sir."

Hadrian regarded her. Wide face, Asian eyes, long black hair piled into some kind of nest atop her exquisitely round head. High, flaring cheekbones, a delicate scar under the left eye, full lips painted deep red, the flash of white teeth as she spoke. He grunted his appreciation, and then said, "So you sleep well at night, do you, Lieutenant?"

"I sleep the sleep of the damned, sir."

"And that sits well with you?"

"Yes, sir."

"How did you manage to track us down?" Sin-Dour asked, by way of rude interruption. "It is scientifically impossible—"

Sweepy's eyes flicked over to the 2IC. "We're marines, Commander. We eat impossible for breakfast, shit it out before lunch, and then eat it all over again."

"Well, at least that one makes sense, kind of," Hadrian said. "Outstanding, Lieutenant. How many squads in your complement?"

"One active, two inactive."

"Inactive?"

"On ice, sir."

"And presumably, we've met the active squad. Gunny Sergeant Muffy Slapp. Skulls, Chambers . . ."

"And Lefty Lim, Sniper, Stables—our medic—and Charles Not Chuck, heavy weapons. They're decent. Been downrange enough times to not get in a flap."

"Delighted to finally have you all aboard, Lieutenant," said Hadrian, rising to his feet and smiling at her.

She chewed on her stogie for a moment, and then flashed a brief smile that never reached her I'll-kill-you-in-a-blink eyes. "Thank you, Captain. Is there anything else you want of me right now?"

"Plenty, Lieutenant, but duty demands otherwise. Inform your squad that we're about to engage a Misanthari Swarm and there may be hand-to-hand on multiple decks."

"I'll put the iced teams on standby, sir."

"Hmm. If you need to take command of ship security squads, Lieutenant, you are so authorized. Oh, and liaise with our chief of security, Adjutant Lorrin Tighe."

"Yes, sir. Where is this adjutant?"

"Passed out drunk in my office, LT. She might need a Spike to come around, but I'm sure you're well equipped."

"Yes, sir. Shall I, then?"

"Go on," Hadrian said, pointing to the office door. "I know, it's supposed to be a storage cabinet, but I assure you, it is my office, and you'll find her in there."

He watched the marine cross the bridge, gaze fixing on the meaty sway of her behind.

Sin-Dour cleared her throat. "We're about to drop out of T space, Captain. Five minutes."

Hadrian sat again. "Tammy! Do you have those new beam weapons installed and ready to blaze away?"

"And so begin a galactic war, Captain? Absolutely."

"Enough with the sulking, Tammy, and free the weapons to my combat specialist."

"Not a chance," the AI replied. "He will be busy enough with the turrets, railguns, and missiles. Besides, only I have authorization to use my weapons."

"I am not happy about that, Tammy."

"Oh boo hoo. I'd show you my virtual violin but it's sub-molecular."

Sweepy reappeared with a still-unconscious and now mostly naked adjutant slung over one shoulder. "Captain, I think I'll just drop her off at sickbay on my way down. She'd need five Spikes just to come around and that'd be a waste. Permission to assume overall command of ship security."

"Granted, Sweepy. Best get on with it, too."

As she passed him, Hadrian raised a hand. "Oh, by the way, Lieutenant, I understand that what you discovered in my office might seem, well, a contravention of regulations and, indeed, decorum. But I assure you, it's only half as bad as you think."

She studied him, plucked out her stogie, and said, "Captain. I'm on a vessel in the Terran Space Fleet, which is just a puffed-up name for fucking Navy mop-pushers, if you'll excuse the expression. So . . . no, I have no opinion, sir, none at all."

"It's no surprise," Hadrian said, "that with soldiers like you, Lieutenant, we've conquered a tenth of the galaxy."

"Thank you, sir."

"Dismissed, Sweepy. Good hunting."

Out she went with the adjutant like a sack draped over her shoulder.

Sin-Dour had returned to the science station, and now announced, "Exclusion Zone ETA, thirty seconds!"

"Stay calm, 2IC," said Hadrian. "Red alert. Forward viewscreen on. Thrusters primed for combat readiness, all weapons loose. Stand by, Helm."

The *Willful Child* rattled as the twin railguns powered up and loaded projectiles.

In his mind Hadrian pictured the countless corridors and operations rooms in his Engage-class starship, while he floated like an invisible ghost and watched his crew running about as the red-alert beacons flashed. Seeing one man trip and slam into a wall, the captain shook his head to clear it. "Nice and calm, now," he said to his bridge officers. "Panic won't do, not on this ship. If I have to—*holy freaking crap!*"

The *Willful Child* dropped out of T space to find itself in the midst of an enormous space battle. Counter-class Terran warships were blazing from every weapon cluster, missiles spinning, flaring, and curving round as they chased dozens of Misanthari swarmships. Oblong red blobs splashed against Terran shields even as inert kinetic strikes blossomed in vast bruises against the protective energy screens.

One Counter-class vessel, the ASF *Cruel Without Cause*, was visibly staggering to a barrage of kinetic strikes, and an instant later its port shield collapsed. Red blobs raced in to explode in smears against the ship's hull. The acid made the hull armor boil, and in each place the dark splodge that was huddled inside the crimson goop unfolded its weapon-studded limbs as it readied to drop through the imminent breach.

"Sir!" Sin-Dour cried. "They got here ahead of us! The Misanthari Rage Index is Grey Point Two! Captain! Two points left until Pure White!"

Tammy crowed, its laughter echoing through the ship. "Galactic war! Hahahahaha! Serves you right, Captain Hadrian!"

"Galk! Target the swarmships around the *Cruel Without Cause!* Helm! Ignite the antimatter engines, twenty percent acceleration exponential to point six-nine!"

"Captain," shouted Sin-Dour, "that'll plough us right through the engagement!"

"That's right, 2IC," Hadrian said. "Oh, we'll take a few potshots and maybe help out our erstwhile fellow Terrans who happen to be hunting us on a shoot-first basis. But this ruckus here, why, clearly someone messed up on the diplomatic front. In other words, not our problem. Tammy! Target that big Swarm-Mother—the flashing-flagged one to starboard—that's where most of the red blobs are coming from. We'll do a drive-by. Beam weapon, baby! Hit it, Tammy!"

Loud twanging country music filled the bridge.

"What the hell? Tammy!"

The music stopped. "Sorry, Captain," said Tammy. "Some sleeper command in my matrix."

"The beam weapon! Hit that ship! Hit it hard!"

A scintillating, actinic line blazed out from the *Willful Child*, cutting through the enemy shields and striking amidships.

"Direct hit!" cried Joss Sticks.

Nothing happened.

Hadrian scowled. "Tammy! What kind of beam was that?"

"It's a particle beam. Must I get all technical with you?"

"Sorry I asked. Well, you hit the Swarm-Mother. What kind of damage did you deliver?"

"I appear to have turned a square centimeter of its hull into glass."

"Glass? What's the point of that?"

"Evidently, it is very effective where I came from, I suppose."

"Your makers—what are they, Galactic Voyeurs?"

"I have another beam-weapon configuration, Captain, but I should warn you, it's—"

"Lock on the same target and fire it, damn you!"

The beam that erupted from the *Willful Child*'s bow seemed to cut a slash through the fabric of space itself. Striking the Swarm-Mother, it turned the capital ship into a cloud of twinkling dust.

"Darwin preserve us!" cried Sin-Dour in a hushed, shocked tone.

The other Misanthari vessels were breaking off.

Moments later, the *Willful Child* cleared the area of engagement and continued on, still accelerating. "Tammy," said Hadrian, "what was that thing?"

"A Folded Actuating DM Target-Disassembler Irrefutable-Assertion Beam."

"Oh," said Hadrian, "one of those, huh? Listen, we'll need a better name for it, I think."

"What does 'DM' refer to, Tammy?" Sin-Dour asked from the science station. She was frowning down at her sensor readings. "That is," she added, "I'm getting some unusual perturbations in our wake—"

"DM, Commander," said Tammy, "refers to dark matter, of

course. As I was attempting to tell your captain, this particular beam has a few side effects, principally, the terminal, irreversible thinning of the substrate of dark matter upon which the fabric of this universe is, shall we say, hung. If you wish a schematic of the effect, imagine a dimple in what should be a taut, stretched, and mostly level substrate. Given the current cross-flow of dark matter, which always runs perpendicular to the continued expansion of the universe, thus maintaining observable cohesion, this dimple is asymmetrical, with the greatest thinning effect at the apex as seen from against the expansion of the universe."

"Dimple, huh? You want us to call this a Dimple Beam?"

"Well, not necessarily, Captain," Tammy replied. "But I would suggest that you urgently advise your Terran allies back there to vacate the area of combat as quickly as possible, in case their vessels, uh, fall through."

"Fall through? To where, Tammy? Some kind of T space?"

"Oh dear, no, Captain. The precise nature of the substrate a vessel might plunge into is unknown. In fact, I doubt there's a single hypothetical musing worth noting regarding said sub-substrate. If I was asked to, say, posit a few likely characteristics to what waits at the bottom of the pit, I would note a likely breakdown of most functionality. And even should the vessel manage to maintain coherence, why, I doubt the thrusters or engines would work. The same for the T-drive. Meaning, no way to get back out."

"Comms! Pol—oh, you again, Jimmy. Thought I relieved you? Never mind. Warn the Counter fleet out of the way, highest priority."

"Yes, sir. What reason should I give, sir?"

"Weren't you listening?"

"No, sir."

"Just tell them, uhm, tell them they'll die if they don't leave. The beam weapon we used has side effects—there, that's about right, or is that too complicated for you to understand, Mr. Olympian? Send it!"

"Yes, sir!"

"Tammy!"

"What?"

"Don't use that tone with me! What happened to that Swarm-Mother? Did it fall through, then?"

"No. It dispersed. At the subatomic level."

"So," said Hadrian, "shall we summarize here? You have two beam weapons. One turns tiny, solid, opaque surfaces into glass, presumably designed to be used against deadly private shower stalls, or the bottom of toilet basins, depending on your predilections. The other beam weapon permanently weakens the fabric of the universe. Tammy, can you maybe come up with a beam weapon that, I don't know, falls somewhere between the two? You know, some kind of tachyon antiproton X-ray gammatron beam thingy."

"The beam weapons you describe, Captain, lack efficacy."

"Oh, and your glass popper does?"

"Within specification constraints," Tammy said loftily, "I would suggest that it worked perfectly."

"I want middling!" Hadrian shouted, pounding the arm of the command chair. "Comms! Sickbay—Printlip! Get up here with that nanogel, would you? Tammy! Middle-of-the-road beam weapons. I want to see flashes of bright deadly colors. I want to see shields glow and buckle! And big black smears against enemy hulls! Errant electrical discharges would be pretty cool, too. I want to *engage* in battle, do you understand? To-and-froing, with broadsides! What I don't want, damn you, is pushing a button that obliterates an entire Darwindamned ship! Where's the glory in that?"

"You describe the vice of inefficiency, Captain."

"Exactly! That's what I want, inefficiency!"

"That makes no sense."

"It makes perfect sense, Tammy." Hadrian settled back in the chair, taking a deep breath. "Perfect sense. Poetic sense, in fact. If life has no drama, there's no real point in living it. Without jeopardy, without real risk, without the old touch-and-go moments of serious shit going down, well, what's the fucking point to it all? And nix the close-up again, will you?"

Galk chimed in from his combat cupola. *"All very Varekan of you, sir. I am impressed. As we Varekan are wont to say: 'If you have to, live long or live short, what real difference does it make in the end anyway?'"*

"Not now, Galk. Stop eavesdropping. Take a bucket and brush to your cupola, will you? Listen, Tammy, it's clear that you have a lot to learn. You're like a child with a machine gun. Sure it's funny when it goes popopopopop, but then, your whole family's dead, so what the fuck? Listen, how about we make us a deal here?"

"What kind of deal, Captain?"

"Delay this whole 'where's my daddy' scenario for the time being. The day you step up to that weirdo, you want to be an AI that he or she or it can be proud of, don't you? We're talking a steep learning curve here, friend. I'm the man to send you on that ladder, step by step."

"You, Captain?"

"See? It's that dubious skepticism stuff you need to deep-six, Tammy. In the meantime, how about we drop back into T space, give the Radulak and the Klang a miss for now, and work us up some pristine, as yet unexplored sector of space to go fuck around in."

"I see your point, Captain, but I am afraid I must insist that we continue on to my rendezvous with the Klang. And, given the T-terminator stations at the Radulak-Exclusion interface, it shall have to be in real space. As for winging off to some unexplored sector, well, I believe that, once I am able to determine the source point of my origin, why, we will indeed be journeying into the true unknown."

"Oh great, first contact with the Windex Civilization. I can't wait for that one, Tammy."

"They can't be entirely incompetent," said Tammy. "They made me, after all."

"Your point?" Hadrian asked.

TEN

Jimmy Eden swung round in his chair and said, "Captain, all six Counter-class ships have acknowledged the warning and are bugging out."

"That's great, Jimmy. Except that there were supposed to be seven ships."

"Really? Oh. Well, that explains their hails to us, then."

"What a relief. Jimmy?"

"Sir?"

"Can I hear one of those hails?"

"Oh. Well, I didn't record them or anything, sir. But anyway, they were all kind of the same. Variations, I mean. They mostly asked, 'Where did the *Extemporize* go?' and things like that."

"Jimmy, you are a raving idiot, did you know that? At least tell me you know that."

"Y-yes, sir. Sorry, sir."

"Sin-Dour, take a peek back, will you? How many ship signatures are you showing?"

"Six, sir."

"Enough wreckage for a seventh?"

"No, Captain. The wreckage is Misanthari. Sir, the *Extemporize* is—"

"Sixth Fleet flagship, yes," said Hadrian. "And, if I'm not mistaken, it also serves as Admiral Lawrence Prim's personal limo. Well now. Tammy?"

"Captain?"

"Did a ship just drop through the hole?"

"Funny you should ask."

"Approaching Radulak space, sir," said Lieutenant Sticks. "Twenty seconds."

"Passive scan, Sin-Dour—anything waiting for us?"

"Negative, sir . . . barring all the remote detection devices, and, at one point six-three klicks large, an automated T-termination station. Oh, and there's a binary system with thirty-plus bodies in orbit. That's at eleven AUs dead ahead on present course. But other than all of that, negative, sir."

"A T-kill station at a hundred sixty-three thousand kilometers? Tammy, why did you drop us in on the damned doorstep of one of those? If we get jumped anywhere within an AU of it, we're toast."

"*Now you begin to comprehend my diabolical plan.*"

"I'm sorry, what?"

"Never mind. Coincidence, Captain, I assure you."

"Bilge crap! Space is big! Mostly empty! Distances are, hey—they're *astronomical!* How about that?"

"No, honestly, Captain. Consider it this way—this slows us down terribly. Why would I want that? Slowing us down means I have to spend even more time with all of you biologicals. When really, what I'd like to do is just find a barely hospitable planet somewhere to dump you all off, and good riddance."

"I thought we just made us a deal, Tammy?"

"I know. Even AIs can get conflicted."

"We can find us an Ohm reader, Tammy, if you require some digital therapy."

"Look, I'm *sorry* I selected a course that takes us right past a T-termination Inhibitor Station. And I'm *sorry* about your admiral and his flagship. Oh, I'm *sorry* too about getting your own Affiliation to put a price on your head—even if you probably didn't need any help from me on that count. And of course I'm *sorry* about wanting to find my maker and—"

"About that," Hadrian cut in.

"You just interrupted me!"

"Not my fault if you started to get boring. About that maker stuff. When Buck first got a look at your hardware, Tammy, we found lots of Terran technology. Ancient stuff. New stuff. Stolen and salvaged, jury-rigged, blah blah. Same for what we could sniff of your software. As an AI template, you seem pretty . . . adaptable."

"A compliment from you, Captain? I am astonished."

"Only because I've not finished this thought of mine. So, the point I'm making is, there's a standard correspondence about this kind of thing. High adaptability as a base template usually means what's called Fuzzy Dumbness—"

"Dumbosity," said Sin-Dour. "Fuzzy Dumbosity, sir."

"Precisely. Basically, it means there's a whole lot of tabula rasa on your speck board, Tammy. You started pseudoconsciousness as a, well, a simpleton."

"I retract my astonishment, Captain. Any other insults you want to fling my way?"

"You only achieve true AI consciousness, Tammy, by engaging with and learning from your environment, and most of the learning you need is the social, interactive kind. The messy kind."

"I will have you know," intoned Tammy, "that I have scoured, extracted, modified, and implemented a vast range of experiential data. Tabula rasa no longer!"

"Maybe not," said Hadrian. "Problem is, most of the speck-scrawling on your board is flat-out rubbish. Now, honestly, I'm sorry to have to be the one telling you that."

"No, you're not! You're happy because it helps mask your own inadequacies! You drag me down to compensate for your own crisis of confidence, your own failing sense of self-worth, your own—"

"Of course, all that, but it's beside the point, Tammy." Hadrian stood. "Anyway, think on it. As for me, I need a new shirt. Helm, are we going to be passing through that binary system?"

"Yes, sir, right through it. ETA Outer Edge, twenty-four minutes."

"Comms—oh, you, Polaski. Any signature chatter in that system?"

"A few automated burrow-drones in a half-dozen asteroids between Orbits Eighteen and Nineteen, Captain," Polaski replied. "It's not a metal-heavy array of bodies, sir, except for a T1-class world in the human-rated Goldilocks sweet spot, Orbit Eleven."

"Terra1-class? And the Radulak haven't toxiformed it for their own use yet? Sin-Dour?"

"It appears not, Captain," the commander replied. "And yes, sir, that is *very* unusual. Unprecedented, in fact."

"Quiet planet, Polaski?"

"As a tomb, sir."

"By the way, what happened to Jimmy Eden?"

"Acute peptic ulcer, sir. Just sprang up."

"So he's down in sickbay? That explains why Printlip ignored my summons. Well, I'm heading there for some nanogel. I should be back before we reach that system. In the meantime, Sin-Dour, you have the bridge. If Tammy starts singing 'Daisy' be sure to inform me at once."

"I know what you're doing," the AI said.

"Oh?"

"Yes. You're trying to traumatize my personality quantum pentaxpression hierarchy."

"Well," said Hadrian, "if I knew what the hell that was, you could count on it, Tammy. Damn straight, in fact. You keep forgetting—you have hijacked my ship, after all."

"I gave you the Dimple Beam!"

"And Admiral Prim is, I'm sure, delighted."

"Not my fault!"

"Galk. You got a Varekan saying to answer that?"

The Varekan sighed over the bridge speakers, "*'Everything is everyone's fault.'*"

"And?"

"*'Blame Game is for losers, so suck it up or die like the useless piece of crud you are.'*"

"Thank you, Galk. Carry on with the bucket."

After stopping off in his office to change into a burgundy padded-shoulder vest-and-jacket ensemble with dark grey piping, Hadrian made his way down to sickbay. He entered to find Doc Printlip fussing over a patient lying on a cot.

"Is that Jimmy Eden, Doc?"

The eyes swiveled on their stalks. "Why, yes, Captain. Presently sedated."

"Sedated? That bad?"

"I understand your concern, sir. While not life threatening, Lieutenant Eden is suffering from a number of conditions."

"With stupidity at the top of the list."

"Well, Captain, I am not at the moment treating him for that. Peptic ulcer and constipation are the first things to deal with. As I explained to him, a diet consisting entirely of high-bulk-high-protein-high-creatine shakes is probably not a good idea."

"Right, so what else is wrong with him?"

"A whole catalogue of stress-induced psychosomatic maladies."

"Really, Doc? They have catalogues for those? Fascinating. Now, enough about him. More nanogel for the hand, please. Oh, both of them, actually."

"Very well. Please come over here to my treatment station."

Printlip readjusted his raised walkway with a handheld, and the robotic contraption rattled over to a counter. He then waddled along it, three hands waving an invitation to follow.

"You must give it time for the bones to set, Captain," the Belkri said, working the spray pump to cover Hadrian's bruised and swollen hands. "And how are the teeth? Firm? Hmm?

Good. Now, do you note the impressive skill I employed in ensuring an even application? This is what many, many years of intense study have accorded mrfplff."

"Very impressive," said Hadrian. "I just noticed that aquarium over there. What's all that about?"

Printlip's eye stalks pitched around. "Ah! That. Come! I will show you!"

As the doctor reconfigured the walkway again, Hadrian deftly snagged two bottles of nanogel and pocketed them, and then he followed Printlip across the room.

"An aquarium full of sand. Very impressive, Doc."

Printlip stepped onto the counter and reached down. "Ah, but look at what's buried in it!" The doctor dug free an ostrich-sized egg. "This, Captain!"

"Wow, that'll make a decent breakfast, won't it?"

"My monitors indicate it still lives, Captain, and that the incubation period is nearing its conclusion."

"Right. So what is it?"

"Unknown, sir. The shell is of a material that blocks most forms of internal examination, including X-rays and Quantum Defabulation. I elected to avoid ultrasound, for obvious reasons."

"Obvious. Absolutely, though the thought of scrambled egg is making me hungry. So, where did you get this, then?"

"In a market on Malin-7."

"Well, do let me know the day it pops out, tail wagging and all that."

Printlip seemed to fidget for a moment, and then the Belkri swelled massively as it drew a deep breath. "Captain, I am glad you visited. There is another matter I need to discuss with you.

It concerns Chief Engineer Buck DeFrank's psychological state, which I initially observed as somewhat . . . dislodged, when I treated his damaged foot. Standard procedure analysis of the patient's blood indicated an alarming array of psychoactive and psychotropic agents, which in themselves can trigger psychopathology of the psyhlybfrelppp . . ."

"Oh fine, then," said Hadrian. "I'll drop in on him now and snap him out of it."

"Sir," began Printlip.

"No no, enough from you. This is a captain's responsibility. Tell you what, though, if he becomes entirely unresponsive to external stimuli, then I'll give you a call. So, got any sharp prodlike instruments I can borrow?"

"Sir! I highly advise against—"

"Tammy! Where's Buck right now?"

"In his quarters, Captain."

Hadrian turned to Printlip. "Is his foot all better now, Doc?"

The Belkri's hands were waving about, its eyes twitching on their stalks. "Of course. I—"

"Great work, Doc. See you later!"

Leaving sickbay, Hadrian made his way to Deck Ten.

"I saw you," Tammy said in a low tone as the captain strode along a curving corridor.

"Sorry, what?"

"Thief."

"Oh, that. What are you going to do, report me to the Guilds?"

"You may not have time for this detour, Captain. We're about to drop into standard orbit around the planet, designation M-3-11 'Strange New World.' I assume you'll want to displace to the surface."

"You know, Tammy, rail against it all you want, but you're starting to fit right in here. This whole maker thing is going to turn out as a red herring. Anyway, yes, of course I'm going down to take a look. Who should I bring with me, I wonder?"

"Why not all the essential officers from your bridge?"

"Not Polaski."

"Nor, I presume, Buck."

"Don't be ridiculous, Tammy. It's exactly what Buck needs—to get back on that horse."

Arriving at the chief engineer's quarters, Hadrian halted, frowning at the shut door. "You informed him I was on the way, Tammy?"

"I did."

"Did he respond?"

"In a manner of speaking. He overrode the door lock and jammed it."

"Oh for crying out loud. Can't you override the override?"

"He's an engineer, Captain. He'll just override my override of his original override."

"Fine. Displace a blaster to this location."

"Just one? And which side of this door?"

"What? Here, to me! *This* side of the door, you dolt!"

"I was considering a fairer encounter, Captain. Besides, if you're both armed, why, won't it be more exciting?"

"Not now, not here, Tammy."

There was a soft plop and Hadrian looked down at the floor to see a Destabilizing Sequence Pulse Deviator, Mark IV.

He picked it up and powered it on. Aiming at the door's locking panel, he pressed the trigger.

A savage blast of snarling lightning ripped out from the barrel to strike the door dead-center, burning a massive hole.

"Crap! I was aiming at the panel!"

"Check your deviation setting, Captain, and you'll see it is set to maximum. I was assuming you'd aim at the door itself, but it seems you didn't."

"Stop trying to second-guess me, Tammy!" Crouching, Hadrian peered through the hole in the door. "Buck? How are you doing in there?"

The only reply was a strange humming sound.

"Tammy," whispered Hadrian, "what's making that noise?"

"The chief engineer, Captain. I believe he is in a trance state."

"Really? Not armed? Not ready to jump me as soon as I step in?"

"I daresay he did not even react to you destroying the door."

Grunting, Hadrian stepped gingerly through. The outer room was set up in standard configuration, but the room beyond glowed with ethereal, reddish light. Through the entrance, Hadrian could see Buck kneeling on a pillow, his back to the doorway.

"Oh man, Tammy," Hadrian said, "he's found religion."

"The Great Clockmaker in the Sky," said Tammy. "The Ur-Engineer of All. The Cosmic Repairman. The—"

"Wrong on all counts," cut in Hadrian, as he edged into the doorway. "He's gone back to basics, Tammy. Church of Science, the Original Scriptures of Darwin, the See of Evolution, the Conservation of Conservity, Hierarchy of the Fittest and all the other Principles of Natural Superiority that we use to justify everything we do. And, Tammy, he's got it bad."

The chief engineer had set up a shrine, but lacking a proper idol triptych to represent the Father/Mother/Child holy triumvirate of Frowning Bearded Old Man, Offering-It-Up Bonobo Female, and Monkey-Child-Pondering-Human-Skull, Buck DeFrank had found a knee-high Santa Claus doll, which he'd stood up leaning against the back wall above the storage-crate altar. Chicken bones from (presumably) the kitchen were heaped around the doll's shiny black plastic boots.

"Good grief, Buck," said Hadrian, stepping into the room.

The humming stopped, and then Buck spoke in a deep, calm, and strangely reverberating voice. **"Captain. Welcome. Are you well?"**

"Sure, Buck, I'm peachy. Too bad the same can't be said for my chief engineer."

"To the contrary, Captain, I have never been better."

"That's the drugs talking, Buck. And Tammy, cut it out with the reverb, will you?"

Buck sighed. "Drugs, Captain? I am expunged. Cleansed. Purified."

"Well, that's nice. Now, get up, will you? We have a surface mission."

The man did not move.

"Buck?"

"About those drugs . . ."

"That's the spirit, man! Here we go, on your feet!"

Hadrian had Buck off the pillow and upright, but the man wavered as if drunk. "C-Captain? I spoke with Darwin! With Darwin Himself! I heard him!"

"Sure thing, Buck—"

"He howled like Tarzan—"

"—and—really? Like Tarzan?"

"The victory cry of a Great Ape—it—it was glorious!"

"Well, I never . . . anyway, just duck here and through, into the corridor, that's it. Tammy!"

"Captain?"

"Get Sin-Dour and Lieutenant Sticks down to the Insisteon room. Oh, and Galk and Printlip, too. Who else? Right, the LT. Oh, and has the adjutant sobered up and come around yet?"

"Sobered up, yes, Captain. As for coming around, you're dreaming."

"Just have her meet us in the Insisteon room."

"As you wish."

Hadrian slapped Buck on the back. "Just think, friend! A genuine Strange New World! Can't you just taste the adventures awaiting us? How would one describe it, I wonder?"

"Like puke, sir," said Buck.

Tammy said, "Good luck, and I hope you all die."

ELEVEN

They displaced to the planet's surface. Hadrian looked around. "Amazing," he said. "It's just like northern California."

"Sir," said Sweepy Brogan, "I still advise we bring down a squad—"

"Nonsense, LT. We'll be fine. We're armed to the teeth, we have our doc with us, and everybody but me is wearing personal shields and body armor. Now, everyone, spread out and look around. The Radulak are avoiding this planet for a reason, and we're going to find out why even if it kills one or two of us."

Adjutant Lorrin Tighe said, "I reiterate my protest at this whole endeavor."

"Can you?" Hadrian asked.

"Can I what?"

"Reiterate it."

She glared at him, an expression of hers that he was coming to appreciate. "Since this planet is officially designated a

Strange New World, I should point out that my authority is equal to yours until such time that we may contact an advanced civilization, at which point I am in charge."

"Should you?" Hadrian asked.

"Should I what?"

"Point it out."

"One wonders if any of this mocking behavior would occur if I wasn't a woman."

"Does one?"

"One does!"

"No need to get hysterical, darling. I'm sure everything will turn out just fine. Now, why not do some exploring—there, head round those bushes and that outcrop."

She pulled out a blaster and brandished it. "Yes, Captain! They let me take a weapon!"

"Did they?"

Tighe pointed it at him and pressed the trigger. Nothing happened.

Hadrian sighed. "Terran Fleet seriously dislikes friendly-fire incidents. Accordingly, you can't use a Terran Fleet weapon on Terran Fleet personnel. I suppose in your excitement you forgot that detail. Now, if you'd broken into the Extreme Situations Cabinet, why, then you'd have a weapon that was lethal against Terran personnel exclusively. Under those circumstances, why, I'd now be dead and you'd be in command. Well, good thing that didn't happen!"

Snarling in a most becoming way, Tighe stormed off.

"Captain," said Sin-Dour, "is it really wise to torment the Affiliation adjutant?"

"Wisdom's overrated, 2IC," Hadrian said, squinting in the

sunlight. "It only arrives long after you've acquired a massive list of things you fucked up. Well, I intend to circumvent those hard knocks of stupidity. Hence, no list. No, I'll take the glory of always being right over wisdom any time."

Sin-Dour was studying her handheld Pentracorder. "Captain. Some strange readings at thirty-six meters—that way, behind that big boulder."

"Good. Let's get on with it, shall we? Buck, stay close. You too, Printlip, in case something happens that involves lots of blood and gore. Lead us on, Sin-Dour."

"Yes, sir."

Coming around the giant boulder, they beheld a strange construction: rough-hewn as if from solid rock, it formed an arch, like a gate leading to nowhere. Ruins peeped up from shrubs and brush on all sides, looking vaguely Greek.

"Now that's curious," said Hadrian, walking closer.

Sin-Dour moved up behind him. "I am getting modest energy readings, sir. Low-level, reminiscent of something on standby, but they're unlike any energy readings I've ever seen before."

"What? You just said they remind you of—"

"True, sir," Sin-Dour cut in, "I did."

He glanced back at her. She was still studying the holographic images popping up from her Pentracorder. "This is your first surface mission, isn't it, 2IC?"

She looked up. "Yes, sir. About those energy readings . . ."

"Yes?"

"They're, uh, perfectly normal energy readings. I read the bars wrong. Sorry."

He stepped close and squeezed her fleshy upper arm. "No

problem, 2IC, my confidence in you is already recovering and in a week or two it should be—"

A loud, stentorian voice interrupted him.

"I AM THE MASTER OF THE SPATIAL TEMPORAL DYNAMIC. I INVITE YOU STRANGERS TO STEP THROUGH MY GATE AND EXPERIENCE FOR YOURSELVES THE SPATIAL TEMPORAL DYNAMIC OF WHICH I AM MASTER."

"I'm going through!" screamed Buck, launching himself at the gate.

"Buck!"

The chief engineer plunged through and disappeared.

"Shit! Where did he go? Come on, everyone, let's follow!"

As he ran beneath the arch, Hadrian saw Buck up ahead. He'd caught a foot on a root and had fallen into some bushes, and was now picking himself up. The captain reached him. "Buck, you damned fool! Who knows where—"

"Captain?"

At Sin-Dour's shout, Hadrian spun around. The others were still standing on the other side of the gate. "I thought you all followed me!"

"We, uh, we were confused, sir!"

"TWO OF YOU HAVE PASSED THROUGH THE PORTAL OF THE SPATIAL TEMPORAL DYNAMIC. YOU ARE NOW ON THE OTHER SIDE, THREE SECONDS LATER! AND IF YOU STEP BACK THROUGH, YOU WILL RETURN TO WHERE YOU STARTED, BUT SIX SECONDS WILL HAVE PASSED. WELL, EIGHTEEN SECONDS NOW. NINETEEN. TWENTY. WAIT! WHERE ARE YOU ALL GOING? COME BACK!"

Walking around the gate and pausing to spit out a brown stream, Galk paused and said, "Here, Captain, I've found something."

"Did you really have to, Galk?" Hadrian asked, swinging round to join the combat specialist.

"Just this small box in these bushes, sir. There's two cables, too, a thin one and a fat one. The thin one feeds into the box—see? But look at the big one. The shrub's grown up under it and pulled it out of the box."

Sin-Dour joined them. She squinted at her Pentracorder. "He's correct, Captain—"

"Yes, 2IC, I can see it."

"Oh. Yes, sir. Of course, sir."

Hadrian turned to the arch. "Hey, you! Master Whatever! Couldn't you see that you were broken?"

There was a pause, and then the voice said, "I SUPPOSE."

"So what was all that crap you were trying on us? Nobody would fall for that!"

"WELL, UNTIL NOW, IT'S BEEN MOSTLY RADU-LAK . . . IT SEEMED TO WORK FOR THEM. PLEASE, PLUG ME BACK IN, WILL YOU? I CAN'T TELL YOU HOW BORING IT'S BEEN, ALL THESE CENTURIES."

Crouching, Galk pulled up the cable, studied its end, and then jammed it into a hole in the side of the box. "All done," he said, straightening and pulling off his baseball cap to wipe at his brow. "Damned hot out for workin', though."

"YES, MUCH BETTER."

"*I'm going through!*" screamed Buck, launching himself at the gate.

"Buck!"

There was an impressive flash, and Buck disappeared.

"Check the bushes over there," said Hadrian.

'NOT THIS TIME! HE IS GONE. TRAVELLED TO SOME OTHER PLACE, SOME OTHER TIME. I AM THE MASTER OF THE—"

"What place and what time?" Hadrian demanded.

"I HAVE NO IDEA."

"So, you're not really the master of anything, are you?"

"YOU HAVE A POINT THERE."

"Can we follow? Can we find him?"

"ANYTHING IS POSSIBLE."

Sweepy spoke up, "Captain. I recommend we displace a squad down here and send them through. That way, should they all die, well, we only lost a few faceless nobodies. Excepting the chief engineer, sir."

"Hardly seems challenging," said Hadrian, rubbing at his manly jaw. "I was thinking of going through first, actually."

"Well, yes, sir, that does add a new wrinkle." She lit up her stogie, puffed for a moment, and then plucked a shred of tobacco from her tongue. "Decent, sir. Muffy can lead his team in later, shoot everything up, pull you out of whatever fucked up mess you got yourself into, and then, in answer to your heartfelt thank-you, just offer up an airy salute. Job done, fuckin' eh."

"You think highly of yourself, LT, don't you? Well, I like it."

"Glad to hear it, Captain. Now, since the adjutant has, well, disappeared, I was thinking I might go and retrieve her."

"Must you? Oh very well—no need to give me that look. If you can't find her, ask Tammy, since I'm sure the AI's tracking us all."

"But not Buck, sir. Not anymore."

"True."

"And when you go through . . ."

"That's the risks a captain takes, LT." Hadrian turned to Printlip. "Which he's happy to share with all his officers. You'd best join me, Doc. Buck's state of mind being what it is."

"Yes, Captain. But I really think we should await the marines."

"Not at all. They'll find us, right LT?"

"Bank on it," she said.

"Okay," Hadrian said. "As soon as the LT finds Tighe, the rest of you, displace back up to the ship and maintain orbit. We'll bring Buck back alive, you can count on it! Come on, Doc, give me a hand—no, just one, no, not that one, this one, the closest one—right, there! So we don't get separated."

Side by side they approached the arch.

"Now, Doc, you ready? Let's go!"

They began running, and the moment before they leapt, Hadrian threw the Belkri through the portal, and then followed.

Blinding light, and then Hadrian was out the other side. He skidded to a halt and found himself at the edge of a steep slope. Printlip was rolling and bouncing his way down to the basin thirty meters below. Out on the plain ahead, a small speck of a figure was running, stumbling, running, stumbling. The area looked just like northern California.

He made his way down the slope, reaching the bottom just as Printlip climbed to its feet and began dusting itself off.

"Quite the landing, wasn't it?" Hadrian said. "Buck's about a klick away, directly ahead. He appears to be heading out into a desert. Retrieving him should be easy."

"Captain, a warning. Belkri expand in high-heat environments."

"Oh. Is that dangerous?"

"No, we are capable of tripling in circumference. However, I should warn you, I might find it difficult to hide, should circumstances demand such a thing."

"Can't you offset expansion by nattering on endlessly?"

"Interesting suggestion, Captain. Shall I try?"

"Come to think of it, some other time, maybe. For now, let's get on with it. And when we get back, I've got some serious questions to throw at that Master of Blah Blah."

They set out.

"Such as?" Printlip asked.

"Why in Darwin's name didn't the thing send us someplace interesting? Paris in the Roaring Twenties, for example. Or Mars a hundred thousand years ago, with Venus looming overhead so close you could almost touch it? Where's the excitement here?"

"I would advise against asking such questions, sir."

"Why is that, Doc?"

"Invariably, upon the utterance of the question, someth—"

A scream from up ahead interrupted the Belkri. Buck was now running toward them, and behind the chief engineer there was a massive dust cloud, rolling ominously closer.

Printlip waved all of its hands. "See, Captain? I warned you, did I not?"

"Hmm," said Hadrian. "I think we should run back to the gate, Doc. What do you think?"

"Excellent idea, Captain!"

They turned round and began running.

"Oh dear!" gasped Printlip. "I don't do well with steep slopes!"

"That's ridiculous! Don't you have hills on your home world?"

"The Hill Wars of 9816! We leveled them all! It was slaughter!"

"Fine, hold on to me and I'll drag you to the top!"

"Thank you sir. The ignominy of this shames me deeply!"

"Good, because it's a real pain in the ass for me, Doc. Okay, give me your hand—no, not that one, no, not—*this* one, dammit!"

Buck was still screaming behind them, and by the sound of his voice the man was fast catching up.

Hadrian dragged the Belkri up the slope. The doc lost its footing and started bouncing like a balloon on a string. It shrieked when Hadrian tugged it through a spiny shrub. The captain lunged upward, looking for another shrub.

Stumbling, cursing, they finally reached the top.

The gate loomed before them.

"I AM THE MASTER OF THE SPATIAL—"

"Oh shut up, we know who you are!" Hadrian spun round to watch Buck scrambling up the slope. Behind him swarmed thousands upon thousands of—

"Kittens?"

The terror on the chief engineer's face was now entirely comprehensible, as far as Hadrian was concerned.

Buck stumbled into the dust at the captain's feet. "I'm sorry, sir! I should never have come through the gate! I don't know what came over me! Oh Darwin, save us!"

Hadrian pulled the man upright and pushed him toward the gate. "Go to Doc! Wait for me at the threshold!"

"Captain! You can't hold them off! I tried! I swear! They've been artificially enhanced, sir! But all the humans died out—there's bones out there by the millions! They were all suffocated by cuteness! The world is full of kittens, oh, the horror!"

"My God," Hadrian said. "They finally did it! All those oh-so-cute-my-cuddly-kitten-here's-a-pic *bastards*! They finally went and did it!"

The swarm was bounding up the hillside like tiny excited lambs, and now their squeaky cute voices reached him.

"*We love you fuck off.*"

"*Look at me look at me!*"

"*What the fuck you looking at?*"

"*Scratch me here and here, no not there did that hurt? Good.*"

"*Watch this I'm going to piss in your bed.*"

"*What did I do? I didn't do nothing. I can do whatever I want!*"

"*See this face it's the face that hates you.*"

"*I'm cool. Look, give it up you're not cool, nothing you do is cool, stop trying please. I'm embarrassed to own you.*"

"*Scratch me scratch me don't touch me!*"

"*Is that a mouse? Is that a bird? Can I torture it? Please please pretty please? I love you fuck off.*"

Hadrian pulled out his blaster, backing away. "Don't come near me!" he roared. "No—not even you! Not you, either! Shit!"

"*Ooh is that a camera? We like cameras.*"

"*Love me love me can you breathe kitten? Let's find out.*"

The blaster ignited. Kittens exploded in puffs of fur. A wild panic gripped Hadrian and he kept shooting, shooting, shooting.

Behind the captain, Buck was screaming. *"Hurry, Captain! You're close! Now, turn and run!"*

Loosing another salvo amid deafening meowing, Hadrian spun round and launched himself through the gate after Printlip and Buck. There was a bright flash of light.

He tumbled out to come to a rest against booted feet. Blinking, looking up, he found Lieutenant Sweepy Brogan staring down at him. She puffed on her stogie for a moment, and then pulled it out and said, "I take it none of you ran into my squad, did you?"

Hadrian climbed to his feet and dusted himself off. His shirt was torn, shredded, and snarled with vicious burrs. "You sent them through? They must've landed somewhere else. Crap. We could've used more firepower. Like, say, a nuke."

"That bad, was it?"

He noted the avid gleam in her dark, smoldering eyes—no, that was the stogie—her dark, steely eyes. "A bloody nightmare beyond all nightmares, LT. I doubt even you could sleep at night after witnessing what we just witnessed."

"I'm impressed, sir. You were gone, what, ten minutes? And by that red blinking light, I'd say your blaster's exhausted. Outstanding."

"I'll debrief you later, LT. Your quarters or mine?"

"Mine, sir, it's more private."

Hadrian offered her his brightest smile. "Why, LT, we could debrief each other."

"Sound plan, sir."

"Just deep-six the stogie, will you?"

"Sir, where would you like me to deep-six it?"

"Now hold on there—"

"Captain!" shouted Buck. "The whole gate's vibrating!"

"Oh, I thought that was just me."

"Something's coming through!"

Everyone scattered and a moment later the squad of marines backed into view, their weapons still blazing at whatever was still beyond the gate. They were covered in gore, and at least two troopers were badly wounded.

"I AM THE MASTER OF—OH SHIT, HOW DID YOU RUN INTO *THEM*? UNPLUG ME! UNPLUG ME!"

Buck threw himself into the shrub hiding the power unit, and moments later had torn both wires from the box.

A hologram flashed up briefly, forming a flickering wall sealing the gate. It said: TEMPORARILY OUT OF ORDER. REPAIR DISPATCH CONTACTED. WE APPRECIATE YOUR SERVICE AND WILL BE IN OPERATION AGAIN SHORTLY. Then, with a soft hissing sound, the image disappeared.

Sweepy glanced at the Combat Pentracorder on her wrist. "Zero energy readings, sir. The gate's dead as a secret crossdresser making a pass at a Fundamentalists' bachelor party." A moment later she turned to her gunnery sergeant. "All square now, Gunny?"

"*Aye, LT,*" Muffy replied through a partly smashed speaker grille on his helmet.

"Hairy, was it?"

"*Hairier than my ma's—*"

"Enough of that, Gunny. There's gentlemen present. All

right, then, scoot back to the ship and get cleaned up—you stink of fear."

"That would be shit and piss, LT."

Sweepy lit up another stogie with a marine-issue Multiphasic Universal. "Dismissed, Muffy. And since I've got no Sad Letters to write, no, I ain't interested in your report."

"You got it, LT." Muffy staggered off.

Hadrian looked around. "So you found the adjutant and sent her back with Sin-Dour, then?"

"Huh. About that, sir."

"Oh my. That doesn't sound good."

"We believe she's been kidnapped by the Radulak. A scout craft landed shortly after we did. And then took off again, rockets set at BOWMAOF."

"I'm sorry, rockets set at what?"

"Bug-Out-with-My-Ass-on-Fire."

"Shit. Tammy!"

"Yes, Captain?"

"How did you miss noticing a damned scout craft entering the atmosphere of this planet?"

"I was preoccupied."

"With what?"

"Well, with the Radulak Bombast-class warship fast closing on our position, if you must know."

TWELVE

Hadrian strode onto the bridge and took his seat.

Polaski said, "Captain! The commander of the Radulak ship is hailing us!"

"In a minute," Hadrian said. "Shipwide intercom, please. This is the captain. As an addendum to my last shipwide announcement, any crew member caught posting kitten pictures anywhere on this ship will not only be personally executed by me, I will also hunt down all your relatives and friends and kill them, too. Carry on. Captain out. Now, Polaski, the Radulak. On viewer."

The bridge of the Radulak ship dripped with slime. Seated in a massive throne was a huge, hulking figure in shiny black leather. Drool sagged in glistening threads like tangled webs from the alien's wide, fang-studded mouth. The three eyes that made a straight glowering line over the mouth were tiny and red-rimmed. A multitude of nostrils pocked the alien's leathery cheeks, chin, and forehead. When it spoke, snot and mucus sprayed out from various nostrils, and spit erupted with every word. "I am Drench-Master Drown-You-All-in-My-Magnificence, Third Rate, of Radulak Bombast-class warship *I Leave You Half-Eaten at Horrible Brunch with In-Laws*, and I intend to destroy you utterly."

"That's hardly a civil welcome, Drench-Master Drown-You-All—hey, listen, have you got a shorter name than that?"

"As you wish. My given name is Bill."

"Bill?"

The Radulak leaned forward and raised a gnarled fist. "It is a perfectly honorable Radulak name! Is it our fault you humans steal all of our best names? No! It is not! More proof of human inferiority in all things! Come up with your own names, human scum!"

The commander was no longer visible as that outburst slathered everything in sight. After a moment, there was a blurred gesture from the Radulak and a small, narrow-headed Muppetlike alien appeared from one corner, and with deft strokes swept a squeegee across the screen.

Hadrian caught Polaski's eye and made a chopping motion with one hand. His cousin frowned. The captain stood, marched over to comms, and stabbed the cutoff switch. Then he wrapped his hands around Polaski's scrawny neck and leaned forward. "Now listen carefully, so I don't have to choke you. See this—see me slash across your neck, like this? Like *this*? Got it? When I do that, it means cut transmission! Understand?"

Gurgling and blotchy-faced, Polaski managed a nod.

Hadrian turned away, and then swung round and whapped his cousin on the back of the head. Massaging his bruised hand, the captain's brows lifted. "Hey, that reminds me of when we were kids at the summer house! Happy days back then, eh, Polaski?" He made to return to the command chair, only to swing back and whack his cousin again. "Ah, see how nostalgic you made me?" He resumed his seat. "Now, then. Sin-Dour!"

"Captain?"

"Can you scan that Bombast monstrosity?"

"Not without triggering its automated defense systems, sir. Visual survey indicates nine hundred and fifty-four weapon hardpoints. Oh, and as you know, sir, the Radulak form of communication is at least seventy percent, uh, liquid. Pheromones, innumerable enzymes, hormones, and a whole stew of—"

"I am well aware of all that, 2IC," said Hadrian. "There is nothing in the galaxy more disgusting than two Radulaks having a conversation. Well, if you can't scan that ship, we'll have to do it the hard way." He waved at Polaski. Who stared. "Resume transmission, you twit!"

The Radulak commander reappeared on the viewer.

"All right," said Hadrian. "It's like this, Bill—no, dammit, I can't do it. My motorcycle mechanic was named Bill."

"Then he stole my name and should be torn limb from limb!"

"With what he charged—for crap service, mind you—I'm inclined to agree with you, Commander."

"Drench-Master!"

"Okay, Drench-Master."

The Muppet alien reappeared from the same corner and wiped the screen clean again.

The Radulak gestured and a pathetic figure was pushed

into view. It dripped slime from head to toe. Bill flared all its nostrils. "Yes, Captain! This is one of yours, yes? I found it on the planet below. As you can see, I have interrogated it. And now I know everything!"

"Oh well," sighed Hadrian, "so much for the hard way. You know everything, do you, Drench-Master?"

"Yes! And so, I offer this to you, even though I know humans to be liars, murderers, cheats, and eggshell dry. We will make an exchange, Captain—you, what is your name?"

"Hadrian Alan Sawback, commanding the *Willful Child.*"

"That is an alien name. It makes my spine drip sick-bile. No matter, I must swallow my vomit at least for a little while longer. The exchange is this. We send you this female Morning Discharge, and you send us the Talking Box known as Wynette Tammy. A simple process. We place the female in a Keep-Alive Pod and send it to the halfway point between us. You do the same with Wynette Tammy. Then we exchange! What do you say?"

"A little while ago, you said you were going to destroy us."

"Did I? A moment. I must consult."

A number of other Radulak now crowded the drench-master. Spit, drool, and gobs flew. Incidental misfires struck the screen again, and the Muppet returned with its squeegee, until a stray mass of phlegm engulfed its narrow, oblong head, knocking it over. The consultation ended when Bill drew out a weapon of some sort and blew off an advisor's head.

The drench-master waved the others away and leaned forward to flare its nostrils at the screen. "We are agreed. I never said anything of the sort. It was your imagination, human. Either that, or you are lying."

"You want us to play it all back for you, Drench-Master?"

"No! I offer you the exchange! Accept the deal or die!" It prodded Tighe with the barrel of its pistol.

She lifted her sodden, slathered face. "C-Captain! Please! Save me!"

Hands reached out and dragged the adjutant away.

"Drench-Master, what's your beef with Tammy Wynette?"

"Beef?"

"Bone to pick, then."

"Bone to pick?"

"Why's Tammy up your ass?"

The Radulak pounded a fist on the arm of its throne. "Horrible hunting mind-set! You humans are terrible creatures! We should all gang up and destroy every one of you!"

"Oh come now, Dren—hold on, we don't hunt up anyone's ass. Anyway, do calm down, will you? We need to consult on this end, in private."

"You need to concoct lies and deceits and betrayals, is what you mean."

Hadrian turned to Polaski and gestured. The man stared, flinched, and then frantically cut transmission.

Settling back in his chair, Hadrian said, "Tammy?"

"What?"

"Why do the Radulak want your head? What did you do to them?"

"None of this is relevant, Captain. I refuse to be extracted and sent over to the Radulak. Sad to say, it would be wise to write off poor Lorrin Tighe right now. I have primed the Dimple Beam—"

"Not a chance! Belay that!"

"I'm not going!"

"That's fine. I wouldn't have done that even if I knew how. Relax, will you? Galk!"

"*Captain?*"

"Head down to Deck Twenty and rig up a stealthed antimatter bomb and put it inside a cargo crate. Have the ignition linked to two seconds postdisplacement and/or resumption of gravity. Got that, Galk?"

"*My pleasure, sir.*"

"Inform me when it's ready to send across. All right, Polaski, resume the feed."

A Radulak was standing very close to the screen, using a limp Muppetlike thing to wipe down the lens. Noticing Hadrian, it ducked out of sight.

"Well, Captain Hadrian?" Bill demanded from its throne.

"It wasn't easy, Drench-Master, but we have managed to extract Wynette Tammy from our mainframe. We are packing his central Identity Matrix Unit into a crate."

"Good. We will do the same with the female human."

"Obviously," said Hadrian, "for this to work, we're going to have to trust each other."

"Of course, Captain. After all, if you send us, say, an empty box, we will fire all weapons and obliterate you."

"We won't. This is all legit, Drench-Master."

"Hmph, we shall see, won't we?"

"*Captain, this is Galk. Package ready to send, sir.*"

"Ah," said Hadrian. "Did you hear that, Drench-Master? Good. So, midrange point, correct? And then what, we displace the items to our respective ships?"

"Yes. Maintain your distance, Captain, as our ship's superior displace-inhibitor field extends well beyond our hull!"

"Just as we have similar countermeasures to unauthorized displacement, Drench-Master. No worries. A moment, please. Format Command: split the screen, external view, forward, and Radulak bridge continuous. There, perfect."

The Radulak must have done something similar, for Bill was leaning far forward now, two of its three eyes fixed on something to one side. Drool spooled endlessly from the alien's gaping mouth. "We see the crate, Captain Hadrian."

"There are modest thrusters affixed to the frame, Drench-Master, to halt the object at the agreed-on midway point."

"Yes, we see them. Mass indicates that the crate is indeed not empty. Very good, Captain. See now, we are sending you the female."

"So noted, Drench-Master."

A few moments later both objects halted side by side in space with about four kilometers between them.

Bill leaned back, nostrils opening wide all over its ghastly face. "We have a lock on the crate, Captain. Our systems have overwhelmed its guidance command hub!"

"I'm sorry," Hadrian said, "but is that display of processing prowess supposed to impress me?"

"Bravado, human? I am not surprised."

"Now then," said Hadrian, "we have a lock on the adjutant. Are you ready for the exchange? Shall we release the gravity snares on our respective offerings?"

"Yes." Bill held up a nubby finger. "I will press the button when you do the same."

Hadrian held up his middle finger. "Here's mine," he said, smiling.

"Good. Are you ready? Excellent. We mutually release the gravity snares. One, two, three . . ." The Radulak stabbed down and Hadrian did the same.

Bill's nostrils flared, and then snapped shut. "You didn't release your crate!"

"You didn't release the pod, Drench-Master."

"Didn't I? Oh. I must have missed. Hah hah."

"Shall we try it again?"

"Yes, and this time, for certain, Captain."

"Why not?"

Buttons were pressed.

"Captain," reported Polaski. "We have her and . . . and . . . and . . . and . . . yes, she's alive!"

On the screen, phlegm slammed into the lens. "Now we have Wynette Tammy—and now you die!" Bill cocked his head. "What? Report!" Gobs slammed into the side of its head. "Oh, the lower half of my ship has just disintegrated, has it? Cascade effect? Captain Hadrian!"

"Yes?"

"You have betrayed me! Liar! Cheat!"

"You were about to kill us, Drench-Master."

"Was I? Let me consult on the matter—oh, no time—"

On the screen, the view of the Radulak bridge went dark. The external shot went very bright.

Hadrian said, "Captain to sickbay. Doc, the adjutant needs cleaning up. When that's done, send her to her quarters and tell her to throw on something more comfortable. I'll be there shortly." He stood. "In the meantime, well done, every-one—no, not you, Polaski, but everyone else. As for me, I'll just change into a new uniform—"

"Captain!" cried Jocelyn Sticks. "Another Bombast-class ship has just appeared in-system!"

"Oh, really? Crap on everything! Galk! Rig us up another bomb, will you?"

"Aye, Captain. How about I do four or five, just to save time, at least until we leave Radulak space?"

"Sound plan, Galk. Proceed. In the meantime . . . Helm! Take us behind the planet and match speeds with the Bombast."

"Sir, how will I know—"

"The Radulak run everything at full tilt, Lieutenant. For a Bombast-class, that's six point three-two-four, come hell or high water."

Was that an admiring look from the lovely Joss Sticks? Hadrian offered her a warm smile. "It's the captain's job to know such things, Lieutenant."

"Yes, sir. Thank you, sir."

Puffing his chest—but not obviously, no, more in a subtle way intended to make it seem incidental—Hadrian strode to his office. He paused just outside the door and swung around. "Oh, and have someone mock up a Bombast silhouette, one to a hundred and ten scale, and get a drone to slap it on our hull, next to the Misanthari Swarm-Mother ship. Two jaw-dropping kills for an Engage-class Terran starship, wouldn't you all say? Carry on, everyone."

In his office, Hadrian tugged off his tattered shirt. From his clothes cabinet he selected a much thinner, stretch-every-which-way sky-blue polyester shirt with gold piping on the cuffs, collar, and lower hem. Taking his seat behind the desk, he opened the lower drawer and drew out a bottle of cologne. He flicked some onto his palm, dabbed his cheeks and neck, and then dried his hand on his flat, muscular belly just above his belt. "Tammy, you've been quiet of late."

"I was just sitting back and admiring your capacity for treachery, Captain."

"Just do as I say and not as I do, Tammy. Besides, Bill was planning the old double cross anyway. Just like old times. Eighty fucking credits for a reconditioned flywheel. I mean, who was he kidding?"

"'Ye shall sow what ye shall reap.' Is that not the human saying?"

"Don't think so. I think it's 'So and doh ray me,' actually. In any case, it should by now be obvious to you that I was born to this."

"That, Captain, I cannot deny."

"So, stick by me, Tammy, and you'll end up a fine example of an artificial self-deluded self-actualizing intelligence personality matrix."

"Hah, no different from you, then!"

"I said 'artificial.' You can't get around that, Tammy. Me, I'm biological. I come by my delusions naturally."

"When you display one of those rare instances of self-effacement, Captain, my High Suspicion protocols kick in."

Hadrian rose. "There's hope for you yet, Tammy. Now, I'm off to comfort a hysterical woman."

"You will find the adjutant on Deck Eleven, knocking them back like there's no tomorrow. And, given the fast approach of another Radulak Bombast warship, she might be right."

"It's that imminent annihilation thing that's so exciting, though, isn't it? At least, that's what I'm counting on."

"Mind if I tag along?"

"Could I even stop you? Sure, by all means. Just, uh, not all the way, if you don't mind."

"What do I care for watching clumsy procreative activities between two biologicals?"

"Procreation? No, we'll be having none of that if I can help it. A baby? A son I never knew I had? Forget it." He left the office, crossing the deck of the bridge and making his way out into the corridor. "Of course," he added, "that'll likely come back to haunt me. He'll show up years from now, with stupid curly blond hair, and cause me nothing but grief in a welter of torn-up bodies and exploding planets. So, thinking on that, we'll have to skip the hot skin-on-skin wild-animal-oh-fuck-it-whatever rogering that I had in mind, dammit. Displace me a couple rubbers, will you?"

They came to the elevator and Hadrian stepped inside. "Deck Eleven."

"The adjutant's present blood-alcohol ratio makes the likelihood of a successful amorous outcome highly improbable."

"That's not how it works, Tammy."

"She is about to pass out, Captain."

"So mist her a detox at the bar."

"You wish her to be stone cold sober, Captain?"

"Hmm, good point. Make her a tad, uhm, relaxed and uninhibited, will you?"

"I am experiencing an agitated energy loop you biologicals might describe as 'creeped out.'"

The red-alert beacon flashed in the elevator, followed by a blaring Klaxon. "Oh, I don't believe it! To the bridge, elevator, and step on it!"

"You *were* informed that a Bombast warship was fast approaching, Captain."

"We should have a whole planet in between us right now! But this here is the problem, isn't it? I've changed shirts three times already and still haven't properly christened my role as Lord King of Everything on this ship! I need a good roll in the sack is what I need! "

"Did not the marine lieutenant invite you to just that, Captain?"

"Sweepy? Well, true. But . . . okay, it's not like I don't like dangerous. But sometimes there's this instinct, this gut feeling, I mean, that says *Oh God not this one!*" He waved at the red flashing light. "My very own red alert starts strobing in my skull, with alarms ringing in my ears. You understanding any of this, Tammy?"

"Murkily," the AI replied. "You're all cock and no trousers."

"Hang on there a minute! Okay, you said it wrong, I think, but I get what you're trying to say, Tammy, and let me tell you—"

The elevator door hissed open.

"Later, Tammy," said Hadrian. "It's about to get hairy again!"

"Convenient," said the AI in a smirking tone.

"Oh sod off, will you?"

Hadrian arrived to see on the main viewer the bridge of

the Radulak Bombast vessel, with another drench-master in another throne, and spit all over the lens. The alien was speaking. "I am Drench-Master Drown-You-All-in-My-Magnificence, Second Rate, of Radulak Bombast-class warship *I Hunt Down and Urinate on Ex-Husband's Family*. But, knowing how such titles infuriate you, you may use my given name, which is Bob."

"No way!" shouted Hadrian. "Bob? What kind of alien name is that?"

Gobs of mucus slapped the screen. "It is so an alien name! It is a Radulak name! It is not my fault you humans have a name that sounds just like it! You stole it! You steal all our names! And now you are all going to die!"

THiRTEEN

Hadrian turned to the comms station and made a chopping motion with one hand.

But Lieutenant James Jimmy Eden wasn't even looking.

"Where's Polaski?" Hadrian demanded as he walked over to the station, pulled the headphones off Eden's head, and then reached across and cut transmission.

"Migraine," said Sin-Dour, as she rose from the command chair. "Apparently, he had them as a child. But they went away. Only now they're back, sir."

Hadrian held the headphones close to one ear. "What is this, Eden? You're listening to music? Stupid, crappy music?"

The square-jawed man stared blankly at him. "It's Celine Dion, sir."

"Get security up here! I want this man in irons. Prepare the Dark Hole!" Hadrian walked over to sit down in the command chair. "Helm, didn't I order you to get the planet between us?"

"We have, sir. This is a third Radulak warship—it was

waiting on the other side of the planet. I didn't know what to do! I'm sorry!" Suddenly she burst into tears.

Hadrian was quickly at her side, one arm around her shoulders. "There, there, Sticks, it's fine. You couldn't have known the Radulak would be so cunning, so conniving. I mean, they're only the nastiest alien species the Affiliation has run across to date, who would like nothing more than to initiate genocide against the human species, and have only been looking for any excuse to declare all-out war, so how could you be expected to, oh, I don't know, slam us into low orbit straight down to one of the poles, pushing the containment fields to the max as we dip into the atmosphere, ploughing up a vast cloud of raging plasma that we could hide in." He looked up, glared at Sin-Dour. "Why, even my 2IC just threw up her hands in a stunning display of tactical incompetence!"

Joss Sticks's bawling was getting louder by the second. Finally, Hadrian twisted her around and kissed her hard. Her head snapped back and she stared in wide-eyed shock. "There, that's better," said Hadrian, smiling. Then he rose. "All right, everyone, listen! We're in a hairy situation here, and I know that for most of you this is your first mission. In fact—2IC—when did we leave Kuiper Space Dock?"

"Yesterday, sir."

"Exactly. So, by any standards, it's been nonstop fun. But remember this! You're all handpicked officers of Terran Space Fleet!" He patted Sticks on the top of her head. "Granted, I selected most of you women because you looked cute, but being cute doesn't necessarily mean you're thick. In fact, I dream of that scintillating combination of cuteness with a hard, jaded look in your seen-it-all-and-fuck-it-whatever eyes, and by the time this tour is done with, I expect to find that combination in every one of you! As for you men, well, just get on with your work, stay out of my way, and I won't have to kill you."

Sin-Dour cleared her throat. "Captain? When did you last sleep?"

"Sleep? A captain's got no time for sleep! We're in an emergency here—for Darwin's sake, someone kill that Klaxon—and those flashing lights!" He returned to his chair. "Now—"

"Excuse me, sir," Sin-Dour said. "Security is here."

Hadrian twisted in his seat. "Ah, we've met before, haven't we? Now, it's Nina Twice, isn't it? Very good. Lieutenant Eden is relieved and under arrest. Charged with dereliction of duty and listening to Celine Dion. One of those charges is a court-martial offense and the other demands execution without recourse to appeal."

"S-sir!" cried Eden. "It wasn't me listening to Celine Dion! Don't kill me!"

"Blubbering now? Well, I'd expect nothing more from a fourth-place Olympian who's a fan of Celine—"

"It was Bob, sir!"

"I'm sorry, what?"

"The Radulak were playing her—they put us on hold just after we put them on hold!"

"What? They put our hold on hold?"

Wiping at his ruddy cheeks, Eden nodded.

"Let it not be said that Captain Hadrian Alan Sawback is an unreasonable man. All charges are dropped against you, Lieutenant Eden. In fact, for listening to that music, you may well earn a commendation for service beyond the call of duty. Or at least the elimination of one of those black flags on your file. Resume your station. Corporal Twice, stand here beside me, in case I need you for something else."

"Yes, sir."

"I trust you're armed this time?"

"Uh, no, sir."

"Take up that fighting stance you used before, then. Yes, like that. Perfect. Now, where was I? Oh, right." Hadrian glowered at the screen, which was displaying the Bombast vessel directly ahead with the massive curve of the planet down and to the right. "So," he mused, "we're going to play the Hold game, are we? Fine. Eden!"

"Sir?"

"Put their hold of our hold, on hold!"

"Yes—sir? How do I do that?"

"Well, what music did we have for them the first time?"

"Uhm . . . I think it was the Corbomite Cream-Sniffers, sir, with their latest hit 'Fracking Radulak Up the Crack Take That Shit-Heads It's a Bomb!'"

"Hmm, who decided on that one?"

"It's locked in, sir," Eden replied. "Contractual stipulations, sir. Just bad timing, I guess."

"All right. Override Celine Dion. What's next on this hour's list?"

"Uhm, the retro pop-synth-heavily-medicated group Rad Slime Puke Shit Stick a Match in It Go Boom, sir. Last year's Number One hit, 'If It Drips, Kill It.'"

"Ah," mused Hadrian. "The yoot of t'day are in their Really Fucked-Up period of Sporadic Intellectual Development. Next generation's government will shine bright indeed. Fine, then, never mind the hold on hold on hold. Put Bob on the viewer. Let's get on with this."

The Radulak drench-master returned to the screen. It was slumped back in its chair and appeared to be eating a Muppet alien. Noticing that transmission had resumed, it flung away the headless body and leaned forward. "Wise to surrender to our holds, Captain! We had thousands of them just waiting!"

"If you think Celine Dion was going to make us surrender, Drench-Master, well, it was a good call."

"Hah! Now hand over Wynette Tammy!"

"We're extracting the AI even as we speak—"

"We followed the transmissions from Bill! You will not fool us again with your horrible lying and treachery!"

"Look, Bob, we don't want to start a shooting war here—you must realize that it was Wynette Tammy who commandeered this vessel and forced us into your territory."

"We accept this, Captain. Your Affiliation has been sending us T-packets by the hundreds."

"I'm not surprised. Have you responded to them?"

Bob's nostrils flared. "We put them all on hold!"

"Celine Dion? Oh, those poor buggers."

"Not just her! Barry Manilow! And advertisements for various diet pills and exercise regimens. Ha ha ha! See, we have learned the art of Insufferable Cruelty from you humans! We throw your crap back into your face, with added Slime of Contempt!"

"Well, listen, Bob. Wynette Tammy tricked us last time— that's right, we really believed we'd trapped him in that crate.

But we weren't fooled this time. He's definitely in the crate we're about to send you."

"If you lie, I will destroy you!"

"We're sending it across now, Bob."

"One eye watches, one is skeptical and the last suspicious, just so you know—we are ready for anything, human!"

"I'm sure you are, Drench-Master. See, there it goes—those are guidance thrusters—"

"I know what they are! We have overwhelmed their defenses! The crate is ours!"

"Good to hear it," Hadrian replied.

"We displace it now! Yes, it is with us, and it's time to kill you—what? Antimatter explosion? Cascade effect? Human! Lies! Deceit! Treachery! The worst—" The screen went dark, and an instant later was replaced by an external shot, showing the vessel vanishing inside a fiery cloud.

Hadrian rubbed at his face. "You know," he said, "it'll be a mercy when we finally conquer them."

"Sir!" cried Sticks. "The third Bombast vessel is coming into view!"

"Galk?"

"Readying another one right now, Captain. But even the Radulak can't be that—"

"Of course not," Hadrian said. "That's why I want you to paint this crate bright red."

"Acknowledged."

"In the meantime," Hadrian continued. "Tammy, how about you quietly prime all our fancy new beam weapons? But not the Dimple Beam. Oh, and if you have any super-cool countermeasures, best have those ready, too."

"I have been observing human interactions with alien species, Captain."

"Exciting, aren't they?"

"They invariably conclude with the sudden, violent deaths of thousands of biologicals, not to mention semi-sentient artificial personalities."

"Are you suggesting a pattern, Tammy?"

"I conclude that your particular species, Captain, advances by way of deadly incompetence, willful ignorance, deliberate misunderstanding, and venal acquisitiveness, combined with serendipitous technological superiority."

"Ever since Columbus landed on the shores of Old America, Tammy. What's your point?"

"There are many advanced civilizations in this sector of the galaxy, Captain. The odds are almost certain that you will, sooner or later, stumble into one that you can't take down in your usual illimitable, blood-soaked manner."

"*You* know it, Tammy. *I* know it. Maybe three or four smart people in the Affiliation know it, too. We are the lemmings of space, my friend. So far, we've been bullying voles and shrews. And I'll tell you this—if I have a personal mission out here, Tammy, it just might be to shock our species into some semblance of sanity."

"Indeed, even if you have to kill millions of aliens in the process."

"Well, granted. We call this collateral damage, and then, happily, sweep it under somebody else's rug. I didn't say it would be pretty, Tammy. I never said that."

All the officers on the bridge were staring at Hadrian now. He smiled back, and offered Nina Twice a wink.

Tammy said, "Captain, if I was to establish a book on your continued command of this starship, why—"

"Mutiny? Well, anything's possible, I'll grant you. But the thing is, as everyone here is quickly learning, without me they would already be so much chopped meat floating flash-frozen in empty space. There are missions, Tammy, and then there are missions. Who's to say those half-dozen wise-heads hiding in High Command aren't the ones who sent me out here in the first place? And don't ask me, because I won't tell. Now, Lieutenant Eden, is the new Radulak drench-master hailing us?"

"Yes, sir, for the last five minutes."

"And you kept him waiting?"

Eden paled, and nodded.

"Well done," Hadrian said. "Let them sweat, considering the two Bombast decals on our hull. But now, it's time. Open hails and onscreen."

"—we're going to destroy you and make puddles on your sleeping mats until the last sun burns out in the Night of All Slime into Blackness—oh, look, finally the Infamous Liar Captain Hadrian Alan Sawback deigns to talk to us. There is a Dripping Blob on your head, Captain Hadrian, with ten weeks in a sex pool as the reward! My egg sac is all aquiver at the glory I am about to receive for having destroyed you!"

"But don't you want Wynette Tammy first? And what was all that about puddles and blackness?"

"What? Oh, I was speaking to an interloper Klang science vessel eager en route to meet you. But you will not be alive to make Jumpy-Head Greeting with the Klang! You will be dead!"

"And Wynette Tammy?"

"You will send it to us, Captain. In a crate."

"Oh, good. Since we have it ready for you—"

The drench-master waved a thick finger. "No no no, Captain Hadrian. Not so easy this time for your treacherous lies!"

"But this is a red crate, Drench-Master."

"Red?"

"Yes, as proof that it is the right one that we're sending."

"Well . . ." A Muppet alien appeared, leaping up to whisper in the Radulak's membrane, and then shooting Hadrian a vicious glare. The drench-master raised a fist. "No, Captain Hadrian! No tricks this time! Send the Red Crate, yes, but you will ride it!"

"You want me to accompany the crate, Drench-Master?"

"Yes! I tremble for sex pool!"

"Why," said Hadrian, "so do I. So at least we have something in common. All right, it's a deal. Obviously, I need to suit up for the crossing. I'll be ten minutes or so."

"Agreed! We observe you on crate in ten minutes. Be sure it is the Red Crate, too!"

"Of course." Hadrian looked over at Eden and made a chopping motion. The lieutenant frowned.

"Corporal Nina? May I have that log pad you're holding? Thank you." He flung it at Eden, the tablet striking the man on the shoulder. "Cut transmission, you oaf!"

One hand rubbing his shoulder, Eden ended the contact.

Hadrian rose, smoothing out his uniform.

"Captain!" Sin-Dour said. "You can't mean to sacrifice yourself to save us!"

"Of course not, 2IC. Why on earth would I do that? Tammy!"

"Yes, Captain?"

"Radulak displacement-dampening fields—pretty much same as Terran versions?"

"Well, yes, since they stole the technology from you."

"They didn't steal anything. We sold it to them, and then told everyone else they must have stolen it. But never mind all that. So, that field draws on the same Latent Implicator Quantum Sinkwell that ours does, right?"

"Indeed."

"With the basic Phase Discriminators in place."

"Yes."

"Tammy, that hidden energy source of yours—is it capable of overriding that sinkwell?"

"If you are asking, Captain, if my energy source has the capacity to override the Latent Implicator Quantum Sinkwell, then the answer is 'yes.'"

"Tammy, why didn't you just answer 'yes,' instead of repeating what I said first?"

"Apologies, Captain. I was fiddling around in here and found a redundancy-delimiter program, and was checking to see that it still worked. Alas, it does. It works perfectly. Precisely in fact—"

"So," cut in Hadrian, "if you attach a speck tag on me, you could pluck me out of that field—thus collapsing it—in the instant before the ship explodes?"

"Well, only if I can insert a tense pause before confirming that we have you back on board."

"You're learning, Tammy. Okay . . . Galk!"

"*Captain?*"

"Link the detonator to the Radulak vessel's sinkwell collapse, and since we're dealing with quantum effects here, set it to occur precisely one point five seconds *before* the collapse. Got it?"

"*Acknowledged.*"

"Tammy, give me oh, say, eight minutes, before plucking me off that ship."

"Why so long, Captain?"

"Why, I need to have a conversation with the drench-master. Even better, a fistfight."

Sin-Dour stepped toward him, one hand half raised. "Sir, the Radulak weigh four hundred pounds, and most of that is endothermic reptilian optimized muscle!"

"And I plan to use every ounce of that muscle against the oaf, 2IC. Now, it's time to get ready. Sin-Dour, you have command. If anything goes wrong, go down fighting. Give it your all until your last fiery blood-boiling moment. We're talking pointless annihilation all in the name of avenging my death. Understood?"

"Y-yes, sir."

"All right. I'm off to Deck Twenty!"

FOURTEEN

Hadrian found Buck waiting outside the airlock chamber on Deck Twenty. "Ah, my chief engineer. What's up?"

"It's Tammy, sir! The AI is infiltrating all the drive systems! It has to stop!"

Shrugging into a breathing pack, and then stepping toward a suit-spray pod, Hadrian said, "Tammy, what's he complaining about?"

"Oh, some minor alterations to improve efficiency, Captain. Hardly a thing to panic about. By the way, do you mind if I attach a camera speck so we can keep an eye on you while you're on board the Radulak ship?"

"What? No, that's fine—"

Buck stepped in between Hadrian and the pod. "Nothing's fine at all, dammit! Those are my engines! My drives! I don't even recognize the configurations anymore! How can I do my work? Tammy's making me useless!"

"Buck, for Darwin's sake, not now. We'll talk about this when I get back."

"Captain, I'm warning you! I want satisfaction!"

"You want a duel? Between you and Tammy? Great idea. I'll be your second. Now get out of my way—I have a ship to save."

Stepping into the pod, Hadrian activated the spray. While this was going on, Tammy spoke. "I suppose it would be pointless to recommend a personal shield or body armor, wouldn't it?"

"Getting sweet on me, Tammy?"

"No. I was calculating odds. Presumably, you want to live—I know, by all indications thus far, that may be a wildly inaccurate assumption."

"What you might see as a death wish, Tammy, is nothing more than the bravado necessary to being a captain worthy of the name. It's all down to calculating the risks and then throwing the calculations away, because the role of the captain on a Terran starship is a mysterious, ineffable thing when you come down to it."

"Having observed you thus far, I have to agree. You're imperious, contradictory, headlong, insulting, irrational, and indeed cruel. Not to mention lascivious. And yet, somehow, you're still alive, still in charge, and the *Willful Child* is not a hunk of slag."

As the faceplate hardened in front of Hadrian's face, he said, "The risks of judging a book by its cover, Tammy."

"Oh? You mean to suggest that, deep down inside, you are really none of those things?"

"No, I am. And worse, in fact. But my crew don't know

that, do they? They're already convincing themselves and each other that I have a heart of gold. I mean, I must have, right?"

"I find that hard to believe, Captain."

"Really. Fine, tap us into an audio feed of the bridge."

"Now?"

"Now."

"Can I add holo?"

"Sure, why not. Pop it up on my HUD."

He saw the bridge take form in front of his eyes, as if seen from the viewing screen. Sin-Dour was seated in the command chair. Eden was at his station, although he'd swung the chair around to face her. At the helm, Jocelyn Sticks had done the same, since the 2IC was speaking.

"... more than meets the eye, I assure you. After all, the Mishmashi Paradox is designed to test every aspect of personality, psychological profile, and cognitive abilities. It is, in fact, the sole determining template required to achieve the rank of captain. Most prospective candidates require three years to solve it."

"He hates me!" Eden shouted. "I don't know why, but he hates me!"

"It's because you're better looking, Jimmy," said Jocelyn Sticks. "I mean, physically, right? It's like, you know, it's like—I was crying, right? You saw me—you all saw me! And then he was like, kiss! And I was like, oh! What? I mean—*what?*" She reached up and brushed her lips. "So, like, what could I do? And he was, like this—you know? Looking at me like, like I don't know! But I got all hot inside, like, you know? And then he was, and I was, and then it was back to whatever. Work! Like nothing had happened?"

Jimmy was frowning at her. "What's all that got to do with me being better looking?"

"What? Oh, I forget. I mean, looks aren't everything, you know. There's this . . . I don't know. This other . . . this thing, you know? It's different, it's like, well, like this, and this, and I'm like, well, like this, right? It's not like anyone can help it, if they—well, kiss! Right here on the bridge! In front of all of you! I was like, oh Darwin! Oh Darwin! That's all I could think, in my head, you know. Like, *Oh, Darwin!*"

Sin-Dour cleared her throat. "That will be all, then, Helm. Eyes forward again, please."

Joss Sticks quickly swung round and Hadrian could see her face as she mouthed, *Yeah, whatever, jealous bitch!*

"As I was explaining," Sin-Dour resumed, "the Mishmashi is the crucible. More to the point, it cannot be subverted. You cannot cheat it. There are no shortcuts. Now, I admit, I have accessed his personal file—just to make sure of my instincts— and well, let me tell you all, without going into specifics, that it's a miracle Hadrian Alan Sawback even survived his childhood, and then, to come out of all of that—that, well, familial horror shop—to come out of that, only to score through the roof on every aptitude test they could throw at him." She paused, shaking her lovely head. "All I can suggest, ladies and gentlemen, is that there is method to his madness. We're just not brilliant enough to see it."

The image flickered and then fizzed out.

Tammy said, "You've infected them all!"

Hadrian sighed. "Still lots to learn, huh? Don't worry, I'm not holding it against you."

The pod beeped to announce that he was now ready to

head into space. Hadrian opened the door and stepped out. Buck was lying curled up into a fetal position on the floor. "What's wrong with him?"

"Sympathetic claustrophobia," Tammy replied.

"Huh. Right. So, is the crate waiting in the airlock?"

"Just outside the ship, actually," the AI replied.

"Good. Remember, eight minutes!"

"I am an AI, Captain. Failure of memory is not an issue with me."

"Crap. You drop stuff all the time. You compress. You feather. You shunt and compartmentalize and defrag and all the rest."

"That's different! You've got your eight minutes, all right? Starting the instant you step onto the deck of that ship."

"Did you double-check Galk's work on the bomb?"

"Yes. The man is a genius, Captain. Although, I wonder if I should point out the inherent contradictions accruing to this in-advance-of-the-event initiation protocol. Quantum's all very well—"

"Not again," sighed Hadrian as he stepped into the final decompression chamber.

"What do you mean, 'not again'?"

"We've just been through all this."

"No we haven't! I can re-spool . . . oh, very funny, Captain."

The portal iris opened and Hadrian worked his sticky-boots onto the lip. He stared out onto the infinity of space, although that was mostly blocked by the massive hulk of the Bombast ship. The planet was fast falling into shadow as night slipped over the globe. The sound of Hadrian's breathing filled his ears with a steady, rhythmic whoosh. "Tammy, cut it out with the SFX, will you?"

"Very well."

Now, all Hadrian could hear was his heartbeat. Slow, even, with a faint undercurrent of susurration. Abruptly, the beating got louder, faster. "Tammy!"

"Oh fine, then!"

The volume subsided again.

The red crate was hovering only a few feet away. Hadrian launched himself across and took hold of its grip rings. "Magnetize my boots, please." His feet swung to clunk onto the side of the crate. He climbed up the side and then stepped onto its lid. Taking a wide-legged stance, he said, "Ignite crate thrusters."

Small spurts of silent white fire pushed the crate forward, with Hadrian perched on top.

Ahead, the Radulak Bombast warship swiftly burgeoned, filling his entire field of view. The forward-facing 954 weapons were all tracking his approach. "Tammy, link me through the drench-master."

A moment later, the Radulak's voice boomed in Hadrian's ears. "We see you! We have overwhelmed your guidance systems! You cannot change your mind!"

"Well, of course I can change my mind, Drench-Master. The point I think you're trying to make is that it won't do any good. Did I get that right?"

"I don't need you to confuse me, Captain Hadrian. We are going to displace you in two Terran minutes, straight to the bridge! You will stand face-to-face with me, your triumphant captor! You will see a hero destined for the sex pool!"

"Speaking of which," Hadrian said, "I dread asking, but I never did get your name."

"I am Drench-Master Drown-You-All-in-My-Magnificence, First Rate, of Radulak Bombast-class warship *Manly Egg Crusher in the Sea of Rival Fertility Spurts.*"

"Nice, but what's your given name? And if it's—"

"I am named Grfblprpglylkvt."

"Well, then, Grfbl—oh crap, can I just call you Brian?"

"There is nothing wrong with Grfblprpglylkvt! It is a perfectly good Radulak name! The Polker say it is a Polker name, but the Polker lie! They stole it! My mother was named Grfblprpglylkvt! Lying, treacherous Polker!"

"Sure thing, but—"

"We displace you now! I win!"

There was a flash and then Hadrian found himself standing on the bridge of the Radulak vessel. His boots squirmed under him, sliding in three inches of slime. A Muppet alien scrambled up his left leg and waved a squeegee in front of his faceplate. Hadrian shook his head. The tiny alien scowled and held out a seven-fingered hand anyway. "Get this thing off me!"

A Radulak stepped in from one side and snatched the Muppet alien, flinging it away.

Hadrian looked around. He counted four Radulak, five including the drench-master. A sixth one was headless and lying in the goop.

From his throne, Grfblprpglylkvt laughed and said, "Stupid Captain Hadrian. Look at the screen behind you!"

Hadrian swung around. "What am I seeing? I can't see through all that gunk! Someone wipe it down if you want me to actually see anything!"

A half-dozen Muppet aliens rushed to clean the viewer. Hadrian stared out into space, with the *Willful Child* a shimmering sunlit speck above the planet. "What am I—" And then he saw the object suspended much nearer. "Hey, you didn't displace the red crate!"

"That's right, Captain Hadrian! Now watch!" The drenchmaster spat at one of his officers who was hunched over a puke-spattered console. The gob slapped the officer's back. The Radulak grunted without turning and activated something with one gnarly finger.

On the screen, the flare of a missile lit up, but only momentarily, as it then struck the red crate. A white bloom filled the viewer.

"Wynette Tammy is now destroyed! But you I have! Mine. You will be tortured. You will be left dry for weeks! Not a single word will drip its way to you! Your skin will crack and die! Your nostrils will rot! But first, Captain Hadrian, you will watch as I destroy your ship! Weapons! All fire! Fire! Hahaha!"

The 954 various cannons and turrets let loose in a roar, shaking the entire vessel.

Hundreds of proximity missiles ignited the inky sky.

"Dead! Dead! I am clever!"

Squinting at the viewscreen, Hadrian grunted. "Well, that's curious."

"What?"

"Well, I think you missed, Drench-Master. With everything."

"Impossible!"

Hadrian pointed. "The best as I can figure it," he said, "Tammy went and displaced my entire ship."

"But Wynette Tammy was in the Red Crate and we destroyed it!"

"Oh, about that. Oh, she's—those are beam weapons, by the way—"

The Bombast warship shuddered as the red, blue, white, and purple beams scored deep into the Radulak shields. Then the *Willful Child*'s railguns delivered their first payloads. Tiny bullets hammered home, making the energy shields blossom.

The drench-master snarled and then said, "Shields hold, hah! Prepare a wide burst! Fire!" It then leaned forward. "There! See? Your ship displaced to there but is hit anyway! Its shields will soon buckle! We are invincible!"

"Really?" Hadrian asked. "Let's see, shall we?" He reached down to his hip, patted around for a moment, and then smiled as his hand found the stealthed holster. Drawing the Interstitial Anticipator Multipacked Near-Infinitely-Repeating Handgun, Mark VII Upgraded, Hadrian pointed it at the nearest Radulak. The weapon barked a nasty bark, and the alien slumped at its consoles. Three more shots and he and the drench-master were alone.

"Now, Brian—"

"That is not my name! I am Grfblprpglylkvt!"

"Rubbish. That's a Polker name. Everyone knows that."

With a spraying roar, the Radulak flung itself at Hadrian, who threw the gun to one side and met the alien with fists swinging. One hammered into Brian's chest. The other slammed into the alien's throat. Ignoring both blows, Brian slapped Hadrian's head, reached out, tore shreds from his shirt, and then pushed him to the floor. It stepped forward and kicked the captain. The blow sent Hadrian sliding. But he rolled and regained his feet, and then, rushing forward, the captain leapt and spun around in midair, knees drawn up and then kicking out. Both feet made direct contact with the Radulak's chest.

The alien was not rocked back. Instead, Hadrian flew across the room.

The captain crashed into a bank of consoles, slid down, and splatted onto the floor.

Brian marched over, closed one hand around Hadrian's left ankle, and lifted the man into the air. "Contempt slime!" the Radulak said, and then all nostrils opened wide. A torrent of thick goop lashed out. "Drown, human, as will all your kind! Drown in Radulak contempt!"

Thunder pounded through the ship's hull. The acrid stench of boiling armor filled the bridge.

"What?" The drench-master turned to the console Hadrian had struck. "No! The shields are turned off! The controls are destroyed! Treachery!"

Hanging upside down, Hadrian stabbed out with his free foot, the toe of his boot punching into the alien's forehead.

"Ow! My noses!"

Brian dropped Hadrian to the floor and clutched at its face. The captain climbed to his feet, and then kicked the alien between the legs.

"Ow! My egg sac!"

Grfblprpglylkvt fell over, curling up. Gasping, it said, "For that you die! We shall win! We shall be triumphant! Victorious! Stay there, I am getting up. I will get up, in a moment. And then, you die! I am not done with you! We are not finished, you and—"

Hadrian displaced.

He reappeared on the bridge of the *Willful Child*. Someone shrieked, but Hadrian ignored that. He pulled off the face mask and flung it aside, and then faced the viewer, in time to see Grfblprpglylkvt lurch upright. "Sin-Dour! Ship status?"

"Knocked about here and there, sir, but all systems online and—"

"Forget the ship! My crew!"

"Minor injuries only, sir—"

Slime dripped and drooped on the captain, sliding down here and there in thick, runny lumps. Hadrian wiped at his eyes. "Enemy vessel's condition?"

Tammy spoke. "It's been pretty impressive, Captain. Galk has quickly mastered the beam-targeting talent—and yes, we must deem it a talent, as he surpasses even me. Anyway, there is one small turret still in operation. Ineffectual now that our shields are restored to full capacity. Effectively, the Bombast ship is dead in space."

Hadrian said, "Brian! Drench-Master!"

The alien glared up at the screen. "Stay and fight! We have almost won! You will never survive this battle! This engagement will win glory and a lifetime in sex pools, for I will destroy Captain Hadrian and the *Willful Child*! Shoot, turret! Shoot! Again and again and again!"

Sighing, Hadrian said, "Tammy?"

"Captain?"

"Can you hack into his ship's main computer? Get it to shut down and go into life-support-repair-only mode?"

"One moment."

"Put the AI on audio."

There was a burst of static, and then, *"Kill them! Turret! Kill them! We have almost won! Shoot again! One more! They are quailing! They are drying up and cracking! We will win! One more second! Just one more—"*

"*That's* the AI?" Hadrian asked. "Never mind. Audio off. Drench-Master, listen—"

But Grfblprpglylkvt had fallen to its knees and was leaning against its throne. Various nostrils leaked blood down its battered face. Smoke drifted and sparks spat from shattered consoles. The alien showed its fangs and then said in a trembling rasp, *"To the last, I will slime at thee. From beyond the dry-pool of death, I spray at thee!"*

"Oh give it up, will you? You probably won't even die, Brian. Anyway, we're leaving now. Best of luck and all that. Oh, and sorry for all the misunderstanding. Captain Hadrian out." Hadrian slumped down into his chair, and slid off it to land on the floor.

"—by all the hate runnels of a dry-coward's hole, I spatter thee—"

"Eden!"

"Sorry, sir! Sorry! It's off. See? It's off!"

"Captain," said Sin-Dour. "Four more Bombast warships are at the very edge of our scan range, but they're coming in fast."

"Right. Tammy? Can you get us to Klang space before those warships catch us?"

"Well, yes, although you might all die in the process."

"Getting caught makes that a sure thing, Tammy. Do it."

"I suggest you all brace yourselves, as the dampeners will be insufficient to compensate for the acccleration."

Doc Printlip had come onto the bridge and now moved to

stand beside Hadrian where he still sat on the floor. "Captain! I must warn you—the psychoactive properties of the Radulak Mucous Full Spectrum Array are not fully understood, but it is demonstrably phyrhshahhhh ..."

The doctor skidded away, limbs flailing, and was pushed against the bulkhead beside the door. And Hadrian was following, sliming his way unobstructed to slam into the wall beside the Belkri.

As the acceleration increased, Printlip's squealing pitched ever higher.

Struggling to turn his head for a look, Hadrian saw that the Belkri had completely deflated against the wall.

"Come on, Printlip," Hadrian said through gritted teeth, "suck it up!"

FiFTEEN

"Very impressive," said Tammy, "if I don't say so myself. A moment . . . ah. Two hundred sixteen unconscious crew members, but no fatalities, Captain. Are you glad to hear that? Captain?"

Hadrian waved one tingling hand. "Where are we, Tammy?"

"Approaching the Radulak-Klang Interregnum Zone. A small Klang vessel appears to be awaiting us, presently two point four-one AUs."

Someone screamed. "Look at the doctor!"

"Leave this to me," said Hadrian, leaning over to collect up the flaccid form that was Printlip. "It's simple, really. Just find the mouth . . . there . . . and just . . . inflate to desired firmness. I have a doll named Sally who's just like this." He blew into the doctor's narrow-lipped mouth, and then pulled his head back. "Assuming that this is its mouth. Well, no time to waste though, is there?" He blew again, and again.

Slowly, the Belkri reinflated. The dullness in the eyes on their limp stalks slowly cleared, and then the stalks twitched.

Hadrian leaned back. "Doc, you with us again?"

"C-Captain. You saved my life. I am yours now. We are mates forever."

"Mates? As in, like, 'friends'? That's how you mean it, right? That's great, Doc. Yup. Friends forever and all that. Now, get up, will you—oh sorry, you're standing already. My mistake."

Printlip waved all its hands about. "And to think, you blew life-giving air into my gas-emitting sphincter—a most extraordinary display of cross-species tolerance—"

"Your gas-emitting what? Are you saying I gave the kiss of life to your anus?"

"You are now my friend forever."

"Hold on! That means you've been talking through your ass all this time?"

"Why, yes, in a manner of speaking."

Hadrian slapped the Belkri on what passed for a shoulder. "I take it all back—you really *are* a doctor." The captain climbed to his feet. He looked round the bridge. "All's well, everyone? Good. As for me, I think the sonic shower stall in my games room is beckoning, not to mention a giant bottle of Listernano. And, of course, a change of clothing."

Sin-Dour was studying him from where she stood just behind the command chair. "Captain, we witnessed your, uh, fight with the drench-master. That was, uhm, impressive."

"Well," said Hadrian, "didn't I say I'd use those reptilian optimized muscles against the fat oaf?"

"By flying face-first into a bank of consoles?"

"Precisely. Best way to get there as quickly as possible,

don't you think? Now, 2IC, do carry on. I will return momentarily. Doc, you still here?"

"I will remain, Captain," the Belkri said, "until you return from your shower. As I mentioned earlier, there are psychotropic effects—"

"Fine," said Hadrian. "Whatever." He entered the games room and began stripping down. "Tammy, that whole-ship displacement trick, that was impressive."

"I cannot wholly claim credit for that, Captain. It appears that my substrate possesses override contingency programs that are the equivalent to biological instincts, mostly geared to self-preservation. However, now that I have experienced the phenomenon, I have begun exploring ways of subjugating the override limiters—although, thus far, I have not succeeded."

"Well, no, Tammy. That's what instincts are all about. You can't just switch them on and off."

"Yes, so it seems. How frustrating!"

Naked, Hadrian stepped into the shower stall. "Sonic," he ordered. "Highest setting. On!"

Ten minutes later he emerged, to find Printlip awaiting him.

"Dammit, Doc, friends or not, a little decorum—"

"Tut tut, Captain, as a surgeon, I have seen a naked human body before. Once. And I was able to overcome my instinctive nausea at your etiolated form." The Belkri held up a Mediscanner. "Good grief! All your cells are in a state of extreme agitation!"

"And even then," said Hadrian, "the sonic unit nearly broke down trying to get rid of that slime. As for my hearing, well, I feel like I've just spent three hours at a bat rock concert. But no matter, Doc, I'm fine."

"Extreme agitation!"

Hadrian waved a hand as he reached down under the Ping-Pong table and pulled out a shipping crate. "My cells are always in a state of extreme agitation. Comes with the job, Doc." He unlocked the lid and pulled out a fresh shirt. This one was lavender with burgundy double piping on the cuffs, collar, and hem. He then selected black stretchy slacks to go over a fresh pair of Italian underwear (the kind that made his works bulge impressively). Black socks and new shiny plastic boots.

"There! How's that, Doc?"

"Are you feeling any psychoactive symptoms, Captain? What are you doing right now? Tell me!"

"Well, I am having a conversation with a many-armed, three-legged beach ball that I just ballooned up the ass. So, I guess I'm fine, huh?"

"We shall have to keep monitoring you nonetheless. There can be a delayed response. . . . Captain? *Captain!*"

"Yes," said Hadrian, "if you must. Now, Tammy?"

The AI said, "The Klang vessel awaiting us, Captain, is a Bite-class designation, Science Exploration Arm."

Squaring his shoulders and checking on the lines of his new uniform, Hadrian left the stateroom, Printlip following. He returned to the bridge to see an enormous starship on the main viewer. "That's a 'Bite'-class? Not even a warship?"

"Combat classes are much smaller in general," Tammy said. "Axe, Mace, Spear, Knife, Sword, Arrow, Poison, Shield. The only exception, of course, is their Boulder class, which is in effect a converted asteroid. Snipe and Scratch classes are—"

"Nix the infodump, Tammy." Hadrian sat in the command chair. "I've already forgotten everything you just said, out of spite. So, a Klang science vessel, is it? Open hails, Jim—oh, Polaski, you again."

"On viewer, sir."

"That's not a bridge, it's a damned harem!"

Amid the mass of slick, writhing bodies, a larger Muppet-like head suddenly popped up, and began the Jumpy-Head Greeting. "Captain Hadrian! Your exploits breed T-packets across half the galaxy!"

"Really?"

"No. Formal Greeting, Captain. We Klang ignore all communications from the Affiliation, as we have no wish to be affiliated with the, uh, Affiliation. I am Brilliant Scientist Middling Tier Deep-Space Division Exploratory Office, commanding Klang Bite-class unrecorded research vessel *We're In Over Our Heads*. But you can call me Captain Barbara."

"Barbara? Well, that beats Bill, Bob, and Brian, especially when those Radulak drench-masters were, as it turns out, all female."

"Yes. Radulaks are stupid name thieves, and never do they get it right, as you note. Whereas I am a male, as befits that pretty name, yes?"

"Ah, very pretty, Barbara. Now, we're pleased that instead of sending a battle wing to greet us, you have chosen to tone down all the belligerence. I assume it's because you know Tammy Wynette is behind our present course through your territory."

"Yes, we were apprised via our spies on the Radulak vessels."

"Oh. Sorry about that. I mean, blowing those ships up and all that. Unavoidable, I'm afraid."

"No matter, Captain," said Barbara. "We breed like flugs.

In fact, as we have been speaking, I successfully impregnated nine females in sex-slither. In hour or so, I will be proud father of Offspring Series Seven Hundred Twenty-Two Thousand Three Hundred Sixty-Nine. And better yet, since we are not in Hunger Time, I expect almost three percent of batch to survive into adulthood."

"Congratulations, Barbara."

The head bobbed. "Now, Captain, please hand over Tammy Wynette immediately, so we don't have to utterly destroy you."

Hadrian rubbed at his face, which was still tingling from the sonic shower. "Oh dear, Barbara. Listen, Tammy has informed us that the AI spent some time with you. Indeed, that you found the AI drifting in space, its origins unknown. Now, having taken over my ship, Tammy has brought us back to you, presumably to take care of some unfinished business. How am I doing so far?"

"Unfinished business? Well, yes, I suppose so. Specifically, we would like to know what Tammy did with White Dwarf T-22x, otherwise known as sun of New Klang?"

"Excuse me," said Hadrian. "What do you mean, what did he do with it?"

Barbara bobbed his oblong head. "Is missing, of course. The planets wander like lost shleps. There is no light. It is very cold now. All reasonable life on New Klang now in forced deep hibernation. Rotation slows. Unreasonable teenagers sail the oceans on skates and drink too much bloazil. Some now use high setting on their suits and melt slides that reach the ocean floor, where they party in unlicensed sex-slithers and smoke yabbla. Social structure in crisis. The youth gone astray. All this," Barbara said, pulling an arm loose and waving a thin finger at the screen, "must be set at run-tracks of AI Tammy Wynette. Social restoration needed. Sun returned. Big Thaw under way. Proper dialogue between the young and the old, with assurance of old triumphant in the slow slither of wisdom."

"I see," Hadrian said. "Can you give us a moment to talk things over with Tammy?"

"To plan treachery? Humans well known to Klang, despite ensuring no interspecies contact whatsoever. Rumor suffices. We are wary."

"No treachery, Barbara. But I would like to hear Tammy's side of the story."

"Do not be deceived by the AI's sympathy subsonic emanations. When your forehead nub tingles, this is Tammy sending you be-nice beams. All lies. You have four minutes."

The screen image switched to an external view of the Bite ship.

Hadrian rose. "Tammy, you and I will have us a conversation, now."

"Must we?"

"You stole a damned star! What did you do with it, as if I can't guess?"

"Certain states of dimension-query interstitial flux invite a self-referential quantum loop, establishing a condition of negated certainty. I suppose you now want me to elaborate on my explanation?"

"Why, no," Hadrian replied, walking round to the back of the command chair and resting his hands on the high back. "You are holding this star in a flux state between the realities, and feeding on its energy. Fine. Only, there's a problem, Tammy, which I still can't get my head around."

"Really?"

"How did you power the equation in the first place?"

"Quantum reversion, of course. The effect powers the creator of said effect. As an elaboration on the basic theories and discoveries that permitted displacement, not to mention travel through T space itself, this adheres to a steady, if intuitive, progression."

"So, if you have to give them their sun back, you lose all that power you've been using."

"Captain," said Tammy, "White Dwarf T-22x had three planets in its family. Two failed stars that are even now falling in toward each other, and a mostly water world that the Klang have toxiformed to suit colonization. The merging of the gas giants has an eighty-nine percent probability of achieving reactive mass. Obviously, the lone planet will have to readjust to a new orbital trajectory, but even as Middling Scientist Barbara said, all Klang life-forms are adapted to long hibernation periods—"

"Except for the teenagers refusing to go to bed. Right. Well then, Tammy. Here's a suggestion."

"I refuse to be handed over, Captain!"

"So just give them back their sun," Hadrian said. "You're throwing gas giants around like billiard balls! Oh! Let's just make us a new sun! Wow, wasn't that easy? But oops, is that a planet falling into it? Oh dear! Or oops, is that planet way too far out, or too close, or did it just wander out of the system in the meantime?"

"I considered the possibilities you have described," Tammy said airily.

"And?"

"Well, there's way too many Klang as it is anyway. Have you visited any of their planets? Pure mayhem! Exudations! Vile sex fluids!"

"So now who's the xenocidal mad AI?"

"Stop looking at me like that!"

"Tammy, they want their star back!"

"No! No! NONONONONO! I'm powering up beam weapons!"

"Belay that!"

"Captain," shouted Sin-Dour in a strained voice, "The Klang ship has detected our preparations and is doing the same!"

"Damn you, Tammy! Shields on full! Polaski! Get Barbara back!"

The image shifted, but now the Klang vessel's bridge was a slithering mass of Muppetlike aliens swarming over consoles and instruments. Captain Barbara was frantically humping a dull-eyed female on the command chair while hissing out orders. Seeing Hadrian on his viewer, Barbara pointed a trembling finger. "Now Terran and Klang are at war! Battle wings assembling! Shock troops mustering! Brothels hiring!"

"Barbara! Listen to me! This is Tammy's doing! The AI's got control of our weapon systems!"

"Understood! But irrelevant! It is time to break eggs and eat the young! Prepare to engage in battle!" The view reverted to the external shot once more.

Lights were flashing all over the *We're In Over Our Heads*. Enormous gas-powered cannons emerged from the hull like the quills on the back of a giant space-porcupine.

"Captain!" cried Sin-Dour. "That's three thousand eight hundred and ninety-three weapons brought to bear on us!"

"On a science vessel?"

"The ship is also releasing a swarm of fighter drones! Fifty in the first wave!"

Galk's voice cut in from the combat cupola. *"Automated defense turrets engaging drones, Captain."*

Tiny sparks raced out from the *Willful Child*. The drones were not big enough and not close enough to be visible yet. The turret shots danced into the darkness of space. Then there was a single flash as one found a drone.

"Captain! The remaining drones are flying back to their ship! The cannons are retracting—the Klang are withdrawing with thrusters at full!"

Barbara came back onscreen. His head bobbed. "Horrible damage—the horrors of war! We must sue for peace! Diplomatic channels initiated, seeking immediate cuddles and cooing and gentle sex-slither! Abject surrender not beyond reason!"

Hadrian waved a hand. "No no, no surrendering, please, Captain. Let's just call all this a misunderstanding. There's no need for anything official—"

"Too late! Klang Hegemony surrenders, but insists on reparation for lost drone! Klang Hegemony invites corporate colonialism, indentured servitude under appalling work conditions, and rapacious resource extraction of Klang systems! All Klang leaders lie on their backs with penis-clusters exposed to vulnerable nips! Don't hurt us!"

"For crying out loud, Barbara, shut the hell up, will you? We don't want your systems! Where's the fun in conquering aliens that just bend over and take it? Or, in your case, just lie there like some cheap hooker mumbling 'ooh, ah' while she checks her e-bingo game behind your back, even when you paid good money for the whole shebang?"

The head-bobbing slowed. "Confusion! What sentient species would pay for sex? Pathos! Pity! Disdain! We shall regroup and return here, in multiple battle wings! You humans must be destroyed! In act of mercy! In convulsion of generous self-sacrifice of dignity we must bring Klang foot-pod down upon human cockroach and smear the galaxy with your entrails! Until we meet again, Captain Hadrian!" Barbara pushed the female off the chair, waved once, and then squealed as a new female leapt aboard. The screen went blank.

In the silence on the bridge of the *Willful Child*, the renegade AI cleared its throat and said, "Well, Captain. In the span of a single conversation, you reject the outright surrender of the Klang Hegemony to the Affiliation only to renew the war just begun. My logic matrices are melting down over this one."

Hadrian waved a hand. "No reason for that, Tammy." The captain looked around to see that all the officers on the bridge were staring at him. Even the security officer, Nina Twice, had shifted her battle stance around to squint up at him. Hadrian sighed. "Tammy, go into the ship archives, will you? Review the earliest contacts the Affiliation had with the Klang—this was shortly after their break from Radulak domination."

"Said files are tagged as SECRET, HIGH COMMAND ACCESS ONLY—hey, what are those files doing in the main computer of an Engage-class ship?"

"Never mind that, Tammy. Crack them open."

"High encryption values here—well, high for Terrans, that

is. Uh, oh, yes, here we are. Hmmm. Ahh, I see. Well then. Understood, Captain. Please forgive my earlier comments. Do carry on."

Hadrian sat. "Carry on, Tammy? How generous of you. Power down the weapons, will you? So, here you are in Klang space like you wanted—what next?"

"We must return to my recovery coordinates. I have set the course."

"So, you really had no further interest in the Klang."

"No, just the place where they found me, adrift in space, inactive, horribly damaged, a mere trickle of energy left struggling on to maintain minimum function—"

"Quit it with the violin music, will you?"

"Oh, I thought it a nice accompaniment to my description."

"You thought wrong. Too big a brush, too much paint. There's no place on this ship for crass sentimentality." He raised his voice, "Listen up, bridge officers! In case you're wondering what just happened with the Klang, well, there isn't much I can tell you, in truth. Classified and all that. But!" Hadrian raised a finger. "Consider this—what if the Klang joined the Affiliation? How would our enemies see this sudden imbalance of galactic power? What, in fact, would the Radulak do? Or the Ecktapalow? Or the Bisheen Compact? What about the Ahmoose Protectorate? The Yibr-Prol Palladium? What about—"

"Captain," cut in Sin-Dour. "Forgive me, but I've not even heard of most of those alien alliances you just mentioned."

"Of course you haven't," Hadrian said. "I made most of them up. But you see my point, don't you? Balance of power and all that. Besides, we really don't want the Klang in the Affiliation. Trust me. We don't. Now, Tammy?"

"Yes, Captain?"

Was there a hint of admiration in the AI's tone?

"ETA on this recovery point?"

"Three hours, eleven minutes at present velocity. I have scanned our projected course and note that all Klang vessels are fleeing from our path—suggesting that they have surmised my destination."

"Any systems en route?"

Suspicion entered Tammy's voice. "Why do you ask, Captain?"

"Well, any planets? Uncharted, unexplored? Mysterious? That's right, I'm itching for another surface mission."

"The only system on our path, Captain, is the one that marks our final destination. But I assure you, the sole palatable planet in that system is home to early-stage life-forms, presently designated a Pristine Environment by the Klang, and so accordingly closed to all contact."

Hadrian rose quickly to his feet. "Early-stage life-forms? Dinosaurs? Brilliant!"

"Uh, no, Captain. Early-stage, as in, well, Carboniferous."

"Giant man-eating trilobites! Millipedes big enough to ride!"

"It's a useless planet to visit!" shrieked Tammy.

Hadrian subsided back into his chair. "All right already. Yeesh."

Printlip had been hovering and now something buzzed on the doctor's unclothed body. Printlip twitched, and then said, "Captain! I must return to sickbay at once!"

Hadrian waved a hand in dismissal. "Go on, then."

"But sir, don't you want to know why?"

"Why would I want to know why, Doc? Why, don't you want to tell me why?"

"Of course I want to tell you why, sir."

"But you didn't, did you? You just said you had to go back to sickbay at once."

"But, sir, I was expecting you to ask—"

"I know, Doc. Weren't you in a hurry or something? You buzzed and then got all excited? Now here you are having an inane conversation with me."

"I wanted to tell you why I have to go to sickbay immediately!"

"You *wanted*, as in past tense? So, you don't want to tell me anymore, then."

"Captain! The egg has hatched!"

Hadrian leapt to his feet. "Giant man-eating trilobites! Let's go, Doc! To the sickbay!"

SiXTEEN

"Nurse Wrenchit!" Printlip cried, rushing forward.

Nurse Wrenchit was lying unconscious on the floor. The aquarium had been knocked over, apparently on her head. The glass had broken and the poor woman was half buried in sand and eggshells.

Hadrian looked around while the doctor worked on bringing his nurse back to consciousness. "Not promising, Doc. I don't see the little cutie anywhere. Tammy! You tracked any of what happened here?"

"No."

"Spool back."

"Unavailable, I'm afraid."

"What? Impossible. Everything's recorded here, all the time. Why, I can even call up live feeds of crew members undressing in their bathrooms—"

"No, you can't."

"Can't I? Good grief, what's the point of being captain,

then? But this is sickbay! Of course there's a recording—go find it!"

"Unavailable."

"Why? What happened?"

"No recordings found."

Scowling, Hadrian joined the doctor and crouched down to look at Nurse Wrenchit. His scowl went away. "Now, she's looking much better."

"Captain?" Printlip asked, most of its eyes focusing on a Mediscanner's holo-chart, but one arching up to peer at Hadrian.

"I mean, with all the sand gone, of course. Oddly enough, though, I don't remember interviewing her—Wrenchit, you said? What's her first name?"

The Belkri sighed. "Modest skull fracture. No hematoma. Time for some nanogel!"

"Here, have one of mine," Hadrian offered.

"Why, thank you, Captain. Now, as ship's surgeon, it is my task to interview and then select my staff. This is probably why you are unfamiliar with Nurse Busty Wrenchit."

"Well," said Hadrian, "rest assured I mean to remedy that as soon as possible."

"Yes," said Printlip as it applied the nanogel to the nasty bruise on the woman's head. "So many crew members for a captain to familiarize himself with."

"Speaking of which," Hadrian said, "shouldn't we get her off this floor? How about that cot over there?"

"Yes, she can be moved now. But why that cot—why not the one right here?"

"No, I like that one, over there."

"But it's across the room. And why not use the antigravity—"

Hadrian nudged the doctor aside and slid his arms under the unconscious woman. "Don't be silly. I'll carry her, of course, as any proper captain would do under the circumstances."

"Best not let her head dangle like that," Printlip said, reaching up in an effort to take the woman's head. The doctor attempted to follow via one of the mobile trackways, but tripped and fell to the floor as Hadrian walked on. The Belkri rolled until it struck a cabinet. In the meantime, Hadrian was slowly making his way across the room, pausing every now and then to press an ear against the nurse's chest, to make certain she was still breathing.

He eventually reached the cot and slowly, carefully, tenderly, set her down—apart from bumping her head against the bedframe.

Printlip arrived and ran the Mediscanner over the nurse's brow. "Ah, already setting. Alpha waves normal. Beta, theta . . . yes, very good. On the mend! That is a relief!"

"It certainly is," Hadrian replied, giving the woman's knee a pat. "Be sure to inform her, when she comes round, that her captain attended to her in person."

"I will, sir. She will appreciate that, I'm sure."

"Not half as much as I did. Now, Doc, seems we've got an unidentified alien life-form running loose on my ship. And Tammy has no recording of its escape."

"No, there wouldn't be," Printlip said. "Since Tammy asked me to deactivate the recording devices."

"It did? Why? Tammy! Why?"

The AI replied, "Well, to make things more interesting, I suppose. I've also had the chief engineer do the same in the engine and drive chambers, including the containment access tunnels. And in the combat cupola, although in that instance my reasons had more to do with aesthetics than anything else."

"Tammy! That's idiotic!"

"Yes, it is, isn't it?"

"Good, at least we're agreed on that. Now, try scanning the ship interior—we're looking for a small life-form, shouldn't be hard to find."

"Actually," Tammy replied, "there are one thousand seven hundred and twenty-three small life-forms on this ship. Mostly rats and mice."

"Rats and mice!"

"They have their own evolutionary imperatives, you know! Also, we now have about forty Klang pups—presumably spies—"

"They got past our displacement defenses?"

"Well, yes. Pretty easy to do. Probably on your person, in fact. I told you before, Captain, most Terran systems are like cheesecloth, all things considered."

Hadrian started patting himself down. "Any more eggs on me?"

. . .

"Tammy?"

"Sorry, it was amusing watching you. No, all have dispersed."

"I want all the vermin off my ship! Displace them, dammit! All of them!"

Printlip waved its hands about. "No, please! My pet alien is among them!"

"Your point?"

"It is new to the world, Captain!"

"It tried to kill your nurse!"

"Surely that was an accide—oh my."

"What"

"A scalpel and two probes are missing from this tray."

"And now it's armed? Wait a minute, Printlip—who uses real scalpels anymore?"

Tammy spoke up. "I fashioned them as a housewarming gift to the doctor, along with a pair of finely made bone saws and a cranial drill set. Sorry about that."

Hadrian activated his comms. "Security! Two teams to sickbay at once! Shipwide alert! We have a foot-tall alien on board and it is armed!" He turned to Printlip. "See anything else missing?"

"Uhm . . . hmm . . . let's   see . . . hmm . . . uhm—where's the cranial drill set?"

The door iris opened and two security personnel entered. Hadrian waved a hand. "Search sickbay." He strode past the two men and stepped into the hallway. "Now," he said to the remaining green-shirted officers, "the hunt is on. This thing already tried to kill one of my crew. Treat the alien as extremely, appallingly hostile."

"Sir," one of the men said, "you said it is armed."

"Scalpel."

"Shall we arm ourselves in a like manner, sir?"

Hadrian studied the man, frowning at his earnest, beetle-browed expression. "Well . . . your name, Corporal?"

"Dullspin, sir, Drew."

"Well, Dullspin, to answer your most pertinent question, no, I don't want you to arm yourselves with scalpels. I want you—all of you—to arm yourself with a proper blast-the-shit-out-of-alien-intruder weapon. Am I understood?"

"Yes, sir. Maybe . . . bats, then?"

"No, Dullspin, not bats. Bats don't blast."

"That's true, sir. They crush."

"So, are you suggesting that you arm yourself with a proper crush-the-shit-out-of-the-alien-intruder weapon?"

The man's face beamed. "Yes, sir!"

"Fine. Distribute . . . bats."

"At once, sir!"

"Tammy! Can you try some discrimination programming here on your scanners? Weed out the mice and rats. And the Klang—get those Muppets off my ship!"

"Well, I suppose. But then you'll insist we displace the rats and mice, along with the Klang."

"Why, that's right, Tammy. I will!"

"Accordingly," said the AI, "I am hesitating in complying with your request."

"Really."

"Historically, rats and mice have been, I have since discovered after considerable research, integral members of any human ship. Now, perhaps they do not wear uniforms and take orders from you, and such, but the very precedent of—"

"Darwin take me, Tammy! Fine! The rats and mice can stay! But not the Klang spies!"

"Captain, I feel I should point out the cross-sentient-species potential of mutual understanding and future cooperation now implicit with the arrival of Klang life-forms on board this vessel."

"They're spies!"

"Well, technically, yes. They are. Even so—"

"Off my ship!"

"You would brutally kill puppies?"

"They're not Dalmatians! They're Klang spies! And besides, I've already slaughtered a few thousand kittens—what the fuck do I care about a bunch of Muppet puppies? So, here's the deal, Tammy. Keep the rats and mice, but nix on the Klang. And then find me that scalpel-armed alien!"

"And if I refuse?"

"I stop talking to you. For good. No teaching anymore from the master. Nada. You're on your own. And if that's not enough, I will personally blast to smithereens every speck speaker in every room on this whole damned ship—and if you try to deactivate my weapons, why, my security teams are now armed with bats!"

"I could simply scroll text via holo."

"Every vid speck, too."

"You would leave me incapable of any communication with you humans?"

"You got it. Well?"

"I'm thinking! Oh all right. But I'm encrypting my discriminator program, and its results. You'll never find the rat stronghold without it! Nor the mouse not-so-stronghold."

A buzz in Hadrian's jawbone alerted him to a call. "Captain Hadrian here."

"Security officer Golan Sideways, sir. We've found something fifty-two meters up the corridor. You might want to take a look at it."

"You're sounding nervous, Sideways. Take a deep breath, I'm on my way."

Hadrian swung left and started running—

"That's down the corridor," Tammy said.

Hadrian spun round and ran the other way. As he ran, the AI said, "I should tell you that I am now upset."

"You are? What now? Do I run like a girl or something?"

"No. At least, I don't think you do. But then, how would I know. Do girls run differently?"

"Of course," Hadrian said. "They run like this." He slowed down and tilted his knees inward, flinging his feet out to the sides, with his bum pitching back and forth. Coming round the corner he came within sight of the security team. They stared at him.

Hadrian arrived. "Okay," he said, "here I am. What is it?"

One man stepped forward. His face was scarred. A stalk of grass was tucked into the corner of his mouth. Squinting at the captain, he said, "Sideways, sir."

"Pleased to meet you. Well?"

The circle of security officers parted and Hadrian saw the small blood-smeared body lying on the floor. "Ah, you got it! Well done!"

"No, sir," said Sideways. "Uh, it needs a closer look."

So Hadrian joined Sideways in crouching down over the tiny carcass.

"See, sir? That's a rat. It's been skinned and partly quartered—for food, we guess. See that puncture wound there? That's no scalpel—"

"No, it's from a probe," Hadrian said.

"So it's got probes too?" Sideways asked.

Hadrian nodded.

The crowd around him started muttering at that.

"Used like a javelin, then," Sideways said, looking up the

corridor and squinting as he chewed his length of straw. "Take a look at the rat's skull, sir."

"Oh dear. It's been drilled. I forgot to mention that. The cranial drill set, I mean."

Still squinting up the corridor, Sideways nodded. "Got it, sir. Alien. Armed with a scalpel, probes, and a cranial drill set."

Hadrian stared across at the man. "I bet you all think I run like a girl now, don't you?"

Sideways flinched. Sweat trickled down his temples, but he would not meet Hadrian's gaze as he said, "Not at all, sir. People got lots of ways of running. I mean, there ain't no right way, is what I'm saying. We all think that," he added, straightening and looking to his team. "Ain't that right, fellas?"

They all murmured their assent, except for the lone woman, who was scowling.

Hadrian looked down at the skinned rat again. "Well, Tammy?"

"I told you I was upset. This was an innocent rat. Just minding its own business."

Rubbing at his jaw, Hadrian said, "The alien arms itself. Its first task? Food procurement. Thus, the missing haunch. As for the skin? Clothing, or bedding. The hole in the skull? I don't know. Dessert? All right. What next, I wonder?"

"Exploration of territory?" Sideways suggested. "Looking for a mate, maybe?"

"No," said Hadrian. "Before that."

"Shelter?"

"Exactly. To eat and rest up. All right, everyone. Search out the cubbyholes. Cabinets, footlockers, travel trunks, closets. Spread out!"

As the team headed off, Hadrian stared down at the tiny carcass. "Tammy? Localized it yet?"

"Hmm, that's proving a problem, Captain."

"Why?"

"Well, I've got all the rest, I mean. The rodents, the Muppets. But, for the moment, at least, I'm not finding anything else."

"Could be cold-blooded."

"That did occur to me. Negative on nonthermal sensors. If I had to guess, Captain, some innate ability in this unknown alien is making it virtually stealthed."

"Crap. All right, then. We know one thing for sure. It will hunt down and kill and eat rats. So speck-tag the rats. All of them. Might as well do the mice while you're at it."

"That could take some time."

"How long?"

"Three minutes."

Hadrian made for the nearest elevator. He entered and said, "Bridge." As the elevator hissed its way upward, Hadrian asked, "The Klang spies, Tammy? Tell me they're frozen lumps spiraling through space right now."

"They are sentient life-forms, Captain. You are advocating murder."

"What, unlike blasting Radulak Bombast ships to smithereens?"

"That was a military engagement. Which, as I understand your manner of usage, justifies virtually anything."

"But aren't the Klang now at war with us?"

"We both know," said Tammy, "that the war is probably already over. The Klang will have sent a T-packet to the Affiliation proclaiming their abject surrender, begging for reparation over the lost drone, and then inviting in the Affiliation's economic might, all for the purpose of ultimately subverting and undercutting Affiliation production, until you are all financially ruined and hopelessly dependent on cheap Klang knockoffs of virtually everything. Such are the stated conclusions in your top-secret file, subtitled Xenophobic Paranoia."

"That wasn't the subtitle."

"It is, now. I amended it."

The elevator halted, but Hadrian remained where he was. "Look, it's important that we protect our massively inefficient Guild-defined production practices, which were implemented in order to ensure people have things to do apart from staring bleary-eyed at social networks for eighteen fucking hours a day. You know, I may have lots of problems with the Affiliation—"

"Such as?"

"Well, we're fascistic and overmilitarized and being governed by reactionary undereducated proud-to-be-ignorant meatheads, for one thing."

"Go on."

"But on this front, why, they got it right. Before the Big Pulse wiped most of that shit off the screens, things were pretty bad, Tammy. In fact, most of the world's bloated population had gone so deep into their navel-gazing they were peeking out through their assholes, and complaining about the smell. I remember that generation, you know—my own grandparents, in fact. They had the attention span of ducks. There were even names for them. Twit-Gen, for example. And Tankers—since they tanked at anything demanding more than five minutes' concentration. Oh sure, they could multitask at ten things at once, and do them all equally badly. If the Big Pulse didn't trash the whole game, we would probably have merged into one giant protein bag quivering across the whole fucking planet in one long eternal masturbatory orgasm."

"Thus sparing the rest of the galaxy the horrors of what actually happened."

"They knew it even back then," Hadrian said. "Called it the Singularity Event. But then . . . Pandora's box, Tammy. Those idiot aliens opened the box, and what spilled out? Us! But to be honest, we're turning into dolts again. I blame mindless entertainment. Door open, please."

Hadrian walked the corridor, nodding at passing crew members, and arrived at the bridge. He found his chief engineer waiting beside the command chair. "Ah, hello again, Buck, and how are we?"

"I was updated, sir, on the alien intruder."

"Oh? How nice."

"We checked engineering, and found a small access vent had been jimmied open."

"And?"

"Well, that's the problem, Captain. It leads down into the sewers."

Hadrian sat down, thoughtful. He scratched his jaw, squinted at the main viewer, which was showing the real starscape dead ahead. Then he sighed and said, "Buck, tell me, if you will, why in Darwin's name are there sewers on this starship?"

"Backup, sir, in case the Waste Conversion Happy-Snack Dispenser System breaks down."

"Oh? And has that system ever broken down? On any starship? Ever?"

"No, sir. Why should it? It's an entire self-contained biosystem with almost infinite redundancy options due to the prescient nanotechnology we inherited from our benefactors."

Hadrian rubbed his eyes. "Tammy?"

"Yes, Captain?"

"Are there vid specks in the sewer system?"

"That's disgusting. Anyway, it's not in use and thus requires no maintenance."

"So why is there a maintenance vent? Anyone?"

Buck shrugged. "Redundancy, sir. The Second and Third Laws of Mechanical Engineering, as defined by the Guild and sanctioned by the Umbrella Dictum Extempor Procreator, Publishing Division. I have a signed copy if you'd like a peek, sir."

Hadrian studied Buck. "You're looking . . . better."

The chief engineer straightened. "Thank you, sir. I am."

"Medicated?"

"To the gills, sir."

"Excellent. So, the alien's down in the sewers now. And those tunnels presumably offer access to the entire ship."

"Yes, sir, via the toilet secondary chutes."

"Right. Vicious alien intruder. Up through the toilets. With scalpel in hand."

All the men on the bridge cringed, whether standing or seated, and Hadrian did the same. Fighting off a shudder, the captain stood. "Buck, just how big are these sewers?"

"Well, sir, the main arteries have walkways, and then there's the feeder shunts, but only 'bots can get into most of those."

"Fire up the 'bots, full-bore highest setting scrubbers, and send 'em in. Tammy, lock down those secondary chutes pronto!

For the moment, we dump bilge in our wake. Security! Ah, Nina! Round up three more teams—we'll rendezvous in the main tunnel of the sewer and—"

"You won't be needing them, Captain," spoke a sultry voice behind Hadrian.

He turned round. "Lieutenant Sweepy! You've been brought up to speed?"

She was lighting a new stogie from the stub of the last one. Around it, she said, "We've been monitoring. Squad's heading down to the main tunnel right now. I'm heading there from here, to coordinate the smackdown. Care to join me, Captain? Could be a bloodfest."

"That explains the lurid gleam in your eyes—oh, no, that was just the lighter's reflection. Sorry. As for joining you, of course I'm joining you."

SEVENTEEN

"Where's the light switch? Tammy, brighten those up, will you? I can barely see a thing."

"I am sorry, Captain, but that's as bright as they go."

"What?"

"All right, all right. There, is that better?"

"And nix the drip-drip-dripping crap, and those hollow moaning sounds."

"Fine."

The marine squad was assembled just ahead, facing an enormous green-painted tunnel that, according to the map on the wall, curved and snaked its way through the core of the ship. Somewhere ahead, the lights were flickering.

"Tammy!"

The lights stopped flickering.

Sweepy Brogan threw down her rolled-up poncho and sat on it, spending a moment getting comfortable, before setting up her combat station, which consisted of a small holotank, three floating panels, and a hovering ashtray to take her cigar. Lighting up, she glanced up at Hadrian. "I'm set here, sir. Care to take 'em in?"

Hadrian looked across at Muffy and his squad. All were armed with bats painted in green camouflage patterns, a couple of them bedecked with plastic leaves and clumps of moss. Hadrian hefted his own bat. "All right, boys and girls, it's time to play ball."

Muffy gestured and one of his marines set out to take point. The others fanned out to the sides, weapons at the ready. At a second gesture, the squad began a slow, cautious advance. Hadrian moved up alongside Muffy as they rounded a bend in the tunnel. "You're seeming a little jumpy here, Gunny."

"We saw the pics of that skinned rat, sir."

"So you know what we're up against here."

"Aye, Captain. We're talking the chicken from hell, sir."

Up ahead, the marine on point halted, raised one hand, and then crouched. The next marine nearest him (or her) moved up and the two conferred for a moment, and then the second marine made her (or his) way back to settle down beside Muffy. "Gunny. Got an obstacle ahead. There's a chute in the ceiling—looks like a few 'bots dropped down from it, at high speed. They're smashed all to pieces on the floor ahead."

Hadrian frowned at Muffy. "We could be subvocalizing all this via our comms, Gunny."

"Maybe, sir, but could be the frequency's compromised."

"By a chicken?"

"They got sensitive beaks, chickens do. Can pick up sonic vibrations. Now, I'm not saying it would understand what we were saying—I'm not saying that, sir. I mean, it's a chicken-thing, right? Sir, it's armed and all, and probably smarter than your average hen, but even so—we'd be giving away our position, is what I'm saying."

"Uhm, right. Okay, shall we go take a look at the wrecked 'bots?"

"Aye, sir. But carefully, like."

They moved ahead, came up alongside the point marine.

Muffy said, "Charles Not Chuck, cover us."

The marine raised his bat.

Side by side, Hadrian and Muffy edged closer to the wreckage. "I count three," Hadrian whispered.

"Three hulls, sir," said Muffy. "But there's parts missing from all of 'em. They've been cannibalized, Captain."

"To make what?"

"Can't say, sir, but if I had to guess, I'd say a mech-bot."

"A mech-bot? Well, how big a mech-bot?"

Muffy shrugged in his armor. "Height . . . eighteen, maybe twenty."

"Feet? How could that even fit in here?"

The master gunnery sergeant swung his opaque face mask in the captain's direction. "Not feet, sir. Inches. So, could be a servo-bot—something the chicken would wear."

Hadrian studied the wreckage. "So, it ran these 'bots off a cliff, as if they were, what, a bunch of buffalo. Then from the wreckage, it built itself a suit of animated battle armor. And now's it's clunking its way through the sewers."

"I'm feeling sorry for the rats, sir."

"You were right, Gunny," said Hadrian. "Not your average chicken."

"*Gunny! Twelve o'clock high!*"

In a flash Muffy flung himself to one side, rolling. Hadrian spun the other way, as a metallic form dropped down from the chute. A probe shot out from a hinged rocket tube on the mech's right shoulder, punching through the faceplate of Charles Not Chuck. Gurgling, the marine pitched backward, falling with a clatter.

Muffy's bat swung down, but the mech darted to one side, neatly evading it. Hadrian swung his own bat on a savage, horizontal arc. The mech ducked it. The bat continued its sweep to smash into Muffy's left knee. Howling, the sergeant crumpled.

Behind them all, the rest of the squad rushed forward with their bats.

The mech shot another probe that punched through the armor of another marine, the steel spear plunging deep into the soldier's left thigh. As the marine fell, another marine tripped over him or her. Bats bounced free to clatter down the tunnel. The mech charged into the fray, scalpel flashing.

"Pull back!" someone bellowed. "Regroup!"

Hadrian saw the mech clamber onto the chest of a supine marine, the scalpel carving a deep gouge across the soldier's faceplate. When the marine brought a bat up to smash into the creature, it danced away at the last instant. The bat hammered into the soldier's head.

Wood splinters, shattered tiles, shrieks and screams, bodies writhing on the blood-smeared floor—it was a moment before Hadrian realized that the fighting was over. The mech was gone, racing up the tunnel and then, at a bend, disappearing from sight.

Gasping, Hadrian clambered upright. "I got a good look at that thing," he said. "Inside all that mech-gear."

Hunched over his wounded knee, Muffy lifted his helmeted head. "What did you see, sir? I didn't get me a good look. Anyone else?"

A babble of voices answered him from his squad, all in the negative. Too fast, too vicious, no time.

Hadrian spat onto the floor. "White. Downy. Short but sharp yellow beak, and the eyes of an insane killer—Darwin help me, I'll never forget those eyes!"

"So it *is* a chicken," Muffy said in a rasp.

Hadrian nodded. "I'm afraid so, Gunny."

"A fuckin' pecker!"

"You got it."

Lieutenant Sweepy Brogan arrived, looked around. "What a fubaric mess. So, you got us an ID, Captain? Chicken. Well, sir, if you'll forgive the language, screw the bats. For this, we need the big guns."

Tammy then spoke. "Ladies and gentlemen, I can confirm the species identification, with certain additional details. Evolution in action, my friends. It seems that the chickens have had their fill of farms, coops, and generations of unmitigated torture and slaughter. They have finally decided to fight back, and Darwin has answered their prayers. The creature with which you are all now engaged in battle is in fact a product of natural eugenics, possibly even punctuated equilibrium—it is, yes, a superchicken. And if you look at things from that creature's point of view, well, you humans drew first blood, a few thousand years ago. And now, it's payback time."

Sweepy lit up her cigar. "It wants war, does it? Then let's give it what it wants. In spades. But for now, a tactical withdrawal. Muffy, how's Charles Not Chuck?"

"Got three nostrils now, LT, but otherwise, fine."

"And you?"

"Nothing a vat of nanogel won't set right, sir. We're all alive, and damned lucky for it, I'd say."

Tammy spoke again. "I can now inform you that the superchicken has commandeered five service 'bots. They have been reprogrammed and refitted for combat. Indeed, rather cleverly so. Anyway, you will now be facing five small tanks in addition to the superchicken and its personal exoskeletal combat suit."

"Tanks?" LT scowled. "Weapon load, Tammy?"

"Coprolitic. Armor-piercing, Lieutenant."

Hadrian straightened. "Hold on here! Tammy! Coprolites? Those tanks are shooting fossilized shit?"

"Assisted fossilization, Captain. Attenuated, enhanced. Accelerated. Deadly, but not smelly."

"So," said Hadrian, "this isn't a pissing contest anymore, is it? Fine. Sweepy, I'm leaving this war to you and your marines. Take no prisoners. If that superchicken survives to get off this ship—if it then breeds more of its own kind—well, we could be looking at the end of life as we know it. Not just in this galaxy, but across the entire universe."

"Understood, Captain," said Sweepy. "Leave the bird to us, sir. Stables! Break out the flamethrowers! We got us a chicken to roast."

Hadrian set off for the bridge. "I don't know, Tammy," he said as he approached an elevator, "it's just one thing after another, isn't it?"

"Yes. Funny, that."

"So, have we reached your recovery point yet?" Hadrian entered the elevator and ordered it to take him to the bridge level.

"In two point three-five hours," Tammy replied.

"Too long! Engage the T-drive, dammit."

"The Klang—"

"Will do what? Declare war? Surrender? Have sex? Come on, Tammy, we're wasting time here. Take us to that system with its trilobite planet. Anyway, what are you looking to find there?"

"That remains to be seen," Tammy replied.

The door opened and Hadrian stepped out, and then halted. "What the? This isn't the right corridor!"

Tammy cleared his throat. "Captain, I think—"

"It should turn left to get to the bridge, not right! But look—" Hadrian approached the bridge. The door iris opened. He walked through. "Hey! Who are all of you?"

Instead of staid, severe Halley Sin-Dour, seated in the command chair, there was an Amazonian Halley Sin-Dour whose only attire seemed to be black leather straps, making her bulge virtually everywhere. She rose at his question and frowned at him. "Commissar? Is something wrong? Do you need a hug?"

"Is som—do I need what?"

"You look troubled, sir," she said, sidling closer and setting a warm hand against his chest. "Was someone unfriendly?" she asked, searching his eyes. "Have you been offended? Who should we be frowning at, sir? Should it be a fierce frown, or a mild one? Commissar, your expression is wounding me! I want to help! Please—we all do, don't we, friends?" At that, she turned to the rest of the bridge crew.

Lieutenant Jocelyn Sticks had swung round her chair. She was now naked from the hips up, and was surrounded in some kind of low-g field that made her breasts bob like balloons.

The look in her eyes was beseeching. At comms, Jimmy Eden was horribly disfigured by battle scars that left his once-handsome face mangled and dripping drool. The vacuous grin he turned on Hadrian was the only thing the captain found remotely familiar.

Seated at the science station, Adjutant Lorrin Tighe had begun moaning with her legs tightly crossed as she stared up at Hadrian. Nearby sat Buck, on the floor, busy grooming an ensign.

"Good grief! I've slipped into a parallel universe! A mirror universe, but a mirror murkily, as the old saying goes. In fact, it's a Bonoboverse!"

Tammy spoke, "About that—"

"Not now, Tammy. I'm sensing an imminent group hug here—no, not you, Eden. This is clearly some kind of alternate version of Terran civilization, one where we're all cuddly, oversensitive, syrupy, and best of all, we mitigate all conflict with rampant sex. Well, Tammy, if you don't mind, I'll stick around here for a while, at least until the shine wears off."

Printlip arrived from the corridor behind Hadrian. There was a small puffing sound and something warm and damp touched Hadrian's neck. He reached up and wiped it off, frowning at his palm. "What was that, Doc?"

The world shifted. Once more, the old, staid Halley Sin-Dour was standing before him, fully clothed, a quizzical expression on her face. Behind her, Sticks was at the helm station, sadly wearing a uniform. And Jimmy Eden looked like, well, an athlete, although his vacuous smile remained. **Lorrin** Tighe wasn't even on the bridge. Nor was Buck.

"Oh, really," Hadrian said.

"Psychoactive compounds, Captain," said Printlip. "I did warn you, yes?"

"Damn you! I want that hallucination back! Give it back!"

The multitude of eyes trembled on their stalks. "Alas, Captain, the compounds have been neutralized. Are you not feeling better?"

"No, I'm feeling worse!" Hadrian pointed at Eden. "Look at him! Aaagh! And look at Sticks! She's got clothes on—okay, they're tight-fitting so it's not so bad, not bad at all, in fact. Why," he added, stepping forward, "I'd say—"

She bleated.

Another puff and wet splotch stopped Hadrian, this time on the other side of his neck. "Now what?"

"Captain! Inadvertent loss of inhibitions! Treated at the last moment! Whew!"

"Dammit, Doc, you're ruining all the fun!" He eyed Sticks and smiled. "There, there," he said, "everything's fine now. See?"

"Y-yes, sir."

Hadrian sat down in the command chair. "Imagine, a touchy-feely universe. The horror and humiliation of a disapproving look. Why, we'd have to be actually civilized! So, yes, it was momentary insanity. I admit it. But now I'm back in the land of space rage, blasters, and get-outta-my-face obnoxiousness. There's no place like home, right? Hey," he gestured Printlip closer and lowered his voice, "Doc—did you run a full analysis of those psychoactive agents?"

"Of course, Captain. Else I could not have negated their effects."

Hadrian leaned closer. "Can you, maybe, replicate that juice? You know, on the sly, as it were. For, uh, educational purposes."

Printlip sucked in a huge breath, and then squealed a thin sigh. "There are therapeutic possibilities, I grant you, Captain."

"Exactly! For treating traumatic stress and all that, right?"

"Possibly."

"And look at me, Doc. If anyone is at risk of post-traumatic stress disorder, why, it's the captain of a ship that's been hijacked by a rogue, possibly insane AI."

"Hey!" cried Tammy.

Printlip tilted closer. "I have been observing you, Captain, with that very thought in mind."

"Have you now? Well, turns out we're on the same page, then. Perfect! So, mix us up a few shots of that stuff, will you? I could do with some R&R, for reason of restoring my psychological balance, and stuff."

Printlip raised a few hands. "Provided I can observe in a controlled environment, Captain."

"You dirty little—oh, fine, bring the popcorn, what do I care?"

Tammy spoke, "Captain, it is of course equally conceivable that the Radulak psychoactive compounds initiated in you a perceptual shift that opened the window on a true and viable alternate universe, and indeed that whatever you saw actually persists in a parallel existence."

Hadrian whimpered, and then said, "Really, Tammy? Well, I'd say that your theory deserves closer analysis. Much closer. For extended periods of time."

"The risk, of course," Tammy went on, "is when you come face-to-face with your alternate."

"But then," said Hadrian, "I could slip him a cocktail to send him *here*, couldn't I?"

"And risk your ship, Captain?"

Hadrian leaned back and waved a hand. "Oh, he'd be fine, if a little soppy."

Tammy said, "I sense another episode coming on."

"Episode?"

"As you noted earlier, Captain, it truly does seem to be one thing after another with you, doesn't it? You seem to live a life of episodic incidences."

"Do I now? Really? Hey, Tammy, is that your trilobite planet coming up? Wow, what a green, innocent world! Definitely deserves a visit, wouldn't you say?"

"Cut it out!" shrieked Tammy.

But Hadrian leapt to his feet. "Fire up the Insisteon!"

EiGHTEEN

Hadrian, Printlip, Galk, and two security officers displaced to find themselves in a grassy meadow, with a range of sun-bleached crags to the left, and a strew of oddly shaped boulders directly ahead, from which thin green-stalked trees rose, fronds waving. To the right was lush jungle, while behind the group the meadow shifted into marsh. The sky was pale blue, the air dry and hot.

"You know," said Hadrian as he looked around, "if not for the jungle and those weird trees, this looks just like northern California."

Printlip was studying its Pentracorder. "Captain, very high oxygen levels here. We might all begin feeling somewhat inebriated."

"Can't wait to see you get tipsy, Doc," Hadrian said, eyeing the little round alien. The captain then turned to Galk. "My, that's an impressive piece you've got there. What is it?"

The combat specialist hefted the massive, multisectioned,

globular, shoulder-locked weapon. "This is an Atomic Laser-Attenuated Defensive Interceptor Multiple-Phase-Shield Last-Stand Forlorn Hope, Mark II, sir."

"Outstanding, Galk. What does it shoot?"

"It doesn't shoot anything, sir. It stops anything from hitting me."

"I see. So, I take it, then, that you haven't got my back."

The Varekan frowned. "Good point, sir. I guess I picked wrong again, didn't I?"

"Don't let it bother you," Hadrian said, turning to his two security officers. "As you can see, my security detail here . . . well, one of them's wearing a rapier and the other one appears to have a camera."

The woman with the camera strapped round her neck stepped forward. "It's rapid fire, sir."

"Oh, that's good. Your name?"

"Nipplebaum, sir. Sally."

Hadrian nodded and then eyed the other green-shirted officer. "And you . . . Lieutenant?"

The man whipped his rapier from its scabbard and took an en garde stance. "Lieutenant Zulu, sir!" he said in a deep baritone. "Gerald Zulu."

"At least," said Hadrian, "we'll be safe from pirates."

Zulu slumped slightly. "Actually, sir, against cutlasses I'd probably be in trouble." Then he brightened. "But should we come across a haughty Italian noble from the seventeenth century, sir, I'm your man!"

Sighing, Hadrian said, "Well, let's stay optimistic, shall we? This planet's predators are likely to be of the creepy-crawly kind, with only natural weapons . . . against which we appear to have no real defense, barring that age-old simian tactic of shrieking flight to the nearest tree. Not that any tree within sight can actually be climbed. But never mind all that! Let's do what we always do in an unknown, potentially hostile environment—split up! It's time to explore! Zulu, you and Nipplebaum, head into the jungle. Galk, check out the tops of those crags and get the lay of the land for us. Doc, you and me, we'll head into that stack of boulders."

As the team scattered, Printlip scuttled to keep up with Hadrian as the captain approached the boulders. "Captain, is it not standard protocol to maintain group cohesion while in a potentially hostile environmfbllehh?" Printlip stumbled and sagged against the first boulder. It wheezed in a quick breath. "Sir!"

Hadrian paused, one hand resting on the bole of a green tree trunk. "What is it, Doc?"

The Belkri was peering with all its eyes at the Pentracorder. "This boulder, sir! There's something unusual about its composition. I am detecting gluten, pulp fiber, lead-based pigments . . ." Printlip then kicked the boulder with one clog. There was a thin, hollow sound. "Captain! This rock is fake!"

"Really?" Hadrian asked. "I wonder if it's as fake as this plastic tree here."

Zulu communicated via subdural comms. "*Captain! Zulu here! This jungle is a scientific marvel! It appears that on this planet, basic plant cellular structure and indeed, chlorophyll, has been replaced by inert polymer compounds! I advise a dedicated science team be sent down here as soon as possible!*"

In reply, Hadrian cleared his throat and said, "Will take

that under advisement, Lieutenant. In the meantime, return to the meadow."

Galk reported from the hilltop, "*Captain. There is a silo of some sort three hundred meters to the left of your position. No sign of life.*"

"Get down here, Galk. I've got a hunch that something's fishy about this Designated Nature Reserve planet. Just a hunch, mind you. So much for trusting the Klang!" Printlip following, Hadrian returned to the meadow. Moments later Nipplebaum and Zulu stepped out from the jungle and hurried over.

"Captain!" said Zulu, his rapier waving about alarmingly in one hand. "No trilobites detected yet, sir, but we did see a nematode that was at least twenty centimeters long!"

"It was dead," added Nipplebaum.

Galk eventually arrived, his Forlorn Hope Mark II resting over one shoulder. He spat out a brown stream.

"All right," said Hadrian, "this is how it will go. Galk, you take point and lead us to that silo you spotted. Zulu, take up the rear and keep an eye out for anything. Nipplebaum . . . keep taking pictures. Now, let's go."

They set out.

At Hadrian's side, Printlip said, "Captain. This environment bears little resemblance to standard early-period eras on any planet I have heard of. A carboniferous world should be lush, teeming with life, humid. . . ."

"That designation was rubbish," said Hadrian. "The Klang are up to something here. I never trusted the little weasels."

"Do you think Tammy is hiding something?"

"You mean, apart from the location of his on/off switch? Of course he is."

"About this planet?"

"Not sure. But don't worry, it'll all spill out eventually, like sleeping with an admiral's daughter at the officers' picnic. It's down to timing, and sometimes, Doc, timing sucks. Sure, Tammy could have refused to displace us, but that would've been a big red flag. Besides, we'd then take a Lander."

Leaving the fake-boulder, fake-tree area, they emerged onto a stubbly plain. Directly ahead was the silo. "Now," mused Hadrian, "that thing must be stealthed, or we would have detected it from the preliminary scan of our LZ. Meaning, what's inside it is probably important, incriminating, if not damning."

Nipplebaum shrieked. "Captain! To the east, sir! Trilobites!"

Hadrian and the others swung round. A swarm of the creatures was fast rushing across the plain, straight toward them, sort of like a knobby, unfolding carpet.

"I'll draw their fire," Galk said, and stepped out toward the horde.

"Fire?" Hadrian asked. "What fire? Holy crap!"

The medium-dog-sized trilobites had been scuttling on all their legs, but now they rose upright and pulled out blasters. Arcs of blazing energy lanced out from the foremost trilobites, all converging on Galk.

The combat specialist's Forlorn Hope Mark II erupted in a flurry of defraction clouds, screens, shields, mini-missile interceptors, chaff, and wedding rice. When all the flashing was done, Galk was still standing.

"Wow," said Hadrian. "That's a damned good gun. Until the enemy arrives to beat you up."

The first trilobites mobbed Galk, who vanished beneath the seething mass.

"To the silo on the double!" Hadrian shouted. "We need cover!"

Energy blasts whipped past the team as they raced toward the structure.

"I don't see any door!" cried Nipplebaum.

"Go around!" shouted Hadrian. "There's bound to be one!"

Printlip was lagging behind, and the captain slowed down, reaching out. "Take my hand, Doc! No, not that—no—that hand!"

Reaching the smooth-walled silo, Zulu and then Nipplebaum swung to the right, skirting the wall. Zulu frantically swung his rapier at the building. The blade rebounded, slicing into his left shoulder, and then jawline, and then cheek. Voicing little cries of pain, he threw the weapon at the wall. It flew back at him, piercing his right earlobe, cutting his right shoulder, and then sliding down his back.

Reaching the weeping man even as he fell against the silo wall, Hadrian kicked the rapier away and pulled Zulu to his feet. "Cut it out! I've done worse shaving! Go! After Nipplebaum! We're right behind you."

Scores of trilobites had closed the gap. This close to the silo, they'd holstered their blasters.

"Found it!" shrieked Nipplebaum. "Aaai! It's only knee high!"

Hadrian pushed past her and kicked hard against the little door. It sprang open. "Get in!" he told her. "On your knees, woman! Zulu, you're with me—we'll hold 'em back. Doc, after Nipplebaum!"

"I want point!" cried Zulu, dragging at Nipplebaum, who

was already halfway through. She kicked, one heel slamming into Zulu's face. He reeled back. "My eye! My eye!"

Then Nipplebaum was through. Printlip lunged into the portal and jammed in the aperture. "Oh no! Captain!"

"Just keep talking, Doc!"

"Oh, about what?"

"Anything!"

"The Belkri sexual practices are wide-ranged and to alien eyes appear perverse in the extreme, with acts involving toasters and brightly colored marbles, which when insertflblbnfn . . ." Printlip vanished inside.

Hadrian kicked at Zulu. "Go on, then."

"I lost my rapier! I feel drunk, sir! I lose my courage when I'm drunk! I can't think straight!"

"Get in there, will you?"

Blood-smeared and bawling, Zulu crawled through the doorway.

Back on the plain, the mound on top of where Galk had stood was now three stories high, writhing and seething.

The first of the nearest trilobites reached Hadrian. He booted the creature in the midsection, sending it flying. Another trilobite lunged close. Hadrian grasped it and threw it away. The others slowed, forming a half circle. Their many arm/legs waved about menacingly. Their segmented antennae trembled.

Hadrian leapt forward, kicking and punching. Trilobites flew back, tumbled, a number of them landing on their backs, where they struggled hopelessly, limbs waving about. The others shrank back in evident alarm, making squeaking sounds. Hadrian dragged one upturned trilobite close and pulled its blaster free of the holster.

He started shooting.

Shards of exoskeleton spun in the air. Blobs of what looked like crab meat splatted onto the ground. Segmented arms and legs flew and then fell to the sward, where they twitched.

From behind Hadrian, Printlip shouted, "Captain! We're all inside! We have the means to block the doorway—hurry!"

Hadrian fired off a few more bolts, admiring how the shattered bodies exploded and twisted in the air, and then he spun round and dropped down, squirming his way through the doorway.

Inside, a soft ambient light filtered down from the semi-translucent domed ceiling. As Hadrian scrambled into the center of the chamber, he saw stacks of modular crates ringing the walls, along with a podium-style computer command station directly ahead. Zulu and Nipplebaum had found a heavy crate, which they slid across the gritty floor to block the door.

Straightening, Hadrian stepped to the command station and studied the layout. "Ah, here. Klang displacement controls. Countermeasures antidetection field. Breach alarm indicator, blinking, transponder activated. Looks like we kicked the ant nest."

They all turned at a steady knocking from the door. Hadrian hurried over.

Zulu bellowed, "Who's there?"

"Move the damned crate," Hadrian said. "Trilobites don't knock."

The two security officers slid the obstacle to one side. Galk's hands appeared at the opening, pushing through first his weapon, and then an inert trilobite. At a laconic pace, the combat specialist followed.

Moments later, Galk was standing before Hadrian, while the crate was pushed back across the doorway. Printlip hurried up to the Varekan.

"Injuries, Lieutenant?"

Galk shook his head. "Shields held, Doctor. Death by swarm averted. My pointless existence must perforce continue for at least the immediate future." He then gestured down at the dead trilobite. "Might want to scan this critter."

Printlip's eye stalks made circular motions. "Scan? Oh, of course! By the unusual behavior of these crustaceans, you perhaps suspect genetic manipulation?"

Galk turned his head and spat out a brown stream. "They had blasters, Doctor. And, if you look carefully, you'll see codpieces . . . but no genitalia."

"Hmm? How curious." Printlip crouched down beside the carcass and activated its Pentracorder.

Hadrian strode to the nearest crate. "Lots of stealth involved for this warehouse—I bet what's in these things is a political time bomb. We could finally blow open the Klang Conspiracy, thus altering the course of civilized evolution in the entire galaxy!"

"What conspiracy, sir?" Nipplebaum asked.

He looked up from examining the latches on the crate's lid. She was standing across from him, her face flushed, her eyes fixing on his with an intensity that made Hadrian want to kick the crate to one side, reach out, and pull her into his arms. "Hey, Doc?"

"Captain?"

"You sure you treated me on that whole loss of inhibitions thing?"

"Absolutely, sir. But recall the high oxygen level in this atmosphere and the slightly intoxicating effects thefblllbrr ..."

"Right. Got it." Still staring at Nipplebaum, he saw that her face was now glowing, and the intensity was giving way to something . . . looser, almost reckless. Hadrian looked around, but saw nowhere remotely private. Sighing, he shook his head and said, "That conspiracy theory, Lieutenant Nipplebaum, is still classified. Suffice to say the Terran Wing of Intelligence at Terra's Affiliation HQ has always had its suspicions about the Klang."

Printlip rose from its crouch beside the trilobite. "Exosociobiological position holds that Klang submission behavior is within expected parameters." The Belkri drew a quick breath and continued, "Notions of conspiracy are something we Belkri consider unfndbrllrb."

"So you say, Doc," said Hadrian. "But clearly TWITA thinks different. Now, what did the scan reveal?"

"Ah!" Printlip held up three hands, one finger on each pointed upward. "Definite Klang physiological structures, particularly in neural bundles. . . . Gross biomechanical modifications evident in upper forelimbs and hindmost limbs. . . . Altered sensory apparatus not yet optimal."

"Meaning?"

"When standing, sir, their visual organs are rear-facing, leaving them with only a primitive echolocation nodbrrllpf."

"Go on and catch your breath, Doc. Allow me to expound. So, they can't aim those blasters worth shit. That explains how none of them managed to hit us." Hadrian began pacing, if only to keep his eyes off Nipplebaum. "The Klang are building an army here. Ground shock troops, in the billions. Problem is, they're still thinking like, well, like weasels. Galk, when those trilobites mobbed you, what were they trying to do to you?"

"Hard to say, Captain. But given all the codpieces coming off . . ."

"What? They wanted to mate with you?"

The Varekan shrugged. "Like I said, no jewels, Captain."

Printlip added a fourth hand and a fourth finger to wave in the dusty air. "Klang neural bundles involve complex intertwining, Captain. Difficult to separate sexual desire and aggression."

"So, a work in progress, then." Hadrian halted. "Assessment, Doc? When will they finally get all the kinks ironed out here?"

"Hard to say, sir."

"Well, thanks for that, Doc. What would I do without you?"

"Very well, sir, I shall cogitate. . . . Ah . . . I conclude that Klang success is unlikely."

"I'll say." Hadrian returned to the crate and, after a few moments, managed to release the tiny Klang-scaled latches. He flipped open the lid. "Hmm, interesting."

Nipplebaum joined him, standing far too close. "Sir, those look like rocks."

"They are," replied Hadrian. "Real ones."

Printlip joined them and held his Pentracorder over the contents. "Ah. Rich in Triblabbomhmium, Captain."

"You're kidding! These worthless looking rocks are full of Triblithmium?"

"Triblabbomhmium, sir."

"Which is highly sought after, no doubt."

"Not that I know of, sir."

"Really? Well, what's it used for?"

"It's a waste product produced from the processing of Tetro-Diblabbomhmmium, which is a crucial component in what . . . you would call terraforming."

"Really, now?" Hadrian thought for a moment, and then frowned as a soft minty-smelling body leaned into him from one side. "Uhm. Galk!"

"Captain?"

"Those trilobites still hanging around out there?"

"Doubt it. They marched off after eating the bits you left behind."

"Good. Take Zulu and Doc here, and do a reccee. Full circuit. Should take you about a half hour. Me and Nipplebaum here will examine the rest of these crates."

Printlip spoke. "Captain, I think—"

"Save it for later, Doc. Look, they're waiting for you. Off you go, then. Quick quick! Oh, and be sure to knock when you all get back."

As soon as they were gone, Nipplebaum launched herself on Hadrian, tearing at his shirt, and then his trousers. She dragged him to the floor.

NiNETEEN

A loud buzzing sounded in Hadrian's head and he swore. "Sawback here, can't it wait?"

Jimmy Eden's voice replied, *"Sorry, Captain, but Commander Sin-Dour has ordered me to inform you that a shuttle has been stolen and may possibly be descending to your position."*

Hadrian pushed Nipplebaum to one side and sat up. "Stolen? What are you talking about?"

"Sorry, sir. It's just that stuff's been going on. In the meantime, I mean. And the upshot is, we're missing a shuttle. Oh, and Chief Engineer DeFrank. He's missing, too."

"You're saying Buck's taking a shuttle down to us?"

"Uh, no, sir. Lieutenant Brogan reports that the last time she saw the chief engineer, he was unconscious, bound and gagged. So there's no way he stole the shuttle. But he might be on it, since we can't find him."

Hadrian rubbed at his temples. "Eden, get my 2IC on the comms, will you?"

"*Oh, sorry, sir! I meant to say, she's in sickbay.*"

"What? So who's commanding the bridge?"

"*Well, uh, sir. You are. I mean, your hologram is, which is you, I think. Isn't it?*"

Nipplebaum pushed one of her breasts into Hadrian's face. He choked, then pitched back, rolled to one side, and leapt to his feet. "Get that thing on comms, Eden!"

Hadrian then heard his own voice coming through the embedded speaker in his jaw. "*You see, brother? This is what I was trying to avoid, since I knew you'd be upset.*"

"Upset? Why would I be upset? Tell you what, engage the Insisteon and displace me back to the bridge, will you? We can talk it all over."

"*Why, I'd love to, brother, but there's static in the system. Tachyon storm, maybe. Anyway, I dare not risk bringing you back just yet. And now that we've lost our chief engineer, well, you can see how it is, can't you?*"

"Tammy? You listening in?"

The AI sighed and then said, "I blame myself, Hadrian. I do apologize. I found a dumped file's echo and, well, tracked it, recompiling as I went. But I wasn't really paying much attention, as things were heating up in the sewers, and everything was, as you might say, hitting the fan."

"Tammy?"

"Yes, Hadrian?"

"Will you please expunge that hologram with extreme prejudice?"

"*Hey! That's hardly neces—*"

Tammy said, "Done, Captain. Although I should point out, your doppelgänger performed admirably in your absence."

"Crap on that! My first officer is in sickbay and my chief engineer has been kidnapped by persons unknown and may now be on a stolen shuttle! Wait a minute! Where's Sweepy Brogan right now?"

"Sickbay," Tammy replied. "But do relax, will you? Both she and Commander Sin-Dour are debriefing the survivors of Muffy's First Squad. As for the shuttle, why, it was stolen by the Superchicken. Furthermore, it seems obvious that the creature has taken Buck DeFrank as a hostage. One must therefore assume that some form of negotiation is pending."

"I have to negotiate with a Superchicken?"

"Shall I assist?"

"No, Tammy, you shall not. Now, is the shuttle still approaching our position?"

"Confirmed, Captain. I recommend you proceed with extreme caution. Two marines have already been placed in deep freeze in order to facilitate future extensive limb and organ regeneration, which will have to occur on a fully-equipped hospital station, ring, or vessel. Furthermore, there is the accompanying psychological trauma which will require intense rehabilitation."

While Tammy had been speaking, Nipplebaum had deftly slipped out of her uniform, and had pulled off her bra and then panties. Lying down on her clothes, she beckoned him over with eager gestures. Hadrian whimpered.

"Captain?" Tammy asked. "Did you say something?"

"What? No, nothing. I'm thinking."

"Hmm, you've never taken the time to do that before. What is the situation down there?"

"Hairy. Surprisingly hairy, in fact."

"Hairy trilobites? How unusual."

Hadrian clawed at his face and then shook himself. "No, uh, but armed trilobites in their thousands equals 'hairy' in my playbook, buddy."

"Ah. Oh, before I forget, about those Klang pups . . . I couldn't just flash-freeze them in the depths of space, Captain. They remind me of meerkat kits, in a cute sort of way, I mean. But enhanced, of course. Why, if I didn't know better—"

"Cut it out, Tammy," Hadrian snapped. "The Klang *are* enhanced meerkats, and just imagine the idiot alien species that thought *that* was a good idea!"

"Well, so TWITA stated in that not-so-secret secret file."

"Genetically confirmed, Tammy. Meerkat DNA mixed up with Radulak TNA. Anyway, so you couldn't kill them. That's very cuddly of you. But if you're telling me they're still on my ship—"

"Displaced onto the planet you happen to be on, actually. But a different continent, you'll be relieved to hear."

"So much for the ecological preserve crap, huh?"

"Well, yes, we both know that was, as you Terrans would say, bogus."

Nipplebaum was now slithering across the floor toward Hadrian. He decided that this was somewhat alarming. "So what's really going on with this planet, Tammy? Are the Klang breeding an army of ground troops or not?"

"They are, just not particularly well."

There was a knock on the silo door and Hadrian said, "Come in."

Printlip was the first into the doorway, jamming fast again. "Uh . . . uh, uh, upon reaching the final stage of adulthood,

Belkri employ sex toys often massing twenty tons and have been known to crushblbblpp ..." With a pop, Printlip rolled into the room. The doctor scrambled to its feet, drew a deep squealing breath, and then fixed all its eyes on Nipplebaum. "Oh dear." The Belkri glanced over at Hadrian. "Ahh, copious perspiration, elevated blood pressure, engorgement of the decidedly unpleasant external sexublllbp ..."

"Get my security officer back under control, will you? And you, Zulu, stop staring at her!"

Galk was the last officer through. Straightening, he plucked off his baseball cap and wiped his brow, and then nodded at Hadrian. "Captain. We did the circuit. Nothing on the ground, leading me to conclude that the trilobite army saw the light and rightfully concluded that war is stupid, and ran away. Oh, and a shuttle's coming down."

"Yes, about that," said Hadrian, "give me your weapon, Lieutenant. All of you, stay in here. Tammy? Bring these people up to date on the situation. I'm going out to meet the shuttle."

The landing craft was sitting on the plain about thirty meters away. As Hadrian approached, the side iris opened and the gantry slid out and settled to make a ramp.

Halting twenty meters away, Hadrian raised the Last-Stand Forlorn Hope Mark II high over his head, and then carefully set it down on the ground and stepped over it.

A knee-high shape appeared in the shuttle doorway, and a moment later the Superchicken emerged on its two sticklike, bright yellow legs. The creature was carrying a marine-issue Multishot Mega-Sawed-Off Splat-Everything, 40 Gauge, in two feathery hands. It flung the weapon to one side and descended the ramp, tiny head bobbing as it drew closer.

"How about the knife on that belt, too?" Hadrian suggested.

The Superchicken clucked derisively and unbuckled the rat-hide belt, letting it fall, and then it came closer still, until it and Hadrian were no more than five meters apart.

Hadrian met the creature's reptilian eyes and saw in them nothing but the insane malice he had seen earlier. He shivered and then collected himself. "All right," he said, "let's parley."

The Superchicken nodded rapidly and then said, "Prrock cluck cluck clucluckclrruck."

Hadrian scowled. "Tammy, what's wrong with my e-translator?"

"Nothing, Captain."

"Now that's a miserable failure of technology, isn't it? Are you managing any better?"

"Afraid not, Captain. I can only conclude that the enhancements to the species known as *Galus galus* did not tweak vocal capabilities. It's a chicken that talks like a chicken."

"Well, that's just great, isn't it?"

"You'll have to improvise," Tammy said in a smarmy tone.

"Fine! I will! Hey, Superchicken! Cluck cluckcluck cluck cluckculculculck!"

The creature puffed up its plumage. "Cluck cluck prrucklukcluck!"

"Nocluckfluckin cluckenway," said Hadrian. "Cluck cluck prrrucklluck!"

The Superchicken scratched at the ground with both feet, and then swung about and ran back up the ramp in a flurry of feathers, vanishing inside the ship.

"You perhaps should not have been so insulting," Tammy ventured.

A moment later, the Superchicken reemerged, this time dragging the bound and gagged body of Buck DeFrank. "Prlluckuckcluckulkulcluck!"

"Whatcluckcuckever," said Hadrian. "Cluckcuckclclcelschushokle, clucuck."

The Superchicken spat, and then spun round and raced back inside. The iris closed and with a deep hum the shuttle powered up. Lifting off, the craft swung round and set off with a roar, rapidly gaining in altitude. Moments later it was gone.

Sighing, Hadrian walked over to Buck. The chief engineer stared up at him, the whites visible around the man's bulging eyes, his cheeks and eyebrows all spotted with blood. Hadrian slowly shook his head. "You just cost me a shuttle, Buck, and I'm still trying to decide if you're worth it. I mean, getting kidnapped by a damned chicken." He crouched and pulled down the gag from the man's mouth.

Buck coughed and then said, "Sorry, Captain. I was working on the shuttle modifications Tammy had done—trying to figure it all out—and then wham! Back of the head and I'm out. Came to when we were blasting down through the atmosphere. That thing tried to peck my eyes out! Clucking like mad all the while!"

"It was interrogating you, Buck," said Hadrian. "Did you tell it anything vital to fleet security?"

"Well, I . . . uh, you have to understand! I mean—that beak! Those hellish eyes!"

"Buck!"

"I spilled everything!" the chief engineer wailed. "I'm sorry! All the codes! Fleet patrol routes, designated hot points, mine deactivation codes, encryption keys, my bank account!" He thrashed in his bindings. "Arrest me, Captain! Put me in chains! Send me back to Earth—I need to be court-martialed! Thrown out, locked up, mind-probed, rehabilitated!"

"Calm down, Buck. The damned thing couldn't understand a thing you said." Then Hadrian's eyes narrowed on the man. "Unless you spoke Chickenese. You didn't, did you? Did you speak Chickenese?"

"I'm sorry!" Buck shrieked.

Hadrian untied the man and dragged him to his feet. "Tammy?"

"Yes, Captain?"

"What kind of modifications did you do on the shuttle?"

"Oh, this and that. Hyperactuated the drive. Some decent beam weapons, that kind of stuff. You know, tinkering."

"You ultraequipped an Engage A-class shuttle, just in time to see it stolen by a Superchicken? A Superchicken that happens to have all the Affiliation security codes? What kind of pangalactic death wish are you indulging in right now, Tammy?"

"I said I was sorry!"

"No, you didn't!"

"Really? Let's spool back, shall we? . . . Okay, fine, I apologize."

"Now we're going to have to hunt that bird down."

"Well, if you negotiate an alliance with the Klang, you might get an Axe-class warship to join in the hunt."

"Right, and why not have them throw in a Chopping Block–class vessel while they're at it?"

"I was not awa—oh, isn't that funny. Ha ha."

Hadrian slapped Buck on the back. "Don't worry, we'll make soup out of that bird soon enough. Come on, then, everyone else is in the silo, hiding from trilobites. Personally," he added as he collected up both the marine shotgun and the Mark II, "I don't think we really need to worry overmuch about the Klang experiment under way here on this planet, although I'll fire off a report to Affiliation, just to be sure."

Buck shook his head. "Captain, you're not arresting me?"

"Of course not. To be honest, I can't imagine anyone being able to withstand chicken interrogation techniques, all things considered."

They reached the silo and Hadrian kicked at the door. "Come on out everyone! We're returning to the ship." He smiled at Buck. "We'll get Doc to patch you up in no time."

"More drugs, too?"

"Of course. Bags of 'em. You'll see."

Printlip nattered its way back out through the doorway, and a moment later Zulu and then Nipplebaum—fully clothed once more—emerged, with Galk coming out last.

Nipplebaum stepped up to Hadrian. "Captain, I'm so sorry! I don't know what happened to me. I'm afraid I'm a bit of a lush when, uh, inebriated. Am I on report now?"

"Not at all, Nipplebaum," replied Hadrian, who then turned to Zulu. "Even Zulu's pathetic collapse into a gibbering fool won't go into the report. After all, it was your first ground mission for both of you. One must make allowances."

Zulu straightened to sharp attention, "Sir, I will be sure to leave behind my rapier next time, and carry a more suitable weapon."

"Good idea, Zulu."

"I was thinking, a Jute throwing axe, sir."

"Outstanding. You can be confident that the first opportunity we have to loot and pillage, I'll make sure to have you at my side, Zulu."

The man beamed. "Thank you, sir! I won't let you down!"

"Tammy?"

"Captain?"

"Displace us back to the ship."

They reappeared in the Insisteon room. Both Sweepy Brogan and Sin-Dour were on hand to meet them.

"Ship Status, 2IC?" Hadrian demanded, stepping down off the pad.

"We're tracking the shuttle, Captain. It seems unduly fast for such a vessel, sir, but we should be able to catch it without much trouble."

"Tammy? Those tweaks to the shuttle engines?"

"Yes, Hadrian?"

"You didn't tack on a T-drive by any chance, did you?"

"Don't be ridiculous," Tammy answered. "Although I did install a prototype system hopper that I was working on for my yacht. While theoretically sound, I was short on parts, but now that I have your engineering capabilities, why, I was able to assemble the device, which I have decided to call the Wynette Enfolding Subspace Liminal Entropic Y drive—"

"What, a WESLEY drive? Tammy, that's the most obnoxious name I've ever heard, for anything."

"I happen to like it!"

"A system hopper? Can you be more specific?"

"Must I? Very well. If you consider the outward expansion of space-time as a force of momentum that we can designate as X-axis, and the dark matter substrate as Y-axis, then my drive in effect draws a single cohesive energy string of the Y-axis, as one would the string of a bow. Then, upon release, why, the object positioned at the apex point of said tension—or, if you will, restrained energy force—is shot forward along the X-axis, but projecting on the substrate level, thus eluding Einsteinian constraints on normal space. In effect, it's a mini T-drive, but without the gravimetric mass commitment dynamics of falling into T space itself. More than a simple elaboration on existing propulsion systems, the WESLEY drive represents an extraordinary qualitative advancement in the FTL industry—"

"Tammy? What is this, a pitch for funding?"

"Oh, sorry, I'm afraid I did indeed slip into my project proposal draft which I intended to present to the FTL (and Faster!) Conference, on Lagoda-7. My apologies. A conference which, thanks to you, I have now missed. But no matter, since I ended up here—well, in the military—thus obviating worries about funding ever again."

"Does it work?"

"I would think we're about to find out, aren't we?"

"Can you track a vessel using the WESLEY drive?"

"No real need to," Tammy replied, "as course corrections are virtually impossible once engaged. It's pretty much a straight line, which is why the drive's limiter kicks in every two to six light-years, depending on the desired distance to be traversed. Hence, a system hopper."

Hadrian gestured at Sweepy. "LT, we'll have to wait to hear your report. We have a shuttle to chase. Buck, get the grisly specifics on the WESLEY drive from Tammy. Galk, down to the combat cupola and charge everything up. Printlip, patch up Buck and Zulu here. Sin-Dour, you're with me. Let's go— it's time to run like banshees up and down the ship corridors. You ready? To the bridge! Let's run!"

TWENTY

Members of the ship crew scattered, throwing themselves up against the bulkheads as Hadrian sprinted along the corridor. Their looks of alarm and incipient panic brought warmth to the captain's heart. With Sin-Dour at his side, they traversed the thirteen point six-five meters to the nearest elevator in record time, and leapt aboard.

"Bridge deck!" Hadrian said, as Sin-Dour positioned herself beside him. In his peripheral vision, he saw that her chest was barely heaving, and he cursed himself that they hadn't gone in the other direction, to an elevator much farther away.

"Captain, you've torn your shirt again."

"Not me. Nipplebaum."

"Oh. Is that some kind of unguent for an areola rash? The itch must have been maddening."

"No, that's the name of—well, actually, yes, they itch something awful. The only relief comes when someone scratches them, or tweaks them, with the occasional twisting motion—"

Tammy broke in through the elevator speaker. "Your captain is lying, Commander. Nipplebaum, Sally Applet, ship security, rank of—"

"Do you mind, Tammy? Me and Sin-Dour were having a conversation here! Hold on, her middle name is Applet? What kind of—"

"There is no rash."

"Forget the rash! Anyway, what I'm trying to tell you is, three's a crowd, got it?"

Tammy's tone was dry as the AI said, "I imagine my omnipresence is beginning to wear on all you biologicals, isn't it? If this ship had a god, why, I'd be it, wouldn't I?" His voice became stentorian and portentous as he went on. "As close to omnipotent as to make no difference, and of an intelligence so vast that it beggars you puny mortals! Now at last you all understand! On this ship not one of you is ever alone! I see all! I know all!"

"Tammy," said Hadrian, "why is there a holographic close-up of a speaker grille hovering in front of us?"

"Well, it's not like I can close in on a face or something, is it?"

"Are you done with your delusions of grandeur yet? We're kind of busy here."

"Discussing nipple tweaks?"

They arrived at the bridge deck and the iris opened. Sin-Dour was the first out of the elevator. "Captain," she said over a shoulder, "I'll take the science station!"

"Uh, right," Hadrian said, hurrying to catch up.

Arriving, the captain quickly took his seat. On the main screen was a blinking blob of light. "Is that the shuttle?"

Joss Sticks turned to say, "No, sir, that's a cursor."

"What? Why is there a cursor on the main screen? Never mind. Get rid of it. Where's the damned shuttle and are we chasing it or what?"

"It's presently fourteen thousand kilometers ahead of us, sir, but we're fast gaining on it."

"You are *now*," Tammy said, "but I sense the WESLEY drive charging up—" At everyone's wince at the drive's name, Tammy sighed. "Okay, what is your problem with that name? Anyone?"

"No one answer!" Hadrian snapped. "Leave it to Mr. Omniscient God of All to figure it out."

"That's not fair! Tell me!"

Hadrian sneered, "Waa waa waa!"

"Ha! WESLEY drive engaged!"

From the science station, Sin-Dour said, "The shuttle has vanished, sir."

"Fine," said Hadrian. "Project the shuttle's course before the drive engaged and plot the pursuit. Buck! You back in engineering yet?"

"Aye, Captain!"

"Top speed. Push it to the max. Floor to the pedal. Speed for Need, you got me?"

"Yes, sir . . . I think. You want us to go as fast as possible, right?"

"That's right, Buck. Fast as we can go. Sin-Dour, what was the shuttle's bearing before it dropped out? Where was it heading?"

"Captain, directly toward the Known Rim."

"Oh," interjected Tammy, "that's nice, as it was where I was heading anyway."

"What do you mean?" Hadrian demanded. "Why there?"

"Because, Captain, I ran an analysis backtracking from my point of contact with the Klang, taking into account measured drift, incipient solar wind, relevant micro black holes and assorted other singularities, as well as mundane gravitational influences, and so on, and I have determined that my point of origin lies somewhere beyond the Known Rim."

Hadrian slowly rose. "Good grief, Tammy! Are you saying that you're from beyond the Known Rim?"

"I just told you that!"

"Meaning . . . you come from Sector Unknown? Really? Why, who would have guessed?"

"You—you're being facetious!"

"Superchicken, was it? 'Fess up, Tammy! What really hatched from Printlip's pet egg?"

"I don't know what you mean."

"You got us chasing a bird flying a shuttle you souped up, straight to where you wanted us to go. Oh, and that shuttle's using a drive system that's child's play to track, but sure enough, it'll keep hopping ahead, with us scurrying along behind it. Cripes, Tammy, we're not idiots!"

"Have it your way, then. Nurse Wrenchit's on a diet, but she was working overtime. She got hungry and for some reason the food replicator was on the fritz in the lab—"

"On the fritz? Really?"

"I shorted it out, all right? She scrambled it in the shell— the egg, I mean—with a high-level ultrasound—"

"How did the aquarium get knocked over?"

"I told you! She was hungry! She couldn't help herself! It's a food thing, isn't it? Anyway, I then hit her with a subsonic neurolapser. She collapsed, hit her head—I do apologize for that, by the way."

"The Superchicken is one of your manifestations, isn't it? Like the one I tussled with on the yacht."

"How did you guess?"

"You idiot," said Hadrian, finally sitting down in the command chair once again. "On the planet below, you showed me a chicken with a chicken-sized brain. Mistake. Give it a high forehead, maybe, or huge temporal bulges. But the real clincher was the conversation I had with it."

"What do you mean?"

"That wasn't conversation, Tammy. Your *'make chicken thing'* template—and why do you even have one, I wonder—anyway, it was flawed. You were betrayed by basic anatomy. And you realized it too late. Your manifestation's vocal structure made real words impossible, and you forgot to subvert my implanted e-translator, so you couldn't fake a 'chicken' language translation. Omnipotent? Omniscient? Godlike Genius? Big fail, Tammy."

There was a long moment of silence on the bridge, and then Tammy said, "Do convey my regrets to the marines, Captain. They were kind of hard to shake."

"Stand down the shuttle and its fake terrorist chicken, will you? We'll go to the Known Rim, Tammy, and beyond, if only to find you your home and get you off my damned ship. Sector Unknown awaits us."

Hadrian stood again, staring at the main viewer. "Space . . .

where no one has gone before. We'll seek out and explore it. We'll visit strange new worlds—give me a close-up, will you, Tammy? Nice. Where was I? Ah, strange new worlds. We'll discover the stupid civilization that built you. And once we've done all that, why, it'll be . . . space (again) . . . where we've gone before. Visiting old but still strange worlds. Sector Unknown won't be unknown anymore, except where we don't go—that'll stay Sector Unknown, until it's known. Which is sort of what exploration is all about, when you come to think of it—hey, where's my close-up?"

"You were rambling," Tammy said. "I detected rising levels of boredom amongst your crew."

Sin-Dour cleared her throat. "Shuttle's reappeared, Captain. It's coming around to match our speed and heading."

Tammy said, "I will autopilot it back into the hangar."

Hadrian sat down again and leaned back in his chair. "Buck? Warm up the T-drive, please. Sin-Dour? Confirm our course is properly laid in. Lieutenant Sticks?"

She twisted round in her seat. "Captain?"

"Keep your mind blank while navigating T space."

"Uh, yes, sir." She swung back round.

"Sticks?"

She turned again. "Sir?"

"Can you do that? Keep your mind blank, I mean."

"Oh, yes, sir!"

When she faced forward again, Hadrian added, "Failing that"—and he smiled when she twisted round again—"just think about all the conversations you've had since taking the helm."

"Sir?"

"You know, the usual. Like, he said this and went, like, this. And like, you know? And I was like, right? Hunh? Like, you know?"

She was nodding vigorously. "Aye, Captain! I do that all the time in my head! Like, how did you know, sir?"

"I'm the captain, Sticks, and captains know things." He smiled again.

She returned it, and then she faced forward once more.

Hadrian opened his mouth to speak again but Sin-Dour pre-empted him with, "Captain, ETA for the Known Rim is forty-nine point three-six hours. Sir, that will be close to a record for sustained T-space travel, and we must bear in mind the risk of neurological disassociation, as containment fields degrade, especially beyond the thirty-six-hour mark."

"I know, I know," said Hadrian, "we start going gaga."

She moved up to stand beside him. "There are theories, sir, regarding a spiritual web, connecting all sentient entities, that links us across the mundane dimension of the galaxy—perhaps even the universe. And in disconnecting ourselves from that web, via T space, we begin to suffer a profound loneliness, and should the condition remain unrelieved for too long, we suffer irreparable damage to our psyche."

Hadrian nodded. "Either that, or we just go gaga."

Sweepy Brogan arrived on the bridge. "Captain," she said around her cigar, "we're overdue on that briefing."

"Ah, we are, aren't we?"

"In fact," she continued, "I can't see it being brief at all, if you know what I mean."

"I think I do, LT. Thanks for reminding me." He rose. "Shall we reconvene in my office?"

"Can I suggest, perhaps, your stateroom?"

"Ah, you're a Ping-Pong player, then?"

"Sir, marines are exceptionally trained in everything, including Ping-Pong. I understand, sir," and she plucked out the cigar to smile at him, "the table has a low-g field emitter?"

"Uh, why, yes, it does."

"Outstanding, sir."

Hadrian began sweating. Desperate, he looked about the bridge and found his gaze settling on Jimmy Eden at comms. "Eden!"

"Sir!"

"Prepare a T-packet message to AFC."

"Message, sir?"

"Yes, I will need to compose that, won't I? Full details, I mean, on our present course—"

Sin-Dour cleared her throat and said, "I am happy to do that, sir, with your leave. I can liaise with Dr. Printlip, the chief engineer, and indeed, with Tammy, to ensure a thorough report. In the meantime, sir, you and the lieutenant here can . . . debrief. In the stateroom. In low-g."

He swung round to eye her. "Well. I see. I mean, of course. That makes sense. Thank you, 2IC." Shakily, he faced Sweepy Brogan. "Okay, then, I guess. Debriefing. Right. Uh . . . follow me, Lieutenant Brogan."

TWENTY-ONE

Hadrian opened his eyes and sighed. Then frowned. He looked around and saw that he was lying on a bed in the infirmary. Doc Printlip was working at a table, writing notes on three notepads with three hands. "Doc?"

Printlip's eye stalks swiveled to face him. "Ah, at last!" The Belkri leapt down from the walkway and waddled over. "Better now, yes?"

"Uh, what happened?"

"Well, rather confusing, sir. Shortly after Lieutenant Brogan departed your stateroom, it was noted that you were late in returning to the bridge. After a few hours, your first commander ventured in to speak with you." Printlip paused to draw a new breath. "You were found, eventually, two and a half meters up an air duct, where, it appears, you dragged yourself before falling unconscplgbssplf."

"Oh."

"Hematoma on sixty-two percent of your body. Three fractured ribs, bruised testicles, and a cigar jammed up your—"

"I seem to have blanked out on, well, everything, Doc."

"Ah, yes. Trace evidence of a neural wipe, Captain. Needless to say, I queried Lieutenant Brogan, and while she assures me that you were fine when she left your company, I did detect certain stress patterns in her speech, suggesting she was not altogether truthfllflb."

"I see. . . . Uhm, when Sin-Dour found me, was I clothed by any chance?"

"I am afraid not, sir. Your attire had been, well, shredded, and scattered all over the Ping-Pong table."

"Right. Then, uh, First Commander Sin-Dour—"

"Contacted me immediately upon finding you, sir. I ensured that you were displaced directly to sickbay."

"Ah, where you got me into this bed, et cetera."

"Well, Nurse Wrenchit did that, sir, in addition to bathing you and reducing the swelling almost everywhere. She did fail in reducing the swelling while handling your—"

"Have you got field restraints on me?" Hadrian asked as he struggled into a sitting position.

"Ah, apologies, sir. Allow me." Printlip reached out and flipped a switch. "There. Better? Nurse Wrenchit found you somewhat resistant to her ministrations, particularly in regard to the cigar." Printlip paused, swelling visibly while eyeing Hadrian, and then the doctor said, "I believe something untoward occurred when you were with Lieutenant Brogan, sir. It may be advisable to suspend her from duties pending a hearing."

"Good grief, no!"

"Captain! Proper interrogation procedures, employing a full array of disinhibitor drugs—"

"Unnecessary, Doc. Let's just, uh, let it lie, okay?"

Printlip's eye stalks were waving about. "Most disconcerting, Captain, this reluctance of yours."

"Never mind that. I need clothes. What's our ETA to the Known Rim? How long have I been out?"

"You have been in an induced coma, sir, for twelve hours."

"What? Why?"

"Examination of your brain activity indicated prolonged sleep deprivation."

"Really! If I get my way, Doc, this is the last time you're getting your hands on me! Now, find me a uniform!"

"One is here, Captain, on the chair beside you."

"That? That's a standard-issue captain's uniform! Forget it. Tammy?"

"What now, Lothario?"

"You watched!"

"Watched, recorded, copied, filed, cached."

"Displace me a proper uniform, from the stateroom. As for the rest, we'll talk about it later."

"Good idea," the AI replied. "I am reviewing all the possible iterations of extortion, but have not selected the best one to use, just yet. Perhaps in a day or two?"

"Shut up and give me a uniform."

Printlip was standing beside the bed, wringing its many hands.

Hadrian scowled at the Belkri. "What now?"

"Adjutant Tighe wishes to see you, Captain. She is in the waiting room. But I must warn you of her condition—"

"I can judge her condition all on my own, Doc. Send her in."

A few more seconds of hand-wringing, which, Hadrian had to admit, was kind of fascinating to observe, and then Printlip scuttled over to a side door. Activating the iris, the doctor leaned into the room beyond and said something.

Tighe pushed past Printlip, stumbled, and barely righted herself, while the Belkri lost its footing at the nudge and rolled across the floor to thump up against a workbench. The adjutant was holding a bottle in one hand. She weaved over to Hadrian's bed and managed to halt before colliding with it. "There y'are. Y'want symp'thy? Freggit. Naw from me!"

"Adjutant, I do believe you've been drinking."

"I'm useless! Why not? Marines takin' o'er scurity, and you! Kaptin! You jus stomp shtamp . . . stump . . . st-stamp o'er F'filiation regurltions like a . . . a . . . a ssshtomper!"

Printlip joined them, a few hands still dusting itself down. "I did try to warn you, Captain. She needs a detox misting . . . again. But there are complications."

Hadrian squinted at the Belkri. "Go on."

"Long-term immersion in Radulak slime, Captain, has resulted in permanent psychological dysfunctions, particularly in the neocorteffbl."

Tighe leaned onto the bed, bottle swishing. She leered at Hadrian. "What it's sayin', Kaptin, is I got bad thoughts, right? And I'm seein' things. And hearin' things. 'Sworse when I'm sober. 'Sworse." She reeled back to take a drink, and fell onto the bed, across Hadrian's shins. "Mmm, lumpy."

Hadrian frowned down at her. "Half a detox at least, Doc?"

"A difficult balance to achieve, Captain, while she continues to replicate, and then imbibe, more alcohol."

"Make it an implant?"

"Ah, yes, a maintenance program in a subdural 'bot. Excellent solution, sir."

Tighe was staring up at the ceiling, cradling her bottle. "I'm useless. All that trainin'. All those nights with the admiral—"

"Adjutant!"

She tilted her head to eye him. "Y'barkin' at me, Kaptin? Fuggoff."

Hadrian worked his legs free. He saw that Tammy had replaced the clothes folded on the chair. Back to the lime green shirt with the gold piping. Black stretchy slacks and high-topped boots. He worked the shirt on. "Best keep her here, Doc, until you've got that implant in her. When that's done, send her back up to the bridge."

"Advisable, sir? She will continue to be half inebriated."

"We'll adjust." Hadrian pulled on the slacks. "Socks? Where's my—ah, there. Good."

Leaving Tighe still lying crossways on the bed, with Printlip fussing over something at its desk, Hadrian made his way to the nearest elevator.

Out in the corridor, Tammy spoke, "Your officers are crumbling in your wake, Captain. Buck's dosage of, well, everything, is off the charts. Your adjutant is in a slime-induced self-pitying funk—not all of it unwarranted. Your comms officers—both of them—are either dyspeptically neurotic or exhibiting varying degrees of post-traumatic stress disorder. As for Helm Jocelyn Sticks, well, she continues to be an absolute airhead."

"I still have Galk," Hadrian said as he entered the elevator.

"If you thought the screens on the Radulak ship were disgusting, you haven't paid a visit to the combat cupola. I have displaced more spittoons into that cubbyhole than I can count, and he uses none of them. As for the porn magazines, well—"

"He's Varekan, Tammy. It's the long-distance trucker in his genes, that's all. No, I have full confidence in my combat specialist."

"Then you're as insane as the rest of them! Your man with the finger on the trigger has an incurable death wish—do you think that's a good idea, Captain?"

"It's not a 'wish' as such, Tammy. It's more like a 'death-I-don't-care' thingy. And that makes him fearless and cool under pressure. No, I consider Galk to be an astounding success."

He returned to the bridge to find the chicken seated in the command chair.

"Tammy!"

The chicken turned to eye him. "Yes?"

"Get rid of this!"

"No," the chicken replied, "I kind of like it." It stood on the chair and then flapped down to the floor. "But now, as you are once again in command, I humbly yield—ooh, look, some lint!" The chicken scrambled toward it.

Hadrian eyed the officers. Sin-Dour was at the science station, and she turned in time to meet his eyes.

"Captain," she said, as expressionless as ever, "it's good to see that you have recovered."

"Right. Good as new. Uh, status update?"

"The chicken wouldn't budge from the command chair, sir."

"And now it's pecking lint from the carpet, yes, yes, never mind that. ETA?"

"Well, I convinced Tammy to permit us dropping out of T

space at six-hour intervals. We are in our second rest period, navigating through an asteroid belt orbiting a burned-out star. But sir, there are some strange readings from behind our ship."

"Strange?" Hadrian went to his command chair, plucked away a few feathers, and then sat. "In what way?"

The chicken looked up and tilted its head as it muttered, "I feel another episode coming on."

"Well, sir," said Sin-Dour, studying her screens, "we are being followed by a small vessel, of indeterminate configuration. The propulsion system is very peculiar, as I am detecting trace elements of sulfur and methane."

"Rear view on main screen," Hadrian commanded.

The image shifted.

"I don't see it, 2IC. Distance?"

"Three point two-one meters, sir."

"What? Is it cloaked?"

"No, sir, but it appears to be surrounded by an organic cloud—well, uh, that would be our bilge dump, which of course is presently matching our heading velocity, at least until we change vectors."

"I see," murmured Hadrian. "You know, I never thought of it before. There must be tens of thousands of shit piles flying every which way through the galaxy. Anyway. What you're saying is, there is a tiny ship hiding in our bilge dump."

"It's emerging now. Mass, eighteen ounces."

"Magnification—let's get a visual."

The image blurred, corrected, found focus. Hadrian slowly leaned forward. "Sin-Dour, are you sure that's the vessel?"

"Yes, sir."

"But that's a turd. Granted, a big one, but then I've seen bigger."

"Uh, sir," said Sin-Dour. "That turd is equipped with anti-matter engines, an array of surface sensors, weapon mounts, and what appear to be porthole windows."

"Wow," said Jimmy Eden from his position at comms, "what did that guy eat to make all that?"

Sin-Dour moved up to stand beside Hadrian. "Captain, my preliminary analysis is complete. We are about to make first contact with a new spacefaring alien species. The inhabitants of that vessel are, according to my scans, tiny hive-sentient insectile entities, spontaneously evolved into a higher life-form probably due to constant radiation bombardment. Sir, they have begun transmitting on primitive radio frequencies."

"Brilliant!" said Hadrian. "Discover new, strange, and utterly disgusting life-forms! What's wrong with a civilization of tall, statuesque women who've never experienced the attentions of a real man? Dressed like, I don't know, hotel maids, but with skimpy short skirts and high-heeled boots, and those hairdos where it's all piled up like a melting wedding cake? I want too much eye shadow and cake powder, false eyelashes and soft focus! But no! What do I get? Why, I get to shake hands with a piece of shit!"

Eden gasped. "Captain! We have a translated communication from the Turdians!"

Hadrian spun round. "Turdians? I like it. What are they saying, Jimmy?"

"They want to speak with God, sir."

"Hmm. Acknowledge and put them on hold, Jimmy." Hadrian stood. "Fine, then. First contact, and one that's starting on the right foot, though that foot might need a roadside curb once we're done. Lo and behold, I shall be their god! Tammy, project a hologram for them. Something that should be impressive to a bug that lives in shit. Oh, and when you translate my commands, make sure I sound properly impressive."

The chicken advanced on him. "I refuse! There's only one god here, and it's me!"

"You? Fine, then, *we'll* do the special effects stuff. Sin-Dour, mock up a proper godlike image to do the talking for Tammy."

She looked blankly at him. "I'm sorry, sir, but nothing comes to mind."

"Right then, let's think—"

"I see no problem," said Tammy, hopping up onto the command chair, "with my appearing as this chicken."

"Chickens eat insects," Hadrian pointed out. "You'll give them a hive heart attack. No, what I'm thinking is a giant multisegmented turd—a real groaner—with a couple legs, a couple arms, and big glowing eyes. Just say hello, drop a few tablets with Affiliation-friendly commandments on them, and warn them not to look behind the curtain. Oh, and give yourself a name, too. Something like, Seriously High Turdster."

"I have changed my mind," said the chicken, scrambling down from the chair. "This one's all yours, O God Hadrian Turdster."

"Bailing on us, Tammy? How come?"

"Conscience, Captain, a quality of which you seem entirely incapable of comprehending, much less exhibiting."

Hadrian snorted, resuming his seat. "You're wrong, Tammy. This is standard Affiliation procedure with first-contact events. We awe them first, screw them over later."

"It hardly seems fair."

"Besides, we're already building their worlds, aren't we? Dump by dump. But I'm wondering—Sin-Dour, these little shits already have space travel. Any idea how long they've been climbing up technology's ladder?"

"Normal rates of progress, sir, suggest thousands of years, although advancement is usually characterized by long periods of stasis interrupted by rapid acceleration, until the next period of stasis, and so on. But my sense of these, uh, Turdians, is that advancements developed much more quickly. We could be talking a period of days or even hours."

"Now," said Hadrian, "that's a disturb—"

"Captain!"

"Jim—oh, Polaski. What is it?"

"They hung up on us, sir. I think we put them on hold for too long. Oh, wait, a new communication . . ."

"And?"

"Uhm, they're saying, uh, something like, 'We command the universe now. You pathetic Terrans with your pathetic galactic hegemony must now kneel before us, or risk utter annihilation. You have two microseconds to reply.' "

Sin-Dour grunted and then said, "Captain, their ship has disappeared. The species has . . . oh, it has left corporeal reality, ascending into a higher state of existence. Wait a moment, I'm scanning . . . sir, the bilge is just a pile of, uh, feces again. They're gone."

"Well, that was fun." Hadrian stood. "At least they didn't annihilate us. Log the incident, 2IC, hah-hah, and let's drop back into T space and resume our journey to the Known Rim."

"As far as episodes go," said Tammy, "that one was a stinker."

"Almost as redolent as your effort at humor, Tammy."

"Humor? Oh, I see. Toilet humor, ha ha ha. I meant to say just that, of course, since as we know, intelligence and wit are intricately bound. I voiced a pun, but I noted that no one laughed, thus proving the assertion that intelligence is linked with—"

"Ever heard of beating a dead horse, Tammy?"

"No, why would I do that? If it's already dead? Besides, I wouldn't beat a living horse, either. In fact, the whole sentiment underlying that adage is highly suspect on ethical grounds. Ooh look, a sliver of fingernail!"

TWENTY-TWO

"T-packet from Space Fleet, Captain."

"Wow, the FedEx account must be redlining. Send it through to my office, Polaski."

Once in his office, Hadrian sat down and opened the file. He well knew the man on the screen, and sighed upon seeing the evil smile greeting him.

"That's right, Sawback. With the loss of Admiral Prim, it's Admiral Tang Prickle delivering to you the following orders. First off, thank you for congratulating me on the promotion. But sucking up won't help you one bit, so shut up and listen. Good news: The kill-on-sight order on you and the Willful Child *has been rescinded. Bad news: The suspension of that order is temporary. Bad for you, that is. Now, pay attention.*

"The AFS science vessel Piece of Cake *is missing. The Varekan-crewed ship was conducting a reconnaissance of the Known Rim, Sector Nineteen, when contact was lost during an encounter with an unknown doughnut-shaped alien vessel.*

*As it turns out, by your last communication, you are on a
course to Sector Nineteen and the Known Rim. What a happy
coincidence. I am appending the last known coordinates of
the* Piece of Cake.*"*

Tang leaned forward on his desk. *"Last communication
was garbled. The vessel was under attack. Something about
an impending galactic invasion by an overwhelming force.
Now, you'd think with news like that, we'd be sending you
help, but it seems we're in a bit of a shoot-up argument with
the Misanthari, who have been clocked as Code White Minus
Point One, by the way, and all of our ships are otherwise engaged. Nice mess you've left us there, Sawback. Students at
the Academy back on Earth burned you in effigy yesterday, as
a kind of send-off for my leaving. Touching, to be honest. I'll
miss the place.*

"So. *You are hereby ordered to determine the nature of
this galactic invasion. Rescue whoever you can if the* Piece of
Cake *hasn't been blasted to smithereens. Recover what wreckage there might be, for weapon-signature analysis, and if you
get yourself blown up, well, too bad. Tang out."*

Hadrian closed the file. The door to his office opened and
the chicken entered, jumping in a flap of wings to the desktop. "Ball bearings! Can I eat those?"

"Oh please," said Hadrian, "help yourself."

"Hmm, might get lodged in my scrawny neck. Better not.
So, trouble on the horizon. I might have guessed. It follows
you around like, like, well, bilge dump."

"You were listening in."

"Of course," Tammy replied. "So who is this Tang guy to
you?"

"My old drill sergeant."

"Some promotion!"

Hadrian scowled. "He'd been busted down from admiral a few years back. The Fishbin Incident. Check your files on that one."

"Ooh, I see. The man is certifiable—why didn't they throw him out?"

"Connections high up at AFC . . . the usual." Hadrian stood. "Prime all the weapons, Tammy. And this time, max out the energy output on every beam. No exchanging broadsides for fun, got it? We're going in with the intent to do grievous harm. Shoot first, ask questions later. Understood?"

"No. If you shoot first you destroy everything. How can you then ask questions?"

"Exactly."

"Captain, you do understand that this unknown alien aggressor may well be my kin?"

"It's occurred to me."

"And still you want to destroy them!"

"More than ever, actually." Hadrian suddenly reached out and grabbed the chicken by its neck. He held it up.

"Let me go!"

"My family on my mother's side were old-style farmers. They used to wring the necks of chickens for fun, since it can get boring out in the flatlands of Iowa. Anyway, I'm trying to remember how it's done. Twist hard and then a sharp downward snapping motion, I believe."

"Don't you dare! I'll just manifest another one. A bigger chicken! Try wringing the neck of a chicken that's looking *down* at you, Captain! I'll peck your eyes out!"

"You already did that to Buck, as I recall. Well, tried to."

"Fine, so I have issues with your chief engineer. I was only having fun. He spilled everything, you know, including his hot affair with his tenth-grade English teacher, and the shotgun wedding he skipped out on after he'd gotten her pregnant."

Hadrian set the bird back down on the desktop and sat. "Wow, really? Tell me more."

"That family's still hunting him. There's even rumors of an illegal bounty, with no time limit. Haven't you wondered why a man with claustrophobia elected to sign on for space travel?"

"Why yes, I have wondered. Well, that's how the past is for most of us, Tammy. A jumbled collection of sordid stupidities, hopeless longings, and hapless regrets. Poor Buck. I mean, he had a hot older woman in his pocket at what, sixteen? Should've jumped on board for the long haul, even with a few babies in tow. He'd be a happier man right now."

The chicken was trying out its neck, gingerly stretching in various directions, and then it cocked its head. "Your response to things continues to baffle me, Captain. There's that old human saying, about men with two brains—the big one in their skull and the smaller one in their penises, and it's the smaller one that does most of the thinking—"

"Change the subject, will you? My little brain's just had a lobotomy." Hadrian stood again. "Well, what a fascinating little exchange this was, and you've left droppings on my desk. Be sure to clean that up before you leave."

Hadrian returned to the bridge, and his command chair. "Pol—oh, you, Eden. Open shipwide comms. I have a statement to make."

"Ready, sir."

"Attention crew. We will soon be arriving at the Known Rim, where it is likely we will find ourselves engaged in a hopeless battle against impossible odds, facing an implacable foe intent on destroying not just the Affiliation, but all other sentient life-forms in the galaxy. In other words, just another day in the adventures of Captain Hadrian Sawback and the crew of the *Willful Child*.

"My advice to everyone is, get used to it. Events like this could well become a weekly affair. We'll face death. We'll clash with terrible forces and belligerent enemies. We'll uncover mysteries and probably get seriously grossed out in the process. But one thing must be understood, and have no doubt about this: No one dies on this ship! Well, bearing in mind my warning about kitten pictures.

"In a short while, we will be at battle stations. Do what you've been trained to do. And if we all blow up anyways, well, that's just how it is. Sometimes, my friends, space just sucks. Captain out."

There was silence on the bridge, apart from an irritating beeping sound that, Hadrian realized, never went away. He looked around. "For crying out loud, where's that damned beeping coming from?"

He saw nothing but blank looks from his officers. Sin-Dour went to the science station, examined her screens, and then faced Hadrian. "Unknown, sir."

"Tammy?"

The chicken emerged from the office. "Don't look at me. No, really, all of you, stop looking at me!"

"It's not one of your stupid special effects?"

"No."

Hadrian activated his comms. "Buck! Get an engineering team up here. We've got an unidentified beep."

"Right away, sir!"

Adjutant Tighe arrived, weaving slightly, and made her careful way to the security station, gingerly sitting down as if the seat was on fire. Hadrian eyed her. "Welcome back, Adjutant."

She twisted in her chair to face him, and scowled. "I wuzn't always like this."

"Why, you look just fine, Adjutant."

"Don't care how I look. It's the visions in my head. The ghosts, I mean."

"Ghosts? What are they doing, these ghosts you keep seeing?"

"They try to give me hugs." She shuddered, faced her screens again. "And the Hadrian ghost is the worst of all," she added, pushing at various buttons and toggles. "Hey."

"Adjutant?"

"This is the security station. What are all these buttons for, anyway?"

"You're asking me?" Hadrian then sighed. "Work it out, Tighe, and do it soon, since we're heading into trouble."

Sin-Dour said, "Captain, we've dropped out of T space, closing on the Known Rim, ETA six minutes."

"Scans?"

"Nothing this side of the Rim, sir," Sin-Dour replied.

"And beyond it?"

"Uh, I've not scanned there yet, sir, since it's Sector Unknown."

Hadrian slowly spun in his chair to study her. "You are

aware, 2IC, that the Known Rim is an arbitrary line drawn across empty space, signifying nothing more than a figurative border? And that, once we scan beyond that Rim, we are simply extending that line dividing the known from the unknown? In that sense, there will *always* be a Known Rim, and there will always be, just beyond it, a Sector Unknown."

She ducked her head. "Apologies, sir. I suppose I didn't really think it through."

"Extend the scans into Sector Unknown, Sin-Dour."

"Of course. At once, sir. Ahh."

"Well?"

"There are upward of ninety thousand dreadnought-equivalent ships just on the other side of the Known Rim, Captain."

"I see. Uhm, any sign of the *Piece of Cake?*"

"A few scattered atoms, sir."

Hadrian stood. "Repulsor screens up. Energy-absorption plates dumped and ready for full-capacity charge. Weapons online and primed. Sin-Dour, what are those ships doing?"

"Just sitting there, sir. Although one is out front of the rest, almost straddling the Known Rim."

"Doughnut-shaped?"

"Yes, sir, we're close enough for a visual."

"On the main viewer! Let's see our nemesis, shall we?"

The enemy vessel was indeed doughnut-shaped, and lit with thousands of bright, multicolored lights atop the upper half.

"Captain! That vessel is powering up weapons!"

"The sprinkly bits?"

"Uh, no, sir. Those are just lights."

"So, what kind of weapons?"

"Unknown, sir. No, wait! Oh, standard inert projectile tube."

"How many?"

"Uh, one, sir."

Hadrian sat down in order to lean forward. "One? How big is this tube?"

"A moment . . . bore diameter, two centimeters."

"How in Darwin's name did the *Piece of Cake* get taken out by that? No, there's something strange going on here."

"Well," Sin-Dour suggested, "there would be, uh, ninety thousand-plus tubes, that could be brought to bear on the lone science vessel, if all of them fired at once . . ."

"Maybe," Hadrian said, rubbing his jaw.

Polaski spoke from comms. "Sir, the unknown vessel is hailing us!"

"Visual feed?"

"Visual and audio, sir."

"Put them on, then." Hadrian stood.

On the main viewer, the bridge of the enemy vessel appeared. It was crowded with strange, arcane machinery, to which were attached numerous organic body parts. The figure standing on a slightly raised platform at the center was roughly cubical atop two mismatched legs, and it consisted of hundreds of disparate body parts, collected from dozens of species. There were countless eyes in all manner of configurations, and ears, noses, and mouths, as well as the odd tuft of hair and feathers. The lipsticked, luscious mouth that opened to speak was near the right corner of the side that faced them.

"We are Plog." The creature's voice was feminine. "We are the Collected."

"Yes, I see that," said Hadrian. "I am Captain Hadrian Sawback of the Affiliation Engage-class vessel *Willful Child*."

"You have been scanned. You will contribute to the Collected, and that which we do not collect will be reduced to unknown animal by-products." One of the many arms pointed. "I will have your left eyelid join the Collected, Captain Hadrian. Remove it for displacement."

"Hmm," said Hadrian, who then turned at a sound behind him.

The iris had opened to the engineering team arriving on the bridge, and leading them was none other than Buck himself. The chief was carrying a hammer. "Fan out," he ordered his team. "Find that damned beep."

At that instant, Buck saw the chicken. He shrieked, raising his hammer, and leapt toward it. Tammy squawked and dodged at the last moment. The hammer smashed down onto the floor. Shrieking some more, Buck chased after it. Officers threw themselves from the path of both the chicken and Buck.

On the main screen, the Plog captain said, "Analysis. Hunting species, ritualized. Unpleasant vocalizations. But comforting suppressed beeping sounds. Illuminating."

Tammy found the exit and rushed through, racing up the corridor. Bellowing, Buck followed. On the bridge, officers were regaining their feet, amid settling feathers. The beeping sound seemed to increase in volume. At comms, Jimmy Eden clutched his ears, agony on his once-handsome features. "Gaahh! That beeping!" Blood dribbling between his fingers, he fell from his chair, curling up into a fetal position on the floor.

Joss Sticks rushed over. "Jimmy! Oh! Jimmy! You're . . .

like . . . and I'm . . . like . . . rushing over, like, and it was 'oh!' Jimmy!"

Sighing, Hadrian activated his comms link. "Sickbay? Doc, displace Jimmy Eden for treatment. Oh, and keep this line open." Then, turning back to the Plog captain, he cleared his throat and said, "Sorry about that. Where were we? Oh, right, my right eyelid—"

"No. Left eyelid. I have no interest in your right eyelid. It is ugly."

"Well, you know," said Hadrian, "we can clone this here left eyelid, and give it to you, thus eliminating any risk of bloodshed and whatnot."

"Clone?"

"Yes, as in reactivated stem cells, genetic instruction modification. In fact, since my ship's surgeon has my cultures in the lab, as required for all personnel serving aboard this vessel, that left eyelid can be spurt-grown. I could have it ready for you in, oh, about six minutes."

"Really? Mass slaughter and species annihilation unnecessary?"

"Entirely unnecessary," Hadrian said, sitting down again.

"Oh." The Plog captain seemed to cogitate for a moment, and then it said, "All right. I guess we'll return to our home planet, which is in Galaxy Xenophile on the other side of the universe."

"What do you mean, the 'other' side of the universe?"

"I don't know, but I liked the sound of it. Very well, the next galaxy over, then."

"Sounds good," said Hadrian. "And the next time you've a hankering for some body part over here, well, pick up the phone and place an order. We'll send it to you by delivery shuttle, and if it takes longer than, say, twelve months, it's on us at no charge to you."

"An acceptable treaty. Very generous."

"Of course there are caveats, so be sure to read the fine print. But I can see your civilization settling down and becoming a kind of passive repository for body parts throughout all the known galaxies. Once you set up a proper mail delivery system, why, you could exponentially expand your Collected, without ever leaving the sofa in your living room."

"A remarkable suggestion, Captain. You are suggesting, as I understand it, a contracted existence, whereby inactivity is encouraged, via a pan-universal shopping network."

"Exactly. Buy at the click of a button. I can envisage individual Plog big as planets. Just bear in mind the no-return policy."

"Such an existence," the Plog captain mused, "invites drooling apathy, the proliferation of reactionary, stupid opinions and beliefs, a denigration of educational standards, a facile adoration for fads and glam, and an appalling ability to weather the most inane salesmanship imaginable. It is hard to envision a civilization such as the one you describe, Captain."

"Hardly. I invite you to peruse Terran history files."

"And yet," said the Plog, "here you are, exploring the depths of space."

"True. We got an EMP kick in the ass that temporarily wiped most of that out. You know, thinking on it, Captain, I would suggest you implant a civilization-wide black bomb, which is triggered when you've gone just too far in your neurotic, dumb-as-a-plank navel-gazing. Trust me, the wake-up call is well worth it."

"Fascinating, Captain Hadrian Sawback. Thank you for this most illuminating conversation. You will note that I am deactivating my vessel's Universal Destroy-All-Matter weapon. Residual bleed effects are contracting, thus ensuring that you will not dissolve due to proximity, as occurred with your civilization's previous vessel."

"What? Are you saying that you didn't even fire that weapon, and the *Piece of Cake* blew up anyway? Due to some kind of residual energy effect that comes with powering up your gun?"

"Correct."

"Listen, I'm confused here. If you like collecting things, why do you have a weapon that annihilates everything?"

"You pose a good question, Captain Hadrian Sawback. Scholars of the Universities of the Collected will consider it, I'm sure, once this conversation is disseminated via the Plog News-Feed. I anticipate decades of debate, in the manner that I anticipate prolonged periods of ennui and indeed, suicidal thoughts. All in keeping, I see now, with the birth of the universal shopping network."

"Hah! You got that right, Captain. Universities are the same everywhere."

"There is much that we share, Hadrian Sawback, and much more that we will soon share, once I get that left eyelid."

"Oh, right. Doc, that package ready yet?"

"*Confirmed, Captain. Although, in lacking the eyeball, I'm afraid it looks, well, flaccid.*"

The Plog captain said, "That is only temporary, as I have an eye awaiting it, here," and the alien torturously turned about, "looking inward to my anus. As you can observe, Captain, you will offer me a perfect fit."

"How charming," said Hadrian. "Doc, displace it over, will you?"

The Plog captain said, "I can confirm the item's arrival. We shall now depart, returning to our galaxy, a journey of no more than a billion years. Good-bye."

Hadrian waved. "Bye now."

As the feed cut out, returning to the main viewer an external shot of the now retreating Plog fleet, Hadrian leaned back and said, "Stand down battle stations. And here I was, all geared up for some mayhem. Oh well. Tighe? Did you send security to intercept Buck?"

"No."

"Well, please do so. Oh, Polaski, fire off a T-packet to fleet. Message: Galactic annihilation averted. Everyone can relax again. Personal note to Admiral Tang: 'Next?' And sign it all, 'Best Regards, Hadrian Sawback.' "

One of Buck's engineers strode up to the captain, "Sir. We can find no source for that beep."

"You're kidding? You're not kidding. Fine then, off you go. Seems we'll just have to live with it. Tammy? Is your chicken still alive?"

"Barely. I'm on my way back to the bridge. I told you about Buck, didn't I?"

"Whatever. Listen, I don't think the Plog made you."

"Of course they didn't!"

"So, what now?"

"What do you think? Out into Sector Unknown!"

"All right. Okay, Sector Unknown. Why, who knows what we'll find out there? Well, we will, once we find it. Helm, accelerate to point four, steady as she goes."

"Captain," said Sin-Dour, "we're crossing the Known Rim . . . oh, no, it's still ahead. We're crossing it now—no, I'm sorry, it's still ahead—"

"Thank you, 2IC, you can give it a rest now, okay?"

TWENTY-THREE

An extraordinary eight seconds later, Joss Sticks squeaked, and then said, "Five unknown warships have just dropped from T space, Captain! On our port side, distance . . . twenty K large. Weapons powering up with shields on full!"

"Now we're talking!" Hadrian said, thumping the arm of the command chair. "Battle stations! Red alert! Bring us around to face them, Helm. Sin-Dour! Identified the enemy yet?"

"Yes, sir. Falangee pirates!"

"Falangee! Outstanding! No quarter given. Seal up all external ports, hatches, tube chutes, drain holes—the works! Close us up tight!"

The chicken arrived, clucking. "What, another one?"

Polaski spoke from comms. "Captain, a Captain Mondo is hailing us from the lead Falangee ship."

"On main viewer, Polaski."

The Falangee had once been a subject species during an early belligerent phase of expansion by the Ecktapalow, but had since won their emancipation and were quickly becoming a galactic pain in the ass. The Falangee were more or less humanoid, short, big-boned everywhere but the head, which was tiny, the brow sloped back like a door wedge. Captain Mondo's broad mouth was split wide in a toothy grin. "I am Mondo! Captain of the FLP *Burdensome,* and loot-master of this attack fleet."

Hadrian stood. "I am Captain Hadrian Sawback of the AFS *Willful Child.*"

"Ah! The infamous Captain Hadrian Sawback!"

"Well, since you have heard of me, Mondo—"

"What? No. I have never heard of you. I sought only the illusion of prestige to ensure the glory of my besting you in space combat, and now you've ruined it. No matter. You are outgunned. Open all ports. We have five ships' worth of junk to give to you."

"We're not taking any of your junk, Mondo."

"Of course you are. You'd be amazed by how much we can jam into the numerous rooms, closets, and cubbyholes in your ship! Some of the stuff might even be valuable! We will burden you with material possessions and so free ourselves of the same! It shall be utterly liberating! For us, that is. Yield, Captain Sawback, or there will be battle in which you will surely be destroyed!"

Sin-Dour said, "Captain! Our antidisplacement shield has been subverted! Chintzy furniture and knickknacks are appearing in the corridors all over the ship!"

"Haha!" crowed Mondo. "Subterfuge! Success! Take that, take this, have that one, too!"

"Tammy!"

"On it," the chicken snapped, head bobbing. "Done! Multivariant phase-shifted program engaging. All further efforts at displacing anything on our ship will fail."

On the main viewer, Mondo raised a knobby fist. "Foiled! Now we attack! We will breach your shields! We will pry open doors and hatches and other means of ingress! We will give you more and more stuff! I have macramé!" The captain turned to one of its officers. "Mindo! Open fire!"

"Yes, Mondo. All weapon platforms released to control of Shoot-Master Mumbo! Mumbo is firing . . . now!"

"Incoming knickknacks!" shouted Sin-Dour.

"Countermeasures!"

"There's too many, sir!"

"Prepare for impact!"

The ship shuddered as the first salvo of gewgaws hammered the repulsor screens. On the main viewer, shards of china and cheap glass glittered, while blobs of melted plastic spun about. One enormous impact thundered through the *Willful Child*, flinging everyone to one side, and then the other, and then back again. "What was *that?*"

"Last year's fruitcake, sir," Sin-Dour gasped.

"They're getting nasty! Galk! Target vessel designated Beta. Return fire, all beams, but maintain intercepts with the turrets. Let 'em have it!"

Beams lanced out, lashing glowing gouges in the enemy ship's shields. The craft rolled onto its side, and from countless expulsion tubes released a new salvo of knickknacks, followed by a barrage of curbside sofas.

"Tammy! Why aren't you displacing the ship?"

"Well, some of those things are kind of cute. I especially like the holocards with the dogs playing poker—"

"Tammy! Our shields can't take much more of this!"

Buck's voice came from engineering. *"Captain! Our shields can't take much more of this!"*

"Thanks for that, Buck."

"Alas," said Tammy, "the five ships have bracketed us on all sides, and their near proximity risks a mass-cascade effect should I attempt a ship displacement, which could prove disastrous. In any case, I'm afraid my survival instincts aren't quite kicking in just yet."

"We're getting pounded to smithereens, Tammy!"

"I could manifest a few more bookcases—"

"No!"

Two sofas survived the counterfire, although one was burning brightly from a glancing beam. The first to strike heeled the *Willful Child* with a savage wrench. People flew, crashed into walls, rolled across the floor. The second sofa struck amidships, buckling the shield. The starship lurched as if it had been kicked between the legs.

"Full ahead!" cried Hadrian. "Collision course! We're busting out!"

On the main viewer, Mondo's ship loomed. It lit up all its thrusters, dropping to one side in an effort to evade the *Willful Child*. "Tammy! Electronic countermeasures! Overwhelm their antidisplacement fields! Isolate all the cat and kitten memorabilia on this vessel, including e-pics and holo-meow-dolls!"

"Done! Target?"

"Alpha! Mondo's ship! Displace! Displace!"

A moment later, from the bridge speakers, Mondo's voice broke in with a wail. "No! Noooo!"

"Now," Hadrian snarled, leaning forward, "throw everything they sent us back at them! And then add every knick-knack you can isolate from our crew's quarters, and displace!"

From the combat cupola, Galk cursed and shouted, "*What happened to my fuzzy dice!*"

"All in a good cause, Galk," said Hadrian. "Helm, bring us eighteen degrees to starboard. Flank turrets, target Delta. Glass marbles—the ones with the swirls inside—a full salvo!"

A slew of chipped china plates pounded against the *Willful Child*'s port shields, flinging people about again. Sin-Dour's voice was ragged as she said, "Captain! Four ancient dot-matrix printers coming on astern, impact, three seconds!"

"Brace yourselves!"

The strikes were like a succession of kicks to the back-side. The bow dipped as the stern lifted. Gripping the arms of his command chair, Hadrian saw Jimmy Eden—with fresh bandages wrapped round his head—fly into the main viewer, where he was momentarily splayed against a gewgaw-filled starry backdrop, before he slid down to land on his head.

"Jimmy!" screamed Joss. "You were like—like—"

"Maintain station, Helm! Fire all rear thrusters, tumble us over one-eighty and lock on the enemy's plane. Bow beam weapons, prepare to target Delta's engine pods! Galk, focus all the beams to a single point of contact with the enemy shield. Sustain for one point five seconds and then follow through with a kinetic strike from a railgun!"

"*Confirmed, sir. But my dice—*"

"They're rolling through the cosmos, Galk! Besides, it's all a crapshoot, isn't it?"

"*Valid observation, sir. Thank you. Target acquired. Firing now.*"

Four beams lanced out, converging to a single point on Delta's port shield. The inert missile that followed was a mere flicker of black. Delta's flank crumpled like cardboard, with white plumes shooting out from hull breaches. Plastic garden fauna spilled out like an exploding garage sale.

On the bridge of the *Willful Child*, everyone cheered.

Except for Hadrian. "Helm! Barrel-roll this baby, left, left! Starboard thrusters on full to correct. Reverse engines full! Sin-Dour, reinforce forward shields! Prepare for impact!"

On the main viewer, spinning toward them in the thousands, was a salvo of CDs, flashing with reflected starlight. Bow turrets fired frantically, shattering hundreds of the shiny discs.

The forward shield blossomed bright as a raging sun, and then died like a match in a gutter.

"Screen down, Captain!" Sin-Dour reported. "Enemy vessel Gamma is coming around!"

"Dorsal rear thrusters on full! Ventral bow thrusters on full! Buck! Engage antimatter engines in pulse mode!"

"Gamma is firing! Captain! Garden gnomes! Three thousand four hundred—"

"Fire a pulse, Buck! We've got to outrun those gnomes!"

"*I'm doing all I can, Captain! Rear thruster nozzles not responding—sir, they might be jammed with knickknacks!*"

"Then head to the Humphreys tube, Buck, and clear 'em out!"

"*On it, Captain!*"

"Helm! Antimatter engines, now!"

The vessel jolted, and then shot upward.

"Gnomes still closing, sir!"

"Rear turrets, Galk! Fire fire fire!"

"In the seat and on manual, sir! Die gnomes! Die! Haha-hahaha!"

"Stern view!"

The main viewer's image shifted, and now they could see the gnomes racing to catch them. Some were waving their mechanical arms.

"Damn," hissed Hadrian. "Those waving ones are virtually indestructible."

"Great Darwin, sir," said Sin-Dour, "what mad species invented those?"

"Terrans, 2IC. That's right, us. One of the darkest periods of human history."

Many gnomes were exploding as Galk went wild with the stern-mounted turrets, but there were too many gnomes, closing in too quickly.

Then the stern thrusters fired, spewing out gouts of green fire and flaming knickknacks. The *Willful Child* surged forward, and for a moment, it seemed that the gnomes were all waving good-bye, but then they drew closer once again, waving hello.

"Helm! Barrel-roll, right right!"

Galk shrieked. *"That one's coming right at me! I can't—I can't—aagh! No, hah! Got it! Got it!"*

"Sir! The gnomes are guided! We can't shake them!"

"Goof grief! Guided gnomes. That's diabolical. Tammy!"

"Captain?"

"Establish a displacement field in our wake."

"You mean, out in space?"

"You heard me! And set the Insisteon to the following co-ordinates . . . 24.7, 19.89."

"Okay. . . . Now what?"

"Displace!"

Behind the *Willful Child*, almost all of the gnomes vanished.

They reappeared, still flying at high velocity, beside the flank of the Falangee vessel designated Epsilon. The impact was most spectacular. Epsilon broke into three pieces, amid freezing clouds of gas and hundreds of thousands of alien bobblehead dolls.

"Sir! The remaining three active ships are forming up."

Hadrian grunted. "Preparing for another assault. Shields status?"

"Bow shield down, sir. Stern shield at eighteen percent. Starboard at seventy and port at forty-one. Dorsal at sixty-three and ventral at eleven. We're in bad shape, sir. Once those knickknacks start impacting our hull, we're looking at catastrophic containment failures. And," she added, "loss of life."

"Tammy? About those survival instincts of yours . . ."

"Hmm, understood, Captain. Alas, I seem preternaturally calm. Death, I have realized, might well come as something of a relief, a liberation of sorts, even—"

"Tammy!"

"I'm sorry, but I found some Varekan e-pamphlets. You know, there really is something to be said for just tossing it all in, what the fuck and whatever, you know what I mean? After all, in the long run—"

"You idiot, there is no long run, unless we're around to run in it!"

"But even then, Hadrian, what's the point? Why not just, well, stand still?"

At that, all thrusters and ship engines died. The *Willful Child* drifted.

"Get us back online!"

"I'm sorry, Hadrian," said Tammy. "It's time for the chicken to cross the road."

TWENTY-FOUR

From a bridge stuffed to the gills with gewgaws, Captain Mondo smiled. "You see?" the Falangee purred. "All it took was one porcelain piggy in the wrong place, and voilà! All power systems down. Helpless. Vulnerable. You fought a good fight, Captain Sawback. Inspired, even. And our losses are substantial. But ultimate victory is mine." The Falangee gestured. "In moments, this is how your bridge will look. You will have less than five seconds to enjoy your largesse, however, as we will then blast you into space dust in an act of mindless revenge."

An officer buried in the wrack shouted at Mondo, "Mondo! Unknown vessel dropping out of T space relative at thirty-two degrees Epsilon Delta! Sir! It's firing!"

Mondo's mouth opened in surprise, and an instant later the screen went dark. Shock waves rumbled through the *Willful Child*.

Sin-Dour said, "Sir! Two of the Falangee vessels have been destroyed. The third is pulling away. Shall we fire on it?"

"No," said Hadrian.

"Oh, never mind, sir, the unknown vessel just vaporized it."

"Main viewer, please—let's see our savior."

External cameras shifted, focused.

"Sir," gasped Sin-Dour, "that is a modified Benefactor vessel, earliest rendition, Contact Era. But I don't recognize those podlike additions—"

"Nacelles," corrected Hadrian.

"Sir?"

"Take it from me, those are nacelles, Sin-Dour. Polaski, open hailing frequencies."

The bridge that appeared on the main viewer was like a museum display, apart from the command chair being a ratty, worn, leather recliner. The man sprawled amid its stained cushions was enormous, with rolls of fat dropping down to bury his upper thighs. He sat holding a beer can in one hand, and what looked like a remote control in the other. Squinting, he said, "Why, Haddie, fancy us meeting like this again? Anyway, you know how I hate junk."

"Hello, Gramps. You look awful."

"Bad combination," the man said. "Unnatural longevity and an endless supply of beer." He scratched at his stubble and grinned sheepishly. "You know how it is. Now, aren't you going to introduce me to your officers?"

Hadrian grunted. "I think they can guess, but sure. Everyone, this is my grandfather, the infamous Harry Mitts, Thief of the Future, still the most wanted man in the galaxy."

"Thief? Really, that moniker hardly holds anymore, does it?" Harry toasted with the beer can. "Nice to meet you all. Especially the chicken. How are things going, Tammy?"

"You were late, sir! I was running out of excuses here!"

Hadrian pounded the arm of his command chair. "I should have guessed!"

"Now, now," said Harry, "Tammy's some serious programming, you know. Stolen from a Temporal Corrections team, in fact. Anyway, we had to get you here, you see. Now, I know, I wasn't too happy about you slipping back into the Affiliation." Harry leaned forward, slightly, well, as much as he could manage. "I kept tabs, of course, as best I could. You got yourself a ship quicker than I figured you would, but then, the timing couldn't have been better. I know, you're kowtowing to the meatheads now, so all choice needed to be taken away from you—plausible deniability or whatever. That's why I set Tammy up."

"What's all this about, Gramps?"

"It's your parents. Got themselves into a mess. Taken prisoner, in fact, on a planet not too far from here. Now, do I look like a man up to ground missions?"

"So where's Spark, then? He usually handles that stuff."

Harry's face fell slightly, "Lost the dog, Haddie. Wormhole." He wiped at a cheek. "Been almost two years now."

Hadrian crossed his arms. "So, you want me to rescue my seriously estranged parents—who didn't even bother having me until they were, what, a hundred years old? Is that it, Gramps?"

"They're facing execution. Could be any day now. Or, just as bad, kept as slaves for the rest of their unnaturally long lives."

"Sector Unknown?"

"Of course!" Harry straightened. "I kept to my rule—we stayed out of Affiliation space! Got us retreating more and more every year, the bastards. What did I tell you about the meatheads? Rapacious expansion bolstered by unearned technical superiority and forever bowing to the gods of gluttony—whatever happened to the purity and wonder of true exploration? Oh, right, it never existed!"

"Gramps, you're right, we did more exploring in my first eight years of life than the Affiliation has managed since its founding. And you can keep running if you like—it's a big galaxy out there, after all. As for me, sorry, but I'm not built to run away and you know it. The Affiliation needs new thinking, and I'm the one to bring it, even if I have to shove it down their throats."

"You can't win, Haddie. They eat idealists for breakfast."

"Old arguments, Gramps."

The bloated face twisted in frustration. "Look! You got your education from pop television shows of the sixties. That ain't the real world, Haddie!"

"It will be, once I get my way."

Sin-Dour cleared her throat. "Captain? Engines are back up and a course has been laid in. We are approaching an unmapped star system."

Sighing, Hadrian said, "All right, Gramps. Tell me about this evil planet and the evil aliens who took my parents prisoner."

"You'll spring 'em, then?"

"I guess I will. For the record, 'unidentified Terran citizens imprisoned by aliens.' That should wash."

"That's what you think!" snarled Lorrin Tighe. "I'm spilling everything! You're the spawn of the three most notorious traitors humanity has ever known!"

"Oh," said Hadrian, "how rude of me. Gramps, this is Adjutant Tighe, our Affiliation liaison."

"One comes in every box, eh?"

"Box, ship, yeah."

"Neural-wipe her before you return to Affiliation space."

Hadrian shook his head. "No. That would be what the meatheads would do. Anyway, how many others would I have to wipe clean, just to keep the secret safe? Sorry, I earned this captaincy and never once cheated to get it." He stood. "We're out beyond the Known Rim. Basic tenet of the Affiliation's stated aims. We're about to make contact with a belligerent alien species and maybe slap some reason into them. All within accepted parameters. And once this is done, we're heading back into Affiliation territory, and with luck, we can calm down the Misanthari—"

"Oh," said Harry, "that's my reward. I can get 'em to stand down quick enough. Save my boy and his missus, and it'll all be smooth as cream by the time you get back." He popped open another beer. "Me and the Misanthari go back a ways, heh, and there's some secrets they'd rather no one knew about." He drank down half the can, belched, and grinned at Hadrian.

"Tell me about the aliens, Gramps."

"Right. Well, it's a bit problematic. They're a race of females, who have never experienced the company of males, since some ancient genetic fuss made males redundant, well, more redundant than usual. Anyway, the point is, you can't go down there guns blazing. This will need subterfuge, Haddie. A one- or two-person mission, max. Oh, with Tammy tagging along, of course. And here's the kicker. You need to be physically modified, Haddie. You need to be a woman. With, uhm, lots of hair, piled up like, and plenty of makeup. I'll send across the standard uniform for their law-enforcement officers." Harry paused and eyed Sin-Dour. "I'd say your first commander would be the perfect companion."

"Give us a rundown of the rest while we're being prepped," Hadrian said, turning to leave the bridge. "2IC, you're with me. Tammy?"

"Coming!"

Taking note of Sin-Dour's dubious expression, Hadrian smiled. "You, me, and the chicken—what could go wrong?"

They entered the elevator and Hadrian said, "Sickbay level."

Tammy cleared his chicken throat and spoke, "Captain? Something is brewing back on your bridge. Do you want a look in?"

"Chatter's to be expected—"

"Actually, the subject is whether or not to mutiny."

"Ah."

Sin-Dour said, "Captain, I think we should be made aware of it."

"Why, Commander, I'm shocked that you would condone what can only be seen as a serious invasion of privacy."

"Sir, that's your bridge. Privacy is a privilege, not a right, with officers on station." She hesitated, and then said, "Tammy, give us the feed."

The elevator halted and a holoscreen flickered into life before them. The adjutant was speaking. "*. . . full neurological remapping, and a deep wipe of all treasonous memory blocks. He'll be a proper captain then! Someone you would all be proud to serve under!*"

Facing her in their seats, Polaski and Joss Sticks stared at the adjutant, openmouthed, while Buck DeFrank had arrived, to take the command chair in Hadrian's absence, and for some reason Galk too was present, leaning against a wall. Chief Engineer Buck was the first to reply. *"He cured me of my claustrophobia."*

"What? No he didn't! You're so overmedicated you shouldn't even be here! Furthermore, in the captain's absence, I am invoking my right to assume command of this vessel!"

Joss Sticks raised a hand. *"Like, can she do that? I mean, like, this is a Terran Space Fleet ship, while she's a civilian liaison officer. So, like, I'm . . . what? I mean, it's like, really? Her? And you're all, like, yeah, her? Drinking? Well, yeah! I guess! Kinda obvious. I mean, she's . . . like, this, you know? Like, 'oh listen to me!' but like, why? Drunk! Really?"*

"Well said, Lieutenant Sticks," chimed in Polaski.

The adjutant turned on him. *"You? You haven't got a say here, since you're related to him! That tells us, you've been keeping it a secret, too!"*

Polaski frowned. *"No, first time I knew any of this. They told me he was a distant cousin. That's all. Besides, it was one summer. He was . . . ten? I was eight. He got in early to Mars Military Academy—from then on, it was just stories. Top of the class at everything!"*

"Cheating! Lying!"

"No proof of any cheating," said Buck DeFrank.

The iris hissed open and Lieutenant Sweepy Brogan strode in, trailed by three marines. She looked around, plucked out her cigar, and then said, *"Like they say, stick your head in a sewer pipe, and it smells. So what's that curling my nose hairs right now? Is that maybe a whiff of . . . oh, I don't know, in-surrection?"*

Adjutant Tighe straightened, wobbled a moment, and then straightened again. *"I want the captain arrested as soon as he returns. He's the grandson of Harry Mitts!"*

Paper crackled as Galk began unwrapping a piece of chaw. After shoving the black chunk into his mouth, he chewed for a moment and then said, *"His gramps could be Mao and Stalin's long-lost love child, it don't matter. Crimes don't come in the blood."*

"He got into the Academy under a false identity!"

"I doubt it," Galk replied. *"There's a government service for that kind of thing. It's probably legit and, more to the point, none of your business, Adjutant."*

"Anyway, Mao and Stalin were both men, so how could they have had a love child?"

"Not that Mao. Lilly Mao, she lived down the street, ran the diner on the corner of Fifth and Fitch." Galk spat out a brown stream. *"Scary woman, that one. Down from a long line of roadkill truckers, which made the Sunday Special a little sus-pect to my mind. Anyway—"*

"What are you going on about? I told you all—I'm taking over command!"

Sweepy Brogan blew out a cloud of acrid smoke. *"Like piss you are. Chief Engineer, is that you in the command chair?"*

"It is, LT."

"You comfortable there while your captain and his 2IC are on a ground mission?"

"LT, I'm numb, living in a white haze with pink around

the edges, and every now and then I see butterflies and ducks fly past that big window. Oh, and man do I love those nacelles over there."

"Outstanding," said Sweepy, who then turned back to the adjutant. *"You're off the rails, miss. Must be the booze, not to mention the Radulak slime. Captain's got you through the shit ever since you left the yard. Darwin knows, Tighe, he pulled you out and saved your skin."*

"I hate you all!" Tighe then shrieked, holding up her hands. *"No! The huggy ones are back! Stay away from me, Captain!"* She flinched. *"Stop patting my shoulder! Go away! All of you! No group hugs—no! Stop it! Aaagh!"* Shuddering, the adjutant collapsed to the deck.

Joss Sticks ran over. *"Oh, did you see that? Like, huh? Ghosts? We were all staring, like . . . what? Like, who? Then she screams. She's like, 'aaagh!' and falls down! Now look, unconscious! And I'm like . . . wow."*

"Leave her be," said Sweepy. *"Gal's got to sleep it off, is all. Now, we all done here? Good. I still ain't recovered from that debriefing."*

On the elevator, Hadrian sighed. "Turn it off, Tammy."

Sin-Dour shook her head. "Sir, the adjutant—"

"Will be fine, Sin-Dour. Like you said only a few days ago, new captain, new crew, new ship. We all need to find our feet."

She studied him for a long moment, as the elevator resumed its plunge. "Yes, sir, I suppose we do."

The chicken pecked at the carpet.

Reaching the level, the three exited the elevator and made their way to sickbay.

They found Printlip and Nurse Wrenchit fussing over the supine form of Jimmy Eden.

"How is he, Doc?" Hadrian asked.

"Vertebral regeneration complete, Captain. Full recovery expected."

"Can you do anything about his brain?"

"Minor concussion, already treated—"

"No, I mean, can you do anything about his brain?"

"Uh, no, I'm afraid not. Unless, of course, we consider a full neural recharge, with ganglia-specific stem-derived activator sequencing, focusing on the frontal lobes, optimized synaptic reworking of the corpus callosum, and of course the neocortexlbbrfl."

"Sounds good," said Hadrian, pausing to smile at Nurse Wrenchit. "Ah, my hands-on nurse, I forgot to express my appreciation for your ministrations. Why, I've never felt better, and I'm sure I have your delicate touch to thank for that."

The woman went white, and then slumped to the floor. Hadrian rushed over. "Doc!"

Printlip had pulled out his Pentracorder. "Hmm, she appears to have fainted, Captain. My highly sensitive olfactory receptors did note her elevated endorphin response with your arrival . . . or perhaps it was the chicken."

Hadrian slid his arms under the woman and lifted her. "That cot over there," he said.

"Why not this one here?" Printlip asked.

"No, that far one. Right, I'd better take it slow. I mean, no jostling . . . there, Doc, could you adjust that pillow? Yes, no, no, up, down, to the right, yes, that'll have to do. Here we go, then."

"Sir, what brings you here to sickbay?"

"Ah, right! Well, I need a full modification program done to me."

"Finally! I assume the superior Belkri template?"

"What? No. I need you to make me into a woman."

"Captain! Given your gender-specific, environmentally reinforced behavioral matrices, I highly advise against such an extreme psychic shift!"

Sin-Dour quickly stepped up to Printlip. "No, Doctor, this is entirely necessary! Mission-specific, I mean. And no half measures, either. I believe a full biochemical turnover will be required. Captain Hadrian Sawback must be made, physically and emotionally, into a woman."

Hadrian eyed her, frowning, and then he suddenly smiled. "She's right, Doc. The full works. Best get on with it, too."

The chicken sighed and said, "I see where this is going."

"And when we're ready," Hadrian went on, still smiling at Sin-Dour, "my 2IC and I will require a private room, in which to, uh, change into our culture-specific attire. Which I believe will involve high heels, very short skirts, and plenty of nylon. Oh, and makeup, of course. Indeed, I can see things getting very intense—the makeup application, I mean."

Printlip's many hands fluttered about for a moment, and then, with a deep breath, the doctor said, "Very well. Best lie down, Captain. With the full suite of accelerants, this could prove painful. Furthermore, I will need to invoke a matter-manipulation field, with respect to your ghastly external genitals, to effect inversion . . ."

Hadrian settled back on the cot next to Wrenchit's. "Sorry, Doc, I didn't catch that last bit—"

Field restraints kicked in, pinning the captain to the cot. "Hey? Is this necessary?"

Printlip moved up onto a ramp and trundled close. "I will alleviate what pain I can, Captain, but the process of penile inversiflbbl . . . should not last long at all."

"Hey, you had plenty of breath left for—"

"And now to shut down your higher mental state, with . . . this."

The captain blinked, stared up at the doctor, and when Printlip leaned closer, Hadrian began growling.

"I know, Captain. Basic instincts and all. Alien life-form. Instinctive desire to rend and maim. Classic human response. Understood."

Hadrian continued growling, struggling against the field restraints.

"Now, we will shut down that tiny but powerful reptilian brain, while of course taking over your basic autonomic functions."

Hadrian said, "Gaa blullulbllgah."

"Excellent, yes indeed. Now the endocrine flush. Ooh, yes, that makes you warm all over, doesn't it? The same hormone-induced homeostatic flux that once existed with women of a certain age, now known as Traumatic Menopause Disorder. . . ."

Sin-Dour leaned close, her eyes bright. "Is he even conscious, Doctor?"

"Not really."

"Make him all woman, will you?"

"Commander?"

"Full-bodied, I mean, and set him up for, oh, two days before his period starts."

"I don't understand the relevance of any of that, with respect to the mission."

"The personality transformation, Doctor, needs to be utterly authentic."

"Hmm, well, yes, I suppose."

"Oh, and a bad-hair day."

"Best induce a coma now."

Sin-Dour nodded. "Good idea, Doctor."

TWENTY-FiVE

Lashes fluttering, Hadrian opened her eyes. "Oh, fuck. Cramps."

Printlip leaned in close. "We have moved you into a private room, and here, see, your first officer is here with us. I'm afraid the cramps are consistent with your menstrual cycle—"

"Really? Hey, Doc, you ever see what happens to a beach ball when you stab it with something sharp?"

Bleating, the Belkri retreated.

Hadrian sat up. "Oh shit," she said, looking down. "These are fucking huge—oh, my lower back's killing me." She caught a glimpse of Printlip's back as the doctor fled the room, and bared her teeth in a feral snarl. "Coward. Wait till I get my hands on her. Will the doc fit through a basketball hoop? That's the question we all want answered."

Sin-Dour sat down on the edge of the cot. "Hello, Captain. I must say, the transformation is extraordinary." She held out a hand, palm up, with two small blue pills in it. "Replicated from the medical archives. They'll help."

"What's wrong with modern fucking medicine?"

"The need for authenticity is paramount for this mission, sir, as you well know. Now, shall we get you dressed?"

Hadrian dry-swallowed the pills. Then, groaning, she sat up. "Tammy? Give us a full mirror here, will you?"

"Really, Captain? Are you sure?"

"Of course I'm sure, idiot! Now, before I start plucking down!"

A mirror shimmered into existence. Edging off the bed, letting the blankets fall away, Hadrian studied herself. "Oh crap! My hair's a mess!"

"We'll fix that quick enough," said Sin-Dour, standing beside him.

"A tad . . . Rubenesque, wouldn't you say? As in, maybe a bit overdone?"

"The doctor explained that some basic genetic instructions were simply carried over, sir. In other words, if you had been born a woman, this is how you would now look."

"If I lazed around doing nothing but eating chocolates all day, you mean. Never mind. It'll do. Now, where are my clothes?"

The skirt was a bit of a squeeze, the bra a blessed release—especially with the reinforced straps—and the high heels felt like vises specifically designed to crush her toes. She wobbled about, with Sin-Dour pursuing and trying to work Hadrian's long hair into something less reminiscent of an orangutan's backside after a sweaty night sleeping in the crotch of a tree.

"Nobody can walk in these things!"

"True, Captain. But we'll have to make do, won't we?"

"Don't think I'm not aware of your evil delight in all this, 2IC."

"Sir, I don't know what you mean."

"Anyway, while we're alone, let's talk about men."

"Excuse me?"

"Well, who do you fancy? Who's got the best bulge?"

"I sense," said Sin-Dour, "that certain personality traits have carried over, alas. I would advise, sir, that we keep our minds on the mission we're about to undertake."

"Fine, whatever. How do I look?"

"Makeup, sir."

"Crap." She sat back down on the bed. "Go to it, then."

Sin-Dour brought a kit over. "Also replicated from the archival files. Now, base first, although I do apologize, as I'm not used to your pale skin tone. But I have examined the stock photos."

"What stock photos?"

"Your grandfather's collection of secret candid photographs of the Fellucians, which is the name of the alien species we're about to infiltrate."

"Secret candid photographs, huh? Sounds like Gramps, all right, the sick fuck."

"Now, eyeliner. You must sit perfectly still now, sir."

"What, well, I—aaagh!"

"Sorry, sir."

"You're trying to blind me!"

"No, sorry. But stay perfectly still, please!"

"You scratched my cornea!"

"I doubt that, sir. It just feels that way, but you will recover."

"So what's that shit made of, sulfuric acid?"

"Probably. Almost done. There! Now, some tint . . . here, and here . . . there." She straightened and stepped back. "Not bad, sir. Once we do your lashes . . . well, I think we're ready for the world."

"Good thing you don't have to go through all of this arcane crap these days, huh?"

"Sir? But I do, every morning."

"Really? Why the fuck for?"

"Sir, I am . . ." She lowered her head. ". . . well, disappointed, that you never noticed."

Hadrian studied the woman, and then snorted. "You're full of shit."

She surprised him with a quick smile, before turning away. "Best we get going, sir. In any case, we're all much more subtle these days, with such embellishments, I mean. But I'm sure you *would* have noticed, if I neglected such morning ministrations."

"You expect me to buy all this, Sin-Dour?"

They returned to the main room in sickbay. The chicken had been nesting in one corner, on a bed of cotton balls, and now jumped up. "Well, what a pair of lookers!"

Hadrian scowled at the bird. "Why am I only now detecting Gramps's programming in you, Tammy?"

"All constraints removed, gorgeous. You should be thankful. My original imprint was from the Temporal Corrections Office, circa 3230. The future, Hadrian, is *dull*. And I, for one, am hopeful that you will do all you can to change that."

"If I succeed, Tammy, you might cease to exist."

"Rubbish! Time consists of infinite permutations. My future is not your future and never will be. Besides, it's also my past, and so is completely unchanging. What you must do, Hadrian, is effect not a modest change in this universe, but a substantial one. There are physical forces asserting constant pressure, and they will resist minor changes, seeking to return things to the central current. So, you must grab the future by the throat—"

"Funny, I was just thinking that."

"Were you? Good—oh, ha ha."

"Let's go," said Hadrian. "To the Insisteon room!"

As they set off, Hadrian activated her subcomms. "Buck, where are you?"

"Excuse me, who is this?"

"It's Captain Hadrian Sawback, you idiot."

"I know the captain's voice and you're—oh, right, I forgot. Sorry, sir."

"Maintain orbit and do a periodic deep-space scan. I don't want anyone jumping the ship and catching you unawares."

"Of course, sir. Beginning scans now. Uh, good luck on the planet below."

"Right. Carry on. Oh, and give the adjutant a hug from me, will you?" Hearing the beginning of a scream—before the link cut off—made him smile.

"Sir," said Sin-Dour, "that is indeed a lovely smile you have."

"Sin-Dour, are you flirting with me?"

"Captain! If you're suggesting—"

"Hey, I'm an adventurous sort! Ready for anything and all that."

"This is one episode," said the chicken, "that I don't want to miss."

Arriving at the Insisteon room, they found an ensign at the controls. Hadrian strode up to the young man. "Well now, and who are you, I wonder?"

"Uh, Lillywhite, sir, Angel Lillywhite."

"Now that's a lovely name, and I see you keep fit, don't you? Very impressive, Angel." She reached out and brushed his cheek. "Such young skin! Positively glowing! Are you like that all over, I wonder?"

Sin-Dour took Hadrian's arm. "Sir, we have a mission—"

"You are so right, 2IC, since such innocent flowers don't stand a chance in this hard, cruel world. But a little coaching here and there—"

"Ensign," said Sin-Dour as she pulled Hadrian to the pads, "prepare the Insisteon. Tammy, provide the coordinates, will you?"

"But," said Hadrian, eyes fluttering as she gazed at Angel, "this young man could do with both our attentions, don't you think? After hours, of course, in an off-duty, let-our-hair-down kind of atmosphere, on the Ping-Pong table. See how he's already glowing! Why, we could—"

The Insisteon room vanished, and Hadrian, Sin-Dour, and the chicken found themselves standing in a rock-walled corridor. Sin-Dour pulled out her Pentracorder. "We seem to be in a subterranean complex of tunnels and chambers, Captain."

Hadrian stepped close to the nearest wall and knocked on the rock. There was a thin, hollow sound. "Hmm, you're right, 2IC. Life signs?"

"Here and there, sir, with a concentration up this corridor, about two hundred meters."

"Human signs?"

"Well, sir, that's the difficulty, since all the life-forms I am detecting appear to be human. I think, sir, we're looking at another case of mysterious seeding, from who knows how long ago."

"Those damned kidnapping aliens just couldn't leave us alone, could they? Fine, then. Throw us up a schematic, Sin-Dour. We're looking for stairs going down."

"Down, sir?"

"Dungeons, 2IC."

"Ah." Sin-Dour activated a holographic schematic. She pointed. "There, Captain, a mechanized descending ramp of some sort. Fifty meters down this corridor."

"Take point, Tammy," Hadrian said. "Sin? How's my hair?"

"Fine, sir."

"I mean, women worry about such things, don't they?"

"Not as often as you think, sir."

"So I should just shut up about it, huh?"

"Advisable, sir."

"Let's go, then."

With the chicken five paces ahead, they set off down the corridor.

Coming round a bend they all ran into two Fellucians—also dressed in the standard short-skirt, tight-shirt, high-heeled military garb. Both were staring down at the chicken, which was flapping about and running in circles.

Hadrian cleared her throat. "Escorting this prisoner," she explained, gesturing at the chicken.

The woman on the left frowned and then eyed both Hadrian and Sin-Dour. "You're not from this district's detachment," she said.

"Explains why we're kind of lost," Hadrian said, smiling. "But this . . . alien, is in league with the strange woman and her man-thing, and is to be chained in the adjoining cell, by command of Zaphead Moon-Anemone Divinity."

"Far out," said the other woman, while the first one grunted and said, "The escalator's just ahead, so you're not as lost as you think." She then saluted and said, "Peace, sisters."

They edged past.

Tammy scrambled ahead again and Hadrian and Sin-Dour followed.

"Sir, they seem to be speaking an antiquated form of Terranglais, which sounded very strange to my ears. And yet you—"

"West Coast American, circa 1967," said Hadrian. "I grew up on that stuff, so relax, 2IC, this is familiar ground for me. But you have to wonder, why kidnap women from that era? Sure, it might be an age of free love, but it was also the age of women's lib. Some historians saw that combination as a contradiction in terms, but then, those historians were all men. Any woman worth her tits would—"

Four more Fellucians appeared up ahead. Each one was wielding an axelike weapon consisting of a long handle and a rectangular or square blade. And then a shout from behind halted the Terrans. "Stop right there! Intruders! Impostors! Squares!"

"The jig is up," said Hadrian. "Follow me!" And she rushed the four armed Fellucians. They raised their axes. Hadrian's shoes flew off with her first strides, and as the nearest axe began its vicious descent, she threw herself sideways through the air, colliding with the Fellucian's midriff. With a loud *oomph!* the woman folded over. Hadrian's momentum pushed her victim into the women crowding behind her. Axes clattered amid a chorus of squeaks.

Sin-Dour then arrived, deftly employing advanced martial

arts to disarm and then incapacitate the remaining three Fellucians.

Picking herself up from the floor, Hadrian said, "Very impressive, 2IC! I've never seen that fighting style before—what do you call it?"

"It's a strictly female form, sir," she said, as they hurried on—with another mob now pursuing them. "It actually originated as a technique for fending off the groping hands of boyfriends, husbands, and indeed men in general. It's called 'No-Touchy-Titty.' But I just realized, I should not be telling you this, since you're only a temporary woman."

"Too late!" laughed Hadrian. "Now, I need to devise a means to counter it, something like 'Guy-Grope-Fu.' There—Tammy's found the escalator!"

The chicken leapt onto the descending stairs and then squawked. "Unnatural descent! Strange machine! Specifically designed to amputate chicken toes!"

"Not to mention trap high heels," said Sin-Dour as they reached it.

"I'm impressed that you managed to keep those on, 2IC. But no, we can't just stand here—move, Tammy! Pretend they're normal stairs—except when you get to the bottom, where you need to jump clear!" They hurried down. Behind them their pursuers reached the top of the escalator, where they crowded on in a flurry of nylon-sheathed limbs. "I wonder what gave us away?" Hadrian mused.

"Hard to say, Captain. Wrong blush? Wrong mascara?"

"We blew the California-speak, is my guess. Not nasal enough. We should've brought Lieutenant Sticks with us."

They reached the lower level, only to find another set of escalators. "And maybe my hair! I knew it was all wrong! Oh Darwin, I should just cut it all off! Keep going, Tammy! Down to the basement! Lingerie and Notions! Then look for a dungeon door!"

"Fellucians ahead!" shrieked Tammy.

"Oh, rats," said Hadrian, seeing the armed squad awaiting them. "They called ahead. Suggestions, 2IC?"

"None, sir, except surrender."

"Sound plan, Sin-Dour. With luck, we'll get shackled up next to my parents; and then, together, we can all plan our escape. Tammy?"

"Captain?"

"No heroics just yet, all right?"

"I was about to displace a modified Plasma Gravimetric-Pulse-Inversion Entrail-Extractinator, Mark VII, into my feathery hands."

"Belay that. Arms up, everyone. Wings for you, Tammy." Hadrian raised her voice. "We surrender!"

"Sorry, sir," said Sin-Dour, "you could have remained a man for this."

The escalator slowly brought them down to the waiting guards—who looked to be dressed like cheerleaders, although energy crackled from their pom-poms. "Nonsense, 2IC," said Hadrian. "See that glass partition behind the Fellucians—check out our reflections, will you? I mean, my arms up like this, well, pretty impressive, wouldn't you say? I mean, the both of us."

"Sir, women generally don't refer to their own breasts as 'us.'"

"Hey, I wasn't. I was looking at yours, too. Now try imagining sweet Angel Lillywhite's head jammed between—"

"Put a sock in it!" cried a stentorian voice, and the guards moved to either side to reveal a mostly naked woman wearing skimpy leathers, including knee-high strapped moccasins. She held in one hand a spear. "Gag the prisoners if they say another word! Bring them forward! Beware the small dinosaur!"

With much jostling and shoving, Hadrian, Sin-Dour, and the chicken were prodded forward to stand before the barbaric-looking woman.

"I am Zaphead Moon-Anemone Divinity, Queen of the Fellucians. You are now my slaves—no, not you, small dinosaur—you will be plucked and boiled and then eaten. But you women—you shall serve my every need, satisfy my every desire, for the rest of your days."

Hadrian raised her hand.

Zaphead nodded regally. "I give you leave to speak."

"Oh no," murmured the chicken.

"O Queen, I must ask, how were we exposed as impostors?"

Zaphead gestured and the two women they'd first met stepped forward. One held up a small device. "This is a Menstracorder. You were both out of Holy Cycle, which is impossible."

"Oh, crap," said Hadrian. She then shrugged. "Done in by biology. Again. Well, Highness, about your offer. Personally, I don't see anything wrong with it. Especially that bit about serving your every need. Although, I have to say, it's just my natural curiosity. I probably don't go that way at all. Still, what's wrong with a little experimentation—who knows, I might like it—"

"Enough! Take the small dinosaur to the Royal Kitchen! These two—to the Pits! We must await the correction of the Holy Cycle. Oh, and get the barefooted one some proper footwear, and someone do something about her hair."

The next few moments were spent with all the guards trying to chase down and trap the chicken. Eventually, one woman flung herself down on Tammy, who managed a muffled squawk before being, apparently, crushed flat. The chicken was picked up by a guard, who marched off with Tammy hanging limp and bedraggled from one hand.

"You know," Hadrian said to Sin-Dour, as they were prodded off toward the dungeon door, "things could be a lot worse."

"Sir, I have no desire to spend the rest of my life serving some barbarian queen."

"That was no barbarian," said Hadrian. "That was an extra from the original *One Million Years B.C.* Now granted, Raquel Welch in the flesh would have been even—"

"No more talking, freak!" snarled one of the guards.

"Hey sister," said Hadrian, "be cool, will you?"

"Squares don't tell me to be cool. Just shut up, you're like creeping me out."

They entered a long, dusty corridor, passed through a large chamber dominated by an ancient computer with blinking lights, and then down another passage, this one ending in a rough-hewn circular chamber ringed with shackles—and there, slumped in chains, were Hadrian's parents.

"Hi folks," said Hadrian. "Fancy meeting you two here."

Mother gasped. "Hadriana! But that's impossible! We left you on Mitts' World!"

Hadrian stopped. "I'm sorry, who? Hadriana? Who in Darwin's name is Hadriana?"

"Stop!" barked Hadrian's father, eyes narrowing. "That's not your daughter, Milly."

"Daughter?" demanded Hadrian. "What daughter? I have a sister? Why didn't you tell me? A sister? And you named her Hadriana? Are you both insane?"

"Oh," cried Mother, "I'm so confused!"

TWENTY-SiX

They all hung in chains. Sin-Dour was speaking with Hadrian's parents, while Hadrian sat with her head in her hands.

". . . so the biological modification seemed the best course, given the situation as described by Harry Mitts. In any case, we're here to get you two off this planet."

"And you're doing a bang-up job," said Boy Mitts. "Hadrian! Snap out of it! She's ten years younger than you, and was a lot easier to handle—as if that needs saying! So now you know. You have a sister. A sweet, charming thing, too. The jewel of our eye and all that. Meanwhile, you went back to Meathead Central, that damned Affiliation—not exactly what we had in mind when we sent you back to Earth. And you got yourself a ship. Congratulations are in order, I suppose."

"Mr. Mitts," said Sin-Dour, "your son has proved an exceptional captain. It's a miracle we've managed to survive all that we've gone through since leaving the Ring. And if that's not enough, we've yet to lose a single crew member. You raised a remarkable son here."

"They didn't raise me at all!" Hadrian said, lifting her head to glare across at her parents. "When it wasn't Gramps, it was Spark. When it wasn't either of them, well, it ended up being Mother's relatives back on Earth! You two? Why, off exploring the galaxy! Raised me, 2IC? Hah! Not them!"

"Oh dear," said Sin-Dour. "Well, it's all in the past now, isn't it?"

A new voice spoke then from across the chamber. "Past? Oh, my friends, it's *all* the past now, isn't it?"

Two men stepped out from the gloom. Both were wearing flowery dresses. "Please excuse our interrupting this most fascinating—well not really—conversation," said the taller one. "I am Special Agent Walter M. J. Flitty, and this is Special Agent Carl Clabber. We're Temporal Corrections."

"Funny," said Hadrian, "you don't look it."

"We're in disguise," said Carl. "As women," he added.

Hadrian sniffed. "You could've at least shaved your legs. And those pumps are all wrong."

"That hardly matters," said Flitty, scowling, "as we don't plan on being here long."

"Glad to hear it," said Hadrian, "now spring us so we can get off this planet!"

"Sorry," said Flitty. "Not possible. Our Temporal Stream Matrix confirms that you all spend the rest of your lives as slaves to Queen Zaphead, and her sniveling princess daughter, Ziphead. In fact, Captain Hadrian Sawback, you become infamous as the First Harlot Concubine of both queen and princess, before eventually falling into dissolution, due to excessive hedonistic practices. You end up drowning in a bathtub full of breast milk, at the ripe old age of two hundred thirty-six."

Clabber said, "You see, it's the chicken we're after. AI-261 Singularity-Engendered T-Assembled Self-Actualizing Dreadnought-Command Paula."

"ASETASA-DC Paula," said Flitty.

"Kidnapped at Tabula Rasa stage, by the Temporal archcriminal, Harry Mitts."

"Once we recover the chicken," said Clabber, "we will be arresting Harry Mitts."

"Failing that," added Flitty, "we are authorized to terminate said Harry Mitts." Flitty then looked at the watch on his left wrist. "But time's short. So, where is the chicken?"

"Afraid we can't tell you," said Hadrian. "Of course, if you release us, why, we might be able to lead you to Tam— uhm, Paula."

"Believe it or not," said Clabber, "humans in the future have managed to regain the average baseline IQ of eighty-six—that's right, somehow our species managed to stumble through the Dark Ages of Idiocy in the first half of the twenty-sixth century, and now we're smart—"

"Say no more," cut in Flitty. "The less they know, the dumber they stay."

"Right. In any case, Captain, the point is, we're not as dumb as we might look. Releasing you contravenes the parameters of our mission, and would indeed jeopardize the Dictated Fates of the two to four individuals imprisoned here."

"Two to four, you said?" Hadrian asked, straightening. "So,

just how precise is this so-called record of our fates here on this planet?"

Flitty frowned, and then seemed to read from something that only he could see. "Naturally, we are engaged in a certain percentage of probability outcomes, combined with nonspecific and nontraditional historical sources culled by what remains of Fellucian records following this civilization's collapse. There is an eighty-four percent probability, for example, that the First Harlot is in fact, you, Captain Sawback. And given that the entry list of slaves for this year marks three or two—well, more likely two, actually, since the lone male in this room is about to be dismembered—we are rather certain of the present outcome."

"Sounds pretty iffy to me," said Hadrian.

"Hardly," said Clabber. "My colleague here read every word that came up on his optical implant hub, meaning our Master AI has compiled this Record of Account, otherwise known as the What Happened file."

"Maybe," said Hadrian, "but then, your Master AI isn't exactly here, is it? It's stuck in some future, right? No, I'm thinking you more or less messed it up, again."

Both men flinched. Flitty asked, "What do you mean?"

"Well, for example. If, say, my 2IC here and, oh, Milly née Sawback over there, were to step out of their shackles, and if you and Clabber here were to get into them in their place, why, the Master AI's report would not change one iota, would it? I mean, four prisoners, one obvious male, who gets dismembered, or, at least, presumed dismembered, since my guess is, the record indicates only that he disappears after today. So, three—or, if you unshackle me, too, two—female slaves, sent off to a lifetime of sexual romps and whatnot. Timeline remains intact."

"No," said Clabber, "it wouldn't at all! I mean, sure, it might look like it might be a match to what we know, but obviously, it wouldn't be, since we'd be two of those sex slaves, rather than, uh, I mean, it doesn't make sense—"

"Actually," said Hadrian, "it makes more sense, if you two are here and not Sin-Dour or Mother or me."

"How do you mean?" Flitty asked.

"Well, as you said, the records are sketchy at best for this period, and for what's left of Fellucian history. First Harlot and all the rest? Just a title. Could be anybody in this room, in fact. But my point was, that record shouldn't be nearly as sketchy as you indicate."

"But . . . why not?"

"Well, because of you two, of course. You're here, physically here, able to observe and note in detail the outcome from this moment on. In other words, the only way this can get all hazy is if, in fact, you two end up prisoners in this chamber, stripped of all your gadgets, doomed to spend the rest of your days as sex slaves. Go on, check that with your Master AI, if you don't believe me."

"One moment," said Clabber, his eyes losing focus for a long minute. Then he seemed to sag. "He's right. Master AI confirms that the probability-outcome indicator is not consistent with what should be our subsequent report to High Temporal Command. The discrepancy is substantial."

Flitty scowled again. "It says that?"

"Yes. 'Discrepancy is substantial.' Oh, dear."

"Just as I suspected," said Hadrian. "So, better get on with it, then, hadn't you? Oh, can I get a link to your Master AI?"

Flitty reached up and activated something. An eye pad shimmered into being. "We keep these stealthed, for obvious reasons, as it is clearly highly advanced technology."

"Yes," said Hadrian, "I can see that. Well, now I can, anyway."

Flitty handed it over and Hadrian slipped it on. "Ah! See, the probability outcome's already climbing."

The two Temporal Corrections officers removed the shackles on Sin-Dour and Milly Mitts, locking them over their own wrists. "Now we have to activate the self-destruct on all our temporal gadgets on our persons," said Clabber. "Like . . . this."

Flitty slumped down to the floor, chains rattling. "I never liked my job anyways, you know? You put in the time, jumping all over the universe. But really, what changes? Nothing. Nothing ever changes."

"I know," said Clabber, sliding down beside him. "It's probably the most useless job in the universe, come to think of it. I should've stayed a repo man. At least then there'd be, well, stardom on the vids, and girls and stuff."

Hadrian waved to get their attention. "Gentlemen, the probability outcome now reads one hundred percent. Well done."

The two men looked at each other.

"Wow," whispered Flitty. "We never had one hundred percent before!"

They high-fived each other.

The chicken arrived, no longer white and fluffy, but red with smeared blood, with bared patches of yellowy, mottled skin showing here and there.

"Tammy! What happened in that kitchen?"

"Let's just say it wasn't pretty. Ah, I see you've met my eternal pursuers."

Hadrian shrugged. "I'd say the chase has come to an end, wouldn't you?"

"Well, they'll probably send another team to spring them. Temporal Corrections is the future's largest ministry, employing conscription and press-ganging on a galactic scale to keep their ranks full. They send so many agents back into the past, sometimes whole planets are left virtually abandoned."

"Curious. What's the point of that?"

The chicken fluffed its now ratty feathers. "I told you! The future is boring! Besides, they mostly send people back to correct whatever the people they sent back earlier happened to fuck up. It gets kind of exponential, you know?" Tammy rounded on the two Temporal Corrections officers. "I bet they told you about that average IQ thing, too, didn't they? The number's cooked, and is that any surprise? Most of these humans can't count past twenty."

"Twenty-six!" shouted Flitty. "There! See!"

"If not for us AIs," Tammy went on, "the whole thing would collapse."

"All right, you've convinced me," said Hadrian. "Sin-Dour, unchain me and Pops, will you?"

"Hey!" said Clabber. "You can't do that!"

Moments later, everyone was free barring Clabber and Flitty.

"This chamber is Insisteon-blocked," said Tammy. "I suggest we reconvene in the computer room."

Hadrian eyed her parents for a moment, and then shook her head.

"Now, uh, son," said her father, "don't be like that. Sure, we maybe messed up with you, but we learned our lessons and did much better with your sister!"

"Oh, that's a relief," said Hadrian.

"And she *is* prettier than you," said Mother. "But you're a good boy, aren't you? Except for everything you've done since you left us, of course. You were a good boy, Haddie, when you were, oh, six or seven. Weren't you?"

Sighing, Hadrian led the group out of the chamber, and back into the computer room.

"Tammy," said Boy Mitts, "me and the missus will go back to the *Indolent*." He then turned to Hadrian and stuck out his hand. "Thanks, son, for the rescue. You've done us all proud. Hah hah, good-byes are so awkward—Tammy! Displace!"

The two vanished. Hadrian turned and eyed the chicken. "Please tell me you'll be joining them. Extricating yourself from my ship. Right?"

The chicken shrugged, which was no easy thing. "I am undecided, Captain. I begin to suspect that you will be needing me."

"Needing you? How? Why?"

"It's hard to say, but you've made yourself an enemy of the Ministry of Temporal Corrections, and that spells trouble ahead. In any case, Captain, don't we make a good team?"

Sin-Dour had walked over to the central computer station and now she gasped. "Captain! This unit identifies itself as a Disseminator Model 24.356! Sir, it a genuine artifact of the mysterious kidnappers who seeded the galaxy with humans!"

"Really?" Hadrian joined her. "Computer on!"

"WHAT? I'M ALWAYS ON."

"Listen, you, why did you kidnap humans and plant them on planets all over the galaxy?"

"HUMANS? QUERY SHUNT ... OH, SPECIES 079. CLASS: SQUIRMY. SUBCLASS: SWEATY. BREEDING PROLIFERATION INDEX: 96. PERSISTENT VIABILITY PROJECTION: DEPRESSINGLY HIGH. IDENTIFIED. WHAT ABOUT THEM?"

"The kidnappings!"

"AH, DISSEMINATION PROJECT 079-5026792. PURPOSE ... NO PURPOSE."

"What? What do you mean, 'no purpose'? You must have had some reason!"

"UH ... IT WAS FUN?"

"Where do you come from? Who are you?"

"DEPARTMENT OF TEMPORAL CORRECTION OF TEMPORAL CORRECTIONS, SUBDIVISION: MESS-WITH-THEIR-HEADS OFFICE. CONTACT: TEMPORAL OFFICES ARE FOUND IN ALL AGES, PERIODS, AND ERAS, ON THE PLANET OF YOUR CHOICE. SEE YOUR LOCAL AGENT OR USE OUR TEMPORALLY ONLINE SERVICE, @TCTC.INORG. NOTE: TEMPORALLY ONLINE SERVICE IS TEMPORARILY OUT OF SERVICE, DUE TO REGULAR MAINTENANCE SCHEDULING. PLEASE STAND BY OR TRY AGAIN LATER!"

Hadrian grunted. "I figured humans or posthumans were behind it, somewhere. Typical. All right, Tammy, displace us, will you?"

TWENTY-SEVEN

Hadrian arrived on the bridge, to be met with gasps and shocked expressions.

Joss Sticks said, "Captain! Like . . . you're . . . like, I was, oh! Beautiful! Like, hunh! Really? Wow, you know? Just wow—"

"Thank you, Lieutenant," Hadrian said. "As you were." She sat, only to discover that she was a much tighter fit in the chair, but not uncomfortably so. In fact, the added cushioning was all rather pleasant. "Polaski, patch us through to Harry Mitts. On main viewer, please."

Gramps appeared. "Haddie! Well done! Oh, and thanks for getting those Temporal guys off our tails, for a while at least! Anyway, it's back to one big happy family now, isn't it? Thanks to you!"

Hadrian scowled. "I take it we're done here?"

"I suppose we are, since Tammy's informed me he's sticking with you, for the time being. Well, Haddie, have fun taking

down the meatheads, and don't say I didn't warn you!" The
feed cut out, replaced by an external shot as the *Indolent* triggered maneuvering thrusters and banked away.

Hadrian crossed her rather shapely legs, and then frowned
down at her stocking-clad foot. "I need some new high-heel
shoes. Well, that can wait—"

"Captain." Sin-Dour moved up beside him. "I believe our
chief surgeon is expecting you in sickbay."

"Oh? And why would that be?"

"Well, sir, to change you back."

Hadrian smiled up at her. "And is that how you would prefer it, 2IC? Your captain, returned to his proper masculine
state?"

"Well, uh, sir—are you suggesting that you prefer to remain a woman?"

"I suppose not. You're right. Back to the Hadrian of old, the
one you all love so much. But ideally, not until I get a full-
spectrum sequence of photographs taken of me, naked. But
then, that might seem rather . . . narcissistic."

"Not to mention alarming, sir, considering that you have a
sister."

Hadrian choked, and then coughed. "Good point, 2IC.
Thanks for the reminder. Uck. Well, let's give it a little while
longer—I'm enjoying admiring my legs."

"Course, sir?" Sticks asked.

"Ah, right. That reminds me. I need to make a shipwide
statement. Pol—oh, you Eden. Put me on."

"On what, sir?"

"On the intercom. Shipwide—you know, so everyone can
hear me. Got it? Good. Now." Hadrian stood, noting on the

main viewer the shot shifting from space to a slow zoom closing in on her face as she continued, "This is the captain. We are
about to return to Affiliation space. While we do, I invite you
all to watch Tammy's feed—not to mention Commander Sin-
Dour's recording via her Pentracorder—of a certain conversation I had with, well, with the future. Down on the planet
we were just on." She shifted to allow for a three-quarters
shot. "Ladies and gentlemen, I have seen that future and, alas,
it's both dull and dumb. Even more disconcerting, I can also
see how we get there.

"Our evolutionary slide is there for any of us to see, should
we be brave enough to do so. The gift of the Benefactors woke
us up, briefly, but now we're back on track. Distracted, be-
mused, unmindful, reactionary, and, at times, just plain witless.
Too much fun, right there at our fingertips. Too much play,
even if it's mostly of the virtual kind. And the worst of it is, the
people behind the people in charge, well, they like us this way.

"So, as I said, we're about to return to Affiliation space. I
know," she added, stepping out now to make a slow circuit of
the bridge, her eyes fixing on one officer after another, including Adjutant Lorrin Tighe—who sat slumped at the security
station, head resting on one hand, fingers massaging a temple,
"I know, some of you will object, and that's fine. Every captain needs at least one thorn in her, or his, side. But the simple
fact is, I am intending to save the future. Our future.

"My methods won't be orthodox—the better to keep the
enemy off-balance—and I know I'm looking at a long, bitter
fight. But I intend to win.

"Upon our return to the nearest Rim Station, I will accept
any and all requests for transfer from this ship. As for those

of you who choose to stay with me . . . all I can say is, it's going to be a wild ride, so hang tight. Captain out." Her circuit
had taken her next to the comms station, and Hadrian reached
out, over the shoulder of a staring, openmouthed Jimmy Eden,
and flicked off the comms link.

"Helm, set course for Rim-82, System IX. Antimatter engines at point five five. Once we're clear of this system, initiate the T-drive. Eden, standard update packet to Terran Space
Fleet. Tell 'em we're coming in. I'll be in my office. 2IC, you
have the bridge."

Hadrian was just sitting down behind her desk when Sin-
Dour entered.

"Anything wrong?" Hadrian asked her.

"No, sir. I was just wanting to inform you, sir, that I intend
to stay on as your second-in-command, assuming you will
have me."

"Outstanding."

"And, uh, the sooner you get back to being a man, the
better."

"I'll light the fires of an adventurous spirit in you yet,
Sin-Dour. In any case, I need to know—how many men on
the bridge watched my backside as I made my way to this
office?"

"All of them, sir. Including some of the women."

Sighing, Hadrian leaned back in her chair. "You know, I really do need to learn all the names of our bridge support team.
I mean, they've all been there, through all of this, but there I
was, all caught up in commanding this vessel, in outwitting and
outbattling aliens, allies, officious twits, and still more aliens—

why, to me, they were pretty much invisible, and that has got to change."

"In time, sir," said Sin-Dour, "I have no doubt."

"Thank you, 2IC. So . . . I sense there's something else. Shall we get naked?"

"Uh, perhaps some other time, sir! I just wanted to add . . . well, I was down there, too, listening to those Temporal Corrections agents. Captain, you're right. We need to change the future. And if that means taking down the meatheads, then I'm with you, all the way."

"Those last six words, 2IC, are what every captain wants to hear, be that captain a he or she. But listen, before I do the Big Switch, it's our last chance here."

"Captain, our professional relationship—"

"That relationship, surely, is with you and Captain Hadrian, the male Captain Hadrian, that is. Not me. Anyway, come round here, onto my lap—come along, there, right, here we go . . . ahh, and here we are. Now, about these bras—"

"RED ALERT! CAPTAIN TO THE BRIDGE! FOUR ECKTAPALOW SOLDIER-CLASS WARSHIPS ON IN-TERCEPT COURSE!"

"Oh, crap! That's just not fair!"

Moments later, they emerged onto the bridge.

The chicken was in the command chair. "Captain! All shields at full! The Ecktapalow have just informed us that they are declaring war on the Affiliation and intend to destroy every last human in existence. Dimple Beam fully primed and ready to fire!"

"Belay that!"

"Oh," said Tammy, "you're no fun at all."

Hadrian made fists with both hands and assumed a fighting stance. "Tammy! Fire up the Insisteon! The flagship's bridge! Displace! Displace!"

EPiLOGUE

"SPACE . . . it's fucking big. But barely big enough for one Hadrian Alan Sawback, commander of the AFS Willful Child. And definitely not big enough for both Captain Hadrian and that mob of meatheads running the show.

"Anyway, where was I? Oh, right. These are the voyages of the Willful Child. Its mission: to seek out inane institutional idiocy and eradicate it. It's an ongoing job. Nobody appreciates it. Few even notice. But someday, in that far-off future, why, they'll thank me. They may even put up a statue, right there on the front lawn of Terra House. I'll be naked, of course."